MIDNIGHT MUSE

VULCAN UNIVERSITY
BOOK 1

LANIE TECH

CONTENT WARNINGS

This book contains subject matter that might be difficult for some readers, including abuse (briefly mentioned), scarring (skin graft, procedure off page), sexual intercourse, and thoughts and feelings of Imposter Syndrome.

To the creatives who don't think they're good enough.
You are.
Trust me.

MIDNIGHT MUSE

CHAPTER 1
QUINN

The bead of sweat sliding down the skin between my breasts is driving me *wild,* but I can't wipe it away because my hands are full.

"I think that's the last one," I sigh, setting down a cardboard box labeled *Living Room* on the stack in the middle of the floor. I immediately dig into my sports bra, shoving the fabric between the valley of my chest to soak up the pesky sweat. The box isn't heavy—only filled with decorative pillows for the cheap futon shoved haphazardly against the wall of windows that leak afternoon sunlight into our apartment—but the tower of boxes sways precariously anyway. My roommate, Rory, darts forward to reorganize them before they all go tumbling over.

We were somewhat organized at the beginning of our move, separating boxes into piles for which rooms they belonged, but as the hot California sun beat down across our shoulders and the temperature rose throughout the day, so did our tempers. The process ended with us trying to get everything into our new fourth floor apartment as quickly as possible, which in itself was an almost impossible feat due to the slow-moving elevator.

Rory huffs, hands on her hips as she surveys the mess of boxes. Her gray-blue eyes are calculating, and the tip of her shoe taps the hardwood floors in a pattern that tells me that my best friend is trying not to let her annoyance of this mess loose from her lips. Neither of us had packed lightly, the same mistake we made last year and promised not to make again, and we both refused to hire a moving company to do the heavy lifting; if there is one thing that Cooper Conroy and Zak Wilson taught their little girls it's that we don't need any men to do anything for us that we can do ourselves.

Yep, our dear old dads have been best friends since their college days, too. Zak, Rory's father, didn't let having three daughters stop him from teaching them how to do any and all tasks that "every man should be able to perform." He didn't want them settling for anything less than average.

My father, Cooper Conroy, has a similar mentality. The only thing that differs between Rory's family and mine is that instead of having two older sisters, I have an overbearing older brother, Sam, who also inherited my father's ability to be self-sufficient. My YouTube history is filled with how-to videos on changing tires, patching holes in drywall (okay, so one party in our dorm last year got a *little too* rowdy, and we haven't hosted one since, *sue us),* and videos of Harry Styles, because hey, I'm just a girl.

And while dad wants me to be able to fix anything by myself, he hardly lets my mother lift a finger. It's as sweet as it is annoying, even though she will playfully roll her eyes at his antics when he takes the serving spoon from her hand to dole out dinner, or is the first to jump from his worn spot on the family couch when she says she has errands to run.

Moving all on our own may have been a mistake, if my

aching arms and legs are any sign of all of the heavy-lifting I've done today.

I couldn't wait to get out of Seattle, where my entire life revolves around my art. I love it, I really do, but I've been keeping this secret for a long time: how I haven't felt that spark—that fire in my soul—for drawing in a long time. I couldn't wait to get away from the questions and the compliments, the pressure put on me not only by my parents, but also myself.

Panting, Rory shoves away a few strands of her dark chestnut hair that clings to her forehead, sticky with sweat. The tresses at her nape curl away from her skin and I'm so glad that she grew out those awful bangs over the summer. I shouldn't have let her cut them herself, but when I refused to assist her in the worst decision ever, she'd stubbornly taken the scissors to her head anyway, and I almost peed my pants laughing at the outcome that night.

It's both one of my favorite and least favorite memories we share. Favorite, because I laughed so hard my stomach ached and the few seltzers we'd snuck from one of her older sisters had threatened to make a reappearance, and least favorite because I had to hear Rory complain about it over the phone all summer long, since her family was on vacation for an entire month.

The loose collar of her cropped shirt is damp with sweat and she uses the hem to wipe at the perspiration beading along her hairline. "Fucking *finally,*" she moans. "I need a drink."

"Alcoholic or caffeinated?" I tease, but I hardly have the energy to laugh. I'm just as drained as she is from carrying all of our belongings into the apartment, and all I want to do is collapse on the navy futon that barely fits two. I'm hot and my clothes scratch my skin from where they're glued to me with sweat. A cold shower, tall glass of something—*anything*—icy, and a few hours of napping will do me well. Maybe I'll even muster up the strength to unpack a box or two before the end of the night.

A grimace works its way onto my scarlet face as I accidentally shift directly into a beam of sunlight, squinting as I shuffle to escape it's sweltering heat. *"Please,* tell me there's air conditioning in this place."

"Already on," Rory responds, stalking into the kitchen. I follow, dodging the tower of boxes and watch as she rips the door to the refrigerator open and shoves her head inside. It's completely empty and I wince, knowing that it's going to be a long weekend while we go shopping for groceries and unpack everything before the fall semester starts in a few days.

I also want to stop by the local art supply to gather the rest of the materials I need for my classes this year. It's another reason that Rory and I have so many boxes with us; half of the ones adorning our apartment are stuffed full of art supplies: brushes and paints of all varieties from oils to acrylics, graphite pencils and kneaded erasers, and canvases too, both blank and filled. I swear, there's an entire box dedicated to sketchbooks filled with random doodles and scribbled ideas for assignments that have never turned into anything more. Rory hadn't been happy with me when she noticed that I left that box for her to carry up.

It's our second year at Vulcan University together, our second year living together, our second year as art majors together…Rory and I have been inseparable since we were young and our fathers reconnected when they were both on a work trip in San Francisco. My mother says that they had planned on meeting up all along and that the trip was really a bluff, but my father refuses to admit it to this day. I don't believe him, either.

When Rory's had her fill of the crisp air wafting from the refrigerator, she hands me a bottle of water from the freezer. It's nowhere near as cold as I need it, but the liquid cuts through the heat of my body as soon as it touches my lips and I almost moan at the cool feeling that washes over me. I had run into the gas station to grab a few bottles of water and candy bars for the last stretch of our road trip while Rory filled the tank of the U-Haul. It hadn't occurred to either of us at the time to buy something with more sustenance until this very moment.

"Ugh," I groan, choking down the refreshing liquid. "Do you have any money left in your account? We should order something for dinner and call it an early night."

"An early night?" Rory retorts, making a face as she sips her own drink. "We have a lot of unpacking to do. *And* our beds aren't even set up yet, Quinnie."

"Fuck us," I grumble, leaning against the marble counter. The surface is cool where it seeps through the fabric of my thin tank top, and I ache to rip off my clothes and press my burning skin to the stone in an attempt to cool myself off. "Let's just find the boxes with the pillows and blankets and sleep in the living room. *Oh*—don't give me that look, Ro," I scold her when she grimaces. "It will be like when we were young again! Except now we're old enough to buy alcohol." I waggle my eyebrows and she cracks a wry grin. "Well, *almost* old enough. But those fake IDs Pipa got for us work like a charm."

"Fine," Rory relents and I cheer. "Dibs on the first shower, though."

While Rory ignores my lame threat and uses all of the hot water anyway, despite it being nearly ninety degrees outside —blasphemous for the end of August in the middle of Southern California—I take the time to move the U-Haul from where she double-parked it outside of our new apartment building. Neither of us have cars yet, but this location is close enough to campus where we can walk to our classes. We saved up what we could from working at a local art camp this summer to road trip to school with all of our things, which our mothers were worried about but our fathers were proud of.

My phone buzzes in my pocket on my way down the rickety elevator to the lobby. Sliding it out, I see that it's my mother calling, probably wondering if we've made any progress on moving in even though I texted her as soon as we parked the truck. I sent a picture of Rory and I for further proof that we made it to school in one piece.

She's what one might call a helicopter parent. While my father is more than supportive in teaching me to fend for myself, my mother is used to being coddled and cared for, so she worries that I'm *too* independent. So what if I've never showed any interest in bringing a guy home to meet my family or going to dances or Friday night football games? That doesn't mean that I'm not interested in any of it…

Except the football, I don't care about the football. At all.

I let the call go to voicemail. I'll return her message later when I've showered, decompressed, and have mustered up the energy to answer her million-and-one questions.

When the contact picture of her and I on vacation a few years back disappears, I check my texts. There's one from my brother, Sam, warning me about how worried mom is and how he's never letting me leave for school before him again if this is what he has to deal with.

Laughing under my breath as I respond to the message, I glance up to the flickering floor number, seeing that I've only just passed the second level. I roll my eyes at the slowest elevator I've ever been on and it creaks as if it knows that I'm being impatient. Rory and I had opted to take the stairs for what we could of our unpacking, trying only to use the elevator for larger pieces of furniture like our beds, the futon, and the TV, taking it up with prayers that the old thing wouldn't give out while we were on it. I can't help but glance at the certificate that says the machine is in running order until its next inspection in two years.

"Is that forged, George Brown?" I mutter, squinting at the paper displayed in the corner with his signature on it. It's frayed at the edges and yellowing, so I'm not all that sure this elevator has been inspected when it says it has.

It comes to a jerky halt that makes me sway when it hits the lobby. Rory's second oldest sister, Pipa—Peep for short, lived here with a few of her friends during their undergrad years; they've now moved on from the shitty apartment buildings riddled with horny college students to a quaint house in town while working on their masters' degrees.

When the doors to the elevator slide open, I slip out as fast as possible, a shudder working its way up my spine as I wonder how many times it's broken down before. I'd hate to be in there alone if something like that happened. Perhaps I'll save my fate by taking the stairs from now on.

The lobby of the building is small. There's a front desk in which no one ever sits, as if there might have been a doorman at some point in time. Mailboxes are pinned to the wall, lining the area behind the counter, and a garbage can sits, stuffed full of envelopes and empty bottles of alcohol and take-away, maybe even a used condom or two.

It's muggy down here, more so than our apartment which

has me wondering why the landlord hadn't turned on the air conditioning when he knew we'd been showing up today. Whatever, I hadn't had to see the greasy man—he'd left the keys on the counter for Rory and I to find when we arrived— and I'm more than thankful for that.

Brushing away some of the hairs that have come loose from my ponytail, I cross the lobby, shoving my phone back in my pocket. The keys to the moving truck jingle on the ring as I swing it around my finger. The hazards of the U-Haul are blinking through the window from where it's parked in front of the building and the skies are turning darker as the sun continues its descent. It's taken us all day to unpack the truck and we're returning it tomorrow morning, so we need to move it to a normal spot for the night.

I push the door open, steps faltering as someone brushes past me like a shadow, my shoulder nearly colliding with theirs. I startle, spooked by the sudden presence. I hadn't even seen them walking this way and my brows furrow as I turn to toss a comment about their rudeness when the words dry up in my throat at the sight I'm met with.

Tugging off the motorcycle helmet, I can't help but stare as his biceps bulge against his skin tight black t-shirt. Tattoos line the length of his arms, but I'm too distracted by his body and can't make out the finer details from my position at the door. The muscles of his broad back glide like butter beneath the fabric as he moves and my gaze travels down his spine to his taut waist, dipping into dark jeans.

His thick soled boots thump loudly as he stalks through the door, stopping at the mailboxes to check if there's anything inside. The tiny door opens with a squeak that has me snapping back into reality, stunned by his musculature. He's in a league of his own, a masterpiece of perfectly crafted body parts and proportions. He has an angular nose and long, dark lashes that match his disheveled hair. He runs his fingers through said hair and tucks his helmet under his arm as he digs through the mailbox. For the first time in a long time, my fingers itch to pull out my sketchbook and pencils from one of the boxes upstairs.

I force my stare away, cheeks heating at the thought of this stranger turning around only to find me drooling over his good looks in the doorway. Pivoting, I click the keys, unlocking the U-Haul, only to stop short when I see that the truck is caged in. A big, vintage Bronco sits parked behind it, and a shiny motorcycle that looks like it moves faster than the speed of light is wedged between the front of the truck and the SUV Rory had pulled behind earlier.

"Hey," I call, ripping the door back open to the lobby. I have no doubt that the motorcycle is his, taking up the only extra space I had to move the truck—not to mention that it's not even a real parking spot. "Is this your motorcycle out front?"

He's already on his way to the elevator, phone stable in the leather riding gloves he's wearing, swiping across the screen, envelopes tucked into his helmet. The elevator door screeches open and he doesn't even bother to turn around to meet my gaze as he punches the button to his floor.

"Nope."

CHAPTER 2
QUINN

"*Nope?*" I mutter under my breath, brows furrowed in confusion. His blunt words—*word*—hasn't quite settled yet, but it forms a coherent thought right as the doors to the elevator begin to grind shut on creaky limbs. My body floods with so much annoyance that my chest aches with it, and I'm shoving myself away from the front door, lunging across the lobby towards the elevator in response.

My eyes catch his when they lift from his phone and my steps falter. They're gorgeous, the color of jade or ferns. My breath hitches in my throat. It's definitely because I'm worked up from the run to catch the doors and certainly *not* because of how pretty his eyes are.

The urge to start dumping out boxes on the living room floor to find my art supplies is both sudden and strong. Recreating those hues is going to be a challenge, but one that will be well worth it.

There is no way I'm going to catch the doors in time, and goddammit I probably look like a fool right now, with my flushed cheeks and blonde hair wild from the move, my forehead dewy with sweat. I'm blazing with intrigue and irritation, embarrassment and exhaustion. The corner of his mouth quirks up in a taunting smirk, as if he too, knows that I won't be able to slip inside of the elevator with him before the doors shut. The machinery is slow as fuck when I need it but now it chooses to work properly? *What's that all about?*

"Fucking *asshole,*" I screech, slapping my palms against the metal doors that separate him from me. I hope that he hears it, feels the ringing of my anger through the reverberating steel beneath my hands. I hope he understands just how lucky he is that I'm not on that side of the doors, making his life a living hell right now.

Releasing a long groan, one that comes from the depths of my tired soul, I press my forehead against the cool metal, squeezing my eyes shut.

The truck doesn't have to be returned until tomorrow morning, but the spot we parked it in is a loading zone, and the last thing we need on our first day back in town is a parking ticket on a rented truck. Or worse, the truck getting towed. We don't even have enough money to pay the bail, and the last thing I'm trying to do is call my dad and ask for money on my second day back.

I trudge up the stairs because I can't be assed to wait for the stupid elevator to return to the first floor. While I take the treacherous trip, I stew in my anger. The effort it takes to climb to the fourth floor helps dispel some of the white, hot annoyance toward the handsome stranger, and I'm beginning to think that maybe I should have expected that kind of behavior from someone as good-looking as him.

I shake the thought from my head as quickly as possible and begin to take the stairs two at a time.

I filled Rory in on the lobby incident as soon as she finished her shower, which took a whole forty minutes *after* I returned from the stairs of doom. In that time, I'd called my mom, updated her on the moving progress and might have complained a *tiny bit* about the boy who wouldn't move his motorcycle. I left out the fact that he was one of the hottest men I've ever seen, and tucked the phone between my chin and shoulder as I began digging through one of the many boxes labeled *Art Supplies,* searching for my case of colored pencils. She told me not to make any vendettas before the semester even started, to which I rolled my eyes and used the perfect excuse: "he started it." It's my go-to response for most arguments in my life, especially when I'm fighting with my older brother. It normally works like a charm then, but not tonight. Apparently, it's my fault Rory parked there and that Mr. Tattoos blocked us in, which only fueled my irritation on the entire situation.

I told Rory to keep checking out the window every so often to see if either of the people blocking us in move their cars before I stalked for the shower.

Two hours later, once pizza fills my stomach and I'm swaddled in my comfortable pajamas, neither of the owners of those vehicles have left.

"Give it up," Rory groans, tossing her half-eaten crust back into the pizza box. It's stacked on top of a moving box labeled *Living Room: Puzzles & Pillows.* I don't understand Rory's packing techniques—if the two are placed in the same box because it makes sense in a way that I can't comprehend or if it's because they both start with the letter 'P.' I'm too tired to care about it right now, or ever.

Groaning, I slump back onto the couch in defeat. The truck remains ticket-less thus far, but the constant nagging of my conscience is keeping me from getting into the reality TV show Rory and I are obsessing over. It's about a bunch of young couples shoved into a house to find love. It's cringey as fuck, but the drama makes for some good entertainment.

My betraying mind wanders into no-no territory again as I wonder just how good Mr. Tattoo would look lounging around in the sun like the people on the show. Is he covered from head-to-toe in ink or are there only a few tattoos scattered across his pale skin?

Quinn, what the fuck are you thinking?

"I'm still pissed off about it," I grumble, picking at the cheese crusted to my plate to distract myself from the thoughts of the man from downstairs. It's gone hard and cold, but I nibble at it anyway. I should have ordered popcorn to be delivered or something. A bottle of tequila, perhaps.

"I noticed," she answers drily. "But you being pissed off isn't going to make the motorcycle magically move." She readjusts herself on the small futon, elbowing me in the process. Rory suddenly sits upright, an idea lighting those piercing eyes of hers. "Oh! Maybe if you *stop* being pissed about it, they'll magically move. Let's try that!"

I roll my eyes, parting my lips to speak, when loud, brash music cuts me off. Rory and I exchange twin looks of confusion, turning to where the sound is coming from.

It blares through the walls. Specifically, the wall that my bedroom shares with the apartment next door.

I whine, shoving my face into my hands.

As if the day couldn't get any fucking worse.

"What the hell is that?" Rory asks, pushing to her feet.

"It sounds like a bunch of metal pans clanging together with a surprisingly nice beat," I answer sarcastically. It's not my preferred type of music, but I can admit that the voice harmonizing with the other banshee is quite lovely.

Rory shoots me a look, pressing her ear against the wall. I don't know what she's trying to do because I can understand each and every word being screamed from my spot in the middle of the apartment. I'm too tired to ask, though, as my attention is more focused on the damn truck sitting outside of the building.

"Should we go over and ask them to turn it down?" Rory questions, making her way back to my side so that I can actually hear her. I sigh. I am *so* tired of today. "That's going to get annoying, fast."

"We can always try not being pissed off about it," I answer, using her own words against her. Rory's lips tighten sourly and she shoots me a glare. Instead, I grin, continuing. "Maybe they'll *magically* turn it down!"

"Shut up, loser," Rory says, her harsh look ebbing a little. "I get it."

Of course, it's fucking *him.*

The bastard from downstairs. Only the person who made my already rough day even shittier would be the person I'm forced to live next door to for an entire year. His onyx hair is wet, unruly like he's only just run a towel through it, sticking up in all directions. It should make him look stupid, but instead he looks incredible. It's the perfect length, a few strands nearly poking him in those bright eyes that are narrowed on mine.

He's dressed in a fresh, tight, black t-shirt that leaves *very* little to the imagination, stretched tight across his chest. The fabric cinches around his taut waist and it makes my mouth run dry. I can only imagine the muscles pointing to what lies beneath his low-slung jeans.

"Can I help you?" He asks, glaring from his spot in the doorway. His voice is a deep, delicious rasp that crawls up my spine. I trade a stunned look with Rory.

Her lips are slightly parted, eyes wide and sparkling as if she's just seen her favorite sculpture come to life. I get it, and felt the same way when I first saw him, but then he went and opened his mouth to ruin the dreamy thoughts I was having about him.

He still looks great, unfortunately.

"Can you turn the music down? We're trying to sleep." I cross my arms over my chest and lift my chin, showing him that I mean business, even if he's looking down at me from his over six-foot height.

His beauty doesn't intimidate me.

Not at all.

That blank, jade stare flickers between Rory and I. He takes his sweet time surveying the both of us, eyeing my loose pajama pants, oversized Vulcan University hoody, and the way that my wet and tangled hair clings to my neck. My toes curl in my slippers under his scrutinizing gaze but I don't allow myself to back down, steeling my spine.

I can't help the way that my teeth grind when he assesses Rory in a similar fashion, a white-hot emotion flushing my veins like a tsunami.

"It's nine-thirty," he responds bluntly, as if we don't know what time it is. The waves stir in the pit of my stomach like a whirlpool.

"We know that," Rory tries, and she must catch the glare I'm stabbing him with because she keeps her tone light. Polite. Or maybe she sees how tightly I'm clenching my jaw at his words. She must have picked up on the fact that this is the asshole I was referring to when I told her all about the lobby incident.

I definitely downplayed his looks when retelling.

"We would appreciate if you would turn it down," I finish for her because he doesn't look like he's understanding what she's saying. Maybe he just doesn't care. I can't tell because I can't seem to get a read on him and the stoic way that he holds himself. I find myself eager to pull *any* reaction from him, and an idea sparks in my mind as I continue. "We've had a long day. People here park like shit and we couldn't get our moving truck out of the loading zone, you know?" I ask, faux innocently, and can tell that he doesn't know where I'm headed with this. His eyes bore into mine, unblinking, and I force back the smirk tugging at my lips. "We had to call the towing company to get them to move that silly motorcycle. Isn't that right, Ro?"

Right *there.* There it is, at the mention of that motorcycle that wouldn't have stood a chance against the big moving truck should I have put it in drive and hit the gas a little too hard on accident. I almost wish that I did, to be honest.

Jade eyes turn from a lush forest to a menacing storm, ripping needles from branches and limbs from trees. It causes my stomach to flip, a shiver working its way down my spine. The light in the hall seems to fracture with his mood change alone and I want to shift my weight with the sudden unease that accompanies it but I won't give him the satisfaction.

Maybe I shouldn't be fucking with him.

Before I have the chance to tell him that I'm only joking, he slips back inside of his apartment and slams the door in our faces.

For the second time today, I have the urge to pound my

fists against the door and curse his name, even if I don't know it.

I don't have to, though, because Rory's doing it for me, rapping her knuckles against the thick wooden door with a frown on her face, her eyebrows slanted downwards in annoyance.

It isn't the same asshole that answers the door this time. No, it's another astonishingly good-looking boy with an aura to him that makes my knees a little weak. Rory flinches away from the door at his sudden appearance, her cerulean eyes shuttering at the sight. His shaggy blond hair swoops perfectly back from his face. It's a little shorter than his friend's, but it suits his sharp features perfectly. His cheekbones alone could cut glass.

Again, I feel the need to reach for my pencils, because the color of his eyes is so deep that it feels like I'm looking into the bottom of the ocean. They're like the opposite of Rory's ice blues that stand out starkly against her dark chestnut hair. I haven't seen anything quite like the color of his, though, and I'm amazed as I stare up into them.

What the hell are they putting in the water here?

Rory's breath hitches as he peeks through the tightly shut door, using the crack he's opened to peer out at us like we're some sort of wild animals come to break it down. His body blocks my view when I try to look around his massive form, searching for his friend. I'd shove right through him if I had any muscle left from lugging my life in boxes up the stairs all day.

"Sorry, ladies," his voice is like silk, and his gaze lights with mischief while he takes a languid look at Rory, drinking her in like she's a fine wine. He barely flicks his gaze in my direction and I tell myself not to take it to heart. There are more assholes out there than this one. His smooth voice drips like honey as he purrs, "We're getting ready for an event tonight, but we'll try our best to keep it down."

Liar, I want to bark at him. I know it not because of the mirth in his tone or the sparkle in his eyes but because of the soft scoff behind the door when there's a pause while the songs change from one screeching metal instrument to the next. My fingers curl into fists and I shove them quickly behind my back.

The blond doesn't leave room for a reply, shutting the door on us with a *click.*

My jaw is clenched so hard that it aches. I take reign of the situation once again, since Rory seems paralyzed by the last boy's looks, pounding so hard on the door that my bones rattle with it. I'm tired of this already. Of this building. Of the motorcycle. Of the fucking elevator. I'm exhausted and irritated and they deserve our wrath now.

Sorry mom, but fuck being civil.

Following a few incessant bangs, the door opens again, and this time my jaw goes completely slack.

A behemoth of a boy stands before us. He's broader than the last two, taller too. And shirtless. His shoulders take up the width of the doorframe he's leaning against, like none of this is bothering him in the slightest. His pectorals flex when he crosses his arms over his chest, and it makes my mind short-circuit as he stares us down. If he isn't on the wrestling team or a football star, I'll be thoroughly surprised. His tan skin on display is mine for the taking and I greedily drink him in like the dehydrated woman I've suddenly become.

Tattoos span across his shoulders, wrapping down his arms and covering one of his pectorals in tribunal pattern that is so intricate I find myself leaning closer for a better look. The muscles of his stomach ripple with silent laughter when I catch myself, rocking away so fast I nearly fall on my ass.

My cheeks go red-hot and I rip my gaze away from the sweatpants hung low around his waist—so low that I can't even see the elastic of his underwear.

I swallow dryly. I don't think he's wearing any.

Rory is silent beside me, and him in front of me. We're all staring at each other, the sound of the loud music seems to drown away as my eyes linger. When I raise them to meet his molten chocolate eyes, I catch him biting his tongue, trying to smother a smile. His russet hair hangs loose around his shoulders and is the perfect length for pulling.

Not that I'm thinking about that, of all things.

"Well, hello there," he greets, his tone a rumble of warmth. His mouth hikes up into a grin that feels welcoming, and my shoulders relax a little at the sight. He seems the most easy-going of the three, and hopefully he'll be the one to listen to our complaints. "You must be our new neighbors."

Rory nods, a dumbfounded look on her face. I'm sure it matches the one on my own right now, unable to form a single word. "That's right."

"Aren't you two the prettiest things I've ever seen," he compliments, and I wonder why it hadn't been him in the lobby when I needed help. Or when we were moving our things upstairs. He's a mountain of a man, and surely, he wouldn't have minded putting all of those muscles to good use.

It's like we're all stuck in our own little bubble out here in the hall, taking our fill of each other. The friendliness of his voice is settling, smooth, and I know it's something that women can't resist.

"Right," I blurt, cheeks flaring as his attention settles on me once more. The tilt to his mouth is as distracting as his naked chest, but the song inside skips to a new one, startling me back into focus. "About that music…"

"Oh that?" The boy rolls his eyes, waving his hand like it's no big deal. "That's nothing. Just wait until later when it really starts picking up. That's when—hey, wait," he cuts off his own eager rant, craning his head around the door to speak to his roommates. "Why aren't we letting them in, again?"

Laughter spills into the hall from the other side and I can barely make out the second boy's response over the music. "They were mean to Knox."

The boy in the door returns his gaze to us, disappointment scrawled across his handsome features. "Ah, sorry, ladies. No one's mean to Knox." He says it softly, like it hurts him to say it. "Have a nice night."

The *snick* of the door shutting is the final nail in the coffin.

The *click* of the lock is them burying it.

CHAPTER 3
KNOX

The party is in full swing. Music beats loudly through the apartment and the rumbling of voices shouting over it cram the room, bouncing off the walls and out the open front door. There are people every-where, crowding the small space. The furniture has been shoved aside to make room for dancing and there's a beer pong table set up between the fridge and the counter that's covered in bottles and red cups. Someone's standing on the countertop pouring a beer into a luge with a frat bro at the other end, chugging. I have no idea how the fuck *he* got in.

The air is thick with over-sprayed perfumes, body odor, weed, and alcohol. I watch from my spot by the window as I prep my latest victim. Working my hands into a fresh pair of black latex gloves for the girl who sits in the chair in front of me. It's one of the rickety ones we have at the dining table that my roommates and I rarely ever use, so it's perfect for this opportunity.

She's excited, the girl in the chair. She's wearing a skimpy dress that leaves little to the imagination. She's sporting a lacy red thong, and straddling the back of the chair.

Her dress is scrunched up over her ass, an expanse of olive skin on display, awaiting me to get to work.

I notice a group of guys standing nearby, leering at her with glossy eyes and beers in their hands, half hard at the prospect of watching the girl get a tramp stamp.

"A little pink bunny rabbit," is what she requested, and I didn't ask why. I never ask why, because people want what they want and I'm here to deliver. I nodded, pulled out my sketchbook, and got to work, drawing a few options for her to choose from.

I'm not proud of the set-up I currently have: tattooing drunken college kids whenever Slate throws a party. It's a normal weekly occurrence for us now that we're juniors and know more than a few people.

To say that I'm completely out of my element is an under-statement, but I need the practice and the students are willing. The only reason I don't have my headphones shoved over my ears, blasting music a little more my own taste, is so that I can hear what's going on and tend to my client's needs should anything go south. I'm preceptive, and will keep an eye out for the hiccuping girl with her dress pulled over her ass, only because I care more about the tattooing than if she's making bedroom eyes at every gaze she meets.

I prep her skin, taking the clean razor to remove the area of any hair. The girl scoffs when she peers over her shoulder to see what I'm doing, but it's protocol for me, and she's happily distracted as soon as someone shoves a drink into her hand. Some of the liquid spills over the rim and I grit my teeth, continuing to focus on my preparations.

She keeps squirming, shouting in the direction of the dance-floor where her group of friends can hear her. Her long, crimson hair that's obviously dyed keeps finding its way back into my workspace, spilling over her shoulder into the area I've just taken the antiseptic to. I sigh when it happens again for the third time, sitting back in my seat, my patience burned to its dregs.

"Get out of my chair."

My voice is so low that she doesn't hear me. She's too busy trying to call her friends over, to brag about what she's about to do. It's incredibly annoying and I've already had a day from hell.

I *hate* knowing that the girl from the lobby lives next door. She's infuriating, aggressive with her words and actions, pounding at both the elevator and our front door, demanding that I move my motorcycle.

She may have been having arguably as bad of a day as I did, given the sight of her unruly hair and tired hazel eyes, their coloring more of a raw umber than burnt. Her cheeks were a soft pink that I wanted to reach out and stroke, if it weren't for both the state of my hands and her shitty attitude.

I came straight home after hearing the news that I hadn't gotten the apprenticeship I wanted at Mystic Mark Tattoos. I thought I had shown an incredible portfolio of work, filled with both drawings and tattoos done in this very living room, without the distractions of beer, girls, and weed. They said I was too young, that I need to work on straightening my lines and that maybe a different style would suit me better.

There had been no parking spots when I arrived home. Normally, I park in front of Slate's rust bucket of a Bronco, my sleek motorcycle teetering on the white painted line a hair before the tow zone. Tonight, there had been a moving truck jammed there instead, which meant more noisy neighbors moving into the already packed building. I don't need to meet more people at mailboxes, fight them for the one slow-ass elevator that might fall if more than three people get on it—two if you're riding it with Slate's enormous build. I don't want to have to fight for a parking spot, either.

Yeah, I might have been feeling a little petty when I blocked the truck in, but I was only planning on leaving my bike there for a few minutes while I dropped my portfolio off at the apartment before turning right back around to ride into the night and clear my head. But then *she* showed up, nearly knocking me over on her way out the door, guns already blazing, rude and looking more than ready to pick a fight.

So, fight we did.

I'll admit, she has some spunk going up against me like that, her attitude much larger than her short frame. I could feel her eyes all over me, goosebumps raised on my skin in response to her scrutiny. She's someone who I might have considered asking out once upon a time, even if her blonde hair was falling from her ponytail, long waves tangled around her heart-shaped face.

I wanted to brush them away and smooth the furrow between her brows, but the way she looked at me—*glared* at me—had gotten under my skin.

With her question, I knew that she was the one who was responsible for the moving truck. Like I said, I had every intention to move my motorcycle until the door to the lobby almost knocked me in the head. She didn't even apologize, snipping at me and commanding me to move my motorcycle.

Her face twisted so prettily when I denied it was mine.

Her demand was my last straw, though.

No, that's not entirely true. My final straw had been finding out she lives next door. When she showed up at my apartment with fire in her eyes and rosy cheeks, I was hardly able to swallow my surprise at the sight of her and her room-mate, angrier than all hell. The very same expression she wasn't able to conceal almost made me smirk, but the threat that she had my bike towed sparked something almost deadly in me. I worked damn hard to buy and maintain that motorcycle. I wanted to grab her, force her down the stairs with me to see if it was still there, maybe bend her over it and—

"What?" The girl asks incredulously, drawing me from the thoughts of my new neighbor. She cranes her neck over her shoulder, that blood red hair touching my work area again.

But I'm done playing around. This had been a terrible decision on my part. I thought tattooing some partygoers would help calm my irritation because art usually does, but tonight it's only adding fuel to the fire.

I stand, already reaching to pack up my things. "Get the fuck out of my chair or I'll tattoo a dick on you," I grunt, ignoring her spluttering confusion. The crimson to her cheeks looks nowhere near as good as it had on *hers.*

"Fuck you," the girl screeches, stumbling to her feet. The group of lingering boys watch on and one even steps closer to help steady the poor girl like I've pushed her. Tears prick her eyes but I don't feel bad about it, if she wanted a tattoo that badly she would've followed my direction, not fucking wasted my time.

She whirls around, tugging the hem of her dress down with one hand, wrenching her arm free from the boy's grasp, and tosses her drink right into my face. I wince as the juiced-down alcohol stings my eyes. I lick my lips and cringe; it's as fruity as it smells. Vodka, it tastes like.

Swiping my now damp hair from my face, I use the same glare that everyone cowers from, but she's already dragging the boy into the throng of people on the dance-floor. Releasing a harsh breath, I take the loss, peeling the black gloves from my hands and shoving my things under my arms.

"Woah, *dude,"* Slate—one of my roommates—says when

25

he stumbles into me on the way to my room. My *locked* room, because I don't need anyone coming in here to fuck or snoop or touch my things. Them being in my apartment is already bad enough. They can fuck in the stairwell for all I care. "What the hell happened to you?"

Slate's pants dare to fall to the ground, button and zipper both undone. His shirt has been shucked off, either because he's spilled beer down his chest or because he's about to get lucky, I don't know which for sure. I don't care. The music is too fucking loud and too fucking poppy, and the air is thick and hot. My skin is sticky from the drink thrown at me and this day comes second to worst out of the twenty-one years I've been alive.

"You invited a bunch of assholes to your party, Slate. What the hell do you think happened?" I bite, tugging my keys from my pocket and sliding one into the lock. I don't have the temperament to even deal with my roommates right now. I just want to be left alone.

"So, she denied you, Knoxie," Slate teases, slurring a bit. The chocolate of his eyes is bright and normally his jokes make me feel better, but right now I'm itching to get clean and get the fuck out of here.

I really should've started drinking.

"Don't start with me," I sigh, shoving my way through the door, flicking on the light. My shoulders loosen when I step inside. My own space, decorated how I like. My bed is on the wall opposite my door, made up perfectly and I'd collapse right onto it if I didn't have someone's drink running down my neck and seeping into my shirt. There's a small table next to the bed, a lamp and books stacked high for late night reading when I'm not sketching.

To the left is my desk, pushed up against the sole window. My school textbooks are shoved as far to the side as I can manage to make room for my art supplies. Outside of the window, I notice the moon high in the sky, calling to me like one lost soul to another. A shelf beside the desk is filled with sketchbooks, their black spines stacked in order of size. No one would be able to tell them apart except for me. I'd love to do nothing more than sit down and sketch something, but with the commotion going on outside of my door, there's no way I'll be able to focus.

I make my way to the desk, dropping off my tattooing supplies before beelining to my closet on the right side of the room. Slate follows me inside and I hear the door shut softly behind him as I rip the soaked shirt from my body. It does little to drown out the noise of the party going on outside of my door, but I'm thankful he's closed it anyway. I toss the shirt towards my laundry basket and reach inside the closet for a new one. My wardrobe consists of dark colors, though most of them are black.

"Hey," Slate pouts, leaning up against the wall as I change. I keep my eyes off of his because it's obvious that he knows something is up with me and he's going to try to get me to stay, to try and make me feel better. He'll probably even recruit Ace—our other roommate—to help out, but who knows what he's up to right now. "You're acting as grumpy as our new neighbor," Slate continues, and I *really* don't like being compared to her. I'd rather call that drunk girl back to finish her tattoo. "Who is pretty cute by the way. What's going on with you?"

My fingers fist the shirt in my hands but I shake my head, pulling it over my damp chest. I won't be able to shower in the one bathroom we have while this party is going on. Someone will either walk in on me or bang on the door until I get out. *Whatever,* at least the shirt will soak up the rest of the alcohol. "Just a rough day, man. Nothing to worry about."

27

Slate doesn't know that it's the understatement of the year.

He frowns, trying to catch my eye, but again, I refuse to meet his gaze, pulling out my leather jacket next.

"It's not like…" He trails off like he doesn't even want to ask this, and my shoulders tense because I also don't want him to bring up the taboo topic I know he's trying to bring up. "It's not like summer break, right?"

I desperately try not to let my body recoil but it does, going completely still. My muscles seize and I squeeze my eyes shut as the memory resurfaces, my chest struggling to pull in air. Two summers ago, when I finished freshman year and returned home for break, my father was waiting for me with a deep frown on his face, something not unusual for him. I took all of two steps inside before he began shouting and threatening me because he found out that I'd been pretending to be a business major like he wanted, when all this time I've really been in art. Dick, my step-brother, had been the one to out me, and I can still remember that smug smirk on his face as my father—

I fled. I took my motorcycle and sped down the winding roads behind his big house, the one where I wouldn't have had to see him all summer if I didn't want to. I hadn't been expecting to see him at all, especially not when I walked in the door. The sketchbook tucked up under my arm hadn't helped the situation one bit. I can still remember my step-mothers cries, as if there was anything that she could do. I wonder if seeing her husband act like that was the first time or if she's been enduring it in the five years they've been together since my mother passed.

I was being reckless out on those roads, scared out of my fucking mind. My face ached from his fists and blood was clouding my vision from the thick cut on my eyebrow, curtesy of my father's wedding band. As I tried to clear my vision, the handlebars slipped from my grip around a sharp curve I hadn't been prepared for.

I don't remember much after that, except waking up in the hospital with both of my hands fucked beyond belief.

My father got what he wanted after all, because no matter how hard I goddamn try, my hands still shake and my art has suffered tremendously because of it.

"No," I answer, voice trembling slightly. I can still hear my father's ugly words sometimes, feel his fists on my face and the burn of my step-brother's snake-like eyes as he all but laughed. Sometimes, memories of the accident visit me in my sleep, the hot road grinding against my skin, the bones in my hands shattering on impact as I tried to brace myself. The helmet I'd shoved onto my already wounded face had hurt at the time, but it had saved my life, for whatever that's worth. I clear the thickness from my throat and try again, ignoring the way my hands tremble. "No, it's not like that."

It's both better and worse, somehow. Better, because no one is assaulting me, and although my father still tries to reach out, there has never been an apology. I don't care if ignoring him only fuels his anger towards me. I lost everything when I ruined my hands.

I've worked hard since then to get back to where I was artistically, but there are differences now that I've had to learn to work through and with. They still shake, and the patches of skin they had to take from my thighs to recover my hands are an eyesore, but I don't care how cut-up I look. I only want to be able to tattoo.

Maybe my father was right. Maybe my artistic abilities aren't good enough to be where I want. Maybe the tattoo parlors denying me apprenticeships only confirm that.

"We can ditch the party right now," Slate tells me, leaning

closer. I know he can read me like a fucking book, can tell that I'm bothered by his question and he's trying to fix it, but all I want right now is to be alone. "Let Ace deal with the party. We can go on a ride and talk if you want to, Knox. We can go down to Rhonda's. I'll even let you drive Cherry."

As much as I would enjoy going down to Rhonda's—our old stomping grounds—I just don't have it in me right now. When we grew old enough to get into bars, both Slate and Ace stopped going to Rhonda's. They don't know that I still frequent the tiny diner not far from here.

I'd like to keep it that way for a little while longer.

I shake my head in response, even with the offer to drive Cherry.

"That's alright, man," I answer, turning to face him. Slate's thick eyebrows are furrowed deeply and it makes me feel bad that I'm ruining his night. I need to distract him, and while he knows me better than anyone, I also know *him* better than I know anyone. He's most likely sought me out for one thing. "Grab those condoms you came in here for and go bag your girl."

The distraction works. Slate curses, his chocolate eyes bulging wide at the reminder. "Oh fuck! Sage! Or was it Paige? Shit, man, I don't even remember her name." He's so frantic I would laugh if I had the energy. There is no shortage of girls for Slate to choose from, even if he seems to be sleeping his way through the school. If this one has bounced already, he'll have no issues finding another girl to spend the night with.

He catches the box of condoms I toss his way with ease, despite the panicky rambling.

"Just call her 'baby,' or something," I advise, clapping him on the shoulder and guiding him towards the door. "They love that shit."

The wind in my ears drowns out the bad thoughts.

This. This is what I love, what I thrive on. Roads untraveled, the night and. wind my only friends. Shadows chase my route and the silence rights my soul. The darkness takes care of me. Always has, always will.

The thrum of the bike between my thighs is exhilarating, especially when it climbs to a speed that makes my heart race faster in my chest.

Yep, not even the accident stopped me from getting right back up, selling my old art to pay for my classes now that my father no longer will, and I was able to save up enough extra money to afford a used motorcycle. It's not as nice as the one I totaled, but with a little elbow grease, it gets me around until I'm able to afford a new one.

It's just me and the world right now: the bike, the moon, and me. No one can catch me, taunt me, insult me, *hurt* me. The middle of the night will never treat me the way that others have.

Shifting my weight, I glide around a curve, slowing the motorcycle to a stop. I've arrived at the hilltop that overlooks the city, glowing brightly in the night. I've found myself here many times since I started at Vulcan University, and it's my favorite spot to come and think.

It's far enough to have a good view of the sky and I count whatever constellations I can, cutting the engine. I shove the kickstand down and pull my helmet off, breathing in the crisp scent of night.

Hanging my helmet on the handlebar, I unzip my coat and peel the leather gloves from my hands. They still tremble under the moonlight, but less so than earlier when I'd had my tattoo gun in my hands.

I clench them into fists, cursing.

Slate has three or four jagged tattoos from me because he's always offered his help whenever someone needs it. When I'd been practicing on myself after regaining the ability to draw and handle the instrument, he was the first to volunteer, even knowing that I hadn't been able to keep my lines straight no matter how hard I tried. Months later, I've improved, but there is still a ways to go.

Most of my roommate's tattoos are tribal, which were easier to work with when he wanted one added, because it was mostly filling in shapes with black. It was drawing those patterns that was the difficult part, and it's not often that I don't think about how fucked up some of the line-work is, as I'm constantly reminded with the amount of times Slate chooses not to wear a shirt around the apartment.

My skin, however, is filled with a different tribute, one of the mythological sorts. Icarus's inevitable fall inked on my torso, because when I truly began reaching out for what I wanted in life, I was burned. I fell. Psyche and Eros intertwined at the top of my thigh, because I, too, should only be loved in the dark, where no one can see my flaws. There are large, bony wings covering the expanse of my back because I always wished that I could just fly away from here, from all of the problems in my life. Others dot my skin, each one curated to perfection, no matter what anyone else has to say. I've spent years drawing, seeking out the tattoo artists who would be the ones to ink my skin with their work, until I was old enough and good enough to do it myself.

I love each and every single one of them.

The breeze blows some of my limp hair in my eyes and I hastily brush it away. I need to get it cut soon.

I slide off of the bike, keeping the headlights on as I dig inside the pocket of my leather jacket for the small notepad and pencil I keep stowed there for times like this. When I need to get away and draw out all of the things filling my head.

Flipping past my previous sketches, I open to a fresh page and put the tip of the pencil to the paper, ignoring the slight shake of my hand. It's something that I'm not sure I will ever get used to, relearning how to make those crisp, straight lines that used to come so easily.

Right now, alone in the middle of the night, none of that matters.

I draw until my wrist hurts and I can hardly hold the pencil, losing the nighttime hours.

Sitting back, I assess my work. There's a warmup sketch of a woman's legs, the tops of her slender thighs covered, peeking out from the hem of my leather jacket. On the next is a bunny, this one a skeleton, and the black of its eye sockets reads *"fuck you."* I also drew a Cerberus showing a full row of sharp teeth as it growls fiercely, two of the canine-like heads gnashing at each other. It has potential to be my next tattoo, actually.

It isn't until the early hours of the morning when I'm sure that my apartment is finally cleared of partygoers that I return home. I take my time, enjoying the last few moments to myself before I enter the town again, where no one seems to sleep. *At least we all have that in common,* I think, racing past an Uber filled with giggling girls who wave at me as I go.

There might not be a point in even returning home, knowing that I won't be able to sleep anyway, but being in my room with my sketchpads and books, easy access to the rest of my art supplies, is a comforting thought.

I'm not expecting to run into my new neighbor on the

way in, but of course, because my night isn't quite done getting on my last nerve, I do.

She's walking back from the parking lot as I swing my leg off of my bike, removing my helmet. Her head is buried in her phone, her long, blonde hair washed and hanging down her back like a curtain of gold. She's wearing a sweatshirt with the school's mascot on it despite the balmy summer night, *but who am I to judge? I'm wearing a leather jacket for fucks sake.* To complete her nighttime look, she dons a pair of sleep shorts that show off her long legs.

I stumble, but quickly recover, glaring at the curb I tripped over as I watched her.

I don't know what it is that compels me to talk to her, to tease her because she's clearly just come outside to move the truck with the flashing hazards now that my bike is no longer blocking it in, but I do. "Finally got that truck moved, huh, Princess?"

She startles at my words, hazel eyes wide with surprise. Her lids quickly fall into a glare and her mouth puckers sourly when she recognizes me. If she weren't mentally planning my downfall, she would look cute. Fuck it, she does look cute, even if she *is* planning my downfall.

"No thanks to you, neighbor," she mutters, trying to avoid crossing into my space. It's impossible, since I'm parked in my usual spot, sans moving truck. I watch the way her eyes drop down my torso, taking in my jacket and I smirk, enjoying the warm tone that spreads across her cheeks at me catching her.

I tut, playfully. "So rude."

"Why would I be a peach when you've been nothing but a jerk since I moved in?" She defends, crossing her arms over her chest. I kind of like this look on her, defensive, standing up to me despite being almost a foot shorter. She's easy to rile and I like that. "I've had a hellish day and meeting you didn't help. Then, you go and slam doors in people's faces and play your horrendous music as loud as fucking possible. *Some people* want to sleep, you know."

I wish I could sleep, too.

"Still salty you weren't invited, Princess?" I deflect.

She scoffs and steps around me, clearly more than ready for this conversation to be over. I'm not, though, spinning on my heel to follow her towards the building. *"As if."*

She stalks for the door but my longer strides eat the distance between us easily. "I think I might catch the elevator with you," I tell her. "Since we're going to the same floor, and all."

I don't know why I'm trying to engage, why I'm egging her on. I've had a nice enough night when I escaped the party, but there's something about her. I *want* her attention on me, even if it's because she's annoyed with me. I want that sharp tongue and dark glares pointed in my direction.

I could easily apologize for earlier, for shutting the door in her face and telling my roommates to do the same, but I think I'll wait. As much as my ride helped calm me down, I'm not ready to make peace with the fact that she threatened to have my motorcycle towed.

I don't play about my bike.

"No, thanks," she responds, all but ripping the front door off its hinges. She's probably hoping that it will hit me on the backswing but my hand's already there, catching it and pulling it wider, trailing her inside.

"More of a stairs kind of girl, I presume?" I ask innocently, referring to her trip up to the fourth floor by stairwell when I had taken the elevator up.

She grits her teeth and I can tell that she wants to take the bait as she jams her finger into the button, calling the elevator.

It's still on the first floor from when she must have taken it down to move the truck. The door opens with a whine that makes me shiver.

"More of a 'don't talk to me' kind of girl," she retorts, nearly growling when I shove myself inside of the metal box with her. Her anger clouds the space, thick and cloying. She keeps to herself during the ride, much to my dismay, glaring at the neon green numbers as the rickety elevator ascends.

"Feisty, Princess," I smirk.

"Do not call me that!" Her scowl is strong. Scary, almost. It has the corners of my mouth twitching upwards.

"Sure thing, Princess."

CHAPTER 4
QUINN

A deep rattling of the walls shakes me from my sleep. It vibrates through my chest, the ardent bass and pounding drums reverberates my bones. The timber of the singer's voice swims in my head, throaty and low, and I'm unable to pluck the words from the lyrics and make sense of them this early in the morning.

I blink once, twice. My eyelids feel like sandpaper and my head is stuffed with tiredness; a sharp pain settled in my skull despite the darkness of my room.

Night still licks the walls and I groan, rolling over. I shove my pillow over my head but it does little to block the disruption coming from the other side of the wall. I have no idea what time it is. If it's still the same night where I'd run into the asshole next door on my way back inside from moving the truck, I'll be absolutely *livid*.

After I noticed the motorcycle was gone, I was hoping that things were starting to finally look up for the rest of my first night at my apartment. Knox—as the third boy at the door supplied—had left while his roommates' party seemed to be winding down, if the three giggling drunk girls on the elevator ride down to the lobby was any sign. They'd been gushing about one of the roommates, Slate. One of the girl's brunette hair was disheveled in her ponytail, as if someone had tried to run their fingers through it, or had wrapped said hairstyle around their fist.

Gag.

"He kept calling me baby," she raved, her voice filled with awe. Both of her friends started squealing in excitement. I could hardly contain the desperate urge to roll my eyes at their annoyance, how they openly talked about the lines of muscle cording his body and the length of his cock with a complete stranger inside of this tiny metal box with them. It's not as if they were whispering. I cut a glance at the girl swooning over one of my rude neighbor's appendages.

Her bright green eyes were clouded with drink and I couldn't help comparing them to Knox's jade ones. I was still itching to draw them, but was much too annoyed and exhausted to do so. Her face was flushed, the top button of her shirt undone. She looked like everything beautifully fucked.

My mouth flattened into a line, wondering which of the remaining two roommates had been the one to claim her tonight.

Eventually, the doors to the elevator had screeched open, but even the shrill noise didn't deter their gossiping. They stumbled out of the elevator with a cheerfulness only alcohol and dick could conjure, laughing their way up the quieting streets.

It was a miracle that I didn't have a parking ticket clinging to the window of the rental truck. I had moved it both easily and quickly, something I would've been able to do if that asshole Knox had given me the damn space when I asked him to relocate his motorcycle in the first place.

And, of course, as I cursed his name for the umpteenth time of the night, he appeared.

Cloaked in a worn leather jacket that clung to his broad shoulders, and what I'm assuming is his usual garb: black pants, combat boots, and t-shirt. There was a tight line to his mouth, his deep eyes reflecting the nighttime sky, caressed by equally dark, thick lashes. He looked as tired as I felt with slight purple rings around his eyes. Knox's helmet, that, when he shucked off, pulled his hair up in the most perfectly disheveled ways, even more so when he ran his gloved fingers through it with that damned smirk on his face, directed at me.

He hadn't allowed my gaze to linger on his handsomeness. A streak of mischief glimmered in his eyes like a shooting star, taunting me. When Knox spoke, his tone was deep and dulcet, unexpected for the jeer that was about to fall from his perfectly pink lips. It took longer than I would admit for my tired mind to grasp onto the words coming from his moving mouth. His asshole-ish smile only widened when I scoffed and took his bait.

Oh, how he had gotten on my nerves.

Again.

And now this: music flowing so easily through the wall at who knows what hour.

I'm so exhausted, I could cry. My body is sore with the efforts of moving, my mind a muddled mess. Tears prick the back of my eyes, my sinuses tightening as I grit my teeth, trying to swallow the feeling back. If my pillowcase wets with a single tear, I will never admit it.

How has the day from hell somehow managed to turn into the night from hell too? Or is it morning again already? *What the fuck have I done to deserve this?*

Even more so, how do his roommates deal with this? Are they all awake and circle-jerking to the music, long bored after their party has died down? Or do they delight in the fact knowing I'm their neighbor and have already complained about the noise once. Why not bother me again when any normal person should be asleep?

Frustration courses through my veins like a lance, hot and unyielding. The rush has tears leaking from the corners of my eyes as I push to my knees, channeling every ounce of burning hot ire and rotting exhaustion into my fists, pounding them against the thin wall.

My chest heaves, burning with each labored breath I take. I wait, hoping that banging on the wall once has gotten my message across to the boy on the other side. There's something nagging at me, telling me that I know exactly which one of the three boys living next door it's fated to be.

There is no response for a breath, two. Then, a thump as loud as my own answers. One singular knock is all I'm gifted back, for a split moment. The music rings louder as he turns the volume impossibly higher. It sounds as clear as day, like I'm standing in the front row to my very own rock concert.

I want to scream in frustration, claw my way through the plaster and tear the speaker to bits. And maybe tear into him too.

What a prick.

Sighing in exasperation, I rip another sheet of paper from my drawing pad and crumple it up with all of the rage and annoyance still cloying my veins. I force so much of my irritation into the motion that I fear it might burst into flames. I want to tear it to shreds and stuff those tiny pieces right up my douchebag neighbor's ass.

Instead, I throw the ball of paper as hard as I can against the wall. I can't hear the sound it makes when it hits its target, nor the soft crunch when it lands on the floor, staring sadly up at me.

Music of my own pounds loudly through the earbuds I stuffed into my ears when it became clear that the raging music next door was not going to be turned down. I considered marching over there to give Knox a piece of my mind, and I even circled back on my idea of punching a hole through this very wall, but instead I opted to play my own music so loudly that if I'm lucky, my eardrums will be affected so greatly that I never have to hear the music from next door again.

Okay, so I might be being a little dramatic, but I'm tired as hell and even angrier.

Art had been my next attempt at blowing off some of the steam turning my cheeks cadmium red. I pulled out the well-worn sketchbook from my bag, along with the colored pencils I always have stuffed in the front pocket, and flipped to a fresh page, trying to allow my mind to unleash *anything* across the creamy sheet.

Except—everything that comes from my hands is trash. My lines are heavy with fatigue and malice, so deep and dark that I've nearly torn through the pages. I've broken the tips on four of my pencils already and I couldn't find the sharpener I swore I put in my bag.

It's as if my mind doesn't know what to draw. The beginnings of sketches quickly turn into shapes of madness and sleep-deprivation, things I can't even make out. There's a hand, bones tearing from the flesh as they splinter into pieces. Another is of a cloaked figure atop a black stallion that makes my stomach clench. A few soft strokes form a pair of lips curved into an incredulous smirk.

My shoulders finally begin to loosen as I work through the piece, but once I come to the realization of who I was subconsciously making the man on the horse's back look like, I tore that drawing out, too.

That had been the very last page in my sketchbook. The black of the back cover stares at me, taunting me, laughing at me.

It doesn't matter anyway, because my stomach has soured with the thought of my final attempt at letting this anger go.

I shove myself away from my desk. My spine is rigid and my bones are vibrating with tension. On the back of one of my scrap papers I began writing a list of art supplies to pick up while out shopping—pencil sharpener, new sketchbook, *earplugs.*

I even managed to unpack most of the boxes in my room before the sun barely tinted the sky with light. Terrible, I know, because I've only managed a little more than an hour's sleep since moving into this hellhole of an apartment. I adore Rory's sister, Peep, but right now I'm cursing her. How could she claim that this was her favorite place to live out of all the places she and her roommates have rented here?

At least I've been semi-productive in the hours since.

I dress in the first thing I pull out of my drawers, a t-shirt and a pair of jeans that never fail to make my ass look great. It doesn't matter though because I'm not trying to impress anyone today, I just need to get out of this apartment for a bit. Maybe the fresh air will do me some good.

Quickly brushing through my hair, I shove it up into a ponytail as I make my way to the bathroom to wash my face and brush my teeth. I look like hell, I notice as I stare at myself in the mirror, all puffy-eyed and paler than normal due to lack of sleep.

I grab my purse and lock up the apartment behind me. Rory must still be sleeping the morning away because there's not a sound coming from her room. *Lucky bitch.*

Trailing the few blocks down to the art supply, I walk the familiar streets of Hardwich, home of Vulcan University. It's a smaller town, one I've become well acquainted with during my freshman year of school.

One entire block is lined with bars and I can't wait to be in there on weekend nights with Rory, drinking and dancing our lives away with our fake IDs. Each one is unique, fighting desperately to draw in the college crowds. There's Revolver, a country bar, Jameson's, an Irish pub, and a dance club called One More. Those are the bars I hear about on campus most often, but there are a handful more I have yet to explore.

I pass small businesses and restaurants, the early morning serene in comparison to how my apartment has been. I can feel my shoulders loosening with each step I take away from the building, my stress ebbing away.

The art supply store—Art Haven—has always been a place of solitude. Being surrounded by fresh supplies is encouraging. The sidewalk is painted colorfully, flowers and vines creating a path to the door, it's *open* sign a vibrant blue where it hangs on its hook.

The large windows are covered with messages welcoming the Vulcan University students back to campus, and there's an eerily spot-on drawing of Perry the Pinto—our schools beloved mascot—with a foam finger on his hand and the other on his hip, his horse mouth pulled into a grin that should seem cheerful, but looks like he's ready to bite.

The bell to the shop rings as I push through the door but

there is no one at the counter to greet me. I don't mind because it's still early and I'm not in the mood to pretend that my morning hasn't been one of the shittiest ones I've had in a long time, and I'm not even hungover.

The scent of the store fills my lungs and I shut my eyes, reveling in it. I can feel the recharging of my creative energy already, my inspiration trying to blossom once more.

Maybe I can talk to the owner and convince them to let me live here instead.

Taking my time, I shuffle up and down the aisles, drinking in everything for all of its glory. Paints lined up by brand and color, a rainbow bursting with life. They're pristine, swollen like plump berries, not yet crusted with use. There's an entire aisle dedicated to sketchbooks and papers of all sorts; canvases larger than my body stacked against the back walls, pencils with graphite of all weights and strengths. I pluck a new HB pencil from its container and admire it. I might come back around for a few more before I leave, depending on my running total. One can never have enough pencils.

A kneaded eraser is added to my quickly growing pile and *aha!* there's the sharpener I need. I sweep back around the front of the store for a basket, dumping the supplies in before I'm rocketing back off to the sketchbook section.

There's a shuffling of noise in another aisle. I gather that it must be the associate on shift. Music begins playing softly through a speaker by the front and it's much less grating than the kind that so rudely woke me this morning. The chill Indie music fills the space with even more life, and combined with the streams of sunlight sliding in through the windows, I think my day might just be starting to pick up.

I end up with three sketchbooks in my basket—a feat in itself not to choose one of each of the gorgeous books calling my name—and I continue traipsing through the store. Passing the sculpting section, I pause for a moment, wondering if I should sign up for a class next semester. At the thought of the clay thick against my skin, constantly caked under my nails and embedded into my clothes, I decide against it.

I grab a can of fixative for when my drawing class starts up and toss it into the basket hooked in the crook of my arm. We're going to be using charcoals for most of the semester, another messy medium I don't care for. I'm not a fan of the feeling of the dry chalk against my fingertips, sticking between the creases of my fingers. It takes forever to get out.

I'm a simple girl with simple tastes, graphite is best, though I do enjoy working with colored pencils every once in a while. I've always wanted to try my hand at painting. Rory's talent with oils is incredible, but I'm sure she's only making it look easy because of her insane talent, and it's much harder than I think it is.

There are so many different types of art I want to try that it's almost overwhelming. Well, anything in my current state of fatigue is overwhelming, but I don't feel like I've found my style of art quite yet. It's something I'm trying hard to figure out this year at college. I've loved drawing since I was a young girl, but as I've grown, my love for the art has become more of a nuisance than fun.

Surely, I will figure it all out someday.

I take the longest in the paint aisle. The different types are astounding: oils, gouache, watercolors, and acrylics. The possibilities are endless.

Tubes upon tubes of color scream for my attention and I admire each one, drinking in their vibrant hues. There are reds of all shades, ochres that remind me of autumn; phthalos and umbers and titanium white stare at me, waiting for me to take them home, squeeze the life from them so they're bursting across my canvas. My gaze snags on a unique color and I lean closer to read the name: *dioxazine.*

I abandon that one, instead picking out a tube each of the most important colors that I can blend together to create any color that I might be in need of. It's like a super power, the ability to mix any shade from only a few, and I love it.

There is a plethora of brushes hanging above the paints and I sweep my fingers across the bristles of a fan shaped one, smiling at its softness.

One of the sketchbooks I added to my basket is for paint-ing, the paper thicker and able to withstand the viscous medium. It's small, something for quick and rough paintings because I want to get used to the material before committing. I've always wanted to work with paint and now seems like as good of time as any.

After adding a few brushes to my basket, I make my way towards the front of the store to check out, halting in my tracks when I see who is behind the counter.

Thankfully, it isn't Knox, but it *is* one of his roommates.

It's the blond. He's leaning against the counter, swiping though his phone without a care in the world. For a fleeting moment I wonder if he's only working the opening shift because the music also didn't allow him to sleep peacefully, but I think better of it. Knox's music is probably a lullaby to him.

His hair is surprisingly neat, brushed back with the damp-ness still clinging to it from a morning shower. He's clad in a dark t-shirt that leaves a plethora of patchwork tattoos on display. There's an over-the-top cup of coffee on the counter that puts my order to shame. His posture exudes an effortless confidence, and when he looks up and catches sight of me staring at him like a deer in headlights, a dimple deepens in cheek.

"Fancy seeing you here, neighbor," he greets.

I bite back the groan at the base of my throat, moving closer. All I have to do is pay for my things and then I can leave. *Sounds simple enough.* I don't have to converse with him outside of the necessary cashier talk, and maybe, if I'm lucky, he won't even try to taunt me.

Yeah, *right.*

"Hi," I grit, placing my basket on the counter. He peers into it and I tense, feeling judged. I have no idea what kind of art he's into, if he even is at all, but I don't like him knowing this part of me, not when he and his roommates have been nothing but rude. It feels a little too personal.

Those ocean blue eyes flicker back to mine, studying me, as if he's deciding—just like I am—if he should be civil or not. I don't balk from his assessment, probably seeing nothing more than my tired eyes and the downturn of my mouth.

I shift on my feet, silently willing him to stop looking at me and start ringing up my supplies. Instead, he smirks.

And there goes my mood.

Much to my surprise, the first thing out of his mouth isn't a jibe. "How are you this morning, Darling?"

Darling? I want to snort. Or grimace, but like the lovely woman I am, I swallow it down in favor of trying to get out of here without my state of mind plummeting further.

"Lovely," I offer, trying for a smile, but it feels forced. His lips twitch higher as he catches me smothering the look. "And yourself?"

"Fantastic."

I nod, pinning the sour remark on the tip of my tongue to the roof of my mouth. *Yes, I'm sure your party was just lovely, unlike the rest of my night.*

Jerk.

"Right…" I trail off, eyes flickering down to my basket in an attempt to tell him to *hurry the fuck up* without so bluntly saying *hurry the fuck up* like I so desperately want to.

"First year here?"

"Second," I answer flatly, praying he starts moving. The muscles of his arms flex where they're on display and he reaches into my basket, examining the first tube of paint he pulls out. Phthalo Green.

Not for anything specific really, like maybe, say, eyes.

I know that I shouldn't be trying to make even worse enemies with the boys who live next door, but I can't help myself. My attitude is on the fritz due to their actions. They should be the ones that have to deal with the consequences.

"I'm a junior," he says, picking up the check-out gun as slow as possible.

"Congratulations," I answer, trying to force a lighter inflection to my tone. He doesn't seem to buy it by the huff of laughter that slips past his lips.

His mirth-filled gaze sweeps over me again and I try not to duck my head, fighting off the fire of both a blush at his attention and my irritation at his less than leisurely pace.

"I'm Ace," he muses, and the chirp of the scanner going off makes me blink. "I think we've met somewhere before."

It's what I've been waiting for; the teasing. I remember him perfectly. The one who answered the door after Knox, leering at Rory like the horndog college student I'd expect him to be, before slamming it right in our faces again.

My temper snaps when he puts the gun down to pull out a bag, taking all the goddamn time in the world to unfold the paper sack. My fingers curl into fists and I can feel my gaze turning into a glare that my brother tells me could cut glass. "Are all three of you always this insufferable?" I blurt, cutting to the chase.

It's a rhetorical question, one that I already know the answer to, but Ace answers anyway.

"Most call it charm," he shrugs, grinning as he moves onto the next item in my basket.

I don't hold back the urge to roll my eyes.

"That's exactly the word I was thinking," I mutter. If he hears it, he doesn't acknowledge.

"So, your roommate is pretty cute," he drawls, scanning another tube of paint. That's two in the span of one minute. He should be fired for all of his lollygagging. I glance at the door, praying that his roommate doesn't waltz right in, because that, I think, would mean that I *actually* have the worst luck ever. "Does she have a name?"

I cut my eyes back to his and narrow them. "Don't we all?"

"And yet, I didn't catch yours." Ace cocks his head and his blond hair flops from one side to the other.

"It's Quinn," I grind through clenched teeth. My already thin patience is now threadbare. Only a few strings keep hold of my sanity, but Ace is quickly sawing through them with his grating banter.

"Nice name for a lovely girl, I'm sure," he teases, but there is nothing funny about his words. These boys might be having their fun, but to me it was never something to laugh at and the situation has only gotten worse. "And your roommate's name? Does she have a boyfriend?"

"Sorry," I bite, "She's not the secret fuck type." Though, she might just be after her breakup with her long-term boyfriend, Max, at the beginning of summer.

Thankfully, my basket is nearly empty. I dig around in my purse for my credit card in haste, wanting to be prepared for when Ace *finally* tells me my total. The quicker I can pay and leave, the quicker I can hole back up in my apartment. Maybe take a nap on the couch.

"Trust me, Darling," Ace says with a wink. "It wouldn't be a secret."

I can't help the splutter of a laughter that bubbles up my throat. He startles, shocked by my sudden chortle as I stare up at him, incredulous. "That usually works, doesn't it?"

I watch his façade falter and I lift my chin with pride. Clearly, I've caught him off guard.

"What?"

"The whole 'Darling' thing. You just expect women to swoon at that, huh?" His smile is hesitant, and he takes the card I hold out to him. "I thought so. Can I have my supplies now, Darling?" I ask, batting my eyelashes a few times for good measure. Ever the face of innocence, I am.

Ace takes my credit card without further comment, running my total. I don't even care what it is right now, I just want him to swipe the fucking card so I can hightail it out of here. His mouth is set in a firm line now, shoulders tense. The aura in the entire shop has changed with my retort, but I don't have the ability to care right now, itching to get away.

When he hands it back to me, I stuff it back into my purse. Ace shoves my bag across the counter with a grumbled, "Knox was right."

"Excuse me?" *Knox was right? About what? The asshole doesn't even know the first thing about me.*

"You are grumpy."

The sheath containing my ire is stripped away. My fingers curl into fists around the handle of my bag, my nails biting into the skin of my palm. The rumble of anger only fuels my irritation and I'm unable to keep the alizarin crimson from staining my cheeks as I glare up at him.

"Tell me you're shitting sunshine when you haven't slept all night because of your roommate."

Ace's answering smirk is cutting, suggestive. It makes me blind with rage.

Spinning on my heel, I shove myself out the door before he can answer my anger with another sly remark.

Fucking assholes, all of them.

CHAPTER 5
QUINN

"All I'm saying is that I think he's pretty cute," Rory scoffs, defensively.

Since we moved in, it seems as though my entire life revolves around the boys living next door to us.

While I finally managed to get the sleep I deserved last night, something had felt...*off.* The other side of the wall was almost too quiet as I laid in the darkness, awaiting sleep to take me in its hold, even though my body had been aching for it all weekend. All night, there hadn't been a peep from the asshole I share my wall with.

I know it's Knox's room on the other side, there's no way in fucking hell that it isn't, but the lack of music blaring through the plaster was almost like a dream.

I shove the thoughts from my mind. It's too early in the morning to be squabbling over our neighbors with Rory.

It's our first day of classes for our sophomore year at VU, and I won't let them ruin it.

The sun shines brightly on Rory and I as we walk to our first class of the day: Drawing 201. It's the only one in our schedules this semester that we share. Rory is delving deeper into her major of oil painting this year, but I'm still on the fence about how I'm going to continue my own when drawing has been so unfulfilling. I yearn for that feeling of pride over my work instead of the existential dread of how I'm not good enough that has been haunting me for years.

Rory has her drawing pad tucked under an arm as she walks. Mine is held in a similar fashion; the obnoxiously large pad of paper bigger than my torso nearly slipping from my fingers as I adjust it. Her deep brunette hair is tied back into a loose bun that she makes look effortless but I know takes at least twenty minutes to make sure all of the strands look "perfectly tousled," according to my roommate. If I were to try to recreate the look, I'd surely resemble a rat with bedhead.

How our conversation shifted to our thunderous neighbors, I'm not entirely sure. We'd seen one of them driving off this morning in his vintage car that somehow always seems to be parked right out front our apartment building. Its cherry paint rusted; the metal rotted through. I wasn't even sure that the car was in running condition because it looks like it broke down there one day and the owner abandoned it, but the vehicle gave a hefty splutter, black smoke trickling from the tailpipe as he rolled down the street.

It was the roommate who had given the final slam of the door in our faces on that Friday night, the one who looked like he could break through the thin wall separating our apartments just by leaning against it. He wore a fitted emerald shirt, and by fitted, I mean that the seams of the fabric were nearly splitting from the force needed to stretch around his broad body.

He had nodded to the both of us, but that was all we were

given before the black puff of fumes wafting from his car made us wrinkle our noses and pick up our pace as we headed for campus. He was the least volatile of the three by far, even if I didn't feel so inclined to return his morning greeting.

The art building is old, but the classroom is spacious and drab. Concrete floors adorned with paint that hasn't come off and dried clay chipping into dust show the essence of creativity within the space, the room shared with many different classes working with a vast array of mediums. The white walls keep the room bright, the sun casting through the windows bouncing off of them, creating a well-lit space to work in. The art horses are lined up in a circle surrounding a mattress with a sheet spread across its lumpy surface. The room smells of both paint and graphite, comforting me, settling me; my shoulders relax as I take in a hearty breath.

Accustomed to the setup from last year, I gather that we're going to be jumping right into the class and will be drawing today. The most memorable moment from last year had been the oldest man I've seen serve as the model. Of course, that was the day the professor had chosen a specific close-up of a limb for each student to draw. I'd so luckily gotten to draw his low-hanging, wrinkly nether region. *Yuck.*

I shudder as the memory resurfaces, following Rory to a seat. Dropping my bag to the floor, I set up my sketchpad, leaning it against the back of the horse as I dig around in my backpack for all of the necessary materials I'll need.

Rolling my eyes in response to her earlier statement, I finally reply, shuffling through my pencil case for an eraser. "I didn't say that they weren't cute, I said that they're assholes."

Despite my quiet night last night, I couldn't help but wonder about Knox. His brooding nature and stupidly charming face plagued my thoughts as I drifted off in the loud silence of my room.

Students trickle into the classroom one by one. A group of girls stride in, laughing about something that happened at a bar over their weekend. Another girl follows, but it's clear that she isn't in their clique. She's pretty, her ice white hair is draped long down her back, the front pushed from her face by the sunglasses sitting atop her head. Her blue eyes flick around the room nervously, searching for a place to sit, and I'm about to call her over because I can use another friend to side with me against Rory over my annoying neighbors when my eyes are drawn to the boy trailing her inside of the classroom.

My jaw almost drops at the sight of him.

Suddenly, I feel like I should have put more effort into getting ready this morning because once again, I'm met with a man who looks like he could stop the world from spinning just by his looks.

He's much more than handsome. I can't even formulate the words twisting my thoughts into knots. Maybe, after my creative writing class later today, I'll be able to describe his sheer beauty. Once again, I wonder what is in the water on this campus. I need to start drinking it down by the gallon because goddammit, how can they all look so yummy?

He has the fluffiest brunet hair I've ever seen and it makes me want to stalk right up to him and run my fingers through it. Its soft waves hook around his ears and curl at the nape of his neck like it's protecting his pale skin from the sun. He's tall, too, an entire head—or maybe even more, *hello*—taller than the white-haired girl he's bounding in behind. His straight nose is flecked with freckles and his fox-shaped features are utterly devastating.

His gaze sweeps around the room before meeting mine briefly. Disappointment sinks my stomach as he continues looking around but suddenly those enticing eyes flicker back to me in a double-take, as if he's as caught off-guard about me as I was him. My feet turn to lead, pinning me to my seat. One of his eyes is a soft caramel and the other is a bright blue. I want to commit them to memory, stare straight into them until I've gotten each hue of his irises perfect. I curse myself for leaving my colored pencils on my desk at home.

He steps towards us and I shoot Rory a look. Internally, I'm screaming *'holy fuck are you seeing what I'm seeing right now?!'* Her eyes are round and pointed as she returns my sudden crazed look with vigor.

"Hi," the boy greets, sliding into the unoccupied seat next to me. I have to look up at him, even sitting, because *wow,* is he tall. "I'm Reid."

"Quinn," I respond dumbly, thrown by the fact that he's sitting beside me right now. This close, he looks even more unreal than he did from the door. I thought you were supposed to be able to see people's pores and blemishes when they're close, but Reid has none. He is perfect down to the bone. "And this is Rory," I introduce, leaning back in my seat so she can wave to him. She's blushing like a fool and between the both of us, we probably look like a couple of clowns. "Nice to meet you."

I fumble with my art case as he holds out a hand for me to shake. I smile bashfully, sliding my palm into his. He's warm, and his hand swallows mine. The longer we touch, the wider his pleasant smile becomes. "You as well," he responds, then shifts to introduce himself to Rory. With his back to me, I make *'oh my God, look at how gorgeous he is'* eyes at her and she responds with an elbow pressed into my side when Reid pulls back.

This year is determined to kill me with all of the handsome men I've seen so far. Reid even more so, with how polite he is compared to the rest.

I can hardly remember what I was conversing with Rory about before Reid entered the class. I wouldn't even remember if one of our neighbors waltzed right into the room—

Fuck.

Of fucking course.

It's the third roommate—the only one that I haven't been forced to learn the name of. He's the one who'd been driving away when Rory and I left for campus this morning. The big, burly, tan one with the biceps made of steel and tribal tattoos adorning his shoulders and arms.

His frame takes up the entire doorway and the room quiets as he waltzes in like he owns the place. It's incredible, the swagger he has as he scans the class. All of the girls are swooning at his carefree yet confident nature. He oozes masculinity, barrel chested and tall. I wonder if this is his *thing.* Knox's is playing obnoxiously loud music, Ace's is that forked tongue of his, and this one's *thing* is filling up any space with his massive body and stealing the attention of everyone in the room.

I didn't know that he was in this class. When Ace mentioned that they were juniors, I figured they would be in the 300 classes, not the 200s.

Now might be the perfect time to ask, though, because his chocolate gaze sparks in recognition when he glances over at Rory and I, before beelining our way.

"Well, hello there, ladies," he greets with a seemingly genuine smile that I'm all too weary of. He *had* been the nicest of the three when Rory and I almost knocked their door clean off of its hinges, but he *had* also shut the door in our faces. Plus, with my not-so-great track record with his room-mates, my body is tense, preparing for the worst. "You're taking this class?"

Rory takes the bait on this one and I'm well aware that Reid is probably listening in despite the fact that he's pulled his satchel into his lap and is carefully unloading his own supplies. "Yeah, it's required for sophomores. Are you in it too?" She asks, way more politely than I would.

The corner of his mouth lifts into a sinful smile. Wolfish, almost. "You could say that," he drawls, and I open my mouth to speak but he's already turning towards Reid, his smile broadening into something practically wicked, sticking his hand out to introduce himself. "I'm Slate, man. Nice to meet you."

"Reid," my seat neighbor responds, gentlemanly. I don't miss the grimace on Reid's face when Slate clenches his fingers in his own. I have to smother the laughter bubbling up my throat because Slate looks like he could break all of the bones in Reid's hand if he applied even a little bit more pressure.

The trifecta is complete. Knox, Ace, and Slate, although I'm not exactly sure what kind of name 'Slate' is. A nick-name, perhaps? Or maybe his parents are really into masonry?

Slate returns that easy grin to Rory and I, asking for our names. When my eyes narrow, he leans in closer, right into the space between our seats. I can feel the heat his body is giving off from the few inches of space between us and goosebumps break out on my arms. He smells earthy, like freshly turned dirt and smoked wood. It's a lovely scent, I'm woman enough to admit that.

"I'm sorry about the other night," Slate starts, and I nearly recoil. I was expecting him to come in here with the same arrogance his roommates seem to share, not with this sincere politeness dripping from his words. His cocoa-colored eyes are earnest as I inspect him, waiting for the punchline. But his smile softens a touch, and it's guilty, if anything. "It's just that, I have to side with my roommates. You can understand that, can't you?"

I share a look with Rory. If our positions were reversed, I know that I would do anything for her. She is my best friend on the planet, after all.

I guess I can understand, even if I don't want to.

Upon seeing our reluctance to accept, Slate continues. "It's not really my place to say, but Knox was having a rough day. And no, that doesn't excuse his actions, but you did threaten to tow his bike, and he doesn't take that lightly. But hey, it had nothing *really* to do with me, so I'm willing to look past the other night if you are."

I sit in my seat, stunned. This isn't the apology I expected, but it's a truce, a peace offering between neighbors. Maybe, if I accept, Slate will be able to pass along the message of *'shut the fuck up after midnight'* to Knox.

Rory and I contemplate, side-eyeing each other in a silent conversation. It seems as though she's on the same page as I am, because she smiles up at Slate, agreeing. "We'd love that."

Slate beams, straightening to his full height. *Fuck, he's huge.*

He looks like he might say something more, but the professor enters the room and calls his name. He shoots Rory and I a cheeky grin. "That's me." He jerks a thumb over his shoulder. "I'll come grab your numbers after class, if that's cool. We should hang out sometime, neighbors," he says, turning on his heel. Before he takes a step, he's winking over his shoulder and tossing out a, "Try not to enjoy class too much, ladies," before he's gliding across the room with an ease someone built like a brick wall should not have.

My gaze follows him as he reaches the professor, all grins and radiant energy. Maybe he isn't like his brooding, rude roommates. The professor asks him something and Slate nods along as if he's done this before and is being reminded of what's expected of him for this class. He roots around in the bag slung over his shoulder and pulls something out as he makes his way towards the door but I can't see what it is.

"Welcome to Drawing 201," the professor greets, clapping her hands together to gain the attention of the room. Her dark eyes are bright, her smile welcoming and happy, as if teaching hungover college students how to draw is her life's passion. I'm thankful, though, because she seems sweeter than honey. "My name is Ms. Woods, but you can call me Beatrice."

It's impossible to miss Slate slipping back into the room while Beatrice briefly explains the syllabus and what's expected of us before shuffling us right into drawing warm ups and best practices for the class.

The charcoal is dry against my fingers, coating them black as I sweep the stick in loose strokes, working on getting Rory's figure down in the one minute we're allotted for this exercise. It doesn't look much like anything, more like a mess of abstract Cheerios that have made it off the conveyer belt in a bunch of mismatched shapes.

The curves of my drawing become more fluid and refined as I fall into the familiar motions of drawing. I never seem to have enough patience and I'm always reminded of it when I'm forced to warm up. The act of letting go and scribbling through warm ups is unsettling to me. I prefer to have a perfect piece as soon as I set my charcoals, pencils, paints to the paper, otherwise I begin overthinking, second guessing my lines, wondering if anything I'm doing is even good enough, if I'm even exploring the right things, if I should even be majoring in art at all…

"What do you think he's doing here?" Rory asks, nodding at Slate. Her gaze keeps flickering up from her drawing pad to our neighbor, where he's once again speaking to Beatrice.

I try to shake the dreadful thoughts from my head, focusing my attention to where Slate is leaning down to hear the professor as if he wouldn't be able to standing at his full height. I mean, sure, Beatrice isn't that all, but I bet she has a set of lungs on her from teaching as long as she has.

I shrug, studying the lines of Rory's face as I dig into my paper with the tip of my eraser, pulling out some of the charcoal to create the highlights on her skin from the lights reflecting off of her nose. "You don't think he's the—"

"Class, this is Slate," Beatrice interrupts, stealing my attention from both Rory and my drawing. It doesn't really look anything like her yet, but I'm trying my best to trust the process, and the few minutes I've used to get something down was nowhere near enough time; which, might be the point, but it leaves me feeling unsettled.

Slate's no longer wearing his loose jeans and tight t-shirt. Instead, he dons a thick, gray robe. The fabric doesn't drape down far enough, his gloriously tanned and muscular legs on display for the class to see. There's an intricate tattoo starting above his knee, creeping up underneath the fabric of the robe, a similar pattern to those on his shoulders. My mouth goes dry at the sight, following the lines of muscle all the way up as Beatrice continues. "He's going to be our model for the day."

I'm not the only one who makes a choking noise at this news. Girls and guys alike are blushing in their seats and avoiding eye contact with each other. Slate looks like he can hardly contain the smug smirk threatening to split his face in two, his bottom lip tucked between his teeth. He winks at Rory and I again when he sees our faces, and we share a wide-eyed look of shock. At my side, Reid scoffs lightly and my jaw snaps shut, heat seeping into my cheeks as well.

Busying myself, I flip to a new page in the large drawing pad propped up in front of me. It's crisp and creamy, not at all as interesting as I'm trying to make it seem as I steer clear of Slate's mirth-filled stare. Smoothing out the paper with my hand, I realize it's shaky with anticipation, a nervous excitement. My new neighbor who has just offered a truce, and I'm already going to see him naked.

Would it be weirder to still be mad at him and stare at his naked form, or now, when a ceasefire has been declared and we're somewhat on the road to becoming friends? Or would he have used his glorious body to sway us into forgiving him? Because I know that his body is nothing short of a Greek statue.

I admit, that might have worked on me.

I don't have the chance to think further on the matter because Slate's moving into the circle towards the long mattress on the floor as Beatrice explains how the rest of the time in class is going to be divided.

There will be a few three-minute sketching sessions where we're supposed to get down as much of his form as we can, while Slate changes poses every time the clock runs out. Following that exercise, there will be two fifteen-minute sessions, a break, and a final, longer session where we will be focusing on more detail than form.

I can't wait.

Slate slides out of his shoes and I swallow roughly as he undoes the ties to his robe.

Thankfully, he's not looking at me, watching how intently

my gaze is pinned to his tanned skin. I might be able to pass it off as using my artist's eye to capture every moment of his body on display, but Slate seems like the kind of guy who can see though obvious lies. He also seems pretty damn comfortable in his own skin, if he's offering to model nude for the drawing classes.

Or, maybe he just wants everyone to know what he's packing.

The fabric slides from his broad shoulders, exposing the muscles of his back. I've seen his tattoos before, when he hadn't been wearing his shirt that night he answered his door, but with the bright lighting of the room shining down on him, I realize just how intricate they are. Ink weaving in and out of each other, sharp, complex lines that form a pattern across his shoulders and creep down his arms. I want to lean forward for a better look.

His waist pulls in tight and I have to bite my lip to hold back the noise threatening to break the concentrated silence of the room. His muscles flex as he moves, corded and thick in all of the right places. I can't help myself, staring unabashed because he's turned away from me, letting my eyes fall from the inky whorls down to the cavern of muscle lining his spine, all the way to his tight ass.

The entire class seems enraptured with his beauty, as if he's a god reincarnated. It's obvious that the boys want to be him and the girls want to be with him.

Two dimples poke in at the base of Slate's spine that glisten as if he's spent hours oiling up prior to class. *Jesus, Quinn, pull yourself together,* I try to remind myself, shifting in my seat and suddenly wishing I'm not currently *straddling* the drawing horse.

Slate shifts, turning, and his cock is on full display.

The stick of charcoal in my finger's snaps in half.

I *hope* I get that facing me for the few hours we'll be here because *holy fucking shit* is that a nice cock.

Next to me, Reid tuts under his breath, but even he can't seem to look away from Slates body any more than I can.

We're all human, after all.

Beatrice breaks the silence by instructing Slate into his first pose before addressing the class. "Alright. Your time begins now."

I have no idea how I'm able to focus on anything other than the cock draped so prettily across Slate's thigh.

He looks as relaxed as ever, splayed out against the gray sheet on the mattress with one arm tucked beneath his head. His eyes are shut in bliss, his breathing even as if he might've actually fallen asleep.

With the late nights I know he and his roommates tend to have, I wouldn't be surprised in the slightest.

I lose myself in the quiet of the classroom, nothing but the sounds of chalk against paper, the scratch of quick sharp lines being drawn or the drag of long strokes being etched into drawing pads. There's the occasional murmur of advice or suggestions from Beatrice as she makes her rounds through the classroom, weaving between students spread throughout the room.

Drawing the contours of Slate's muscle is no easy feat. Packed layer upon layer from years of hard work spent in the gym, I rub the dark soot into the paper. It's calming: sweeping the charcoal over the white space to create the shadows the lighting paints across his body.

His tattoos take some effort, even though Beatrice had

said not to worry about them, that getting his form down is more important, but I can't help myself. I'm interested in his tattoos and the stories behind them, the significance or possible lack thereof, despite not having any of my own. I draw them with extra care, trying my best not to make up any reasons of why he might have them. Now that we're trying to be on friendly terms, maybe I'll have the chance to ask him about them myself.

Eventually, Beatrice's timer goes off. It's the same ring-tone I use for my alarm in the mornings and when it shrieks loudly throughout the room my body reacts as if it's this morning again, my stomach twisting in response to its annoying chirp.

I place my charcoal down as Slate sits up, dusting my fingers off and admiring my work, comparing it to the model once more before he slips back into his robe and covers that glorious body up.

Rory stands to stretch, her back popping as she twists around. I snag my water bottle from my bag, allowing the crisp drink to wet my parched throat, eyes trailing Slate as he leaves the room to change back into his clothes.

Reid leans over, his brunet curls bouncing as he does so. He studies my work and I clam up at his intense gaze.

After I've almost drained my water to the dregs, he smirks, blue and caramel eyes lighting with a tease. "You have quite the eye for detail."

I splutter and he bites his lip, trying to smother his smile. He pastes on the most innocent look he can muster, but he doesn't know that there's a retort waiting on the tip of my tongue already, just as soon as I stop choking.

"You sound a little jealous there, Reid."

Rory giggles as he gasps dramatically, clutching a hand to his chest. "Maybe, a little."

I can't help but to laugh along with them. It's nice to now have made as many friends as I have enemies, with Slate extending his apologies.

The class packs up around us while we converse, joking around about little things as if the three of us have known each other our entire lives. It comes naturally, and there's an openness to Reid's demeanor that makes him easy to talk to.

I stuff my extra sticks of charcoal back into their case, along with the cloth and eraser. I feel confident in the work I've done today. I've spent a lot of time trying to find my love for drawing again over the summer when I wasn't too busy testing out new mediums and working with Rory at the art camp our town has. It feels so much easier to create art that the children *ooh* and *ahh* at, a simple mask made out of a paper plate and string and colored like a tiger will do just that.

Flipping my art pad shut, I gather Rory's for her and walk with Reid to the cubbies we've been assigned to store our materials in.

"So, are you an art major?" I ask, waiting for the crowd to disperse.

Reid cuts me a suspicious look, but it's a playful one. "You obviously didn't get a good look at my drawing, did you? I suppose I can't blame you with a model looking like *that,* but what I drew is entirely awful," he states and I stare up at him in disbelief.

"Surely, it can't be that bad," I argue, and his lips thin a little as he flips open his drawing pad just enough for only me to see. It's…yeah, it's exactly as bad as he was hinting at and I have to work to keep my face carefully blank.

He puffs out a breathy laugh that eases my shoulders. "I told you it was shit; your face only confirms it!"

There's no lying my way out of this one, so I decide to play into it instead.

"Okay, so it's not great, but I've definitely seen worse. You should've seen my work from last year."

Reid rolls his eyes, stepping forward in line. "Oh, I'm sure it was nothing like the gorgeous drawing you've managed to pull out of your ass in only two hours today," he scoffs, and my elbow flies gently into his side. I rear back when I realize that we've only just met today, but Reid's laughing nonetheless. "Your drawing literally looks like a photograph!"

It most definitely doesn't, but my cheeks heat with the compliment anyway.

I brush off his flattering remark. "I might've been doing this a little longer than you have," I defend. Since I could hold a crayon, to be exact.

He huffs, stuffing his pad into a drawer and offering to help me with Rory's and my own. Reid pulls the drawer open and I slide the sketchpads inside, stepping out of the way so others can crowd him as he closes the drawer and follows me back to our seats.

"Well, you might have to show me the ropes because I thought that taking a few drawing classes would help me with my rendering for architecture, but those are all straight lines and circles and this is all curved strokes and cock."

I'm unable to hold back my laughter this time, and it comes out in a shocking burst that has a few students glancing my way. I duck down, still giggling as I lean over my chair to pack away the rest of my supplies. Rory's all ready to go, her bag slung over her shoulder and her face buried in her phone as her fingers fly across the keyboard.

"You know, if you remove yourself from what you're looking at, this is all just lines and circles too," I answer Reid when I finally catch my breath.

He slings his satchel over his shoulder, staring down at

me with those mesmerizing eyes. "Would you want to explain that further sometime, Quinn? Over coffee, perhaps?"

I'm a little stunned by his bluntness, but I grin and nod nonetheless, sliding my phone from my pocket to snag his number. "I'd like that."

CHAPTER 6
KNOX

"So, you think you're free to do as you please, when you please?" My neighbor's grating voice startles me from where I'm elbow deep trying to change the oil of my motorcycle. The drain plug slips from my fingers and I wince as it falls into the oil-filled pan below.

I'd noticed that my bike needed servicing and this is nothing I can't take care of myself, though Slate *was* supposed to meet up with me after the only class I had today and he hasn't shown yet. He's pretty handy when he wants to be, *has* to be with that old beat-up Bronco of his. He offered his help when I texted him what I was doing after class, or to at least sit outside the apartment building with me and pester me, whichever he felt like participating in when he arrived.

Apparently, he isn't feeling much like showing up at all, which is fine because I know what I'm doing and I *was* enjoying listening to the sounds of the world while I worked: the birds chirping as they chase each other from tree to tree, the students and citizens of the city happily chatting as they walk down the streets, and the occasional rumble of cars driving up the block. It's easy to focus on something so simple, and I'm feeling a lot looser than I have as of late, but it seems like it isn't meant to last very long at all.

I wish Slate was here to be a buffer right now.

What I don't understand is what she's doing here. Obviously, I know very well that she lives in the same building as I do, but after the harsh few meetings we've shared, I'm not entirely sure why she's approaching *me,* of all people.

Grimacing, I reach my glove-covered hand into the dark oil pan, feeling through the slick liquid for the plug I dropped. I need it and I didn't have any intention to get this dirty while working, but at least I have boxes and boxes of gloves to use at my disposal—it's not like I've been giving too many tattoos these days anyway.

I squint against the sun, eyeing her. Her bright blonde hair lies across her shoulders, curling up at the ends. Her arms are crossed over her chest and her hip is popped like she's going to scold me. With the scowl she's wearing, she just might.

Her face looks exactly how it had when we ran into each other almost a week ago. A frown tugs the corners of those pretty pink lips and this time she's glaring down at me with those hazel eyes instead of up at me.

Actively avoiding her has only lasted a handful of days, it seems. It's inevitable that we would run into each other again, with us living next door to each other and all, but I was hoping she would at least try and keep away from me like I am her.

I even kept my music at a lower volume than I'd normally like. Okay, so, it's only one click lower, and it hasn't exactly stopped her from pounding on the walls late at night, but I've been trying to be nicer about it. I've actually listened to at least one of those knocks, I think, turning the music off completely to shove my headphones over my ears instead.

Seems like nothing can make this one happy.

"Am I disturbing your afternoon, *all the way out here,* Princess?" I ask, tacking on the little nickname I know she despises.

Her foot taps against the asphalt, showing her annoyance just like I knew it would, and I smirk. The rhythm reminds me of the bass line to one of my favorite songs, and as I glance at her feet, I realize that she's not wearing any shoes. My brows furrow as my gaze slings back up to hers, enjoying the purse of her perfect lips. I want to touch them, see if they're as soft as they look, but I duck my head instead in case my face betrays those thoughts, watching the oil slowly drip into the pan.

"I *told* you not to call me that," she growls and I blink at how cute she sounds, flicking a glance upwards because there's no way I can't *not* look at her when she sounds like this. Her nose is scrunched with distaste, crinkles accompanying the move. "I don't think you're supposed to be doing this in front of the building."

"That's funny," I snipe, because why can't she just leave me alone? "I didn't ask you."

Her cheeks glow. I brush it off, grabbing a few paper towels off the roll I brought out and wiping the oil plug clean. Now she's on my nerves, and all I wanted to do was to fix this one little thing before hiding away in my apartment for the rest of the night.

I'm meticulous with my work, ignoring the glare I feel like a dagger in the side of my head. Maybe, if I ignore her for long enough, she'll leave me the fuck alone.

Once I'm sure all of the threads are clean, I set the piece aside to wipe off my gloves. I snatch a new filter from the box and remove the packaging, patiently awaiting her to decide if she's going to stalk off or bite back.

I tense as she sighs, even more so when she plants her ass on the curb. *What the fuck does she think she's doing?*

My unspoken question is answered a moment later. "Look, I locked myself out of my apartment and my phone is inside. Can you maybe text Slate and have him let Rory know the situation? He has her number."

I cut her a glance but promptly remove it from her now softened features. I don't need to see what she looks like when she isn't irritated. *Since when does Slate have either of their numbers? Since when did he even start talking to her?*

I remind myself to ask him about it later, and my mouth betrays me when I blurt, "He should be here in a little while. You can ask him then."

What the fuck are you doing, Knox?

Surprised by myself, I carefully return my attention to the task at hand. Removing the old filter, I toss it into the pan with the used oil and clean up my hands once again before reaching out for the new filter to replace. It slides in easily and I cap the drain.

She huffs like it's the most inconvenient answer in the world, but I don't want to get oil on my phone and I don't want to take my gloves off right now. Not ever, but certainly not now that she might be able to see the traces of the accident that still mar my skin.

"Please, can you not be a prick right now? I'd rather let her know as soon as possible so that I don't have to be around you."

Ouch, Princess, I think sarcastically. It's not exactly the response I was thinking she would give, but it sparks my irritation nonetheless.

"I'm not being a prick. I'm working on something and you're interrupting me because you've made the mistake of locking yourself out. Maybe you should take your phone the next time you go to the landlord's office to complain."

Her face flushes and her mouth falls as she gapes at me in surprise.

Yeah, I want to bite, *I heard all about that.*

I return her previous glare, unscrewing the fresh bottle of oil with a little more force then necessary. Some of the liquid sloshes over the rim of the jug but I don't care anymore, I want to be done and far away from *her.*

"You're right." My grip falters on the bottle at her words, so soft that it throws me off for a second. "I'm so—"

"Now here's a sight I never thought I'd see." Slate's voice echoes down the street, starling the both of us. I cut her a look and find her already staring at me, both of us averting our eyes to watch as my roommate appears, grinning like a fool. I will the oil into the hole faster because I can't bear seeing Slate being all buddy-buddy with her. "Knox and Quinnie, sitting on the curb," he sing-songs, and I want to fucking throttle him. He looks as if he's going to continue despite my warning glare, but he catches sight of her—*Quinn's*—bare feet. "What are you doing out here with no shoes on?"

I watch her response from the corner of my eye. Her hazel gaze is turned my way but disappears just as quickly when she shifts her attention to Slate. Her shoulders droop as if she's feeling defeated, and a pang of sympathy burrows in my gut.

"I, um, got locked out of my apartment and left my phone inside. I was just asking Knox if I could borrow his to message you, but here you are," she explains with a weak smile.

I can't help but note the way my name rolls off her tongue. She's been paying attention, too.

"Here I am, saving damsels all day long," Slate jokes,

offering Quinn a hand up off the curb. I have to drag my eyes away from how they look together when she accepts.

She laughs at his lame ass joke and the bottle slips from my grasp again because it sounds like the best song I've ever heard in my damn life.

I quickly fix the spout back into place.

"Need some help, Knox?" Slate asks, but I shake my head.

"All good here, man."

"Great. Quinn, why don't you come on inside and I'll wait with you until Rory gets back. Maybe we can pick up where we left of in class," Slate says, waggling his eyebrows. I don't know what the fuck that's supposed to mean, but I don't like it. Quinn rolls her beautiful eyes and allows him to sling an arm around her shoulder. He grunts dramatically at the playful shove she gives him and my hand tightens around the empty bottle on its own accord. I don't like how friendly they're being with each other.

And she has a class with Slate too? Something hot flares in my chest. I don't like that either.

Not. One. Bit.

It's not right.

Nothing is ever *fucking* right.

The tattoo gun in my hand shakes and the line squiggles, array, just like my thoughts.

It's well into the night, yet I'm unable to find sleep again. I tried—I really, truly, did. I was exhausted, laying down in my bed as I shoved my headphones over my ears, praying that the music would keep my haunting thoughts at bay.

Flashes of memories shattered the songs, menacing words in my father's voice slipping between the lyrics, slicing into my brain like spears no matter how loud I turned up the music.

I tossed, turned, and did everything I could to fight away the nasty thoughts, but nothing worked.

After the oil incident with Quinn, I'd cleaned up, disposed of the mess, and headed up to my apartment for a quick shower. Neither she nor Slate were anywhere to be found, so I dipped into the bathroom, feeling greasy from working out in the hot sun.

When I had finished, I'd returned to my phone only to see a message awaiting from my father. I hardly read the first three words before I was swiping it into the trash and trying to shove the reminder of his existence from my head.

My hands shook for a lot longer than I'd ever be willing to admit to anyone, not that I have to worry about it becoming a topic of conversation brought up by me or my roommates.

By the time the pizza arrived that Slate ordered, Quinn was gone and he was calling Ace and I from our rooms, there was only a slight tremor, one I could easily hide.

Still, I wasn't in the right headspace throughout dinner and I retreated back into my room as soon as I finished my last slice, ignoring Ace calling after me, asking if I wanted to watch a movie with him and Slate.

A part of me did. I want to be able to forget everything in my stupid head and give my full attention to a movie, but tonight isn't the night for that, apparently. Not with my thoughts aching to be relived like a harrowing film of their own.

So, I'd put my headphones on as to not disturb my room-mate's movie night and pulled down one of the many sketch-books from the neatly stacked shelf beside my desk.

It had been my therapist's idea: the sketchbook. That was

long before I stopped calling her, but the comfort of drawing always took me away, let me be free. I've been practicing since I was young, and the more time I spent doodling on the corners of my homework and tests, the more I fell into it, until, eventually, I decided I wanted to make a career out of it.

Thank you to the therapist I don't remember the name of, for telling me to buy a sketchbook and use it for when I'm feeling shitty.

Most of the time, when my hands shake or ache with the memories, I push through it, drawing *something, nothing, anything* I can think of when I'm like this. There are pages shaded completely black, some with random things when I tried forcing myself to think about anything else. Some are of the accident.

Staring at the drawing I just finished, it stares right back, taunting me with its dark, shaky lines and sharp-fanged smile. My chest constricts as I peer into the eyes of my father, the man who hadn't been able to control himself, keep himself from beating the shit out of me when he found out my lies. His words echo in my head and my fingers tighten around the charcoal pinched between them.

With my breath caught in my throat, I shove away from my chair, slamming the sketchbook shut and binding it with its leather cord, knotting it so tightly that I don't know if my fucked-up hands will be able to untie it the next time I need to escape these thoughts.

I consider throwing it off a cliff. I considered burning it, tossing it into the lake, digging a hole at the state lines and burying the damned thing. I haven't done any of that, yet, even though I so desperately want to.

Once my breathing has calmed and my hands stop trembling, I tuck the sketchbook back onto its shelf. I shouldn't keep it with the rest of my collection in case the drawings in there taint the others, but I choose not to keep it away from the rest for one reason specifically. If someone comes snooping in my room despite the lock on the door, there's a better chance at them picking up one of the others before that one.

It's also why all of my sketchbooks look the same.

Now, with the memories of drawing those silly fucking pictures, my tattoo looks like a piece of shit.

And the tattoo gun in my hand still shakes.

"Fuck," I curse, tossing it onto my desk. The clatter cuts through my headphones as it slides, skidding to a stop once it's knocked into the cup of pencils and sticks of charcoal. A plume of black puffs from the chalk falling from the rim and I glare. "Fuck this!"

Swiping at the jagged lines of the stag I've been inking below my kneecap; I scowl at the bite of pain that follows my harsh action. The raggedness of my lines is minimal, but too much for any shop in town to want to hire me. If I can't figure out how to straighten them, there's no hope for an apprenticeship at all.

Of course, I have my charcoal drawings to fall back on and the exhibition I have for them is coming up in a few months, but I've never wanted anything more than this. I've dreamed of becoming a tattoo artist; I love it and I don't want to give up everything I've been working towards.

I slump back in my seat, ripping the latex gloves suctioned to my hands off. I run my fingers through my hair, squeezing my eyes shut tight, swallowing the lump in my throat as I try to breathe deeply.

In. Out. In. Out.

The music is no longer helping. I remove my headphones and shove them into the top drawer of my desk, out of view. I grit my teeth as I catch sight of the decimated skin of my hands, all patched back together like I'm fucking Franken-stein's monster.

Before I can do something irrational—like smash all of my things to bits, a noise suddenly draws my attention.

It's not coming from the living room where Ace and Slate are watching some action-packed movie. I can hear the sounds of reckless driving and explosions creeping from beneath my door. This sound, however, has something zipping up my spine, my ears perking as I turn my head, listening intently.

A low moan, muffled by the thin wall connecting my room from Quinn's. It's soft and sweet, has my back straight-ening in my chair, my cheeks growing hotter when I realize that it's her and the noise is a sensual one.

She must not think I'm home because I'm not blasting music, or maybe she doesn't care if I am. Maybe it's her way of getting back at me for all of the times I've been rude to her since she moved in.

A low curse emits from her side and I would think she was in pain if I didn't recognize the sound of lust lining the noises she's making, the way she seems to be begging for it, chasing her pleasure.

I can imagine her writhing in her bed, hazel eyes hidden behind shut lids and stupidly perfect lips open wide as the filthy noises eke out of her. My cock twitches when Quinn keens, and it's then that I realize how much of a fucking pervert I am for listening in on this.

I can't sit here, can't listen to this. I can't humanize her or listen to the sweet sounds she's making through the wall. It's too weird. As much as it interests my cock, it feels all too wrong to be listening to her pleasure herself though the wall. My body is coiled tighter than it was when I was thinking of the worst moments of my life, and I don't even realize that my hands have finally stopped quivering.

Springing from my chair, I slip out of my room like my ass is on fire. The warmth coursing through my veins isn't one of annoyance right now.

I don't think I'll ever be able to think about her the same way again.

"Took you long enough," Slate complains when I plant myself of the couch beside him, tugging a pillow onto my lap. I need something to hold onto, is all.

Slate shoves a bowl of popcorn my way. I take a handful to distract myself, stuffing the buttery goodness into my very dry mouth. "You've missed all the good parts, but we're watching the sequel next," Ace says. "Slate will fill you in on what happened before we start the next one."

"No, I won't," Slate protests, completely engrossed in the car chase that's happening. "He didn't want to watch it when we asked, so it's his loss."

That's fine, really, because the movie is the furthest thing from my mind.

I can barely focus on what they're saying, on the bright-ness of the movie that forces me to squint against every fiery explosion. It's so different from the soft lighting in my room where I worked.

I refuse to look at anything but the screen but my eyes are unfocused as my mind wanders. When I force them back into clarity, I'm staring right at the door to my room as if I might be able to see past it and through the wall inside.

CHAPTER 7
QUINN

Things slowly begin to enter a new normal.

In the span of a few weeks, I get into the groove of classes, learn that Art History is *not* my thing, and I only had to reach out to Slate three times with mildly threatening texts to relay the message to Knox to keep the music down. It's always followed by the slamming of his door and the revving of his motorcycle on the street outside my window, then a deafening silence that keeps me awake the rest of the night.

Progress.

Part of me feels bad for it, that he can't stand being in the room without the need for music to drown out whatever nightly thoughts consume him. Are they that terrible that he can't just put headphones on instead? Where is he even going so late at night?

On the other hand, Knox obviously doesn't feel at all bad about it because he continues to do it, not picking up on any of the hints I'm sending his way: the slightly aggressive texts, pounding on the wall—which only causes him to hit right back—turning the music up a few more notches until my walls shake with it.

Perhaps he uses the music to mask the noises he makes when he has special guests over. When he's pinning them to the bed and smirking down at them as he slowly teases his cock right against their entrance—*No, Quinn. We are* not *thinking about Knox and how he fucks right now. Bad.*

The other part of me wants to figure out the very reasoning behind the notes that hang heavy in the air.

Now that the semester is under way, projects for my classes begin pouring in and I can feel myself slowly becoming more and more stressed as all of my insecurities stack up.

I yearn for the ability to have confidence in my style, to gather inspiration from anywhere and everywhere. From a children's character to war, from comics and landscapes to vehicles and buildings to even a pound of butter—inspiration from a fucking Campbell's soup can. None of those things speak to me, make my fingers itch to sketch or paint or sculpt. Everything I create is a series of overthinking, and it shows. Every stroke of the brush or line I make with a pencil is over-examined, again and again and again, until the final piece is complete and there isn't an ounce of pride surging through my body.

I hate it and I certainly don't need Knox's night-time shenanigans adding to all of the pressure I'm putting on myself.

As artists, everything is open to interpretation. We draw the way that the model sits, paint the way the still-life stands, mold the clay into shapes and forms that will inevitably be placed in galleries for all to judge. Interpretation means shit. It's just a glorified word for judging the fuck out of something. People think they have to attribute meaning to every-thing in life and I wish it wasn't all that serious sometimes. There is so much pressure to create something that has mean-ing, something objectively beautiful, and I'm not entirely sure I have that in me.

I feel utterly and completely average in comparison.

Sometimes, I sneak peeks at the others while they work. Reid, completely new to life drawing, understands the human body in a way that's completely different from me. I can see his architecture background in the more technical approach he takes to drawing: perfecting the proportions of the model's limbs as he goes. Instead of using the points on his pencil to gauge the length of an arm or a calf, he's using his scale to proceed in a more mathematical sense, doubling or tripling the calculation in his head so he knows exactly how large to sketch the image. He's drawing in that functional way that architects have, and it's unlike anything I've seen thus far during my time in art school.

Rory, on the other hand, works in a vastly different way. There's a fluidity to her lines that Reid doesn't possess, as if each stroke is meant to express emotion rather than to serve a larger purpose. It doesn't seem like she has to overthink anything, relaxed and with a soft smile on her face as she works, letting the charcoal guide her. It's like she's a vessel for the art flowing from her fingertips, wicked with a pencil, lethal with oil paints.

In Rory's work, there are specific elements that she emphasizes, and other times she's drawing a perfectly propor-tional model, confident enough in her craft that she knows exactly what her intentions are when she makes those artistic choices. Rory's signature is adding a tweak of vividness with her colored paints: bright eyes, pointed teeth, sharp ears, and I can see that she's brought that quirk over to drawing class with her, making the models' eyes or lips pop.

She's had her style figured out for years, since she was old enough to understand what made others unique.

And me? I don't feel like there's a specific way to approach things. Or, if there is, I haven't cracked the code on it yet. I just...*do.* There is nothing special in the way that I draw the models, there's no splash of color like Rory nor technical elements like Reid.

I'm just me.

So, when we receive the first project of the semester from Professor Beatrice, I'm kind of already fucked.

"What are you thinking of drawing for the assignment?" Reid asks after class one day. We're walking with Rory towards the local coffee shop, the desperate need for caffeine a priority since it had been another sleepless night for me. Tiredness weighs heavy on my body in a sluggish cloud, but the lack of sleep isn't from the jerk on the other side of the wall this time. I couldn't sleep because of the impossible thoughts filtering through my head, fighting for the first-place spot in my mind. All of the assignments I'll be working on this semester and how poorly I feel like I'm doing in Art History already despite the fact that we haven't had a single assignment because the only grades in the class are the three tests we're taking this term. There's no hope for extra credit either. I don't know what the fuck I'm going to do there.

Add in the creeping sense of imposter syndrome, and I didn't sleep a fucking wink.

I shrug, my lids scraping against my eyes when I blink slowly. "I'm not entirely sure yet."

The assignment should be a simple one, yet here I am once again with no clue what I'm going to do. My mind must not be all that tired because a fresh spike of anxiety claws its way up my throat.

All we have to do for the assignment is copy the work of a well-known artist as close to the original as we can. To imitate and learn how the greats once created their art. The task sounds simple enough, but it isn't, because there are millions of artists crafting works in a million different mediums and styles, all renowned in their skills. Popular names with perfect pencil marks or paint strokes, sculptures and prints.

I'm not all that confident I'll be able to recreate such things, to be honest.

"How about you, Ro?" Reid asks, holding the door open for the both of us to pass into the coffee shop. I thank him, perking slightly as the delicious scent of roasted coffee beans attacks my senses.

Caffeine is probably the last thing I need right now, but hell, I'm going to get it anyway.

The line inside of the coffee shop isn't long, but it's also not the shortest I've ever seen it. There's a warm glow reflecting off of the terra-cotta floors, the emerald tiles of the counters, and the backsplash is bright in contrast. The warm wooden tables and booths make Sip & Savor a popular spot amongst studying students and the patrons of Hardwich City alike.

"I'm planning on doing something by Élisabeth Vigée Le Brun. Her work is breathtaking. I could only *wish* to create something half as good as hers someday," Rory sighs in admiration, long and forlorn. Both of them trail me into line. "But I'm not sure if I want to do one of her landscapes or portraits. How about you? Did you pick anyone yet?"

"I'm choosing something by Santiago Calatrava for sure," Reid's features light up like they always do when he talks about his major, and I wish I was as excited as they are. The emptiness in my stomach only hollows and I grip the straps of my backpack tighter, silently willing the line to move faster. "I think he's brilliant in the way he combines architecture and art. I think it will definitely help me work on bettering my skills."

Sounds perfectly planned, I think sourly, then immediately feel bad. Why am I bitter about their excitement just because I haven't figured out what I'm doing yet? It's fantastic that they have their projects decided, but it makes me feel worse than I already do. More negative thoughts form thorns in my head, woven around my brain like a vicious poison.

If I can't get my emotions in check, I'm not entirely sure what will spill out of my mouth, and I *really* don't want my friends to be on the receiving end of them if they come slipping out.

The line is moving slowly enough to set my teeth on edge. The wait allows the volley of thoughts to grow stronger, and Rory and Reid's continued conversation about the upcoming art project isn't helping.

As I part my lips to interrupt them—to desperately change the topic to something that isn't school or art related—the bell above the coffee shop door chimes and my stomach completely drops to the floor beneath my feet as Ace appears.

He's wearing a cable knit sweater even though the autumn heat is sweltering today. There has been a tease of cooler days to come, but summer must have put her winds back to rest because it's positively scalding today. There doesn't appear to be a droplet of sweat on that angular face of Ace's though, no dampness beading the hairline of his perfectly unruly blond hair.

I watch his gaze sweep over mine, those ocean eyes

lighting in recognition. It's as if his stare is drawn to Rory like a magnet, taking a leisurely fill of her while she chats with Reid, completely unaware to the newcomer. There's a cheesy grin on her face and as I quickly glance back at Ace, I catch his lashes lowering slightly, the corners of his mouth turning downwards at the sight.

Studying him, I analyze the threat of him being here. If he's standing in the doorway, the other two are sure to be close behind. Would I rather have a large cup of coffee or be subjected to whatever teasing is bound to happen, completely tarnishing my already irritable mood?

Slate sweeps into the coffee shop as if I've just thought it into existence. His frame blocks the sun cresting over the trees lining the street and people turn to stare at the sudden shift in lighting. The glow of his tanned skin shines brightly, giving him an ethereal radiance that rivals his easy smile. He is as all of the poets describe: tragically beautiful.

The door clangs shut behind them as the pair move forward and my shoulders sag in relief for two reasons. One, because Knox isn't completing their little trio today, and two, because of the wide grin Slate greets me with, paired with the hug that makes me feel like a small child in the crook of his massive frame. It has me releasing a breath filled with the tension of a thousand wildfires.

"Hey, you," Slate says, and I allow myself a moment to soak in his warmth because who doesn't want to feel all smothered and protected by a handsome man? *Sue me.*

"Hey, Slate," I respond, moving up in line when it shifts forward. I avoid looking at Ace, who seems to be trying to catch my eye from around Slate's shoulder while he says hello to my friends. Thankfully, the latter is broad enough that it doesn't take much effort for me to keep my eyes locked on the back of the person in front of me.

One more customer and then I'll have my coffee.

My group of friends—and Ace—are all smiles and laughter. I don't know what they're talking about, I don't care to focus on the conversation even when I see Reid shooting me a questioning look from the corner of my eye. I keep my gaze pinned to the menu, roving across the chalkboard writing as if I'm actually reading it and not skimming over the words because I already know exactly what I want.

What I definitely want is for everyone to leave me alone.

"So, if the football team wins homecoming this year— which they're going to, because we're undefeated—my sister, Peep, is throwing a party at her house afterwards." I catch the tail end of Rory's sentence and frown. She's grimacing at the thought of her football-star ex. Rory already mentioned it over dinner earlier this week when she was complaining about Peep betraying her boycott of the football team since her breakup with Max. I wasn't expecting her to extend the invitation to our rowdy neighbors. Reid, sure. I can even see her asking Slate, but Ace too? Why is she inviting him when I told her what happened at the art supply that day? Shouldn't we be discussing a truce instead of just offering it up? I'm still pissed at him, too. "If you want to come with Quinn and I."

Please say no, please say no, I beg, shoving the thoughts at them and hoping they take root in their heads.

"Sounds like fun," Ace answers. He's still staring intently at Rory, but before I can think about it too much, I'm called forward.

"Hello! How can I help you?" The girl behind the cash register asks. She's pretty, her dark hair pulled back into a clip at the base of her neck, a few fly-aways looking effortless as they frame her long face. Her deep, espresso eyes are intimidating but soft, and her smile is bright for a fleeting second before it falters when she takes in the rest of my group.

"Hi," I answer politely, putting on my best smile even though it takes a lot more effort than I'm willing to admit. "Can I have a medium mocha with an extra shot, extra whip, and light ice, please?"

"Of course," she presses the buttons on her tablet and returns her attention to me. "Can I have a name for your order? Would you like any pastries?"

I shake my head. "Quinn. And, no, thank you."

"My pleasure." She sounds sincere. "Your total is $6.23."

I tug out the cash I stuffed into my pocket after class ended when Rory asked Reid and I if we wanted to grab coffee. It's a little crumpled and a smidge damp from the heat of my body and the warm end of summer, but it does the job, the barista taking it without complaint.

She hands me my change and receipt, then flounces away after letting me know that it will be ready at the other end of the counter. I slide the loose change from my palm into the tip jar and begin shuffling down to the pick-up area when Reid stops me with a hand on my shoulder, frowning in disappointment.

"Did you pay already? I wanted to buy your drink."

I blink up at him, not exactly sure I enjoy the extra thump my heart beats at his words. A pang of guilt gleans in my chest. Here I am, letting my negative thoughts consume me while my friends are attempting to distract me and cheer me up. I wonder how unlike myself I've been acting for even Reid to notice after only a few weeks of knowing each other.

The vibrant contrast of his eyes is breathtaking, even when his chestnut brows furrow, casting shadows across them.

I cough, realizing I've been staring for a beat too long

when the cashier is calling the next customer up to the counter. Rory looks over to see if Reid is going to take the spot, but he waves her ahead, returning his attention to me.

"Yeah. I, uh, just ordered. Sorry," I stutter, feeling like a fool.

"Don't be," he replies easily. "I'm the one that's sorry. I'll make it up to you next time."

"Thanks, Reid." I can't help the heating of my cheeks at his words. "You don't have to, though."

I can't help but notice how Rory's watching us from her peripherals, staring at the hand Reid still has on my shoulder. I wonder what she's going to say when we're back at our apartment. If she'll encourage me to stay friends with him or maybe pursue this...*whatever* is going on here.

I let out a shaky breath, willing the redness from my cheeks to go away. "Okay, then. Next time."

He stares at me, looking a little suspicious, like as soon as he turns away, I'm going to take it back. Luckily, my name is called and Reid reluctantly releases me.

The feel of his fingerprints lingers even after I've taken a sip of the deliciously cold and chocolatey coffee.

It cures absolutely nothing.

Not quite like Slate's hug or Reid's touch did, anyway.

It's when everyone has gotten their coffees and we've all made it outside the shop that everyone stops to chat more.

And more.

And more.

It's overwhelming at this point, and not even the cold pressing through my fingertips nor the chocolate coffee goodness I'm swallowing by the lungful is doing anything to quell my flaring annoyance. Not even the whipped cream or chocolate shavings help. Paired with the heat of the sun and the bag across my back, and the looming fact that I still have

Art History to trudge through, I'm more than exhausted of today.

Ace is telling some *hilarious* story from the other day when he was working at the art supply store, and to everyone but me, it's probably funny. I, however, am still annoyed with the way he acted when I was there, how he all but called me foul names. My views on his charming personality have been tainted since then and I don't plan on hearing an apology from him anytime soon.

"And then she was rude to me about the paint colors when I specifically told her that alizarium and cadmium are two completely different reds! Wait, Quinn," I hear him call as I spin on my heel to head back to campus. "Where are you going?"

Shit. I was hoping I'd be able to sneak away without anyone noticing.

Cringing, I twist around to face them again. "I have to go," I answer awkwardly, jerking a thumb over my shoulder. "I have Art History."

Rory breaks off from the group, leading me a few steps away.

"Hey, are you okay? If you want to skip Art History, I'll walk back to the apartment with you," she offers, ocean eyes filled with a concern that makes my shoulders droop. Rory, my best friend, is simply the sweetest, always making sure I'm okay. "We can order food, pig out, and watch reality TV."

"As much as I'd love that, I really can't miss this class," I sigh, but refuse to tell her how much I feel like I'm struggling already. Like I'm so far behind, despite not having any assignments. I should've taken it with her last year but I'd been stubborn and took Contemporary Art instead. "Professor Dolf is kicking ass already."

"Ugh, you have him? I heard he's the worst," Rory says, then cringes. "Sorry."

I can't help but laugh. "Thanks, Ro."

She bites her lip, looking like she wants to say more. Whatever she sees when she studies me, I hope she finds. Hopefully, she's not taking in the mauve rings around my tired eyes.

"Okay," she relents, and I want to cry in relief. "But text me when you're on your way. I'll order something. Chinese sound good?"

"Sure, that sounds perfect," I nod. "I'll see you later."

When I move to leave, it's Reid who calls my name next. My fingers flex around the cup with annoyance because all I want right now is to be left alone, build myself up before I walk into Art History and get torn down by the information overload I know I'm going to be receiving.

"Yeah?" I call, turning to face him as he catches up to me. Behind him, Rory, Ace, and Slate are all laughing over something, lost in conversation once more.

"Can I walk you to class?" He asks, so endearingly that it's going hurt to say no. I just need a few minutes alone, though, so I have to decline.

"Sorry, Reid, I'm already going to be late as it is," I aim for joking, no matter how much I don't feel like being chipper. "I don't need you seeing me after I run across campus with my backpack in the heat. But I'll see you at the party this weekend, right?"

I don't give him the room to argue. I want to walk to class alone and thankfully he takes the hint, nodding. "Yeah, I'll see you this weekend."

I smile, waving, finally releasing the pent-up breath in my chest as I stride back towards campus. There's no fucking way I'm running in front of any of them. I'm not that desperate to get to class yet, so I walk into the lecture five minutes late but feeling slightly better from the space.

I slide into the back row, next to a boy whose head is tucked deeply into his notebook, writing down more notes than Doff seems to be sharing on his screen. Maybe I should befriend him, he seems like he'd be willing to help with the intent way he's diligently taking notes.

He wears tortoiseshell glasses and they frame his warm azure eyes that track me as I take the empty seat next to him, quietly trying to get my notebook out of my bag. His blond fringe hangs as he leans down to continue his notes, and his broad shoulders pulled in tight like I've left him no room to stretch out.

It makes me feel a little bad.

"Excuse me," I whisper, snagging his attention. I'm nervous, not sure what kind of attitude I'm going to get from the boy as I disturb his work. "I'm sorry for bothering you, but would you mind filling me in on what I missed?"

His gaze flickers to the coffee on my desk and I immediately feel judged. He doesn't get to draw conclusions as to why I'm late for this dreaded class. He doesn't know how much I desperately needed the coffee to get through this, and frankly, it's none of his business.

"Sure," he agrees, and I could cry with joy. "If you bring me a coffee next time."

I scowl, because what the hell? But then Doff switches slides and the boys hand flies over his paper, scribbling down all of the notes in what appears to be the nicest handwriting I've ever seen coming from a man.

"Fine," I huff.

He looks up from his notebook to grin at me before returning to the paper. "Sick. I'm Odie, and I'll take whatever that is because it looks good as fuck."

I let out a startled laugh that has a few students glaring our way. I sink back in my seat, opening my notebook to a fresh page, jotting the words on the screen down. "You have yourself a deal, Odie," I mutter under my breath, "I'm Quinn, by the way. And the coffee *is* good as fuck."

He snickers as I'm shushed and I duck my head, glaring at the words about art in a time period I don't understand a thing about.

CHAPTER 8
QUINN

When I was a little girl, I was obsessed with drawing. So much so, that when my school would host art shows, my parents would invite all of my extended family along to see my work. The ribbons and congratulations made me feel ecstatic at the time, like I was an unstoppable force. It was a reminder that I was good at what I loved, which brought smiles to my family's faces.

The constant praise made me feel like each piece after needed to be better, and the next had to be even more breathtaking than the whatever came before it. It was a vicious cycle I found myself stuck in, always striving to create something more superior than the last. On and on it went, until sometime in the middle of high school, I completely burnt out.

Of course, I didn't tell my parents this—I didn't tell anyone, not even Rory. Art doesn't mean the same to me as it did back then. Somehow it went from something I loved spending all my time doing to something that I felt *had* to do. It was me, and always has been, forcing myself to keep up with the demands that my family and I set for myself.

Five years later, I was relieved to be out of Seattle—from under my parents' thumbs—hoping if I could explore a few classes, something might strike my creative match again. Last year, I took most of my general education classes and Drawing 101, just to keep up with my skills, but for most of freshman year, I took a break from drawing and allowed myself the time to just be a student, to make friends and have fun.

Now, as I delve further into the art sphere, it still doesn't feel right. I *want* to be in art, I love it with all of my heart, but there is no excitement anymore, only a nervousness that I pretend not to show.

I often sit in class and compare my work to those around me. Even my friends'—I can feel a thousand happy things when I look at their pieces but when I study my own, it doesn't feel good enough. It never feels good enough. *I* don't feel good enough.

Which is why I find myself lingering around the art building after my Critical Thinking class on Friday afternoon, the night of Vulcan University's homecoming football game. I'm spending my time *critically thinking* about all of my life choices right now.

I stare at the work that past classes have made, hanging throughout the otherwise drab halls of the establishment. This building used to house most of the art classes, is the second oldest building on campus, but in all of the years of its occupation, no one has decided to stray from painting the walls anything other than the one shade off of pure white that they are.

Walking down the corridor, I admire the different techniques used to create them. Most are drawn with charcoal or pencils, black and white renderings of a still life. I remember doing that last year in Drawing 101. It had been nice to sit and work on something that didn't move, didn't change or judge me or use too much brain power. It was practical, the items tangible and something that couldn't necessarily be screwed up.

It had been our challenge to work on proportions and perspectives. I liked that mine was different from everyone else's because no one sat in exactly the same spot, didn't have the same angle that I did. Each piece was meant to look different from the start, and sure, I could compare technique, but I couldn't compare my viewpoint against my classmates.' It had been easy to lose myself in the simplistic set up of the bowl of fruit.

The drawings end as I round the corner. My ears perk up at soft music flowing down the halls. Looking ahead, I realize I've turned down the hallway to the ceramics and sculpture classrooms. It's another art class I'd been contemplating taking this semester, but didn't line up with my schedule.

I follow the sound of the upbeat music down the hall. The closer I move, the more I pick up on the familiar sounds of someone working on a masterpiece. The whirring of the pottery wheel drawls soothingly under the music. The splashing of water as the artist wets their hands, it draws me in like the busybody I am, peeking my head through the door.

It's a large classroom, much like the drawing room. Afternoon sun pours in through the windows, painting the atmosphere in a golden light. It's crowded with large tables and chairs, walls lined with towering racks for the students to hold their pieces. Pottery wheels sit in perfectly straight lines and I immediately spot the one being used, my surprise at who it is has me blurting his name.

"Slate?" It comes out sounding accusatory, even though I don't intend it to. My friend startles from where he's zoned in on his work, the clay between his hands crumpling as he jumps.

He frowns down at his piece and I wince. I didn't mean to frighten him and now his work is ruined. Slate doesn't seem all that bothered by it after a few long seconds when he smashes it back into a clump of clay and turns to grin at me.

"Quinn, hey! Are you taking ceramics this semester?"

I respond as I step into the room. The sleeves of his shirt are pulled high to his elbows, the gray substance speckling those toned arms all the way up. He has on an apron so the material doesn't get on his clothes, but from the way that his large thighs frame the pottery wheel, the fabric isn't doing much to stop the clay from splattering the inside of his jeans. "Ah, no. I just heard your music playing and thought I'd come check it out. I'm sorry for wrecking your piece."

He shrugs, offering me an easy grin. "No worries, was just messing around, really." He gestures to the pottery wheel beside him and I take a seat. "You ready for tonight?"

Ugh, the homecoming football game. We're not going to the actual event but the pre-games are supposed to be wild. Plus, Rory volunteered us to get to Peep's early and help out with decorations.

I don't even know why Peep wants to decorate—or host a college party at all, really—because everything is likely going to be trashed come the morning.

Quite possibly, myself included.

I avoid looking at him when I answer, staring at a few flecks of clay left abandoned. They're dry and I have the urge to pick at them, but I keep to myself. "Yeah, should be fun."

"Sounds like you really mean that, too," Slate chuckles, and I find myself smiling with him, elbowing him softly. "What's on your mind?"

I sigh, long and forlorn. I'm not really sure I want to talk about my frequent feelings of imposter syndrome with him. We've only known each other for a few weeks now, and none of our conversations have encroached on something so intimate. I don't even know anything about his personal life, either.

"Just tired, I suppose," I say, watching as he begins working the clay again. The substance oozes between his fingers but he kneads it into submission easily. If I had more energy, I'd be staring much harder at those large hands and how they move and my pussy would be begging for those fingers to work *me* into submission.

Slate's frown returns and it doesn't look right on his face. He's the kind of guy who's always smiling and joking around, cheeky through and through. This doesn't suit him.

"Is it Knox again? I'll barge right into his room and tell him to shut the music off if it is," he says and he sounds like he genuinely would if I asked.

That means a lot to me.

"Don't worry about it too much, Slate," I answer with a soft smile. Maybe he can see through me in the time of our short friendship. I change the subject, not wanting to wallow in my sour feelings and have them carried with me throughout the night. There's no way Rory or even Pipa will let me escape this party, no matter how hard I consider trying. "What are—*were* you making?"

Slate's beaming smile rivals the bright sun outside. His brown eyes glitter like goldstone and it warms me how thoughtful he is. "I was making my mom a set of teacups for her birthday," he answers happily.

I want to cringe again because that sounds like quite a nice gift I've managed to ruin, but he's giving me a look that tells me that I shouldn't be worrying about it at all. "That's nice," I comment sincerely. "Have you been into ceramics long?"

"Since I first tried it in high school," he explains proudly, sticking his thumbs down the middle of the wet lump of clay, parting it easily. Slate continues shaping, curving his fingers outward to form a bowl shape. "I took pottery because I thought it'd be a blowoff class and at least I could get a little dirty. I fell in love with it my first time on the wheel." He says it like he's reminiscing about the first love of his life and that yearning feeling is back in my chest again, striking fast and hard. I wish that I could feel the same way about my own art. "Have you ever thrown before?"

"Yeah, when I was in the third grade, I made a mug," I grumble. It was hard and my piece turned out badly. Unfortunately, my mom still keeps it on her desk, using it as a pencil holder. It never fails to embarrass me when I'm home to see it. My eyes widen when Slate stops his pottery wheel abruptly to cut at the block of clay sitting beside him. He slaps it on the empty slate in front of me and I stare at it like it's going to mold itself into a pair of fangs and bite me. "What are you doing?"

Slate's smirk spells trouble. "We're upgrading you to an ashtray or a vase today, yeah? Come on, go grab an apron and I'll show you how the professionals do it, Quinnie."

He gives me a stern look when I'm about to protest and I snap my mouth shut, staring wearily at the lump in front of me. I *have* always wanted to try my hand at pottery and I don't have anything else to do until the game starts, so might as well redeem my third-grade self.

Standing, Slate gives me an encouraging thumbs-up as I head over to where the aprons are draped over a rack on the wall.

Why the hell not?

It turns out, spending a few hours in the ceramics room with Slate was exactly what I needed to turn my day around.

He had been the best distraction, naturally funny and a great teacher, too. Somehow, he talked me into making an ashtray, which is something that I don't need, but was easy enough to make with his direction.

It was nice feeling the slimy material bend under my will, to really get in there and squeeze the life out of it until my frustration had eked out of me enough to finally mold it into the circular shape Slate was showing me. He didn't comment or tease, just let me do what I needed to do while he worked with his own piece until I was settled and ready to create something that I wouldn't mash to bits.

He said he'd let me know when it was time for glazing, and we could set something up after class hours so we can paint our pieces before they go into the kiln.

I feel like there's residual clay clinging to my skin and under my nails that I'll have to wash off in the shower before I get ready for the party with Rory, but I kind of can't wait to try it again. The giddy feeling has me excited for the rest of the night.

"Thank you, for that," I say as Slate and I reach my apartment door. Ever the gentleman, he'd even offered me a ride back home *and* a trip through the drive-through of my choice, but Rory mentioned something about ordering pizzas with Peep before the end of the game, so I had to politely decline.

"Anytime, really," Slate answers as I stick my key in the lock. "I'll text you when we're ready to glaze. It was really nice hanging out with you, Quinn. I'll see you later?"

"Absolutely," I agree as he continues to the next door down. "Later."

When I open the door, the TV is blaring loudly and I wonder why Rory has it turned up so high. Maybe she's getting ready in her room and wanted to listen to something in the background, but she could have just played music on the speaker instead...

Kicking the door shut behind me, I finally look up only to freeze when I spot a figure sitting on the couch, scrolling aimlessly on his phone.

"Sam?" I ask in confusion.

My older brother is at Vulcan University, sitting on my couch right now. We have the same hazel eyes but he's been gifted with our mother's brown hair, a few shades darker than mine. It's unruly from where he's clearly been running his fingers through it from the sheer boredom he's currently experiencing, if the loud but relieved groan he lets out when I arrive tells me anything.

"Finally, you're home." Sam springs off the measly futon and winds his way over to me for a hug. I wrap my arms around him, still confused as to why the hell he's here right now, and I let my backpack slip from my shoulder when he pulls away. Sam frowns, poking my nose as he teases, "You don't look too happy to see me, Quinnie. What's that all about?"

"No, I am happy you're here, I'm just confused. Why this weekend?" I ask, trailing him back to the couch. Sam collapses against it, grabbing the remote to pause the movie as he laughs incredulously.

"You think I would come down here the same weekend as mom and dad? Hard pass, Quinn. I'm here for parties and fun, not lectures and Pictionary."

I cross my arms over my chest, narrowing my eyes at my

brother. Last I knew, he loved playing Pictionary with our family and nearly broke a vase when he lost to me by one point.

Sam relents with a sigh. "Fine, so Peep might have invited me down for this party she's having and I thought I'd stop by and see you."

A shit eating grin appears on my face as Sam ducks his head back into his phone to avoid eye contact. He and Peep have been skirting around each other for *years.* The Wilson's and my family have been close for a long time now, and I think we all knew that one of the Wilson daughters was bound to have a fling with Samuel Conroy. Or more.

Looks like that lucky lady is Pipa.

My brother is a fantastic guy most of the time, when he and I aren't arguing like the siblings we are. He's kind, smart, and funny, all of the attributes most women want in a man. He's in his final year at Brownstone University up in Connecticut, which is certainly a long flight from Vulcan U, settled down here in Southern California.

"All this for a weekend trip?" I pry, and he shoots me a glare.

"I don't have much going on this early in the semester." He brushes me off, but I know it's a lie. Biology majors are always busy with school. Peep must be one special lady if she's gotten Sam to fly all the way out here for one of her parties because he's never come running when I've asked. "So, what's the plan for tonight, then?"

I roll my eyes at my brother's impatience, pulling out my phone when it buzzes in my pocket. "Where's Ro?" I ask, frowning as I read the message from Reid telling me he's been summoned to a family dinner that he cannot escape. I type back quickly, sending him Peep's address just in case along with my condolences. If he can get out of the dinner early or slip out after, he should be able to arrive in the thick of the festivities.

"She went to go pick up some pizzas with that guy she was hanging out with," Sam says, texting someone as well. I try to squint to see the contact's name, but he locks the phone too quickly for me to read. I'm pretty sure I saw a heart emoji and with the smile he's trying to smother, I'm almost positive he's texting Peep. It's nice of him to stop by and see me before he falls completely into her for the rest of the night. "Ace, I think."

I make a face without realizing it which causes Sam to laugh. "You don't like him, I take it? He did seem kind of cocky, had an attitude when I showed up, but at least he's better than that Max guy. Man, he was such a dick."

I hum in agreement. He hadn't been good for Rory, but she's been caught up in him like a tornado. Her first college fling that hadn't ended as well as the school's football season did, which Max is on. They were pretty steady during the end of fall semester last year and well into spring, but when summer finally came around, Max broke it off, not wanting to be tied down during the time off from school.

From what I hear now, he's all but making it clear he wants Rory back, which he should because she's amazing, but I pray she doesn't start fucking around with him again.

If she's out picking up pizza with Ace, that must mean that they're joining us for dinner before we all head over to Peep's later, which no doubt means that Slate and Knox will be there.

My stomach tightens at the thought of seeing Knox again. He'd been right to call me out the other day, but he didn't have to be so harsh about it. I couldn't stop staring at his hands as he worked, the sliver of skin I noticed when the sleeve of his shirt tugged up a little too much—

"Earth to Quinn! Hello?" My brother sings annoyingly, waving his hand in front of his face. "What's going on in there?"

I bat his hand away, standing from the couch. "Nothing. Just watch the damn movie and wait for the pizza, I'm going to get ready."

He grumbles something under his breath that I don't care to listen to as I make my way towards the bathroom to shower.

It's going to be a long night.

CHAPTER 9
KNOX

"Listen, kid," the tattoo artist across the table from me sighs, and I already know what's going to come out of his mouth next.

The interview for this apprenticeship hasn't been going well since the moment I walked through the door to Carver's Ink. I should have turned around as soon as I stepped inside and felt the vibes were off instead of wasting my fucking time. But I need an apprenticeship badly, so I stayed.

I'm officially regretting that decision right now.

The man conducting the interview had forgotten he was even meeting with me today, and I had to wait thirty minutes while he finished with his client before he had free time to speak with me.

He's lanky and tatted with some of the worst ink I've ever seen—*is that a clock dripping blood for fuck's sake?* There's a lion head on his arm and he's judging me over my art? I bet if he pulled up the sleeves of his flannel any further, he'd be showing a collage of gears forever marked onto his pale skin, too.

He—Chad? *Vlad?* Something or other, hasn't listened to a

single word I've said while I spoke about my time tattooing. That it's my passion, that I want to make a career out of it. Instead, the guy kicked his sneaker clad feet up onto the edge of the table as he flipped through my portfolio, brushing off the explanations of my work.

I saw the look he gave me when I pulled out my collection of art from my backpack. The way he openly stared at the scars on my hands, running up my forearms. The patches of skin they'd taken from my thighs to cover the gashes ripped open across my palms and up my arms that I'd gotten during the motorcycle accident two years ago. It hadn't been pretty, still isn't really, and I fucking *hate* when people stare.

At this point, I don't even want to apprentice here anyway, not after all of this, but I'm running out of tattoo parlors to apply to in town. I'm not against riding out to the next city over because I have a reliable source of transportation, but driving all the way out after classes is something I'd rather not have to do.

I set my jaw at his words. I already know it's going to be bad news so I slip my phone out of my pocket and check the time. Only a few more hours until I'll be surrounded by a bunch of drunk students with the neighbor I can't get out of my mind.

I see Quinn more than I'd like. When I'm home, she's home. When I'm in my room trying to work on my assignments, she's in her room banging on the wall. When I'm trying to hang out with Ace or Slate, they already have plans with the girls next door.

It's annoying as fuck.

I've had better interviews with the same result. The fact that I keep putting myself through this proves my determination, but I'd be lying if I said that the handful of noes I've received isn't more than a little disheartening. I feel like I've come a long way with my tattooing since my accident, when I'd essentially had to relearn how to hold my pencils, charcoal sticks, and my tattoo gun.

All of that pride I've built up is slowly deteriorating like an age-old painting.

So, I'm more than ready to pack my things and leave, maybe even swing a fist at the fucker on my way out when he says, "I think you're very talented with your sketches, but it's not translating into your tattoos." He scratches his patchy beard and sucks his teeth but it doesn't get rid of the cluster of food jammed between them that I've been talking to for the past half hour. Yeah, I really don't want to work here. Not only is this guy an ass, but I've seen at least three violations since I walked in.

Imagine if you had to put up with this shit every day.

The man continues because he clearly doesn't know when to shut up. "Your lines are all jagged, and we can't have that. I'd be happy to look at your work again next semester when you've had more practice."

No. Fucking. Thanks.

I grind my teeth because there's nothing else for me to do. How many times have I heard this line before? I *know,* God help me I fucking know that my lines aren't the straightest, but I've come a long way, and my more recent tattoos aren't suffering as much because of it.

Why won't anyone just give me a fucking chance?

"I understand," I nod tersely, and it takes a lot more effort than I thought to keep my tone neutral.

I'm thankful he can't see how white-knuckled my fists are under the table.

"What made you want to get into tattooing, anyway?" The man flips my portfolio shut with a harsh snap. The way he asks it makes me feel like I'm about to be told that I should find a backup plan. Based off the way this—and every other interview—has gone, I have one, but this fucker doesn't need to know that.

"Every tattoo has a story," I answer simply, because it's something I believe with my entire heart, and maybe, just maybe, this man can relate to that.

The idiot has the audacity to cock his head, questioningly. "Is that so?"

"The one's that I get do," I respond stiffly, hoping that this interview is over because I can't bear to sit here a moment longer. What's with all of the follow-up questions? He already said no, so why the hell is he still interrogating me?

I'm being looked at like I'm some dumb college kid with no idea what I want to do with my life and I fucking hate that. I know exactly what I want to do when I graduate and that's to be a tattoo artist, hence trying to find an apprenticeship at a local shop. I'm not going back home, and I'm not working at my father's company, no matter how often he tries to reach out to me.

"Well, I appreciate you taking the time to meet with me," I say, gathering my things. The guy looks at my hands again and I know the question is on the tip of his tongue so I hurry, shoving my portfolio into my bag and rising from the chair.

"No problem, kid. Like I said, work on it and maybe next semester—"

"Right," I interrupt, forcing a smile like I've never forced one before. It feels like I'm cutting steel and I'm sure it looks more threatening than genuine. "Thanks."

I dip out of the shop before he can ask me anything else.

I'm glad I didn't even care to remember his name.

I didn't know I was going to walk into *this.*

Quinn and Rory don't seem like the type of girls who would be able to pull this kind of party off. The music is blaring, putting the volume I listen to mine on to shame. There are colorful strobe lights flashing in the windows of the small house and out onto the lawn where a few people are playing some sort of drinking game that looks much too complicated for even a sober mind to figure out.

Bodies pack the house, spilling in and out of the door when I finally arrive, and I'm pretty sure the cops have already been called and stopped by more than once.

Apparently, Vulcan University's football team has won their homecoming game.

Go Pintos, I guess.

I had taken my sweet time getting here, but as I glance around the yard while I make my way up to the craftsman that Rory's older sister is renting, I can't help the churn of nerves in my stomach. It's been a while since I've been to a party of this proportion; besides the ones Slate throws, I haven't really been much into the partying scene at all. It's a waste of my time and drinking only accentuates the trembling I sometimes experience in my hands.

Like right now, as I shove myself into the throng of people, looking for any sign of my friends. It's more packed than the stadium probably was for the homecoming game itself, students more interested in getting shit-faced than watching dumbasses run back and forth with a ball.

There's no one I know in the living room, but everyone is screaming out the lyrics to a song that is engrained in every college student's mind. The furniture has been shoved up against the walls and the crowd is going wild, jumping up and down with the beat. The floors shake beneath my feet as I worm my way through the first archway I reach.

My shoulders droop a little as I enter the kitchen. There are less people in here and I admire the interior decorator's quirkiness as I take in the baby pink tiles and blue walls. This must be every girl's dream, a colorful kitchen with bottles upon bottles of alcohol lined up on the butcher-block island in the middle of the space.

My friends are here too. Slate's cheeks are ruddy with drink, his eyes bright and glossy. He looks like he would be two seconds away from slipping into the living room to find a girl to spend the night with if he wasn't already openly flirting with one of the girls in front of him. I can only assume she's Rory's sister's roommate. Ace is leaning against the countertop, his deep cerulean eyes settled on Rory where she's giggling with her sister over something. They keep sneaking glances between him and the boy who has his arm slung over Quinn's shoulder.

My steps falter as I stare. She seems happy, laughing and elbowing the guy in his side when he leans down to whisper something in her ear. *Sweet Jesus,* that smile is…something. Her rosy lips are stretched wide, showing off those perfectly straight, white teeth. Paired with the glint to her eyes and the crinkle to her button nose, she's gorgeous.

"Knox," Slate cheers, bounding over to me. I blink, peeling my gaze away from Quinn before she can catch me in the act of observing her. He shoves an open beer into my hand and it sloshes over the rim, dripping over my skin. "You made it!"

I glare for a second, hastily licking the drink from my hand, before flicking my gaze quickly back to Quinn to see how she reacts to my presence. She was probably hoping that

I wasn't going to show up, that I ditched them all. I bet she was happy, cuddling up to this guy who's refilling her cup with liquor.

Those blazing hazel eyes are glued to me, watching me as I tongue the droplets of spilled beer off of my skin.

Her throat works around a swallow and something in my chest tightens at the sight.

Suddenly, I want her throat to work around swallowing something else.

Fuck, maybe I should stay away from drinking tonight if this is how it's going to go. She doesn't even like me for fuck's sake, and I'm not too keen on her, either. Or, at least, I'm not supposed to be.

"What's up, man?" I greet back, focusing my attention on my roommate so I don't smirk at Quinn like I want to. I can still feel her eyes on me, following me as I move deeper into the kitchen, nodding politely at everyone Slate introduces me to.

"Isn't this house sick?" Slate grins eagerly, "It's Peep's. She's Rory's older sister and her name is really Pipa, but they call her Peep for short. Isn't that the cutest?"

"Yeah," I agree, distractedly, taking a swig of my drink. I can't control myself, glancing back over to Quinn where she's now taking shots with Rory, Ace, and that other guy. "Super cute."

Slate catches what I'm looking at and makes a noise of outrage, barreling past me and shouting about how they promised not to do shots without him. I shake my head fondly at my roommate, trailing him because I don't know anyone else here and the way one of Pipa's roommates is making eyes at me has my skin crawling.

I catch the tail end of their cheers. "Riding with pride since 1869!"

"That has to be one of the worst school slogans I've ever heard," the guy I don't know laughs. He seems to be sticking to Quinn like glue and I'm not sure why it's bothering me so much, but it is.

He has sandy brown hair, and strikingly similar eyes to Quinn's. His sharp jaw is covered in scruff and he looks like an actor that I can't quite put my finger on. Either way, I already don't like him.

"Really? It's one of the best I've heard," Slate grins, slamming his shot glass back onto the counter. "It's like, my life motto."

Quinn grimaces at her drink and I bite back my smile of amusement. She's only managed to down half of the shot, choking a little before slyly dumping the other half into the nameless guy's cup.

He catches her and shoots her a look but she only ducks her head, offering him a sheepish grin.

"Knox," Ace calls, snapping my attention away from her. He's holding out a shot to me now and I take it, ignoring the questioning look he sends me when he notices the finite tremble of my hand. "You need to catch up," he continues, although now there's a weary twinge to his tone. I need Rory to come over here and distract him before he starts questioning me.

Plastering a fake grin on my face, I take the shot. I immediately want to spit it out because *what the actual hell am I drinking right now?* Maybe Quinn had the right idea, after all.

Speaking of, the music in the living room switches to something different, something with a little more beat and a little less words. It's the kind of song that makes everyone want to grind, and apparently, Rory and Quinn are no different because the former is dragging the latter out of the room with the biggest smile on her face.

The guy that was all over Quinn slinks over to Pipa and her roommates, seamlessly joining their conversation. My eyes narrow when he sidles up a little too close to Pipa, but she doesn't seem to mind, and even bats her eyelashes at him when he smiles at her.

"Who's the guy?" I mutter, and I hate that I care.

"Oh, that's Quinn's older brother, Sam," Slate fills me in, pouring another round of shots for Ace and I. Ugh, I really hope it's something different than whatever hellish liquid I just had in my mouth. "He flew in specifically for this party. I think he has thing for Peep."

Of course, now I feel like an idiot for thinking they were something more when they have the exact same eyes. The longer I study him the more I realize that they do have other similar features: the shapes of their faces and the strong lines of their noses. How did I not notice before?

Because you were blind with jealousy, my mind supplies. I toss that thought back with another swig of my drink.

"C'mon, Knox," Ace warns, and I don't even realize that I'm still glaring at Sam until I see the sharp look on his face. The one that tells me not to do anything stupid, which is stupid in itself because I wasn't going to do a damn thing about some random guy with his arm around Quinn's shoulders. I wasn't going to do a damn thing at all. "It's your turn to make a toast."

I don't want to but Slate's looking at me like an eager puppy, more than ready to turn this house upside down.

I'm not good at making toasts and I don't want to, so I say, lamely, "Go Pintos."

"Yee-haw!" Slate slams his back like a pro, and I know it's going to be a long night.

Yee-haw, indeed, I think, and then I take my shot.

CHAPTER 10
QUINN

For the first time this semester, I feel at ease.

Sitting in the middle of the commons on the lush grass, I'm leaning against one of the biggest oak trees on campus. The bark is rough where it presses through the fabric of my shirt; it's like my own little acupuncture therapy while my head is buried deep in my sketchbook, the urge to draw lingering from the weekend.

I'm waiting for Rory to arrive so that we can spend our lunch hour together. She texted me saying she would bring sandwiches and snacks and meet me after my Art History class ended, so here I am.

That's right, not even horrible Art History can wreck my mood today. The rest of the weekend had been good. Peep's party was a success, especially when Rory and I caught her and Sam pressed up against the wall in the hall, making out. Yeah, it was a little gross watching my older brother with his tongue down Peep's throat, but hey, if something happens between them and they end up together, Rory and I will be in-laws, so I'm rooting for them!

There was something about the party that stirred up this

sudden inspiration. Through the bits that I can remember, I could always feel Knox's eyes on me. When I was in the kitchen with Sam's arm slung over my shoulder, when Rory and I went to dance in the living room, when she and I snuck off to the bathroom together because—*hello?*—power in numbers.

Slate dragged Ace and Knox into a tight circle with us at one point, and I remember laughing and laughing until the happy ache in my cheeks went numb with alcohol. I think it had been Slate's goal to distract us with each other because I'm pretty sure he disappeared sometime shortly after that.

The intensity in which Knox had looked at me hadn't been lost on me. It made me nervous, from his normal harsh glare to when he eased up the more he drank. I hadn't been able to decipher his expression then, but it's been stuck in my mind since.

Hence, the drawing.

I'm adding the finishing touches to those thick, dark lashes of his, so intently focused on the piece that I barely notice the sound of footsteps approaching before a sudden, "I'll see you later," startles me from my stupor.

Looking up, I scramble to snap my sketchbook shut when I see it's Rory. She's not alone, Ace, Slate, *and* Knox trail her, though the latter of the group looks betrayed as he glares at his roommates. My stomach falls with disappointment at his scowl. He clearly doesn't want to be in my presence.

It's a good thing he's distracted because I can't help but stare. Knox is in his usual garb, wearing a black long sleeve shirt, covering the beautiful tattoos that line his arms. I think he does this to hide the very things I'm interested in seeing. That scarred skin I've only seen a sliver of while he was working on his bike a few weeks ago has piqued my interest, even though I'm still irritated by his previous actions.

Knox turns, shoving his hands deeply in his pockets as if he can feel my lingering gaze, but Ace stops him with a firm hand on his arm, dragging him to a halt. I watch Knox's body go still, his spine straightening as his entire demeanor changes.

I can't hear what they're murmuring to each other but Rory's stepping forward to settle down across from me, her arms loaded with our lunchtime essentials.

I take the sandwich she offers me, murmuring a thanks. I wonder what Ace is whispering to Knox because he looks almost apologetic, carefully removing his hand from his friend's arm. Knox rolls his broad shoulders and relaxes slightly, muttering something back to Ace before the three roommates join our circle.

To my utter surprise, Knox sits beside me. I think it's because Ace flanks Rory's other side and Slate takes up the space of two grown men, but he shoves himself down onto his ass nonetheless. Knox's dark brows are furrowed deeply as he scowls at the grass. He looks about as enthusiastic to be joining us for lunch as a sculpture with its arms cut off.

I set my sketchbook aside even though this is the first burst of inspiration I've had in the handful of weeks since classes have started. I've missed that familiar feeling rushing through my veins, the one where I lose hours upon hours drawing, not wanting to break from my work until it's done. It's refreshing and long-awaited and I want to bask in it.

If only it hadn't come from the boy sitting beside me.

Unwrapping my sandwich gives me something to do, something to look at instead of Knox, who's making it clear by his silence that he'd rather be anywhere else but here. I wonder why he's staying when he's a grown man and has the ability to leave and sulk elsewhere.

Slate is the perfect distraction, with his buoyant attitude.

He's a good guy, one of the best I've ever met, and I'm thankful to have found it in myself to accept his apology when he extended it. I doubt Ace and Knox will ever grow up enough to admit their wrongs and apologize, though I do find myself avoiding Ace's gaze as often as he tries to catch mine, but I can be civil when they are.

I peek at Knox from the corner of my eye, back to studying him. He's pulled out his own sketchbook, his sandwich abandoned next to him, still wrapped tightly in its parchment. His head is bent close to the paper, black hair falling across his brow from the tilt of his chin.

There's an arrogance even to his drawing form. No, not arrogance, but a confidence that I'm entirely envious of. He seems to know exactly what he's sketching, utterly enthralled with whatever is being etched onto the page. He's quick about it, as if the image in his mind will disappear at any moment if he doesn't get it down on the paper.

I feel weird for staring, but there's something about him that's drawing me in, now more so than ever. No one else seems to have noticed yet, so I take a bite of my sandwich as I watch. His tongue pokes out of the corner of his mouth in concentration and I ignore the way my heart thrums at the sight.

Finally, my gaze moves to his hands, squinting when I notice the scarring around some of his fingers, winding over the backs of his palms. It's on his other hand too, the one propping his sketchbook up for a better angle. Across the top of his hand is a long patch of skin stretched so tightly I can see the muscles and bone structure as he works. I follow it upwards where it creeps under the long sleeves of his shirt. It's still pink and irritated, and the bite of sandwich in my mouth turns sour.

Whatever happened to him, it must not have been good.

The conversations of our friends pull me back to reality before I blurt out something I shouldn't, like questioning Knox on how he got those scars.

"Quinn, back me up here," Slate exclaims, nudging me with his elbow.

"Ow," I bite, because the fucker is sharp. He needs to pull his strength, too, because he probably punctured my lung. "What?"

"Ace said that painting is messier than sculpting, can you believe that? Asshole doesn't even know what I go through to make such masterpieces," Slate huffs dramatically. When I stare blankly, he continues with a scoff. "Yes, I know. Someone as glorious as me *is* multi-talented. I both sculpt and model. I'm really easy on the eyes and even better with my hands."

I nearly choke on my lunch, swatting at Slate as he tries to sneak a grape from the bag I'm opening simultaneously.

Making that ashtray with him *was* messy as hell, but so much fun.

Swallowing, I answer, "Ew, Slate, I'm trying to eat!"

"Picturing me back in class, huh?" He responds cockily, wagging his eyebrows.

I shake my head in response. *He wishes. "As if.* You could only be so lucky to be in my thoughts. And I agree with you, sculpting is *way* messier than painting."

Movement beside me draws my attention a little too easily. Knox is sitting back now, admiring his piece as he reaches for his sandwich. There's a slight curve tugging at his lips that makes my mouth dry and all too aware of my own heartbeat. I wish I could see what he's drawn, but form the angle of the pad, there's no way I'm seeing shit unless I ask.

Which I refuse to do.

"I told you!"

Ace says around a chip, with a smugness so thick, "Not the way I use it."

"You fucking *dog,*" Slate howls with laughter. I bite back the amusement trying to thread my lips into a smile because Ace's joke *wasn't* funny. Instead, I stuff a bite of food into my mouth.

Slate's chortling is so loud that it draws the attention not only of Knox, but half of the students in the courtyard as well. He doesn't seem to care though, doesn't give the slightest fuck about what anyone thinks about him, and I envy that. "That was a good one, Acey."

Rory's cheeks are rosy and my brows furrow when she avoids my questioning gaze. She seems much more interested in peeling the skin off of a ripe, purple grape.

Ace and Slate continue with their banter in a way that is brotherly and warm. A few times they try and goad Knox in as well, but he seems pretty content with watching and the sketchbook in his hands. I wonder if he ever joins in with them, lets loose enough to crack a joke every once in a while. I can't imagine him acting so *guy-like,* but I suppose anything other than glaring and brooding would surprise me. I can't seem to be able to separate him from the moody, irritating, monotonous neighbor I met him as.

"So, you're picking me up tonight, right?" Slate asks with a lazy grin, stuffing another bite of sandwich into his mouth. It's stacked so full of meats, cheeses, and veggies that it's exploding from the bread, but Slate seems to have no trouble fitting it inside that big mouth of his.

"Slate, you're the one that offered to call the Uber, shouldn't you be the one picking us up?" I ask, pulling out my buzzing phone. *Shit.* I was supposed to call my parents between classes and debrief them on homecoming weekend. I might've accidentally let the beans spill about Sam showing up when I drunkenly sent them a picture of Rory and I forming a heart with our hands around our siblings who stood in the background. They were about two seconds away from kissing, but as far as my parents know, they were just talking *really closely.*

I send my mom to voicemail before shooting her a quick text, letting her know that I'll call after my last class of the day.

Slate answers with a prissy tease. "Only if I'm ready first, which is unlikely, because I like to be fashionably late."

No one mentions that he's wearing jorts.

"You don't need to be fashionable; we're getting drunk and painting pottery. It'll probably get messy." His smirk widens and I shoot him a glare, tossing a grape at him. It hits his chest but he catches it on the recoil, popping it into his mouth. *"Don't.* I know how it sounded."

Slate's only response is a wink.

My knock on the boy's apartment door is answered by the one and only, my worst nightmare, Knox.

"Can I help you?" He grouses, and he doesn't sound or look outright disgusted by my presence, but he doesn't seem thrilled to see me at his door either. He's wearing the same long sleeve from earlier, and it's hard not to follow the stretch of the fabric as his muscles pop when he crosses his arms over his broad chest, staring me down with those bright jade eyes.

There's a fifty percent chance I'm about to have the door slammed in my face again.

I tilt my chin up, as intimidating as it is to stand my

ground, it's just as much to look up at his towering form. "Are Slate and Ace here?" I ask, attempting to be civil. The half glass of wine I've already had churns in my stomach.

Knox doesn't say a word. His gaze dips, trailing the length of my body and it makes me want to cross my own arms over my chest as goosebumps break out across my skin. I don't like that I can't tell what he's thinking: if I'm revolting to him or maybe he's just doing this to spite me.

Before I can call him out for his wandering eyes, he steps aside, holding the door open and allowing me into their apartment with a sarcastic sweep of his hand.

So much for the civility we had going at lunch, but at least Knox keeps his mouth shut.

I shiver as my arm brushes his, the warmth of his body zipping beneath my skin, jolting my heart rate like a set of jumper cables. I want to jerk away but instead I lengthen my strides into their home.

Their apartment is similar to mine, worn hardwood floors that are stained with the alcohol of a hundred parties. The black granite counters suits them, and someone's painted the cabinets to match. It pulls the light of the room in like a void, whereas mine and Rory's apartment has white cabinetry, reflecting the light—or lack thereof since the sun set hours ago—and makes the room feel bigger.

Their couch looks much comfier than the cheap one Rory and I found online. It seems like the perfect place to hunker down for a movie marathon, and I don't even notice any odd stains on the dark fabric. Of course, their TV is colossal sized, and I think I'll have to convince Slate to host a movie marathon sometime.

"They'll be right out." Knox's voice startles me and I jump, unaware that he'd been standing so close. I peer up at him over my shoulder and it's only now that I realize just how tall he is, nearly a whole head above than me.

I nod because my breath is caught in my throat.

I watch him move back to his seat at the counter where he must have been before I knocked on the door. Spread out across the dark stone are large pieces of drawing paper and an entire box of charcoal. They must be assignments that he's putting the finishing touches on.

I bet being up all night surely helps him stay ahead of his coursework.

I stand dumbly, halfway between their kitchen and living room. I want to move closer, look over Knox's shoulder to finally catch a glimpse of his artwork, but I don't want him biting my head off about it, either.

"What are you doing with Ace and Slate?" Knox asks, and I'm shocked because it's not said rudely. I didn't know he had another tone besides annoying, or that he would ever deign to ask *me* of all people what my plans are for tonight.

"We're all going to Tipsy Canvas," I answer bluntly, because it's more of an answer than he deserves. Knox seems content in his refusal to apologize to me, and that's fine, but I can't help the pang of remorse I feel, knowing that Rory and I are taking his friends out and he'll be left alone tonight. I tack on, softer at the sudden guilt I feel, "You can join if you'd like."

He looks up from his artwork, settling those beautiful eyes on me once more. Their coloring rivals that of a grassy knoll, waist-high strands that I could see myself frolicking in.

Although he doesn't know it, Slate comes to my rescue, sliding out of his room while he tugs a shirt over his head. I allow myself to be distracted by the muscles of his abdomen that are sadly being covered up.

I'm sure he'd be more than happy to take his shirt back off if I asked.

Slate shakes his wet hair out like a dog and Knox grimaces when a droplet hits him in the face. I smother my smirk, tucking my lip between my teeth.

"Oh, time for Tipsy Canvas already? *Please* tell me there are going to be naked ladies."

I roll my eyes because he already knows exactly what happens at Tipsy Canvas and that nude models are a no. But Slate truly loves nothing more than a naked body. "I don't think they'd like it if you got naked at Tipsy Canvas, Slate."

Ace emerges from the single door on the left side of the apartment. It must be his room, and even without having seen Slate enter from his own, I would know who the last room belongs to. The loud ass music that I share a wall with. It's surprising, actually, how Knox isn't in there right now with the noise amped up to *astronomical.*

"Wrong," Slate answers flippantly, flicking me on the nose as he passes, making his way towards the door for his shoes. Knox frowns. "Everyone would love that, don't kid yourself, Quinnie. Although, you already know what I'm working with. You can put in a good word for me if I see any pretty girls, right?" He bats his eyelashes at me. "Present company excluded, of course."

Before I can snark back, Slate's plucking his keys from the bowl by the door and sauntering out of the apartment. I hear him barge through my door a second later, shouting for Rory.

I take a breath to steady myself. I can feel eyes glued to the back of my head and I know that it's Knox because Ace is following Slates steps and grabbing his wallet from the counter. I don't want to be left alone with either of them, so I crane my neck over my shoulder, making direct eye contact with Knox. "You in?"

Ace's steps falter as if he's surprised that I'm extending the invitation. It makes me wonder what exactly Knox told his roommates about me that night we met.

He doesn't break my gaze as he contemplates, and after a moment, he nods, standing from his chair and following Ace and I out the door.

I can't help but feel like we're moving a step in the right direction.

CHAPTER 11
QUINN

Okay, so I was horribly wrong.

I'm currently on my second glass of wine—which is really my third because I chugged the other half I started with at my apartment before we left—and stuck sitting between Knox and Slate at Tipsy Canvas, and I am *most definitely* tipsy.

Why we chose to do this on a Thursday night instead of the actual weekend, I'll regret tomorrow.

Ace and Rory sit opposite me at the table, their canvases hiding their faces. I can only see them when Ace leans over to whisper something to my best friend or when Rory leans over with a calculating look on her face as she assesses his work. She's failing to bite back her flirtatious smile and I bring the glass of wine back to my lips as the realization sets in that her crush on Ace might not be as little as I once presumed.

"Hey, let me borrow some of your blue," Slate says, leaning over me to grab at my palette. We haven't even begun using that color yet, per the instructor's tutorial, but somehow the entirety of Slate's canvas is painted a deep shade of cobalt.

How the hell did he mix that *color?*

His shoulders are so wide that when I lean back in my chair to avoid him, I almost teeter out of it. Knox is the one that saves me, a firm hand gripping my bicep as I begin to flail. I'm stunned when he rights me and Slate has disappeared from my space, staring at him in shock. His hand is still locked around my arm and Knox looks as confused as I do.

The warmth of his hand on my arm is nice. I can feel every single one of his calloused fingers pressing into my skin, electricity branching from his touch through every nerve in my body.

"Blue," I blurt, like a total idiot. It snaps him out of whatever stupor he's in because he removes his hand just as quickly, turning back to his painting. It already looks amazing, the sand of the beach we're supposed to be dotting in looks like Knox found a cup of it and thrown it at his canvas for effect. I continue sputtering nonsense because I can't focus on anything but the lingering feeling of his hand on me. "I have to get more blue."

Stumbling from my seat, I pluck my palette from the table as I spin on my heel, off to retrieve more paint from the counter at the back that's filled with bottles of it. It's conveniently placed next to the bar, and I'm clutching my wine glass to my chest, so I may as well get a refill while I'm at it.

Setting my things down on the table, I flip the cap off the bottle of paint, squeezing it a bit too hard when a figure suddenly appears by my side, startling the fuck out of me.

"Hey, Quinn," Ace says, eyes bugging when the paint squirts out, splattering onto the other colors. The container makes the loudest squelch while there's a lapse in conversation throughout the class and my cheeks burn bright red. The only sound to be heard is a snort of laughter from Slate, but I don't dare turn around to see if every single set of eyes is on us right now.

Maybe I can convince the bartender to let me take the entire bottle back to my table.

Ace glances down to my mess of a palette before meeting my gaze. He looks like he doesn't really know what to say, so I busy myself with capping the paint while he gathers his thoughts.

"Sorry about that," is what he goes with, taking my palette and trading it with his own. "Here, you can use mine."

"Thanks, Ace," I answer sincerely, taking note of how all of his colors are full. He didn't come over here to get more paint, he came over here to ambush me because I've been avoiding him like the plague.

Great.

The chatter of the class picks up again and he glances over to our friends nervously, as if needing reassurance in my presence. He looks embarrassed, almost, as he plays with the blond hair curling at the nape of his neck. His eyebrows are pinched, like whatever is going to come out of his mouth next is as painful to say as it's going to be for me to hear it.

"I, um, wanted to apologize," he mutters, and all of a sudden, it's him that can't look *me* in the eyes. A surge of gratification has me standing taller, biting back a smirk because he *should* feel like an ass for treating me the way that he did at the art supply shop weeks ago. "For, you know..."

I raise a brow, waiting. He may be taller than me, but I feel a whole lot more confident right now, even more so with the wine flowing through me veins. "No, I don't."

Those ocean eyes meet mine and I can tell he wants to sigh in frustration. But he knows that he's going to have to work for my forgiveness if he wants to continue pursuing my best friend like he so blatantly is doing.

"I'm sorry for being a dick."

"Which time?" I ask, cocking my head to the side and feigning confusion. That's right, I'm going to play this apology out for as long as I can so I don't have to go back to sitting next to Knox.

At least, that's what I tell myself.

Ace's gaze grows sharper, but it's not quite a glare yet. He studies me like he's looking at the exact same girl who'd gone blow for blow with him at the art shop. In a way, I suppose he is. I'm still annoyed about the situation and he's acting like I'm the one that owes him something, not the other way around.

"I'm sorry I called you grumpy," he relents, shoulders slumping a bit with the movement. He doesn't seem all that rushed to get back to his seat, but that's probably because he and Rory are miles ahead of the class, being the painting majors they are.

"And?"

"And?" Ace echoes, incredulously. His eyes are wide and if he and I were better friends, his surprise would make me laugh. I watch him scramble for something to say, puffing out an amused breath when he answers, a very unsure lilt to his voice, "And I'm an asshole?"

Slate appears suddenly beside us, reaching between Ace and I for that damned tube of blue paint. For someone so large, I'm not sure how he moves so silently.

I startle back a step and run into a solid frame behind me. Peering over my shoulder, I swallow harshly when Knox's intent green gaze locks on mine.

Great, it's a party over here now.

"I would've said dickhead, but that's just me," Slate supplies, overhearing the tail end of our conversation. Ace rolls his eyes and I laugh as I shift subtly away from Knox, accepting Ace's apology with a nod and a soft smile in return. It feels nice to be on the good side of two of my neighbors. Now I just need to find common ground with Knox and half of my worries will be gone.

Ace snatches our palettes as I grab my wine glass for something to hold onto. Knox's abrupt appearance has unsettled me. All we're missing is Rory and—

There she is, grabbing my hand with a tipsy grin and dragging me over to the bar. My saving grace, this girl, and she doesn't even know it. I'm sure we're all about three seconds from getting kicked out of this class if we don't return to our seats, but I don't think any of us care all that much.

Glancing over my shoulder once more, I find Knox's eyes still on me while Ace and Slate turn to make their way back to their seats.

I can't fight the shiver that crawls up my spine at his piercing gaze.

I register the ding of my phone in the distance and I groan, reaching out blindly for it. It must be nearby if the alert had been that loud, slicing through my unconsciousness like a hot blade through butter.

My knuckles rap against the edge of the coffee table and I grunt, clutching my aching fingers to my chest. Peeling my eyes open, I blink blearily until my living room comes into focus.

I must have fallen asleep sometime between Rory leaving for her study group and after Knox's music had started up again next door. It's less loud than it would be if I was in my room, but the song strums a much lighter tune than his usual playlist. It must have helped lull me into a slumber, my hangover from last night still vignetting the corners of my mind.

Somehow, after my nap, I feel both better and worse. Less like I got hit by a truck and more like maybe it was only my foot that had been run over instead.

Or, my knuckles.

My phone dings again and this time, I'm able to reach it without injuring myself. There aren't many new notifications; one from Slate who tagged me in a picture on Instagram, and by the thumbnail in the corner of the notification I don't even want to open that. There's an excess number of messages from Ace, who, after I accepted his apology, thought it necessary to request to add me on every social media platform he could find me on.

I roll my eyes at that.

There's also a message from my dad, another handy-dandy YouTube link, and he's telling me to watch this video on how to snake the shower drain. *Ew.*

Maybe Rory and I can start a new trend of shaved heads instead.

I'd had a surprisingly good time at Tipsy Canvas last night, drinking wine and painting our sad beach scenes. Well, mine wasn't the worst, but it definitely wasn't the best with two painting majors in our group. Even Knox's had looked amazing. Slate's and mine looked like we spent most of our time drinking instead of painting, which, in all honesty is the truth, but still.

The final message I see is a text from Reid that says:

REID:

On my way, be there in 20.

"Fuck," I grunt, shoving myself up from the couch. I

squint through bleary eyes to read the time. 6:45. Only fifteen minutes until Reid said he'd be arriving.

When I stand, I'm thankful that the room doesn't spin as much as it did this morning when I was getting ready to go to class—*total win to have made it out of bed at all*—but I still stumble on my way into my room.

I may have been a little ambitious when I told Reid he could come over to my place to work on our projects for drawing class together, but I also hadn't been four bottles of wine deep with my friends when we initially made the arrangements.

And I'd stupidly told him that I would cook us dinner, which, along with my entire existence, I'm regretting right now.

Muttering reassurance to myself, I rifle through the dresser for something more appropriate than my current garb, a t-shirt two sizes too big and my favorite cotton pants that have more holes in them than Swiss cheese.

It's a nostalgic save, but these pants have gone through so much with me and I'm comfortable as fuck, so no, I won't be getting rid of them until they can no longer cover my coochie.

I opt for a pair of comfortable jeans and a plain t-shirt instead, shoving it over my mussed hair as I trip over to my dresser, plucking my hairbrush from the top. I wince as it catches in my locks but I power though it until there are no more knots, twisting it up into a clip as I assess myself in the mirror hanging off of the back of my door.

I look like…hell to put it nicely. There are purple circles beneath my eyes and it looks like my cat nap hasn't helped. Mascara still lines the bottoms of my lashes from where I hadn't taken it off properly in my haste to fall into bed last night, and my bright eyes have a dull edge of tiredness to them.

Quickly, I scrub my face clean. I'd rather be late with dinner than look like even more of a mess than I feel. I don't need my image reflecting what's surely going to be my project soon, something not as put together as I try to come across as. I've already decided to make a simple meal that will hopefully impress Reid, and I'm sure with how nice he is, he won't mind or mention otherwise.

A few swipes of mascara and blush later, I'm running to the door, flipping the lock so Reid can let himself in when he arrives. I've forewarned him about the blasted elevator and he laughed at the time, but he'll find out soon just how dreaded it is.

It will give me a few extra minutes to work with, and I send a quick prayer that he does decide to take it.

Setting a pot of water on the stove for pasta, I slide over to the cabinets, pulling out the ingredients I need. A cutting board, knife, garlic, and onion follow. Slowing down so as not to cut my fingers, I chop the onion and slide it into the skillet with some butter. The sizzle fills the otherwise quiet apartment, and it's now that I realize Knox's music has stopped playing while I was napping.

I toss in the freshly chopped garlic after a few minutes, along with salt and pepper. My stomach growls as the savory aroma begins to fill the air.

Of course, just when everything seems to be going well, it all starts taking a turn.

Puncturing the tube of tomato paste, I go to squeeze it into the pan and it explodes all over my shirt.

Fucking fuck.

"Why *wouldn't* it fucking explode," I growl, lowering the flame as I carelessly wipe at the mess on my shirt. It's already ruined, and there's no saving it, unless I ask my father for another YouTube video, so what do I care? Abandoning the red-smeared paper towel, I shove the shirt up and over my head as I aim for the laundry, careful not to get any remnants of the red paste on my face. Thankfully, I have a fresh load of clean laundry in the dryer from yesterday.

In my haste to shove my dirty shirt into the washing machine, I don't hear the door creaking open until I slam the washer shut and raise my hand to get to the dryer. Someone's whistle makes me jump.

Not someone. *Someones.* As in, Knox and Slate, standing wide-eyed in the door as they stare at me, shirtless.

I freeze like a goddamn deer in headlights, gawking right back at them. My heart thumps heavily in my chest as I watch Knox's jade eyes shift darker as they raze down the length of my body in a motion that burns me all the way through.

Something between my legs tingles and I like it entirely too much.

Slate, of course, is the first to break the charged silence. "Don't stop on our account."

It snaps me right the hell out of my staring contest with Knox, my cheeks feel like they're as red as the tomato paste.

"Oh my God! What the fuck are you doing here?" I shriek, scrambling for the dryer. Yep, I've gone full into freaking out mode. *Great.*

The door to the machine gives easily and I snatch the first thing I come in contact with. Thankfully, it's another t-shirt and there are no cringey graphics or an excess amount of fabric involved. I turn my back on Knox and Slate as I shove it on hastily before spinning back to them and pinning them both with a harsh glare that rivals my mother's whenever she is angry with me.

Knox still hasn't said a word. His grip on the doorknob is white-knuckled and he doesn't look like he could speak right now if he tried. It kind of makes me feel giddy. He's much too focused on holding my gaze.

Slate's hands find the air quickly in a display of surrender, almost as fast as the words fumble from his mouth. "We thought it was our apartment, honest! We didn't mean to walk in on you like that."

I groan, slapping a hand to my forehead. It makes my head ring a little in the aftermath of my hangover and I grimace. I'm officially embarrassed. "Just get out, *please.*"

"Yes, ma'am," Slate responds, quickly grabbing Knox and shoving him back into the hall. On his way to slam the door shut behind them, Slate pops his head back inside with a final comment. "Oh, one last thing. There's a pair of panties stuck to your shirt, Quinnie. Nice ones, by the way. Great color."

He ducks out of the apartment before I can throw the nearest thing I can find at him.

Sighing and completely mortified over what just happened, I pluck the scarlet, lace panties clinging to my shirt and shove them into the front pocket of my jeans.

My concoction on the stove pops, drawing my attention.

"Fuck me, truly," I sigh, snagging the bottle of vodka off of the counter on my way back to the stove. If I add more alcohol than I should to my sauce, no one needs to know.

And if I take a shot to try and burn away the feeling of Knox's eyes on my body, no one needs to know that, either.

CHAPTER 12
KNOX

uck me.

F I want to shove the tip of my pencil through the paper when I fuck up my drawing once again.

It's not because of my shaky hands or the fact that I can hear Quinn giggling through the wall with Reid, who Slate and I had conveniently run into after falling back into the hallway following the incident of catching her unaware while she was half naked.

All I needed was one look at the brunet haired boy she invited over, well dressed in his olive slacks and gray sweater vest, to know that I don't like him. The collar of his button-down white shirt popped dramatically against the colors, and with each of his eyes a different splash of butterscotch and sky, it was entirely too much for me to handle. Especially when I noticed the bottle of wine loosely hanging from his grasp, even though he tried to tuck it behind his leg like he was trying to hide his intentions going to Quinn's apartment.

I'd turned on my heel, something hot and heavy slicing through my veins and settling in my stomach like a boulder. I walked right into my own apartment while Slate extended niceties with Reid in the hall. Into my room I went, snatching the dark bound sketchbook from the shelf above my desk and the pack of my favorite pencils. I flopped onto my bed, staring up at the ceiling with the familiar book clutched to my chest.

"Who was that?" I ignored Slate's question when he stuck his head into my room, demanding I play a round of Call of Duty with him.

"That was Reid. He's in Quinn and Rory's drawing class. Architecture major, I think. Seems like a decent guy."

Architecture major? How pretentious.

I declined the game and Slate huffed, leaving my room grumbling something about how Ace would've accepted, which is why I'm currently sitting in my bed, attempting to draw while my mind keeps wandering back to Quinn.

If we hadn't gotten off on the wrong foot, I probably would've pursued her.

She had a bra on, a rather nice, maraschino colored one that matched those rosy cheeks of hers. The body that she hides under those clothes…*my fucking God,* I hadn't expected her to look like that. The perfect handful of plump, round breasts, the tease of her stomach between her bra and the waistband of her pants.

I hadn't been able to take my eyes off of her.

Those gorgeous hazel eyes blazed with the heat of a thousand fires when I was finally able to make my way back up to them, and the intensity of her harsh glare made my heart stutter in my chest like I was a kid with a crush. I watched the way that look in her eyes faltered, and I swear I saw something raw, like she was feeling the same thing I was experiencing: a hot, unyielding need coursing through my veins. But those walls were back up as quickly as they dropped and I was shoved out the door by Slate.

I find myself wanting to hear those foul words rolling off her tongue as she cusses me out. I want her to fight with me again.

It's not difficult to picture the way she stood there. My artist's memory keeps that image fresh and my cock rouses when I draw it back to mind. How Quinn's shoulders curled in on herself with her surprise. The color of her bra stuck in my head like it's tattooed there forever. I saw entirely too much of her: the creamy skin of the tops of her breasts, spilling from her bra, the curves of her sides, rounding out at her hips.

Fuck, do I feel like a pervert right now, thinking about her body—how she'd move under me. What shapes I'd be able to fold her into as I feed her my cock. Would she look at me in that way that makes my stomach tight? Would she fight me every step of the way, vying for control?

Charcoal clings to my fingertips. My kneaded eraser is dark with use, the number of times I've had to go back in and erase is unusual for me. I've always prided myself on being able to put on paper exactly what is in my head, but with the noises on the other side of the wall distracting me, I'm feeling more than frustrated.

Quinn laughs again and I desperately want to shove my headphones over my ears so that I don't have to hear her so happy. Her laughter is a beautiful sound, one I think she should make more often, but I've only known her sour mood, thanks to my actions toward her.

I don't wear my headphones because as much as I'd like to drown out the low rumble of her date's voice, I don't want to miss out on any of the noises slipping past her lips.

I hate that I want to listen in.

Teeth clenched, I force myself to go back in with my charcoal for a third time, and finally, I perfect the line I've been working on. The touch of the chalk is a comforting weight in my palm, and when I smear the medium into the paper, I can almost picture my hands tracing the curves of her body, leaving darkness in their wake.

Something causes Quinn to gasp dramatically and I have to squeeze my eyes shut. My mind wanders back to the time when she was in there all alone and the noises that she made. Pleas of desperation, as if she wasn't the one doing it to herself.

Fuck. I shouldn't be here. I should go see if Slate still wants to play that game, or get out of the house, maybe go to a local bar or have dinner at the diner. Ace is nowhere to be seen lately, so he's out of the question.

Slate's likely to see right through my ploy because I don't usually want to go out and do things. I prefer being in my own space. I never was one to want to get wasted off my ass like the other drunken college kids our age. Working on my art and tattooing—*oh,* I bet I can convince Slate to let me practice on him.

I get up from my bed, and when I leave my room to knock on his door, a neon sticky note plastered to the front stops me.

Gone to get laid. BRB. Love you Knoxie!
P.S. You should think about getting some
yourself ;)

As if I wasn't just thinking the same thing.

Deflating, a noise from the other side of the wall tears my attention away from Slate's note. I frown because I don't know if it's a noise of pleasure or pain, or perhaps a bit of both. I only know that I need to get out of here before the sounds Quinn is making drive me completely insane, or before I barge into her apartment and rip that fluffy-haired fuck right off of her.

They're so fucking annoying, these thoughts that are clogging my head. I don't even like her, and yet, here I am, wondering what she's doing with the guy who'd been standing outside of her door.

Fucking whatever.

I snag my jacket on my way out. The worn leather is a comfort in my hands as I stride to the elevator. It's time to take a ride because if anything, I know that the wind against my body and the open road will wipe the thoughts from my mind.

I don't see Quinn for the rest of the weekend, and her side of the wall is suspiciously silent.

I know this, of course, because I've been listening.

I'd be lying if I said that I wasn't doing it on purpose. My fingers haven't itched for the button on my speaker nor the app on my phone for the songs I play on repeat because it's the only thing that keeps me from spiraling.

It bothers me, I find, not seeing Quinn.

And it isn't until late in the week one night that I do.

It's pouring buckets outside when I finish my classes for the day. I curse because of course I hadn't checked the weather this morning. It's fucking California for fuck's sake; it hardly ever rains here.

Slate and Ace are probably both at the apartment by now and I know that they'll be reluctant to pick me up when lightning flashes brightly across the dark sky. There's a hole in the floorboard of Slate's rusted-as-fuck Bronco, and water will get in it if he drives it in the rain, so that's not an option. Ace's parents said he's not allowed to have his car on campus until he's either a senior or has all straight A's, even though they're rich as hell and his Beemer is collecting dust down in Colorado.

And, well, I'm also stubborn as fuck.

Thankfully, I don't have any of my drawing materials with me, having stored them in the classroom for the night since I'm ahead on most of my projects.

With a sigh, I run to where I parked my motorcycle, two buildings away.

I'm drenched by the time I reach it, but probably not as wet as the girl I see with her head hung, trekking down the block like a drenched campus squirrel. Squinting hard against the rain, I can just make out Quinn's face when she lifts her head, seemingly to curse the skies above.

Fuck. My heart thuds heavily in my chest. Her blonde hair is plastered to her head and she has her arms wrapped around herself as if she's trying to keep warm. She's not dressed for the rain either, in her jean shorts and soaked-through t-shirt.

I'm a prick, but I'm not that much of an asshole. My conscience won't let me sleep for the rest of my measly days if I don't offer her a ride, no matter how much I fear she's going to say no.

"Princess," I call, and want to bite my tongue off for the stupid pet name that rolls out of my mouth so easily. I started calling her that because she was acting like an entitled princess, parking her moving truck where she did and ordering me around right after. Plus, I know it gets on her nerves. But right now, I don't want to fight her, I want to get her back to her place where I know she'll be safe and warm.

When those familiar hazel eyes lift to mine, I add, "Need a ride?"

I see the moment she wants to bite and I have to swallow my smirk. After all of this trying to be civil, here she is, continuing to go to bat with me. "No, thanks," she says, although her teeth are chattering. "I'm all set."

I can't help the way my eyes trail down the length of her. Yeah, she looks all set alright, standing here soaked to the bone. "I see that," I say, drily. "Come on, Princess, don't make this more difficult than it needs to be. It's just a ride. Get on."

Convincing, Knox.

Her mouth falls open as if I've just said something totally obscene, and I start to think about the way her lips are parted so perfectly. Before I can delve further into that thought, her voice pitches and she's shrieking. "Just a ride? Are you kidding me? That thing is a death trap and it's pouring out!"

Ah, so she's scared. I can work with that.

"Is it really?" I mock, veins lighting up with the harsh glare she's sending me now. It's too much fun, teasing her like this, but I'd rather get her out of the rain. "I noticed. Now, come on. I'll drive safe."

She scoffs, rolling her eyes, wincing when rain sluices into them. I watch with a carefully straight face as she blinks rapidly, dispelling the water. "Yeah, knowing you, I doubt it."

Something preens in my chest at her words, knowing that I have her attention. But she doesn't know a thing about me, yet.

"Do you really think you know me, Princess?" I ask, amused. Quinn's lips part again but nothing comes out.

I win.

"I know you well enough," she huffs, but I can see that

she's slowly giving up the fight. Her gaze flicks between me and the motorcycle at my back.

I jerk my chin, gesturing for her to get on.

Her feet betray her, taking a single step in my direction, and that's two points for me.

I do something that I've never done for another girl in my life. I shed my leather jacket, ignoring the chill of the rain that causes goosebumps to break out across my flesh. The rain soaks through my black shirt within seconds, but I don't give a fuck when I catch Quinn's eyes raking the length of my body. That's the look that always makes me shiver.

Helping her with her bag, I hold the coat so she can slip her arms through the sleeves. It should keep her somewhat protected from the rain and wind while we're driving.

It hangs long on her body, across her thighs. She looks good in it. A little too good.

I help Quinn slide her backpack across her shoulders and give her my helmet. My heart thunders in my chest like the storm raging around us, but my hands don't tremble as I tighten the buckle beneath her chin. She looks pained, almost, avoiding my eyes the entire time. I swear I hear her sharp inhale of breath when my fingers brush her skin, but I'm not sure.

"Thank you," she says quietly when I step back. I don't answer because I can't, the words cling to my throat as I turn and swing my leg over the seat of the bike, trying to let the familiar feeling soothe me.

Extending a hand to Quinn, I watch her examine my scarred skin. Well, I assume she's looking at my scars but it's difficult to tell with the visor pulled down. My hand doesn't shake, and I allow her to take her fill, helping her onto the seat behind me when she finally grasps it. She rests her feet on the pegs and I'm suddenly all too aware of how her body is pressed against mine. I can tell she's experiencing some-thing similar in the way that she tries to sit back as far as she can but as soon as the motorcycle roars to life beneath my fingers she's squeaking, winding her hands around my waist and holding onto me for dear life.

Quinn's touch sets me on fucking fire.

Fuck, I can feel each and every single one of her fingers where they're pressing into my abdomen, the hot feeling of her thighs flanking me is like a brand to my sides. I peer at her over my shoulder and all I can think is *shit, shit shit...I am* so *fucked.*

The visor prevents me from looking into those perfect hazel eyes that I'm suddenly yearning to see. Her body is rigid with tension, probably because of our close proximity. *We aren't friends,* I have to remind myself, turning back around and shoving the kickstand up. *It's only a ride home and then we'll go back to hating each other, just like it's supposed to be.*

My motorcycle jerks into motion and the jolt sends Quinn's body sliding closer to mine. Every inch of her is wet, but she's incredibly warm. Her arms tighten around my waist as I pull into the street, taking it at a slow pace since the rain is hitting me directly in the eyes.

I haven't ridden in these conditions since I got my first bike and was stupid enough to drive it everywhere, all the time. I thought I was invincible, and I was addicted to the feeling of the wind against my body, like I was flying down roads without a care in the world. Thankfully, I smartened up before the accident.

I shove the harrowing night from my mind, focusing on the road ahead. I don't accelerate too fast, avoiding the puddles gathering in the roads so we don't slip. I know the way to the apartment like the back of my hand and I'm careful with the precious cargo holding onto me for dear life. It's hard to focus when Quinn's hips are pressed against mine like this, clenching when I take a turn. It's hard not to think about her thighs squeezing around me, making me wonder how hard she'd hold onto me if I was plowing my cock into her.

Rain beats down on the both of us but the warmth of her body keeps me from completely freezing my ass off. I'm soaked through, but it doesn't register, especially not when her fingers accidentally skate under the hem of my shirt when I take the last turn to our apartments, dancing against the skin of my stomach.

My entire world fucking flips.

The rear tire skids, slipping on the wet asphalt. Quinn gasps, clutching onto me for dear life. My heart spikes painfully in my chest as I act quickly to right the bike, shifting with it and keeping it from falling over. My heart hammers in my chest and my breathing turns ragged as I'm transported back two years ago when I had been going at much faster speeds but hadn't been able to control my motorcycle, resulting in the worst accident of my life.

I sense the tension in Quinn's body and it keeps me from reliving that nightmare. Her thighs are trembling around me and I know this has given her a good scare. Now that the bike is one again steady, I slow down even more, slipping one hand down to give her thigh a quick pat and a gentle squeeze, a silent reassurance for her as much as it is for me.

Her arms locked around my waist tighten in response.

I roll to a stop in my usual spot, the same one where I'd blocked her moving truck in the first day we met. The tree offers little cover, but the rain is lighter than it was when we left campus.

Right now, Quinn doesn't seem to care about anything

other than getting out of the blasted weather. I cut the engine and swing off the motorcycle, helping her next. I drop her hand as soon as she has her footing and we're racing toward the building, ducking inside as I hold the door open for her.

She grunts, trying to pry the helmet from her drenched head. I laugh softly, helping her undo the straps. When she slips from the helmet, poor Quinn looks like a soaked cat.

Her blonde hair is plastered to her head. Her skin is rosy and there's mascara running down her cheeks but I refrain from mentioning it because of the way she's looking up at me. I don't want to break whatever this peace is right now. I want to revel in it.

"Thank you," Quinn says softly. She wrings her fingers together and I offer a nod in response. She looks like she wants to say more but she doesn't, so I lead her toward the elevator. She needs a warm shower for sure.

For once, the elevator is on the floor I need it to be on and it opens with a screech. Quinn and I cringe before stepping inside. I punch the button to the fourth floor with my knuckle and the doors slide shut, encapsulating us in silence once again.

Until the elevator starts climbing upwards with a jarring groan, at least.

It sounds horrendous, like the ghosts of tenants past screeching for help. There's a chill inside that isn't because of the silence between us, prickling the hairs at the nape of my neck. It's awkward, and even if we were verbally sparring right now, I think it would be better than the complete silence we're standing here in.

The ascent to the fourth floor is a long one, but neither of us break the quiet. The events of the day hit me full force: the lack of time I've had to practice my tattooing lately is catching up to me, my schedule is quickly filling up with assignments and artwork for an exhibition I'm preparing for at a local gallery. I have a few more pieces to finish up for that in the next coming weeks as well, which will put my search for an apprenticeship on hold.

The soft protest of Quinn's stomach rumbling gathers my attention. She's blushing hard but refuses to look my way, content with staring at the glowing floor button as we rise.

I bet she's silently cursing the elevator to hurry up right now.

Finally, the doors open and Quinn almost sprints to her door. I catch up within strides because my legs are longer than hers, but I keep a few feet behind because whatever magical tension from the metal box from hell has followed the us into the hall.

She shoves her key into the lock before turning to face me, speaking hastily as she twists. "Thank you again, Knox."

Before I can respond, she's shoving her shoulder into the door. It gives easily, but the loud moan that fills the hall as soon as it cracks has the both of our eyes widening.

"Oh God, *Ace!*"

"Holyfuckingshit," Quinn exhales in a single breath, and I thought that the elevator ride up was the most awkward part of tonight.

Seeing Rory and Ace going at it on her couch is *definitely* not something I was prepared for.

They don't seem to notice us, I don't think, and Quinn shuts the door as quickly as she opened it, wincing as it slams loudly. If they didn't know we saw anything then, they sure do now.

Quinn locks it once more, jolting away from it like it's on fucking fire, and she stares at me, her eyes wide in disbelief.

"Was that—"

"Yes," I breathe. "Yes it was."

Quinn runs her fingers through her hair as if she can't believe what we just saw. It tangles easily from the rain and she frowns, ripping her hands from the knots. "That's *my* couch!"

I try to hold it in, I really do, but my laughter bubbles out of me without permission.

Quinn looks more shocked at my laughter than she did at the explicit porno she just walked in on.

After a second, she joins in.

"That's what you're worried about?" I wheeze. "Your couch?"

"Hey," she scowls, the smile still lighting her face even as she glares at me. "I paid good money for that! Half of it is mine!"

I shake my head, more than amused.

A noise from the other side of the door startles her and she stumbles back a step. Apparently, Rory and Ace aren't letting our interruption affect their night.

"Come on," I tell her. "You can hang out at our place until they're done."

Quinn looks reluctant, but she has no other choice, so she follows, muttering, "Who knows how long that will be."

"You'll know it's safe when you can't hear them through the walls anymore."

An entertained smile curves Quinn's lips but falls when she finds me staring. She turns away but I still catch the way her cheeks go pink. "Right."

I open the door to my apartment and it's all I can do to pray that Slate isn't here for once, enjoying the easy laughter between us. I don't want a buffer. The apartment is dark and silent when we enter and I mentally cheer knowing that I get to have more of Quinn's attention on me. Maybe I can finally right the entire mess from the day we met.

I duck into Slate's room, double checking to see that he hasn't just fallen asleep. When I find his bed empty and the blankets a crumpled mess as always, I know he hasn't arrived back from class yet, either.

Drifting over to the hall closet, I pull out two towels, tossing one to Quinn where she's still standing awkwardly inside of the threshold, clutching the fabric as tightly as he can.

"Slate isn't here, yet," I explain, sliding my phone from my pocket. I shoot off a text to my friend and set it on the counter. "You can take a shower here, if you want to warm up. I can get you some clothes. I don't know if we have any of that fruity scented shampoo that you probably use, but I know Slate has a three-in-one mix you should stay away from."

Laughter spills from her lips and she looks almost affronted that she wasn't able to hold it in. "Knox, did you just make a joke?"

"I don't know, did you just laugh at my joke, Princess?" I retort, amusement filling my tone.

Quinn can't hide her smile now. For the first time, she seems to actually be enjoying my presence, and I'm not about to take that for granted.

"Yeah, I think I did."

CHAPTER 13
QUINN

"What the fuck do you think you're doing?" I groan at my reflection in the mirror.

I'm currently locked in Knox's bathroom after he handed me a fluffy towel and offered me their shower. I'm staring into the mirror, fingers white-knuckled where they're curled around the edges of the counter, totally freaking out.

I look as much of a mess as I feel like. There's a part of me that appreciates Knox for not mentioning my state, but the other part of me is fucking mortified that I'd been talking to him while looking like a drowned raccoon. My mascara has run from the rain, streaking dark down my cheeks that are pale from the cold. My hair hasn't fared much better—glued to my head from Knox's helmet. It's tangled in knots around my shoulders.

Of course, Knox had looked like a fucking God when he'd run his fingers through his own drenched hair. It had stuck up in all different directions but he only managed to make the hairstyle look even better. And worse, the black t-shirt that clung to his skin only showed off his impressive arms and the tattoos lining them. It gave me a closer look at his forearms and the scarred patches of skin crawling from his hands up.

My staring didn't last long, and although I wanted to ask him about the scars that look like lightning, erratic threads in the sky, I managed to keep my intrusive questions to myself.

I covered myself with the towel he handed me as I slipped out of his leather jacket, returning it to him with a grimace. It was heavy with rain, and I hope it's not ruined. The fabric of the towel helped cover my pert nipples, hard from the cold and Knox's glorious presence before me. It didn't stop the shiver from raking down my spine and collecting between the apex of my thighs when Knox leaned over to stretch the jacket across a nearby chair, showing off the impressive expanse of rippling muscle lining his back.

I'm standing in the bathroom, completely beside myself. I shouldn't be here. I should've sprinted right past Ace fucking Rory into the couch and locked myself in my room. I should've shoved my headphones into my ears and turned my music all the up to drown out the sounds of them having sex. It would've been way more mortifying for me, but at least I wouldn't be in the situation I'm currently in.

Huffing out a breath of frustration, I slide my phone from my pocket. The case sticks against my damp jeans and I nearly drop it onto the tiles below my feet when I manage to pry it free. My heart races in my chest as I catch it, clutching it even tighter. Thankfully, it has made it out of the rain unscathed, but the battery is running low.

Quickly, I pull up Slate's contact and shoot off a text before I can really think about it, asking when he'll be returning to the apartment. When the message reads delivered and there isn't an instant reply, I tack on that he's missing out on hot gossip because I know that will draw him home like a bee on honey.

"Okay, you can do this," I mutter to myself, taking a breath to calm my nerves. "Just take it one step at a time. A shower, first."

There's a pile of clothes that Knox found for me, folded atop the counter. Sifting through them quickly, I wonder if I should be thankful. There's a plain black t-shirt and a pair of boxer shorts, not forgotten garments of the three boys' conquests or items left behind from rowdy partygoers that may have been a little too drunk to remember all of their clothing.

Drunk. That's what I need to be right now.

Snagging the wash cloth from the top of the pile, I twist the knob on the shower until steam begins filling the small room. For a bathroom in a college boys' apartment, it's cleaner than I thought it would be. There's a shower mat placed outside of the tub and they even have a shower curtain. Surprisingly, the toilet seat is also down.

Three towels hang on hooks around the room but that's the only disorderly thing about it. A brown one hangs on the back of the door next to a robe, and I recognize it as the same one Slate had worn to my drawing class the day that he modeled for us.

It's shocking that I actually remember what he was wearing that day.

There's a gray towel slung along a rod nailed beside the shower and a dark azure one hanging from a hook next to it. Wondering which towel belongs to which roommate helps keep my mind off of my internal freakout.

Stop distracting yourself.

Right. The shower.

I'm still shivering a little when I strip down, peeling my

wet clothes from my body. It's hard to wiggle from my jeans with the way they're clinging to my legs and I nearly trip, biting back the noise of fright that tries to free itself from my throat when I stumble.

Righting myself, I take a moment to ease the racing of my heart. I pray that the hot water will relax my tight muscles and clear my head of all my worried thoughts.

The spray is delightful. Near scalding in temperature, I relax almost instantly under its prefect pressure. They've clearly replaced the shower-head because this is utterly fucking *therapeutic.* This one is heaven sent compared to the leaky one in my apartment. I release a sigh of enjoyment at the way the water warms my aching bones.

When it's time to shampoo, I eye the products lining the built-in shelf. There are enough that I'm surprised, immediately trying to discern what belongs to each roommate. I eye the three-in-one Knox mentioned was Slate's and laugh because with hair like his I wouldn't expect him to be using that, but hey, whatever works for him.

There are three other bottles of shampoo, along with hair oils, expensive looking conditioners, razors, shaving cream, and face washes all lined up nicely—presumably in the order they're used on the shelf. Reading the bottles of each one as the water pours soothingly down my back, I tentatively pick one up and take a whiff of the product. The label reads *hydrating* but the overpowering lavender scent that consumes my senses nearly makes me gag.

Next.

The second bottle smells like actual heaven. It's deep, musky, and masculine. There are hints of pine and something I can't really describe as anything other than *man.*

It's every woman's wet dream.

It's a little robust for me but I use it anyway because I

haven't gotten any in months and I want to smell like I've just been cuddled up to the most gorgeous, amazing-smelling man in the world. Seriously, I'm debating stealing this for when I finally get a boyfriend and force him to bathe in it.

I lather it in my hands and scrub it into my scalp, breathing in deeply when the heady scent fills the room.

I work as quickly as I can so Knox doesn't have anything to complain about except the lack of hot water because I just can't help myself. I'm cold and I want to marry his shower-head.

If it were detachable, I'd absolutely take it down to the courthouse right now.

My stomach twists at the thought that the products I'm using right now might be Knox's. We've been arguing less, and if it weren't raining, I might admit that the ride on his motorcycle was nice, minus the near topple we had when we turned the corner to our street. My heart had kicked out of my chest when we slid, but then Knox's hand caressed my thigh, squeezing it like I had been the one to save us from falling when all I did was try my best not to scream. His reassuring touch had made me wet for a completely different reason than the storm.

After I finish cleaning up, I shut the water off and dry myself off. I feel much better already, no longer shivering from the cold.

The clothes Knox gave me make me look like I'm drowning all over again. The shirt drapes long down my legs and I frown, tucking the side of it up into the waistband of the boxers so if anyone happens to walk in on me here, at least they'll know I have pants on.

I don't understand how the shirt can fit him so tightly but is so loose on me.

The steam from my shower has revealed a message

written on the mirror that reads '*hurry up, fucker.*' It's been left by Slate, no doubt, and I smile, thinking about him sneaking in here while Ace or Knox were showering to leave them this note. Only he could have such scraggly writing like this. His entire persona screams sneaking into the bathroom while his roommates are showering just to leave them cheeky messages.

The novelty of the joke doesn't last long when I hear rummaging from the other side of the door. It hits me once again exactly where I am and who I'm with.

Enough, I scold myself. It's now or never. I only need to stay here for as long as it takes Ace and Rory to finish fucking or until Slate comes back so he can be the buffer between Knox and I, even if he isn't being entirely intolerable tonight.

After making sure my panties are folded as small as possible and tucked tightly into the middle of my wet clothes pile, I scoop them from the floor and exit the bathroom.

The smell that slaps me in the face is *incredible* and my stomach agrees with a loud growl.

The sight might be even better.

Knox is standing over the stove, shirtless as he stirs something in the pan that smells like heaven. My mouth waters and I blame it on the aroma of whatever he's making and not the fact that his back looks just as good as I imagined it.

Two, large wings are tattooed across the expanse of his shoulder blades, dipping down to caress the line of his spine. They flex when he moves, reaching to stir something in a different pot, and my knees wobble as all of the warmth from my shower converges deep between my legs.

He's changed his pants, I notice, into a pair of light gray sweatpants that hang so low on his hips that I can see the cutting lines of muscle where they triangle into the waistband. There's no line of underwear to be seen, but the two dimples at the base of his spine call out to me and I want to press my tongue into them.

Knox turns, heading for the fridge, freezing when he sees me standing two feet out of the bathroom, ogling him.

The jade of his eyes stirs and my cheeks go molten. They're so hot I can probably fry an egg on them while Knox takes his time looking me up and down, just like I'd been doing to his backside a second ago.

Of course, his chest looks even more magnificent than his back. I knew he was muscular but I wasn't quite picturing *this*. The cording of his muscles, arms bulging with little effort, the tight abdominals and taut waist. The expanse of tattoos lining Knox's skin are inked exactly where they belong, an effortless addition to his beauty that even Monet would be envious of. I need to take a step closer, get a better look at them. He's glorious, and it makes me want to drop everything and draw him, trace those lines with my pencils, my fingers, and my tongue—

"You can put your clothes in the dryer," Knox croaks, and his words startle the both of us into action. My brows furrow until his sentence catches up with me and then I'm looking down at the bundle of wet clothes I'm holding so tightly to my chest, even my clean shirt is wet with it. It also gives me something to lay my eyes on instead of his illustrious body. "If you want to."

I nod because I don't trust my voice right now. Shuffling quickly to the dryer, I stuff my clothes inside, reminding myself that I should not be ogling the noisy neighbor who just happens to be the most handsome man I've ever seen.

And he's most certainly a prick underneath all that glory, so there's that.

"Thanks," I murmur once I've started the machine. I dare

step closer to see what he's doing in the kitchen but when he glances at me from the corner of his eye, I freeze all over again like a fucking deer in headlights. "What are you making?"

"Chicken and pasta," he says as if he's making something as simple as a bowl of cereal, which would have sufficed. With the scents filtering through the room, I know it's not as simple as chicken with pasta, but I refrain from asking. "Hopefully you're hungry."

I don't question why he's making something so extravagant but I also won't complain. I'm hungry as fuck, and Knox is kind of...*pleasant* when he's not being an utter dick.

"It smells incredible," I offer politely, testing the waters with him. I'm not sure if we're drawing up some sort of continued peace treaty, but the petty part of me still wants an apology out of him. A girl is hungry right now, so I can wait a little longer. "Can I help you with anything?"

Knox shakes his head. "Almost done, Princess. Have a seat."

I do as he says, ignoring the nickname he refuses to stop calling me. I find a spot at the counter and the both of us fall into a peaceful silence as I watch him plate the dishes. He seems completely focused on the task at hand, rinsing the pasta and serving it into wide bowls. He seems confident in every step that he's taking and a pinprick of envy pokes holes in my stomach.

I shift uncomfortably in my chair the longer I think about it.

"Do you think Slate will be back soon?" I blurt with sudden unease.

Knox doesn't glance at me when he responds. "I'm not good enough for you, Princess?"

"Considering you've been a grumpy prick since we met,

I'd say that answer is pretty obvious. And I told you to stop calling me that," I snap, taking the bait. "I hate it."

Naturally, my request is denied as Knox tops the sauce with some freshly grated cheese and slides a bowl across the counter to me. "Here you are, Princess. Enjoy." *Holy hell.* I thought it smelled orgasmic, but it looks even better. My mouth is watering already and I can't wait to dive in.

Knox rounds the counter, sinking down onto the barstool next to me with his own serving. He slides me a fork and sets a stack of napkins down between us, eyeing me as I stare between him and the steaming dish in front of me like the mess that I am.

"Why are you being so nice to me?"

Nice one, Quinn, really. The fuck did you have to say that for? Just shut up and accept the food.

In what I'm learning is typical Knox fashion, he lifts a brow, watching me with that intense gaze of his. "Do you prefer it when I'm rude, Princess?"

I huff, cheeks burning as I stab my fork into the pasta, spearing a chunk of chicken coated in sauce. I don't even know why I asked because of course he was going to have a snarky answer in response. I should know this about him by now.

"You know, you don't have to be so volatile all of the time—oh my *God.*" The moan that accompanies the flavor bursting on my tongue is completely unnecessary and unlady-like, but the dish Knox made is just that damn good. And surprising. I stare at him in bewilderment. "What the fuck? This is fantastic!"

He startles in his seat, not expecting my compliment. I can't blame him because I would react the same if he compli-mented me. There's a faint dusting of color to his cheeks that makes me want to grin smugly but I'm much too busy twirling the pasta around my fork and shoveling another bite of delicious food into my mouth.

"What was that, Princess?" He taunts, and I duck my head. I refuse to give him the satisfaction of repeating myself.

"I'm not saying it again," I grumble. The chicken is perfection, juicy and flavorful from how it soaked up the sauce he finished cooking it in. The pasta is delicious and the dish warms my entire body happily.

I'm taking this meal *and* the shower-head down to the courthouse.

I don't notice the way Knox's shoulders shake with silent laughter until I'm able to spare a second to look up from my bowl. There's a self-satisfied aura to the air around him that I just want to burst.

I ignore him, because the food is much more important right now.

When my bowl is clean, I feel like I can fall asleep right at the counter, full and satiated. The entirety of my day, from my classes to the review I had with Beatrice about my project, to being drenched in rain mixed with my anxiousness of being in Knox's apartment, are all catching up to me. Slate still hasn't answered my texts so I'll have to grill him about where he's been when I see him next.

I might have to chew Rory out for not warning me that she had someone over.

Or the fact that she decided to have sex on the couch. With Ace.

Sure, it's obvious that there was something going on between them, but I thought it was innocent flirting, not full-blown sex! Why wouldn't she tell me?

Knox takes my dishes, holding the bowl out of my reach when I try and grab for it.

"I can clean up," I protest. "You cooked!"

He shakes his head, dumping the dishes in the sink. "Don't worry about it. I'm more than capable."

I scoff. *"Clearly.* Doesn't mean that I'm rude, though."

He tosses me a look over his shoulder like he doesn't believe me and I scowl in response. It bothers me, those little looks he gives me, like he's trying to bait me into arguing. I don't want to start something after the civil dinner we've just shared, but the way that he acts like everything leading up to this moment is my fault gets to me.

"No, but threatening to have my bike towed wasn't the nicest thing to do."

Oh, so he really wants to do this right now? *Okay, then.*

"Neither was parking in front of the truck I was *just* about to move!"

I swear I hear him mutter "whatever" under his breath and I grit my teeth. Standing from my chair, I swipe my phone from the counter.

"I think I should leave now."

"I think that would be best," Knox responds flippantly from his spot at the sink.

It makes my head spin, how we can go from having a semi-civil conversation to snapping at each other's necks like rabid dogs.

As I move to gather my things from the dryer, a loud moan cuts through the wall, making the both of us freeze.

How the fuck are they not done yet?

I certainly have some dumb fucking luck.

Maybe I can still leave and call Slate out in the hall. Worst case scenario, I think Peep might let me stay over at her house if I need, but she'll probably tell Sam all about it and I know I won't hear the end of it from my brother until I explain why I had to stay over.

Stubbornly, I head for the dryer. Knox doesn't say a word

as I pull the door open and he doesn't look up from the sink when I gather my warm clothes into my arms, holding them as close as I can to keep what remains of my temper. What is it about Knox's attitude that always has me reacting like this?

"Wait," Knox sighs, finally daring to speak when I'm about to snatch my wet shoes from the floor by the door. They're still soaked and there's no way I'm putting my bare feet into the cold fabric.

Pausing, I wait for him to continue, because really, I'm not all that confident about my other options.

"I cannot, in good conscience, kick you to the street," he says, shutting off the water and wiping his hands clean on the kitchen towel. I watch him as he does, once again drawn to the marks on his hands and forearms.

He catches me looking and his jade eyes harden, but he doesn't shift away or hide his hands, as if he's used to people staring. I feel guilty, anyway, with the way he's assessing me.

Knox looks a little like he might kick me to the curb, after all.

So, I build up that wall, fighting back like I always do. "You? A good conscience? As if."

"I'm doing it more for Slate than for you. If he finds out I let you leave with no place to go, he'll pummel me into the ground."

I study him. He doesn't break my stare, allowing me to search for whatever it is I'm looking for in those hillside eyes. I don't even know what I'm hunting for, but I welcome the challenge.

"Afraid of Slate?" I taunt.

Knox crosses his arms over his chest and the sight of his muscles flexing makes me weak, my gaze trailing the movement. My mouth runs dry but my pussy is dripping and there's no missing the way that his eyes melt with heat before I can snap myself out of it.

Knox shakes his head, the corner of his mouth tilting up, and it eases the tension a bit. "Have you seen how big he is?"

My shoulders slump at the ease that's returned once again. It's like a tennis match between us, the highs and the lows, volleying for attention. "Yeah," I agree. "I have."

His jaw flexes and he turns slowly, as if he's afraid I might actually go running from the apartment and he'll have to chase me down. *I kind of want him to,* I think before immediately cutting that thought off. No need to be thinking about a shirtless man running after me through the halls of the apartment complex and wondering what he might do if he catches me.

Shit.

When Knox is sure that I'm not going to leave, he returns to washing the dishes while I stand by the door like a fool. I can bear it for all of one minute—which I pride myself on—and then I shift on my feet, drawing his attention once more.

"You can sleep in my room. I'll take the couch."

That's not at all what I was expecting him to say.

My throat dries right the fuck up because *what?* My gorgeous—albeit an asshole—neighbor is offering me a ride, shower, food, *and* his bed? I'd marry him right now too if I didn't know that he has the personality of a brick wall.

Truly, a shame.

Knox doesn't look my way while he offers this and I'm thankful because I feel like melting into the floor with how hot my cheeks surge.

"No, no," I respond hastily, "I'll take the couch. I'm not all that sure I'll be able to sleep with the image of Ace's ass in my head, anyway," I word vomit, mind scrambling to put letters together as I imagine what the inside of Knox's room looks like. "Was that a tramp stamp I saw?"

Knox bites back a smile that makes my heart race and my knees wobble.

"Sure was, gave it to him myself."

"Shut up," I squeal, before we both break out into laughter.

It's nice, being on Knox's good side. He has a great laugh, a low rumble that wraps around my bones like warm honey.

"At least take Slate's room, then," he offers. "I'm sure he won't mind."

I wrinkle my nose. "Are the sheets even clean?"

His quiet chortle is melodic, husky like he hasn't laughed in years.

It makes me ache for him.

"That's a gamble you'll have to take if you don't want to sleep in my room."

God, he really does make it sound appealing.

"Right," I answer rather awkwardly, because now all I'm thinking about is being in Knox's room *with* him and what his bed must be like and how he— "Thank you again for dinner, Knox. And the ride." I inch towards Slate's room even if the urge to get a glimpse of the real Knox is tempting.

"Pleasure's all mine, Princess."

"Stop calling me that."

"Not a chance."

I shut the door to Slate's room with a frustrated noise that puts the affable night to rest.

CHAPTER 14
QUINN

The ceiling has never been more interesting.

I say this because I'm currently laying in Slate's bed, staring at the ceiling, and have been for the past four hours.

I'm avoiding the inevitable, which is seeing Knox again.

Another night of no sleep. I should be used to it by now, and where I'm normally all achy bones and gritty eyes, this morning is different. I'm wired—restless.

It's not Knox's fault that I hadn't been able to sleep this time. Not intentionally, at least. He wasn't blasting music on his side of the wall—which, Slate also shares, so he must be able to sleep through a zombie apocalypse if Knox's loud metal playlist doesn't bother him while he's sleeping—but I couldn't rest because he was just simply there, existing in the room next door.

My mind wouldn't allow me to stop thinking about him over there. If he found it as difficult to fall asleep as I was. If the thought of what I was sleeping in was as vivid in his head as it was in mine.

Did he go to sleep in those sweatpants? His boxers? Or

briefs? I'm not judging, just making an educated guess because of the boxers he gave me to wear for the night. Unless they're Slate's or Ace's, but why would he give me one of their pairs without asking? That seems rude. They *have* to be his.

Jesus, Quinn, look at what you've become.

Anxiousness weighs heavily on my body as I slip from the bed, looking around the room with the sun peeking its head through the windows. Slate's room is utterly Slate. His bed dons ocean colored bedding, matching comforter and all. I thought that he might have something a little quirkier, like cowboys or even a plaid pattern, but then I remember just how much Slate likes bringing ladies here, and I figure they wouldn't want to have sex on bed sheets that scream *Wild Wild West.*

Whatever happened to saving a cowboy and all that?

He doesn't have much in terms of furniture. There's a tall dresser next to the door with clothes spilling out of the drawers as if he's rifled through them in a rush like a raccoon through a garbage can. He has a desk but I don't think the surface of it has seen the light of day in years with how much crap is piled on top of it. I don't know how it's possible that Slate has accumulated this many things in the matter of weeks since the semester started, or if he hasn't cleaned it off in the entire time he's lived here.

There's a photo placed on the table beside the bed and I pick it up, admiring the three roommates, arms around each other. They're dressed in their usual attire, Slate in his low-cut jeans, showing off the deep lines of muscle pointing straight to his crotch. In the photo, he's wearing a jersey of some sort, cropped above his navel. The bottom of the number 15 is cut off and I think it might be a Terrapin's rugby jersey, not that I know too much about the sport nor what they wear.

Ace is wearing a pair of slacks and a t-shirt tucked into the waistband of them. He looks like he's just rolled out of a mob fight with his unruly blond hair. There's a single strand that hangs down in front of his mischievous ocean eyes and I actually think he looks kind of cute here.

Go Rory.

Knox looks exactly the same as last night, with a little less muscle. It has me wondering how old this photograph is. Maybe they had taken it on their first day of college at Vulcan University. He's dressed in all black, with the hood of his sweatshirt pulled up over his head as if he's trying to hide from something. His cheeks are swept with pink and his hands are stuffed deeply into the pockets of his hoodie, but the white that peeks out from the bunched-up sleeves has me squinting, trying to get a closer look.

They're bandages, I realize, wrapped tightly around his forearms and my stomach rolls.

This picture was taken around the time of whatever happened to his hands.

A noise from outside of the door startles me. It's coming from the kitchen, and the sick feeling doesn't lessen when I figure out that it's probably Knox, and that he's probably making noise because he wants me to get the fuck out of his apartment.

I find a mirror leaning against the wall behind the door and assess myself. I don't look much different than I had last night. My hair is messy, but at least I don't have mascara streaming down my face anymore. The tired lines of my features show, but there's absolutely nothing I can do about that.

I'm sure Slate has a brush around here somewhere but I

rake my fingers through my hair quickly before stepping out of the room.

Slate's bedroom opens directly into the kitchen and once again, I'm met with a delicious smell. It's sweet, like overloaded sugary breakfasts usually are. Knox stands, his back to me, at the stove as he flips a pancake.

He doesn't even glance over his bare shoulder as he greets me. "Good morning."

"Morning," I echo, tentatively working my way into the room. My clothes are folded on one of the stools where I left them last night, and I really should just snatch them up and run the fuck right out of this apartment before I have to endure a truly awkward breakfast that screams 'morning after' despite the dislike we share for each other.

"Sleep well?"

Not at fucking all. "Yeah," I lie, inching closer. Maybe, if I'm quiet enough, he won't even notice my disappearance. I can return the clothes he's let me borrow to Slate later.

If Knox feels me spiraling, he doesn't show it. He's busying himself with whisking a bowl full of eggs, adding a touch of water to make them fluffy.

Perhaps he's ignoring me. Maybe I've misread the situation entirely, thinking that he's making me breakfast. He could just be making it all for himself. He's built, so it wouldn't be a surprise, and I make it all the way to the door, about to reach for the lock when it turns from the other side. I startle backwards as the door swings open.

Ace and Rory freeze from behind the threshold and I'm staring at them all wide-eyed like I've just been caught robbing the place.

"Well, good morning to you, too," Ace greets, ushering both Rory and myself back inside. I go reluctantly, shooting her a pleading look before slumping down at the counter and resting my chin on my pile of clothes. All of a sudden, I'm exhausted, and I contemplate how much of a fool I'd look like if I do decide to run out of the apartment right now.

Ace moves straight over to Knox, their conversation quiet as he begins assisting his friend.

Rory looks like she's hesitant to take the seat next to me and she should be because I can hardly even look at her without replaying what I saw last night. Her legs pitched up above Ace's shoulders as he—she's my best friend for good-ness' sake but there are even some things I didn't need to see.

I knew she was flirting with Ace, but I didn't know how far it had gotten, fucking on the couch like bunnies.

I have so many questions for her but the betrayal in my gut and the tiredness stroking my back keep me from speak-ing. I wouldn't interrogate her in front of the boys anyway, that would be cruel and mortifying for the both of us.

How long have they been fooling around? Why hasn't she talked to me about anything more than saying he was attrac-tive? Was it because of my own attitude towards Knox? Was I so volatile that she couldn't even confide in me about her relationship with our neighbor?

"Hey," she greets awkwardly, and her cheeks are rosy. I wonder if she thinks the unpleasant tension is because I'm upset about them having sex on the couch.

It's so much more than that.

"Hi," I answer with a weak smile. Rory looks like she wants to say more but the door is bursting open with an unruly Slate stumbling into the apartment. Half of his brunet hair has fallen from the bun he has it shoved into and his chocolate eyes are tired with sleep, but he perks right the hell up when he sees all of us in the kitchen.

His grin turns wolfish.

"So, everyone got laid last night? Fuck yeah! Where's the whiskey, we all deserve a shot!"

Everyone seems to groan in unison and I'm the one that answers.

"Slate, it's too early for all that."

He scoffs in response, ripping open the cabinet as he searches for liquor. "Right, and? There are breakfast shots, Quinnie, very good ones too. Plus, it's almost the weekend, so why the hell shouldn't we have a little celly? I swear, you've got to start acting like the college student that you are."

"Celly?" Knox grimaces. "Where the fuck did you learn that word?"

Slate shrugs, "Overheard some guys saying it at one of our parties. I kind of like it." He finds the bottle and slams it down on the counter with a little too much force. It makes a dull throbbing between my eyes form and I watch wearily as he spins on his heel and dives into the refrigerator next. "If I give you some orange juice and a piece of bacon, will that be considered an appropriate morning time shot for you, Quinn?"

I huff. How everything always gets pinned on me is unreal. I should've just kept my damn mouth shut.

Rory snickers next to me and I cut her a look, trying my best to smother my amusement. She must see it sparkling in my eyes because her grin widens. "Yes, sir."

"Ooh, I like it when you call me that," Slate winks. "How's the bacon coming along, Knox? We're in dire need of alcohol over here!"

"I think that's only you, Slate," Rory laughs.

We watch as Slate places five mismatched shot glasses on the counter. That doesn't seem to be enough because a clamber of five additional glasses joins the fray and he begins filling them with various liquids, cussing when he shakes the orange juice canister and the cap flies off, spraying all over his arm and shirt. Rory and I burst into laughter while Knox and Ace roll their eyes, shaking their heads at their roommate.

"Who didn't put the lid back on the orange juice?" Slate whines, whisking off his shirt.

Hello, chest.

Knox tosses over his shoulder, *"You,* idiot."

"Thanks, fuckhead," Slate retorts, balling up his shirt and tossing it towards the washing machine. It hits the wall with a soft thump, falling lamely to the ground. He turns that bright gaze back on me as I ogle his tattoos and his smirk grows. "Like what you see?"

Blushing, I dip my head, but it's too late, the damage has already been done.

"No need to be all shy, Quinnie. We've already seen each other naked. Want to feel them?" Slate asks, gesturing to the hard muscles of his abdomen. He flexes, then does the same with his pectorals.

If I had a drink in my mouth, I'd surely be spluttering it all over the counter right now.

"I was *not* naked!" My retort is pitched, because really, I wasn't. All he saw was me in my bra and it wasn't even my nice one.

Knox glances at me but I can't make out the expression on his face. He turns away too quickly for me to catch.

Of course, Slate has a witty retort. "Want to fix that?" He winks. "Or—" his eyes trail down my shirt and the boxers I'm wearing and I wish the floor would open up and swallow me whole. "Did you already have your fill?"

"Fuck, man," Ace almost growls. It's a little mortifying, how far Slate's taking his jokes this morning. "Cut it out."

"She slept in your bed." Knox's voice sounds like gravel. He doesn't turn around, even when Slate groans, loud and disappointed.

"The *one* time I don't answer my phone." He sighs, refocusing on the task of pouring breakfast shots when Ace brings over the plate of bacon he'd been manning. "I'm sorry, Quinn. Let me make it up to you." Slate slides me a shot of whiskey, a glass filled with orange juice, and gestures to the plate of bacon. "I'll let you have the first one, even."

I relent, because I need this breakfast to be over as fast as possible and the best way to do that is by keeping my mouth shut. Taking the first shot means I have to make the toast and I'm much too tired to be dealing with all of this right now.

Even Knox accepts the drink Slate hands him, flipping the last pancake onto the stack and sliding the entire thing to the center of the counter.

Raising my glass, the others follow, but I'm unsure of what to say. As I look at each one of them, I kind of get the feeling that everyone would rather be split off, doing their own things. Knox doesn't meet my gaze and I ignore the pang I feel in my chest. Rory looks weary as well, and Ace's eyes are on her, whereas Slate is the only one that doesn't balk away from me.

"To Slate, who gives me more headaches that I ever thought possible." Glasses chink as they're knocked together, cheers all around.

"Did I hear you say head?"

"When were you going to tell me about you and Ace?" I ask Rory sometime later. We've decided to get an early start to the weekend, skipping our classes for the rest of the day. As much as my Art History grade won't thank me, grilling my best friend is much more important right now.

She winces, ducking into the fridge to pull out a container of strawberries and the bottle of whipped cream as I slide onto the barstool. "Never."

"Never?! Rory Judith Wilson, what do you mean *never?*" I exclaim, watching her squirt some of the creamy substance onto a plump strawberry and bite into it. The whipped topping clings to her nose and she wipes it off with the end of her finger, sucking it into her mouth.

She rolls her eyes. "Ugh, I hate it when you call me that."

"Don't care, Ro. Best friend privileges. Spill. *Now.*"

I hook a finger around the rim of the bowl, tugging it towards the middle of the counter so I can reach better. The fruit is red and ripe, juicy when I bite into one of the berries before plucking out another, this time adding whip on top.

"I don't know," she huffs, rolling a strawberry between her fingers like it's the most interesting thing in the world. She deflates a little, resting her hip against the counter. "We aren't even dating. We were just…" Rory shrugs helplessly, muttering. "Hooking up."

The way that she avoids my gaze tells me she's keeping something from me.

"Rory," I elongate her name with a whine, letting her know that I know there's more to that truth.

She sighs, "Please don't make me tell you."

My brows pull tight in confusion. Why wouldn't she want to tell me about this? We've been best friends since we were eight! We tell each other *everything!* I even told her about that mortifying hook up my second weekend of classes last year when I made out with the Vulcan U mascot. He had a wicked way with his tongue but the Perry the

Pinto body wasn't the sexiest or easiest thing to maneuver around.

Why would she want to keep this a secret from me? I understand if it's because I've done little more than complain about the rude boys living next door, but we've come a long way since move-in day! I was even civil to Knox when we all hung out at Tipsy Canvas. That alone should have scored me points for trying.

"Why wouldn't you want to tell me?" I ask, and I sound more hurt than I'm trying to.

Her bright eyes soften and she rounds the counter to sit beside me. "I—" Her voice catches and she peeks over at me. Her cheeks are pink with embarrassment and it makes the cerulean of her eyes pop. My heart stings at the way Rory's acting. For the first time since I've known her, we've both been keeping secrets from each other.

I don't like the feeling.

"I know you don't like Ace."

I sigh, trying not to let the frustration I'm feeling lace my words. The last thing I want to be arguing with my best friend about is the boys next door. Make that *boys,* period. I fumble with the lid of the strawberries, pulling it closer so I have something to focus on instead.

"He's growing on me," I admit, and Rory scoffs. "What? I'm trying! We didn't start out on the best foot with any of them and I've only just found out that the two of you have been fucking—" Her nose scrunches in distaste and I have to bite my tongue at the audacity of that. "For who knows how long. But we've talked and hung out and I think Ace and I might finally be on the same page."

"Okay, that might be true, but what about Knox?"

I stare at her incredulously. "What does Knox have to do with this?"

She shoots me the same look back. One that I duck away from.

Fuck.

"Quinn. You hate the guy."

"Not true," I say a little too quickly for my liking. I did hate Knox when I first met him, and he's still not my particular cup of tea, but I'm beginning to think there's more to him than I once thought. He's not all dark tattoos and sharp attitude anymore. And, I've always found him attractive, if that counts for anything. "If I hated him, I wouldn't have spent the night at their place last night."

"Really?"

Double fuck.

I turn the conversation back on Rory because I don't feel like talking about Knox anymore. What's going on between us is for us to figure out. That doesn't mean I can't be happy and supportive of my best friend. "Ace was just a dick to me at the time and I really didn't want to like him," I admit. "And now, walking in on what I did the other night, I feel like shit because my best friend couldn't even tell me that she was hooking up with our hot neighbor."

Rory's answering smile is contagious. I bump her shoulder and she nudges mine back as we burst into giggles, throwing our arms around each other for a tight hug.

"You think he's hot?"

I roll my eyes, pulling away. "They're *all* pretty hot, Ro. I can't lie about that, even if I wanted to."

"They are," she huffs wistfully, handing over the can of whip to me. "It's not even fair. What are they drinking over there?" She asks and *that's what I've been saying!* There's no way they all look that perfect without drinking *something.* We share a look because we know the liquid on constant flow in the apartment next door is alcohol.

Grinning at each other, I shove a berry into my mouth. "I cannot believe we've seen Slate's dick."

"I can't believe he's built like a fucking statue," Rory sighs dramatically, spraying a dot of whipped cream on the tip of her finger before licking it off. "Like, he's literally cut from marble! He's a Bernini sculpture come to life!"

She needs to stop before I start choking. I'm laughing too hard for it to be safe, but everything she's saying is true. Slate's form is *impeccable.*

I'm happy to have had this conversation with Rory and not let the awkwardness build between us. Arguing over boys is something that I don't ever want for our relationship. We didn't even do such silly things when we were in high school.

Rory's eyes soften. "I'm sorry for not telling you, you know."

I offer her a strawberry that she accepts with a smile. "I know."

"So," she starts with a feisty grin and I'm sure I'm not going to like where this is going. "I'm pretty sure I just heard you say that you think all of our neighbors are hot. Does that mean you think Knox is—"

A knock on the door interrupts and I've never been more grateful. I'm not expecting anyone and from the look on Rory's face, she's not either.

Sliding from the stool, I make my way to the door. As far as I know, Knox, Ace, and Slate had all gone to class after the breakfast they made us. I guess it wouldn't be unusual for Slate to change his mind and come calling the second he gets bored, though.

Pulling the door open, my face falls when I'm met with four sets of stern eyes.

My parents and the Wilson's stand in the doorway,

frowning at me like I've been caught with my hand in the cookie jar before dinner.

"Mom, dad, hi," I laugh nervously. Thankfully, I've changed out of Knox's clothes from last night. That would've made this situation *much* worse. "You're here."

I'd forgotten this weekend is parent's weekend, but they're *way* early. I expected them to arrive at least mid-day tomorrow.

My father gives me his famous unimpressed look and I have the feeling I'm going to be grounded. "Why aren't you in class, young lady?"

CHAPTER 15
QUINN

"I don't have class right now," is what I decide to go with, but the lie is easily detectible. I've never been great at skirting the truth to my parents, and the look my father shoots me as I let them inside tells me he knows it, too.

"Hi, my baby, I've missed you!" Rory's mother barges into the kitchen, racing to her youngest daughter and throwing her arms around her. I try not to roll my eyes. Of course, I would be the only one getting scolded for skipping out when we're both supposed to be in class right now.

I hug my mom on her way in and am about to do the same with dad but he stops in the doorway, assessing me as if he's taking note of all of the things that have changed about me in the two and a half months I've been away from home. To me, he looks the same, brownish hair peppered with gray streaks, those familiar laugh lines crinkling when he squints at me as if I'm about to reveal a secret truth to why we aren't in class right now, but I don't break his hazelnut stare.

Finally, he relents, grinning as he pulls me into his arms. I release the door and fold myself into his warmth, familiar and comforting and loving. Tears prick my eyes as I squeeze him as tightly as I can. I've missed my parents so much. Talking on the phone has nothing on this.

"How's my girl doing?" He asks as he pulls away, ruffling my hair. I scowl, batting his hands as I reach for the door to shut it. The sound of the elevator dinging draws our attention, my father grumbling about the age-old contraption and how he and Zak could have it in perfect working condition before the weekend ends.

I'm sure my landlord would love that, actually.

"I'm good, dad," I answer, distracted by the doors opening. Why I thought our neighbors would go to class is my bad. I should know them better by now.

Knox leads the pack, Slate and Ace on his heels. They're all laughing about something and my breath catches in my chest at the sight of Knox's easy smile.

I'm not sure I've ever seen something better.

Said smile slowly falls when he sees me standing in the doorway to my apartment. His steps slow and that's when Ace and Slate finally take notice of me as well. They're all carrying cases of beer like it isn't eleven in the morning on a Friday.

Knox's jade gaze flits over my shoulder where my father stands at my back. It dawns on me then, eyes widening, that I need to shut this door right the fuck now before my dad puts together that these are the noisy neighbors I've complained about so many times.

It seems that he does realize that it's them.

"So, you're the boys that have been keeping my daughter up all ends of the night?" My dad asks, puffing his chest and crossing his arms. I want to slap my hand over my forehead as embarrassment flares. Slate is the only one that can't force back a snicker, and my father scowls.

Knox's stare burns me to my core, the minuscule slash of amusement he allows me to see. I blush—*hard*—and something takes flight in my stomach the longer he looks at me like that.

"Wow, dad," I mutter, shoving him desperately into my apartment before turning back toward the hall. I glare at the three boys before shutting the door in their faces, and yeah, it does feel kind of good, actually. I can't blame them for doing it to me and Rory. Except that I can, and I will. "Only three minutes in and you've already mortified the fuck out of me."

"Language," my mother scolds and I roll my eyes before diving into her arms.

"I've missed you, but you're early. A little warning would've been nice."

She pulls away, scolding me lightly. "Why? Because you would've actually gone to class?"

I shake my head. I'm never going to live that down now. I really wish Sam was here so I could blame this on him somehow, but the fucker already visited me and his refusal to fly down for parent's weekend still stands.

Older brothers.

I bet if Peep came calling, he'd rush out here like a chicken with its head cut off. He's been ignoring my prying every time we've spoken since her party and it's more than annoying because I'm his sister—he should *want* to tell me things. Then I remember how I accidentally let it slip to our parents that there's something going on with them and now both sets of parents are trying to force this thing between him and Peep even further.

Oops.

"I know, I know, I should've gone to class. It won't

happen again, I promise," I say, guiding them further into the room. Rory and her mom are already hastily making plans, while her father roots around in the fridge. "Is there anything else you want to hear, or can we start having fun now?"

My mom shoots me a reprimanding look, shaking her head before twirling a strand of my hair around her fingers as she admires me. "Look at how long your hair has gotten," she exclaims, eyes getting teary, "My baby girl, looking so grown up."

"Mom," I whine, easing myself from her grip. "You don't see Mrs. Wilson doing that to Rory, do you?" I ask, gesturing to where my roommate sits with her mother who is doing exactly that.

Okay...moving on.

"How about you girls give us a tour of the campus?" Mrs. Wilson suggests, and I've never been quicker to agree to something in my life. Anything to get my parents out of our apartment before the wild boys next door start cranking their music, or worse. I don't need my dad barging over there and embarrassing me even more than he already has.

Knox's amused gaze still lingers in my mind.

"That sounds like a great idea, Mrs. Wilson! Let's go!"

Spending the weekend with my parents is great, but now that I've had a taste of the freedom of college and setting my own rules and limits, it's difficult to fall back into theirs like they expect.

As shitty as this might sound, I'm excited for my parents to go back home tomorrow.

Mom, dad, and the Wilson's had all traveled down

together, taking a road trip from Seattle in a rented car. All weekend they gushed about the scenery they saw, showing me blurry photos on their phones of the same pit stops Rory and I had stopped at during the same trip a few months ago when we moved back to Vulcan U.

It's as endearing as it is annoying, because if I have to scroll through one more photo out of the million my mom hordes on her phone, I might take this steak knife and stab it right through the screen.

"How are classes going, Quinn?" My father asks, sipping on his glass of whiskey. As much as I could use a drink of my own after this very long weekend, I can't out Pipa in front of all of our parents by using the fake ID she got me to order the strongest liquor that they have. She looks like the epitome of relaxed with her mojito in her hands.

I envy her.

I wet my suddenly parched throat with my *lemon water* to avoid answering dad's question. If I close my eyes hard enough, I can pretend there's a bit of tequila at the bottom of my glass. When I open my eyes, even the Wilson's are looking at me like they can't wait to hear all about my classes, and Rory ducks her head as if that is somehow going to save her from getting grilled next.

Luckily, I'm responsible for my own grades now, and my parents don't see anything I don't want them to: namely, my unimpressive Art History grade. I've already signed up for the study group happening next week, and I pray it won't be completely filled with people like me who are on the verge of failing and that there's at least one person who knows the difference between Gothic, Romanesque, and Baroque cathedrals. I swear, they all look the fucking same no matter how long I spend staring at the pictures.

After that, I have to try and learn the names of all of them.

I am *totally* fucked.

"Things are going well so far," I answer with a polite smile, fingering the corner of the menu for something to do. We haven't even ordered mains yet and they're already drilling me? It's going to be a long meal. "I like them so far."

"And how's drawing?" My mom questions and I want to groan. I knew they were going to ask me about this and I knew I wasn't going to like it. I've been on the edge of my seat all weekend, waiting for them to bring it up. Little Quinnie, drawing extraordinaire. "I can't wait to see how your portfolio has grown by the end of the semester."

Maybe I will order that drink, after all.

It's not that I don't like drawing, I *love* drawing, and have since I was a little girl. It just feels different now. When I was young and didn't have a care in the world and all I needed was my drawing pad and pencils, and I would draw to my heart's content. My parents saw that passion in me and signed me up for competitions and when I started winning awards, they only entered me in more and more. It was fun, until drawing started feeling like work. I was always trying to put out the most perfect pieces, all to try and make my parents proud.

They are, and I know they are, but forcing myself to constantly strive to be something better made me lose the creativity I once had when I was just drawing for myself. I was no longer drawing what I wanted and instead making what people wanted to see, what would look good for the judges and win me those awards.

I stopped creating art completely over the summer, started hiding my sketchbooks because most of them are blank anyway. Every time I want to put my pencils to the paper, my mind empties, waiting for the rules, the theme of what I'm supposed to draw—the *instruction*.

It's like I don't even have a mind of my own anymore.

The only thing that's made me consider wanting to draw again is the short burst of inspiration I feel when I'm around Knox.

I don't want to draw for just anyone—I want to draw for me...if drawing is still what I want to do. I haven't exactly decided that yet.

My parents don't know that and it will break their hearts if I tell them.

"It's good," I nod, trying to make eyes at the waiter when I see him. I need him to come over and interrupt this conversation right fucking now, please. "Rory and I made a new friend. His name is Reid."

It's a poor excuse to try and distract them when I fail to catch the waiters gaze. Luckily, it does the trick because my mother and Mrs. Wilson start gushing over him immediately.

"Is he boyfriend material?" Mrs. Wilson asks with a wink.

Rory and I share a look, one that tells me she's as ready to roll her eyes as I am. "Just because a guy talks to us, does not mean he wants to date us," Rory explains, and I jump in quickly, adding my two cents.

"And, *no,* just because a guy looks at us, doesn't mean he likes us either," I tell my mother pointedly, because she keeps making weird faces at me every time the waiter walks by.

I'm pretty sure he's staring at Peep's chest, anyway.

"Oh, you girls," my mom scolds playfully, brushing off our antics while I tuck back into my menu. I already know what I'm going to get, and yes, it's going to be a steak because I haven't eaten one since I left for college and if my parents are willing to pay, then damn right I'm going to take advantage of it. "You know, when I was your age—"

Thank the motherfucking heavens the waiter chooses right now to interrupt.

"Do we need a few more minutes or are we all ready to order?" He asks politely and I almost cut him off with how quickly—and desperately—I answer.

"I think we're all ready," I smile, glancing around the table to gage where everyone's at. I garner mostly nods of agreement, so I continue. "I'll start."

CHAPTER 16
QUINN

By the time my first class on Monday rolls around, I feel like I'm spiraling.

My parents' words kept swirling in my head throughout the rest of the weekend and well into the evening. I hadn't been able to focus on my assignment for drawing class that's due this morning. I stayed up all night forcing myself to draw, to put the damn lines down on the damn paper and not think about touching them when they all felt wrong anyway.

I definitely didn't stare at the project for thirty minutes, picking out everything I loathed about it before I rolled it up and snapped a rubber band around it, tucking it next to my backpack before stumbling into bed.

I didn't wake up late or have to rush to take a shower because there was graphite smeared all the way up my arm and on my face from where I'd been leaning on my hand while I slept. I didn't skip breakfast, coffee, and makeup while Rory yelled at me to hurry up so we could make it to class on time.

Just kidding. That all happened.

I sit at the end of the row, having dragged my chair to the furthest possible spot allowed after tacking my work to the wall with the rest of the class. The drawing room today looks like a gallery, the overhead lights spotlighting our creations, cheery chatter happening all around as we spent the first thirty minutes of class roaming throughout the room, examining each other's projects.

Rory sits to my right, Reid on her other side. I hardly greeted him when we met up for class and I could tell that he wanted to sit next to me, to talk to me, which is why I shoved my chair between Rory's and the wall and slumped in it like the nervous wreck I am, chewing on my lip until I tasted blood.

It's not the action of being critiqued that I'm worried about. It's a drawing class for fuck's sake, I've been getting feedback on artwork for years, it's engrained in my system by now. I'm fretting over the fact that there's nothing I like about this piece and I don't want to show it off at all, even if it's just for a measly grade.

I don't want anyone looking at it.

"Who wants to start?" Beatrice asks from her own chair, looking around the room expectantly. I wish presenting last meant that there might be a chance time would run out of class before we could get to mine, but with just less than three hours here, there's no way anyone is getting left out of critique today.

The bright side is, we might get out of class early and then I can run to the coffee shop and down the four espressos I'm in dire need of before Creative Writing. It's going to be a late night on campus for me with my Art History study group tonight, and I'm already dreading it.

"I'll go," Reid offers, raising his hand. Sweet Reid, always up for anything.

Beatrice gestures to his work and the class quiets down as he explains his piece.

Our task for this project was simple: draw a composition of the human body in any position, along with the skeletal form in a similar pose. This helps us learn about the structure under the form that supports the human body. The skeleton is used as a guide that helps with proportionally placing parts of the human figure.

Reid's drawn a female form that's lying on her side. Her long hair is swept over her shoulder and I examine it for a while, wondering if this is a reference photo he'd found on the internet, or something he's captured in real life.

It's none of my business, but I'm curious nonetheless.

The skeletal form is drawn a few inches above the figure, and he's done an extremely good job of sketching it. I can see the straights where he's gone in with his ruler, Reid's signature technique, and I admire the flat, sharp lines that he's brought over from his architectural studies.

"The first thing I see when I look at this is the placement of the figure," Wynter says when Beatrice asks for commentary. She twists a chunk of her brilliant white hair around her fingers as if she's nervous, her cheeks a dusty pink. "She's lying down and looking relaxed, which stands out amongst the group because when the models are posed, they're usually stiffer, making the form appear less natural."

Reid's freckles disappear with the blush that overtakes his face and I know that his project is not based off of an internet picture.

I shift in my seat, nervously. That hadn't been anywhere close to the first thing I noticed about the drawing, and if this is how every comment is going to be, I'm so screwed.

I sink further into my seat when Beatrice begins calling on other students for their critiques.

By the time we reach my piece, we're in the middle of the group of works and everyone seems to be getting into the flow, adding comments and rewording critiques that have come before. Size, color, brightness, subject, contrast, and more are all mentioned, and we breeze through my project without any groundbreaking comments. After Rory's we're allowed a fifteen-minute break before we continue with the rest of the class.

"That wasn't so bad," She says when we stand to stretch. Her back pops as she twists and I wince. That sounded painful.

She and Reid trail me from the room because I'm in dire need of water before I fall asleep in my chair. Most of the class is milling about in the hall, chatting softly to one another or hiding their heads in their phones as if the most important thing has happened while we were in class.

Ironically, my phone buzzes and I slide it from my pocket, opening the group chat Slate has made and named *Noisy Neighbors Club.*

SLATE:

Any1 want 2 grab lunch?

I see Rory checking her messages too and lock my screen, tucking back into my pocket. I'm not in the mood to see anyone right now unless they have a coffee the size of my head in their hand.

"I really liked your project, Quinn," Reid says when I stand from the water fountain, wiping the droplets from my chin with the back of my hand. Classy, I know, but a girls gotta hydrate. "That pose was impressive."

I shrug, trailing slowly back to class. We still have a few minutes before we're due back. "Eh, it's nothing special." It's really not. Rory's male form on his knees is better than the simple yoga pose I put mine in. I refrained from wondering if her form was based off of a similar pose she put Ace in. If so, she's a lucky lady.

I should've recruited Slate to help me with mine. He has experience holding a pose for an extended amount of time and he would've happily done it if I offered him a few beers until I was done. My mind wanders to Knox, if he would've helped me if I asked. There are a thousand positions I'd love to see him in, namely, one with him—

"Just take the compliment, Conroy," Reid argues, slinging an arm over my shoulder and bumping my hip with his. I stumble, unprepared for the move but Rory's flanking my other side and wrapping her arm around my waist. It's more than a little comforting, like my friends know that I'm not feeling very cheery today.

I don't deserve them.

I duck my head as we stalk back through the classroom doors.

"Thanks, Arlet."

"I'll be back late tonight," I grouse with a hefty sigh. I'd actually love nothing more than to lie my ass in bed right now and bury myself in my phone on social media to avoid my own life for a bit, but, as a less than exemplary college student, I have things to do, classes to study for, et cetera, et cetera.

Except, the internet is fake anyway, and I'll likely spend the time comparing myself to every photoshopped, filtered picture and video out there. Maybe I should take up reading instead. "I have study group for Art History tonight."

"Bummer," Rory wrinkles her nose. She knows exactly what I'm going through right now, having taken the class last year. Professor Doff, the literal bane of my fucking existence. He's an ancient man with what I swear is the goal to fail the most students Vulcan University—or *any* university—has ever seen.

He's winning by a fucking landslide. I know this, of course, because compared to two months ago when the class began, almost half of the hundred students have already dropped.

"I know," I sigh, rubbing my tired eyes. It's going to be a long fucking night.

Rory offered to help me study, but I want to do this on my own. And by on my own, I mean complaining with whatever students come to the study session tonight. Hopefully, one of them knows their shit. Otherwise, I might have to schedule a meeting with the TA or Doff himself, and I would rather one of those ancient buildings crumple on top of me than do that.

If none of that works, *then* I'll ask Rory to help me.

"Ace and I are going to order in," she says, and it's adorable how she blushes when she says his name. They're not officially dating yet, but they've been hanging out a lot more recently. I bet he's going to ask her to be his girlfriend soon. "I'll get you something."

"You're a real-life angel, Rory Wilson," I grin, splitting off from her as I head towards the library. "Don't forget to lock the door or Slate will sniff you down like a bloodhound."

Rory's laughter follows me for a few steps and my mood feels a little lighter because of my best friend. I'm happy for her; she seems smitten with Ace, and she deserves it after that asshole Max treated her like trash right before summer started. She'd been miserable and it hadn't been a good start to break. She seemed down even when she left for the famous Wilson Family Vacation, but was in better spirits when she arrived home, more than ready to finish our summer with a bang.

A little TLC always helps, and I sure could use some of my own right now instead of lugging open the library doors and searching for the reserved study room.

When I arrive, there's only one other student there. I can't blame anyone, because who the hell wants to go to a study group on *Monday* nights of all nights? The weekend just ended and people are still getting over their Sunday Scaries.

The blond head looks up from his book and when he recognizes me, his grin grows wide.

"Quinn."

"Odie," I match his blank tone, and when he pulls out the chair next to him, I plop down into it with a defeated sigh. "Fancy seeing you here."

He's wearing a Vulcan University sports jacket and there's a patch with two hockey sticks crossing over each other. I figured he was a jock by the way I have to hunch in my chair when I sit next to him in class. His shoulders take up two seats alone, but now that I know he plays hockey, the weary part of my can finally relax. Thank fuck he's not on the football team. Rory would never forgive me for fraternizing with the enemy, even if all we're doing is studying.

"Fancy? Me?" He teases, leaning back in his seat. "Not like those coffees you like, Quinn. Now *those* are fancy."

I laugh, digging around in my bag for my book, but come up empty.

Fuck. Me.

"It seems like I've forgotten my textbook at my apartment," I say bashfully, nervously glancing at my classmate. "Do you mind if we share?"

Odie shakes his head, chuckling. "First, you're late to class, and now you forget your textbook? No wonder you're coming to this study group, Quinn." He slides the book between us and I stare down at it. The page is open to something that I can't say I recall seeing before in class.

Oh, I'm so screwed.

"Hey," I exclaim, like he's not completely hit the nail on the head. "You're here too."

He snorts. "I'm running the study session."

My jaw slackens and my cheeks turn bright pink. "Seriously?"

Apparently, Odie's not done laughing at me because he nearly keels over as a new wave hits him. I sit lamely in my chair, tapping my foot as I wait patiently for him to finish. His laughter sounds so similar to the one in my head, the one that accompanies a symphony of *'you can't do this,'* and *'you'll never be good enough.'*

"Yeah, really," he says, wiping a fake tear from his cheek. *Asshole.* "I'm a history major, which means that every kind of history is my jam."

"Oh, Odie," I beg because that's the best fucking news I've heard all day. Who would've thought that a hockey jock would actually be my guardian angel in disguise? "Please, help me. I'm completely useless at this shit."

He gives me a pitying look, planting the front legs of his chair back on the ground before slinging an arm over the back of mine. "I'll make you a deal. You write down that coffee order of yours so I can get it every time I go to the coffee shop from now on, since you've still never brought me one, and I'll help you pass Doff's class."

I stare at him, wide eyed. "That's it? That's all you want?"

His smirk turns wicked and he winks when he asks,

"What else are you offering me? Want to come be a cheer-leader at my game this weekend?"

I elbow him in the ribs, enjoying the way my shoulders ease with our laughter. Odie has been a real saint since the day I was late to class, now so more than ever.

"Nope, no," I cross my arms over my chest, glaring play-fully at him. "You already said what you wanted. There's no changing now."

Odie rolls his eyes and I turn back to the book, startling when I catch sight of someone standing outside the glass to our study room, staring directly at me. I'm surprised to see Knox, dressed in a black cable knit sweater and his usual dark jeans. His brows are furrowed, onyx hair tousled in a way that makes my heart stir.

My lips part and I feel like I've been caught doing some-thing that I shouldn't be. Knox stalks away before I can even let out a breath, but it doesn't matter because every word has eddied from my head anyway.

"You know that guy, Quinn?" Odie asks, staring after him.

I shrug a shoulder, "He's, uh, my neighbor." My voice comes out more nervous than it should. I blink hard, shaking myself out of the funk I've suddenly slipped into. Knox looked like he actually cared who I'm sitting with and he didn't look very happy about it. Dragging my gaze from the window to Odie's book, I ask, ignoring my confused and muddled mind, "So, what are we starting with?"

CHAPTER 17
QUINN

"Tell me again why you and Ace *had* to have sex on the couch?" I gripe, planting myself on the carpet, bowl of popcorn balanced carefully in my hands. I cringe just thinking about it, how pale Ace's ass was in comparison to the rest of his summer-tanned body. I've learned—against my will—that Ace loves to pamper himself. It had been his expensive shampoos and soap in the boys' bathroom. One would think that with how much he enjoys taking care of himself, he would splurge for a full body tan instead. "Your room is five feet away for fuck's sake!"

Now I have to live with the image of his full moon in my head forever.

Rory has the movie set up, paused on the title screen while I made the popcorn and gathered the drinks. The ominous font glows crimson, painting the living room in red light. It's a horror movie the both of us had been wanting to see since we moved in, and since it's finally October, we figured we should kick the month off with it.

After another busy week of classes, I asked Rory if she

wanted to have a girl's night because I've missed my best friend. She was immediately on board with the idea, gushing over face masks, wine, candy, and binge watching the list of movies we made on her phone.

We've been spending a lot of time with the boys next door lately and I can finally say that I don't think Knox hates me anymore. He even laughed at one of my jokes at lunch the other day, though he seemed reluctant to admit I'm actually as funny as Rory claims I am.

The chocolate we picked up from the local grocery after class is already half eaten; tiny balls of tinfoil tossed in a haphazard garbage pile from where we'd both dug into the bag while we waited for the popcorn and set the movie up. We're splitting the bottle of wine, maybe more if the *'drink whenever someone makes a stupid decision'* rule we came up with is to be followed.

Rory tosses a pillow at me that I dodge it like it's on fire. I've been avoiding the couch and anything that could have been on it while they were…*canoodling* for days, not even so much as sitting on the other side where Ace's ass hadn't been.

I don't trust it.

"I was trying *not* to have sex with him until I figured my shit out, but," Rory shrugs sheepishly. "I couldn't resist. He's so charming." The way that a smile cracks her mouth without her knowledge tells me everything I need to know about her feelings on this new relationship with Ace. Her grin is glowing brighter than the damn screen!

I'm not at all jealous, I'm just really happy for my best friend who has now been in two relationships during our time in college. That's two more than I've been in.

Nope, not jealous at all.

I hum in agreement, ignoring the twang in my chest. I'm

familiar with that silver tongue of his, and I'd thought the same of him when he was trying to sweet talk his way into my favor at the art supply—*not*. Ace has gotten a lot better since we'd all gone to Tipsy Canvas.

I have to give it to him for his persistence. He's proved he's wanted to be more with Ro despite her worries about Max, and even my grouchiness hasn't been able to scare him off.

I do wonder if he calls her Darling, too, or if that was reserved for the ones that came before.

"You're an 'us' now?" My question is sincere, and I look at her over my shoulder when she reaches into my lap for some popcorn. Her cerulean eyes glow in the light from the TV and even without the sinister crimson pouring from the screen, I know just how pink her cheeks are.

Rory brushes her dark hair over her shoulder, blowing the shorter strands that keep falling in her face away. I bite back my laugh when I remember how bad they looked at the beginning of summer.

I'll never stop reminding her of it.

"I think I might be starting to see where things could go with him."

I squeal because I really can't help myself. Rory looks shocked for all of two seconds before she's screaming along with me. Seeing her so giddy over a guy is contagious. I haven't seen her like this since she first gushed about Max asking her out last year. Rory had fallen hard and fast for the hotshot quarterback from Vulcan's team. He'd broken her heart by the end of the year and Rory hasn't really been the same since.

Getting revenge on him and his frat helped a little, though.

"Is he hung?" I blurt and we stare at each other before we're both falling into a fit of laughter until Rory manages to calm herself enough to smirk over at me.

"Didn't you see it when you walked in on us? You tell me."

"Ew, *no!* I only saw his ass," I scrunch my nose, tossing a piece of popcorn into my mouth. The buttery goodness nearly makes me moan. "Which, I must say, is not that impressive."

I reach for a chocolate, unwrapping the foil with a crinkle. It melts against my tongue and I pair the sweetness with a sip of wine.

"Not as impressive as, say, a certain roommate with an affinity for parking like shit's ass?" Rory teases and I groan, tossing a handful of popcorn her way. There's already who knows what kind of fluids staining the fabric, what's a little popcorn to go along with it?

"Slate's ass is quite nice, you already know that," I sigh dreamily, trying my best to distract her from conversation surrounding Knox. I *so* do not want to be talking about him or his ass right now, not when I'm so unsure of my feelings about him. The look on his face when he saw me studying with Odie is still fresh in my mind. His confusion turned into what I can only call jealousy. We're supposed to be having a peaceful night. "And I don't think Slate's parking is *that* bad, Ro. It's questionable at best."

Rory takes the bait, agreeing with a pleasant hum, settling into the couch. She tucks an arm behind her head, posing exactly like Slate had during the time he'd modeled for our class. "So biteable, and he's hung as fuck. Any girl would be lucky to have him."

It's true. His cock is *huge.*

Snorting, I reach for the remote. "If she can put up with all of his dirty jokes."

"You're damn right about that," Rory says, then joins me on the floor as I press play.

The treats run out long before the movie is over.

An empty bottle of wine stuffed with the balled-up wrappers from our treats sit on the coffee table and I'm beginning to regret playing this little game because the wine is only making me more terrified of everything that jumps out at us.

I'd given in and risen from my spot on the floor with the irrational fear that some monstrous creature's claws would creep out from underneath the couch and snatch me up. Rory had been the first to cower into a ball on the futon, blanket pulled up to her shoulders. I'm surprised she's even watching the movie still, but the half full glass of wine she had has been abandoned.

I sit on my own blanket as far away from where I'd seen her and Ace's sexual activities as I can, and I'm wondering now out of all of the moments, while the victim hides beneath her bed, why we thought a horror movie would be the best genre to watch tonight.

Holding my breath, the murderer stalks down the pitch-black halls of the house on the screen. He's already killed three of the five group members in the most gruesome of ways, and I know that she's the next to go because it's obvious to everyone but her that she can totally be seen in her hiding spot under the bed.

"I can't watch, I can't watch," Rory complains, but a quick glance to my side shows that her blanket sits just over the bridge of her nose, her eyes wide with horror and glued to the screen in anticipation.

The killer enters the room, stalking on silent feet, and just as he leans down for the jump-scare of a lifetime, there's pounding at our door.

Neither of us can contain our shrill screams. Rory almost jumps out of her skin, launching herself across the couch to clutch at me like a terrified child. I'm faring no better, my heart pounding so hard in my chest that my head goes dizzy with it.

It takes me a few harsh breaths to realize what the sound is, only because the knocking becomes more urgent with our screams.

"Fucking hell," I mutter, lunging for the remote as the girl gets dragged out from under her bed. Her screams have nothing on the ones Rory and I just let out. Pausing the movie, I notice the bass blasting through the walls as I make my way to the door.

Rory stumbles up from the couch, stopping me with a firm hand on my arm. "What if it's the killer?"

I know she's somewhat joking, the small lift to her lips tells me that she knows it simply can't be, but I'm wearier than I'd like when I twist the knob.

I have an inkling of who it might be on the other side, but I check the peephole before I do anything else, groaning when I see who it is.

Slate stands on the other side, brows furrowed in concern. "Are you ladies alright? I heard screaming."

"Yes," I huff, frustrated. "Because of *you,* Slate."

Stepping aside, I allow him to enter the apartment. Rory's already settled back onto the couch, all of the fear fallen from her shoulders as she's now engrossed in something on her phone. Or someone, if her shit-eating grin is anything to go by.

"Neither of you answered my texts, so I came to see what all the screaming was," Slate says easily, though when he sees what we're watching his face lights up. "I can't believe you're watching *Red Grave!* Why didn't you tell me? I would have definitely canceled this party to protect the both of you." He's distracted now, peering down into the popcorn bowl, frowning at its emptiness.

"Party?" Rory questions, and now she's the one frowning. "Ace didn't tell me you were having a party."

"Well, maybe that's because you weren't answering your phone," Slate sing-songs.

"Well, he could've been the one to come get us," she responds with a pout. Her gaze is already glued back to her phone and I watch the way her eyes widen a little at the messages he must have sent her because she's shutting her screen off and hiding her cellphone in her lap.

I can feel the heat from her cheeks from where I stand, five feet away.

I predict another couch episode happening in the very near future.

"Someone has to play host," Slate grins wolfishly. "Besides, if I sent him over here, he wouldn't have come back. There's too much temptation on this side of the wall."

Rolling my eyes, I cross my arms over my chest. "And you're less likely to be tempted?" I question flatly. I know Slate too well; his cheeky attitude is second nature. He looks like he's ready to settle in, scouring the coffee table littered with candy wrappers for more. He truly looks like a vulture on the hunt, cocoa eyes sharp with precision as he sorts through the brightly colored foils.

"I knew you had your eye on me, Quinnie," Slate winks and I gag. It rolls off of his shoulders like any of my teasing does, before he's reaching down and plucking a candy off of the table. My brows scrunch in confusion because I swear that Rory and I had eaten all of the chocolates while we were engrossed with worry while the murderer in the red hood tortured his second kill. "Want to be my date to the party? I know you've already been in my bedroom but we can make sure you're well-acquainted tonight."

"You're incorrigible."

"I thought you liked that," Slate flings back, and although his tone doesn't suggest anything of the sort, I can't help it that my mind turns to Knox.

Yes, he's been completely and utterly *irritating* since day one, and *no,* I don't like it one bit.

I wonder how many times I have to keep repeating that before I believe it.

I can't pretend that I have no idea what Slate is talking about. I shove the thoughts from my mind before I can think about it too hard. I've had way too much wine to be thinking at all right now, yet somehow also not enough.

I suck my teeth. "I think we need more drinks."

"May I interest either of you in a seltzer? A vodka cran? How about a tequila shot?" Slate rattles off drinks, eyes already gleaming with the few that he's downed. "Need my best drinking buddies with me." He nudges my arm with his elbow and I scoff in response.

"I thought you lived with your two best drinking buddies," I retort, more than ready to plop back onto the couch and finish up the movie.

Slate waves flippantly, searching for more sweets. He looks seconds away from sucking the popcorn kernels into his mouth for a taste of the salty, buttery goodness still coating their shells. He refrains, luckily for us. "Ace is busy moping and Knox isn't home yet."

Before I can tell my brain to shut the fuck up, it's already wondering what the stoic man might be doing. Has he stayed late on campus, working on a project? Is he taking a night drive out past the city limits?

Is he on a date?

The last thought makes my mouth sour and I look at Rory to see how much she's been influenced by Ace's texts and Slate's words.

It really is a shame that she's looking at me with wide eyes, the pleading pout more than an answer to my unspoken question. She looks like an innocent deer, with her eyes round like that. I don't want to give in, but maybe attending the party will help get my mind off of Knox, and more importantly, off of the movie that I'm sure to have nightmares about tonight. It's not like I'll be able to sleep anyway, with the music blasting through the wall.

Rory knows before I even open my mouth that I'm going to agree and she's springing from the couch, squealing happily. She rounds the sofa and Slate stumbles back, startled by whatever seems to be possessing her right now.

She grabs my wrist and tows me towards her room. She hardly looks over her shoulder as she calls back to Slate, standing confused in the middle of our living room. "We'll be over in a bit, Slate. We've got to get ready!"

"I was beginning to think that you weren't coming," Ace smirks when he opens the door. A rush of heat wafts from the apartment behind him and the music is ten times louder. So loud that I hardly hear his quip.

The way that his ocean eyes trace Rory's body, filled with

fire, makes even me shiver. He's looking at her like he's going to devour her and worship her at the same time.

It makes my chest ache.

Slate doesn't seem phased by the public display of eye-fucking we're witnessing. He shoves his way past Ace, my wrist firmly in his grip. The moss green of his shirt stretches tightly across the muscles of his back and I'm surprised he hasn't already taken it off to use his washboard abs to gather the plethora of girls stuffed into their apartment.

Speaking of, the number of glares I'm receiving because Slate's hand is wrapped around my arm is astonishing. I've never seen so many sharp looks, glares, and envious stares as I am right now. It makes my skin itch, yet I smirk at all of them in return, following Slate to the keg where a boy with tawny skin and a curly head of dark hair is tipped upside down, the crowd around him cheering as they count the time he's been chugging from the nozzle.

"Let's go, Lynx!" Slate chants, immediately distracted by the events happening in the small kitchen. I must say, I'm impressed as well, but after about three seconds, my gaze wanders, looking for a certain boy with onyx hair and piercing jade eyes. I already know that he's not here, but I can't help searching the crowd anyway.

Something in the corner of my eye catches my attention. I blink at the sight of a boy passing out a round of shots, and when I squint to make sure what I'm seeing is correct—

"Slate, those drinks are on fire!"

My friends head turns sharply, releasing a curse.

"Yo, asshole," Slate shouts, thrusting himself through the crowd, sights set on the boy with the flaming tray of shots. My stomach curls and I'm not sure why, but Slate's reaction to the havoc tells me more than I need to know. He's not normally such a stickler, so if something has him reacting like this, carefully disarming the boy from the tray and grabbing his collar, alerting Ace to the drinks as he hauls him from the apartment, it must be serious.

I watch Ace disentangle himself from Rory, quickly making his way to where the flaming liquor has been left unattended on the counter. He walks so smoothly it's almost like he's gliding, each step filled with purpose.

He takes the tray and quickly disposes of the fire. There are a few moans and groans about the wasted alcohol, but the razor-sharp look in his sparkling eyes shuts every last one of the party-goers up.

"Sorry about that," Slate apologizes when he returns. He offers me a cup of beer now that the boy is no longer deep-throating the nozzle, and I realize that I have no idea how long he stayed up there while I was distracted by the two roommates fussing over the flames.

"No, thanks," I wave the cup away.

Slate grins and I don't like that one bit. "Ah, right. You wanted something a little fruitier."

"How about a little *stronger,*" I counter, and the gleam in his cocoa eyes paints a target on my back. All of the girls in the kitchen openly glower at me.

"That's what I like to hear," a female voice says, startling me. I turn to find one of the prettiest girls I've ever seen.

She's blonde, with perfect waves falling long down the length of her back. Her brown eyes are like molten chocolate, warm but gleaming with mischief. She's clad in what I think is the tightest dress known to man, red and latex and hugging every perfect curve. It's hot in the apartment but she's not sweating at all; in fact, her skin looks dewy and healthy.

Her cherry red lips curl upwards as I all but gape at her.

"Mandy," Slate shouts, tugging her into his side. He plants a firm kiss to her forehead that has all of the female attention that was on me, sliding to her. With a quick glance around the kitchen, I see that the girls look envious, not only because of Slate's arm around her, but because of Mandy's perfect looks as well. I totally get it. "I didn't know you were in town this weekend! What gives?"

She purses her lips as if trying not to smile, shrugging like she doesn't have a care in the world. "Wanted to surprise my cousin and meet the girl he's been gushing over."

Slate bellows so loudly it rumbles the floor with its bass. He releases Mandy and hands me a drink, introducing me to the mysterious but gorgeous girl. "Quinn, this is Mandy. She's Ace's cousin. Mandy, Quinn. She and Rory live next door."

"Neighbors?" She questions, bringing her own cup to her lips. Her gaze is curious as she assesses me and the look has me bringing my own drink to my mouth for something to do. I don't break her stare, though, interested in what she has to say. "Knox didn't tell me that."

I don't understand it, the way my heart stutters at his name. Or perhaps it's the alcohol I'm currently choking on, because whatever Slate poured into my cup is just that—all alcohol and no chaser. Yeah, that's surely the reason my heart is doubling in pace, from the shock of straight tequila to my system.

That knowing look on Mandy's face has me boldly swallowing another sip of my drink. The cheap liquor tastes like gasoline going down, but for some reason, I feel like I need the liquid courage for whatever else is going to happen tonight.

"Where is he, by the way?" She continues, cocking her head. She doesn't know that she just asked the very question I've been wondering, but too cowardly to ask myself. The longer she stares, the more forced her charming smile seems, carving a blood-red slash across her otherwise glowing skin. She's looking at me like I'm a threat and I don't know why.

"Dunno," Slate responds, and it's clear by his wandering eyes that he's more than done with conversing with us. His brown eyes are already lingering on two girls grinding in the living room. "Said something about a date, I think."

CHAPTER 18
KNOX

I don't know why I fucking lied.

I do and I shouldn't have, because now I'm sitting across the table from the man I'm a carbon copy of, and I don't like it one bit.

Travis Foster, my father, types something on his phone. His thick, gold ring catches the light above the table at Rhonda's diner. His gray suit is pressed perfectly and his sunglasses are pushed up into the dark hair that he has been religiously dying since his first gray popped up.

I haven't seen him since the accident. Since he took his fist to my face when my dickhead of a step-brother ratted me out. Travis thought I was a business major here, because that's what I told him I was, knowing that he wouldn't approve of me wanting to be in art.

I didn't think I'd almost lose my life over it.

My father wanted me to follow in his footsteps, take over his business of buying, renovating, and selling or renting out buildings. Sounds fucking boring to me and always has.

My passion lies with art, with tattooing—something I'm

not even sure that I can do anymore because of the motor-cycle accident that followed the beating.

I shift uncomfortably as the memory resurfaces at his presence alone.

Blood was running down my face, blurring my vision in my haste to get away. I could taste it in my mouth. My heart was beating too furiously in my chest and my hands shaking where they were clenched around the handlebars of my bike as I flew down the streets, trying to get away. My tire to slipped, and my entire world completely shifted in a matter of milliseconds as the bike kicked out from under me.

The helmet I had on saved my life.

I shouldn't have lied to my roommates about my where-abouts tonight, but I couldn't think of a better excuse. They would have told me to ignore him, not to go, but he's been calling and texting me for months now, and Travis doesn't take no for an answer. He showed up to campus without warning, or if there was, it was another message that had gone ignored.

I hated the way he was touching my bike, admiring the piece of shit I built from the ground up. The accident didn't stop me from climbing back on, saving enough to get another motorcycle and living my life.

The only thing the accident is threatening is my ability to tattoo.

I took him to Rhonda's because it's a comfort to me, and I knew he would hate it. I was proved right when my father slid into the seat across from me with a crinkle of disgust to his nose.

I almost smiled at that.

My hands tremble in my lap. I'm not scared of the man, not anymore, but I'm shaking with rage because he showed up unannounced, demanding to meet with me.

If this is what it takes to get the fucker to leave me alone, I will answer this one request.

"What are you doing here?" I ask, after a long ten minutes of sitting in silence. I only ask because I know that he will wait me out, and I want him gone as soon as possible. I have a life to get back to.

There's a fresh cup of black coffee sitting in front of him, untouched. He doesn't bother with niceties when he finally speaks, and I'm happy, because they'd be lies anyway.

We have merely put up with each other ever since mom passed, and that continues to this day.

"I'm interested in an opportunity in town," he says, finally tucking his phone into the interior pocket of his suit jacket.

"And?" I ask, bored. I don't fucking care, but the idea that my father might be in Hardwich more often makes me want to squirm.

I won't give him the satisfaction.

He pins me with a scathing look. One that used to terrify me when I was young and he was yelling at mom.

Now, it only makes me hate him more.

"And—" he taps his thick ring against the ceramic of the mug impatiently. The sound makes me grit my teeth. "I want to know about the area." His gaze flickers down to where he can't see my hands under the table. Something passes through his gaze but I ignore it when he sucks his teeth. "If you'd consider it profitable."

"Take a walk around," I wave lazily towards the windows. There aren't many people milling about this late in the evening, and I hope the lack of them drives my father away from this town. "I certainly don't have the time to do it."

"You don't have the time to do it between drawing those

stick figures and nonsense you ruin your body with?" He quirks his brow, always unimpressed.

Oh, he knows that I'm still not taking the classes he tried forcing me into. I don't want a fucking thing to do with this man or his business, even if I'm owed it by name when he retires. He wouldn't dare give it to his step-son, Dick, because they're not related by blood. I *know* that he won't do that.

When I refuse to answer, Travis continues. "I'm looking at Third Street Apartments," he says and my world comes to a screeching halt. My breath catches in my throat and I'm lucky that he doesn't clock it, too busy sneering at the interior of the diner.

That's my apartment building. Mine and Ace's and Slates. Quinn's and Rory's.

Ours.

And by the smirk on my father's face, he knows it too, even if I've been paying my own rent through odd summer jobs and selling my artwork.

"It could use some updating, and when summer rolls around and there aren't as many students on campus, it will be the perfect time to renovate the building, don't you think?"

My stomach shrivels. If he buys the building and is wanting to renovate during the summer, that means he'll be evicting everyone, and Slate, Ace, and I will be out of a place to live. Not only that, but Quinn and Rory will be thrown out, too.

I don't like the thought of that at all.

But my father doesn't care. He's already taking the first and final sip of his coffee and grimacing at the taste. He looks around the diner as if he might just buy this place next. I swallow harshly, suddenly regretting bringing him here.

"If the deal goes through, you might be seeing a lot more

of your old man around this summer." It's said like a threat. He stands, staring down at me. "Wouldn't that be nice?"

I glare, glued to my seat. I throw every ounce of hatred at the man who fathered me because there's nothing that I can do about it. If he's talking about buying the building that means that the plans are already in the works.

I'm truly and utterly fucked.

Travis Foster throws a twenty-dollar bill down on the table. "This should cover that. You can keep the change too, son, spend the rest on some paint, or something."

Fuck, do I want to bare my teeth at him right now.

My stare doesn't leave his back until he's settled into his sleek, black sports car. My breathing is heavy, fingers clenched so tightly that I know they'll be aching when I uncurl them.

As I sit alone in the booth, I still can't help but wonder why I lied about going on a date.

The wind against my body and the rumble of my motorcycle beneath me makes my night slightly better.

I try to let the meeting with my father roll off of my shoulders with the current pressing against my body, but it isn't happening.

Usually, I enjoy the ride. The way taking the curves a little too fast makes my heart stutter in my chest, the smooth asphalt beneath my wheels wiping my worries away, but there's something about tonight that has me feeling like I'd rather just put on some music, wallow in my bed, and work on my drawings for my upcoming exhibition.

I'll show that fucker.

I almost pass the apartment building while I'm distracted with my thoughts. Slate's big, beat-up Bronco is a red flag waving at me from its perpetual spot in front of the building. Literally, the crimson rust bucket is an eyesore and I'm surprised we haven't gotten any complaints from the landlord about it bringing down the value of the building.

Especially since he'd been looking to sell it, apparently.

I jerk to a stop and back up my motorcycle, parking it in front of Slate's car. He always parks closest to the corner so that no one can block him in. I didn't know if it had been a jab from when I trapped Quinn and Rory's moving truck in on their first day here, but I laughed nonetheless.

There are a handful of people wandering in and out of the building, typical for a weekend. Giggling groups of girls and guys carrying racks of beers on their shoulders, hooting and hollering, eye-fucking the girls in their short skirts as they wait for the elevator. There are parties throughout the building every weekend, and I pray that for once, Slate has decided to wander down a few floors to find a fuck instead of hosting another party.

My prayers are not answered.

Shoving through the stairwell out onto the fourth floor, the music hits me like a truck. It's bass-heavy, blaring down the hall like a goddamn rave. I groan, pushing my way through the people loitering in the hall, ignoring the more than interested looks I receive from a few girls staring me down like a pack of hungry hyenas.

Fuck, I really don't want to deal with this right now.

It's late enough that the pregame should be finishing soon, but knowing Slate, this party is only just beginning.

I stayed at the diner after my father left, ordering something sweet because I couldn't leave until my hands stopped trembling. It hadn't helped much, waiting out the shakes, not even when my favorite waitress—Rhonda herself—brought me a fry on the house and added an extra cherry on top of my milkshake, then proceeded to sit with me to check in.

I adore Rhonda. Slate, Ace, and I used to frequent her diner often during our freshman year, when we had no transportation and were broke art students. Rhonda has always taken care of us, even now that the tradition seems to have dwindled as we've gotten older and are able to attend bars and have money for restaurants that don't only serve smash burgers and shakes.

I'm pretty sure I'm the only one that still visits.

The apartment is packed to the brim with partygoers. I can smell the alcohol and sweat in the air and the stench makes my nose scrunch. *I could use a fucking drink right now,* I think, even though I try to refrain from alcohol altogether because it only makes my hands tremble and that's the last thing I need right now.

At first glance, I don't see either of my roommates, but suddenly, Slate is barreling through the crowd as if he has a sixth sense for knowing when I enter a room.

"Hey, man." He grins widely, tossing an arm over my shoulder. The drink in his cup sloshes precariously close to the rim of his glass and I grimace at the thought of it spilling on me.

His eyes are blurry with the alcohol in his system and he's swaying, leaning his body weight against me. Slate is not a light man, and I hope he hasn't tripped and crushed anyone with his sheer size because it wouldn't bode well for the person trapped underneath the behemoth.

"Hey, Slate."

"Are you setting up tonight? There are these two chicks that want to get tatted up. *Underboob.*" Slate wiggles his eyebrows and grins like he just caught a glimpse of heaven. *"Matching."*

"Not in the mood," I grunt, shoving past him. I hate every second of pushing through the crowd, bodies plastered against my own like the ink on my arms. I wonder if the loud music is bothering Quinn on the other side of the thin wall, and I shake that thought straight from my mind because I simply don't care.

I can pretend that I don't, anyway.

She's probably here, if I had to guess. Somewhere in this crowd with a drink in her hand and that gorgeous smile on her face. I bet her cheeks are red with liquor and her perfect hazel eyes are all wide and glossy. She's probably dancing with Rory, or maybe not, because Rory's probably off somewhere with Ace. Maybe Quinn's dancing with someone else, grinding those generous hips against his—

I clench my jaw, digging in my pocket for my keys so I don't look over my shoulder to seek her out.

I shove the key into the lock, twisting more aggressively than I need to. I added a new one to my door after our first party when I found a couple in my room about to fuck on my bed.

I'm the only one that gets to do that, even if I haven't touched another girl in *God knows how long.* I had a few flings and hookups freshman year, but after my accident I've become too much of a surly asshole to even want to pursue a random girl. I know they wouldn't want me touching them with my fucked-up hands anyway, despite the eyes made at me in the hall.

There's really only one set of eyes I want on me.

Someone bumps into me and it causes me to nearly smash my head into my door. I choke back the growl threatening to crawl from my throat and decide against whirling around to bark at whoever has run into me. My grip on the doorknob tightens.

A soft light emits from the room when I push my way inside. The lamp beside my bed is glowing, though I don't remember leaving it on. I release an exasperated huff to try to ease the tension in my shoulders, but it skyrockets when I notice the lump tucked tightly beneath my blankets.

I move closer and my steps falter.

It's Quinn.

Two thoughts run through my mind so quickly I can hardly grab onto them before they're zipping away.

What the fuck is she doing in my bed?

Who the fuck let her into my room?

Okay, so the second question is easier to answer than the first. It's obvious that Slate must have let her in here because I'm pretty sure the fucker made a copy of my key the second he found out I put the lock on the door. I hadn't let him in when he was trying to get me to smell four different colognes he got as samples from a magazine, so Slate took it into his own hands to make sure I could never be in my own room in peace.

The first question, however, makes no sense. She lives right next door for fuck's sake, so what the hell is she doing here?

I stare. I can't help myself; I'm frozen in the doorway until Slate's belting voice complaining about the pop song that the playlist has switched to snaps me from my stupor. I quickly duck inside, shoving the door shut behind me and flicking the lock back into place.

I genuinely don't know what the fuck I'm doing.

I gawk at Quinn's sleeping form like she's only pretending, armed with a weapon and hoping I'll move closer; she'll pop up and scare the shit out of me and then Ace and Rory will fall out of the closet laughing and Slate will use his key to burst through the door, clutching his chest in hysterics.

But she's not moving. Quinn is curled up on her side, and a plastic bowl sits on the table next to my bed, my stack of books spilled over haphazardly. One is face down on the floor.

There's a glass of water next to the empty bowl, and I don't like that it's sitting so close to my books, despite the cup only being half full.

My bag falls from my shoulder and I sling it over the back of my desk chair, all while keeping my eyes pinned on Quinn. The dark sheets rise and fall shallowly with each breath she takes, her pink lips parted slightly, completely unbothered by the intrusion and the loud music shaking the walls, sleeping through it like a cursed princess.

She must be used to it by now.

A few strands of her blonde hair fall across her cheek and I ache to reach forward and push them back, tuck them behind her ear. I want to see if her skin is as soft as it looks. I want to wake her up and watch those hazel eyes find focus on me as she tries to figure out how she ended up here.

This is weird. This is so fucking weird that I don't even know what to do with myself but my feet are pulling me closer against my better judgement. No, it's beyond fucking creepy now, with me looming over her like this, watching her sleep.

Flexing my fingers, I suck down a few breaths, my mind spiraling.

Doing so doesn't stop the feelings that curdle in my chest. The one where I want to feel the familiar pencil in my hand, charcoal coating my fingers. There's a blooming feeling in my head, inspiration swiping the foulness of meeting with my father away. The urge to get my sketchbook and flip it to a clean page and start by drawing every curve of her—

No. I scold myself, shaking my head furiously, backing away from Quinn. I trip over her shoes, discarded in a pile on the floor, but luckily, I don't eat shit. Maybe if I did, it would help clear my mind of whatever is happening right now—the way Quinn's presence has erased my tainted night. It should be adding fuel to my anger, to see her occupying my sacred space like this, but instead, she calms me.

Fuck. I shouldn't be looking at the way that my sheet is draped across her body. She's still clothed, and I'm more than thankful for that. I shouldn't be admiring her quiet, peaceful side, not when I'm so used to seeing that crease between her brows and the frown tugging her lips whenever I'm around.

I bolt from the room, but not before making sure I lock it behind me. I'm feeling frantic again, like my skin is stretched too tightly over my bones. I need to find Ace because the music is making my head spin and I'm so, *so* close to completely spiraling right now.

Stumbling across the living room to the other side of the apartment, I reach Ace's door. I hope that it's unlocked, because being alone right now sounds even better than having to be around anyone right now.

It's fucking locked.

I pound on the wood. There's an urgency to it that Ace must hear because he's cracking open the door and I'm met with the oceanic blue of his eyes and his bare chest.

"Knox?" He frowns, immediately concerned. "What's up? I'm a little…busy at the moment."

I don't need to peek over his shoulder to know that Rory is waiting for him on his bed right now.

I don't care, though. I shove my way into his room and slam the door behind me. Rory squeaks, pulling his duvet higher over herself, but I'm not looking at her as I pace the length of his room, back and forth and back and forth.

"Knox," Ace warns softly, raising his hands like I'm a rabid dog he's trying to leash. "Are you okay? What's going on?"

I ignore him, running my fingers through my hair and pulling on it in distress. I don't know what the fuck is going on but I'm fucking reeling right now and someone needs to help me stop it.

"Did you know that your roommate is passed out in my bed?" I turn on Rory, ignoring Ace's question.

"What?" She sits up, concerned, and the blanket drops to reveal her collarbones. She's wearing a bra, but Ace scowls, helping her into the first shirt that he can find. "Is she okay?"

"Think so," I mutter, retracing my steps. "She's sleeping."

"And you weren't the one that put her there?" Ace asks and I'm halting my frantic pacing to stop and stare at him. Rory pins him with a glare as if she's telling him not to go down this road, like this is something they've discussed before.

My voice is quiet when I respond. "Why would you assume I put her there?"

Ace is staring at me like I should know exactly why they think that, but I have no idea. Quinn and I haven't done much other than bicker and fight since she moved in. Our petty nights where I play my music loudly and she bangs on the wall in response is our preferred form of communication. When she makes those little noises of pleasure and I slam my door when I storm out because I can't stand the thought of another man—

"Oh, Knox," Rory says softly at whatever look is on my face. I don't like the way that she's staring at me all empathetic. It makes my hackles rise even more. "You like Quinn, don't you?"

My mouth opens to deflect, to reject that with my entire being, but I can't. Nothing comes out.

Nothing comes out because it's true.

"I—" I start, but when the words get caught in my throat, I spin on my heel to escape.

I hear them calling after me but I'm already making my way through the crowd again. I spot Slate somewhere in the middle of the living room with a group of girls rubbing their bodies up against his. They're so close together that they look like a pack of sardines and Slate is the king fish. He's laughing, making suggestive eyes to at least three of them.

I wish I could be that carefree, but all I can think about are my *feelings* toward Quinn.

I *definitely* need a fucking drink.

CHAPTER 19
QUINN

Everything fucking *hurts.*

My head is throbbing like someone has been hitting me repeatedly with a hammer all night. I can't open my eyes because the dots of light clouding my vision are swimming in circles, and I'm pretty sure even if I could crack my eyes open to squint around the room, I'll surely lose the contents of my stomach, which is still housing all of the alcohol I'd stupidly drank last night.

Groaning in agony, I curl further into myself, tugging the blankets up over my head, trying to block out as much of the sun as I can.

I test a deep inhale to try and ease my stomach. With it brings the scent of a calming freshness, like midnight and pine. The smell is so perfectly balanced, familiar and crisp in my aching lungs that it almost lulls me back to sleep. It's effortlessly masculine and with another luxurious inhale, my brain connects the scent to its familiarity. It's the same soap I used when I was forced to stay the night at the apartment next door while Rory and Ace had been having their public nudie show in my living room.

I want to snuggle into it, wallow in its comfort all day, but my mind is quickly catching up to me, running that thought back for a second time, *really* spelling out all the words.

My eyes snap open and my body jolts into an upright position that makes my stomach roll. I shove my head quickly between my knees so I don't make a complete fool of myself before I fully realize where I am.

Fuck. I drank *way* too much last night.

I blink away the bleariness, the dizziness from my vision, staring down at my lap. I'm still wearing the t-shirt and tight jeans I ambled over to Slate's party in, and the fabric sticks to my skin uncomfortably. I feel like shit all around, sick from the alcohol, dirty from the night spent dancing and sweating, and I'm pretty sure my breath smells like I licked the floor of the local dive bar.

Another blink brings the sheets into focus, certainly ones that are not mine. These are a deep charcoal color, softer and smoother than anything I've ever touched. The thread count must be in the thousands. The mattress beneath my aching body feels like a cloud, and all of the effort that went into curating such a lovely bed surely shouldn't be wasted.

I'm impressed for a few seconds until I lift my head and realize where I am.

Knox's room.

It's easy to tell because last night's memories are slowly rolling in like I'm flipping through the pages of my sketchbook.

"Look," Slate grunts as I stumble again. He rights me back on my feet. He's only faring slightly better than I am right now, but only because there are women to flirt with. "I know our friendship is still kind of new, but if you keep hanging all over me like this, you're going to scare away the ladies."

I can't help but laugh. It feels good, so good that my chest aches with it. I can feel the blistering heat of my cheeks from the drinks I've downed, but it's a nice warmth, one I want to bask in.

"Where are your keys?" Slate asks. His hands are hot on my hips where he's trying to keep me from falling flat on my face. Maybe the last shot we had taken together had been one too many. "Can I pat down your pockets?"

"I know you wanna feel me up, Slate," I slur playfully. His name sounds snake-like with the way I drag the S.

"Of course I do, Quinnie girl. Any man would be stupid not to want you," he comments but his words don't register because the floor is slipping out from under my feet again.

"Rory has the keys," I hiccup. Then, "Are we on a roller coaster? The room is spinning."

Slate curses, and there's more movement that I can't keep up with. My eyelids are shutting slowly and I can barely muster the energy to keep them open.

I've wilted into Slate's chest, rubbing my cheek along the soft fabric of his shirt as he digs around in his pocket for something that jingles nicely. After puttering around with something, he guides me into Knox's room.

"Oh, my fucking God," I groan at the memory, holding my head when my curse rings in my ears. Of course I'm in Knox's room, because I'm fated to end up in situations that will make him hate me even more.

Slowly, I manage to shove the blankets away, slipping my legs over the edge of the bed. The good news is, I feel like I've slept for one hundred hours. The other good thing is that I haven't thrown up anywhere in his room that I can see, or smell.

Yet.

The bad news is that I don't actually know where Knox

is, I'm thankful nonetheless that he's not here to witness me rising from the dead.

He probably stayed the night over at his date's house. As much as that makes a hot wave of jealousy roll like a tidal wave in my stomach, it's much better than him being here. *So* much better.

Blindly, I reach for my phone, patting across the table next to the bed. In the back of my throat there's a lump that I consciously have to work to swallow down. Later, I might regret not purging the rest of the sickness from my body, but the last place I want to do that is here, in Knox's room. What the fuck did I end up drinking last night? I remember the flaming shots and Slate throwing out the partygoer who made them, but the rest of the night is a Mad Lib of surprises.

There was Mandy, who told me all about Ace while they were growing up over a few drinks. The longer Slate forced us to talk, presumably so he could sneak off to flirt with girls while I was distracted, the more Ace's cousin seemed to relax around me. Those cutting looks had turned from pinning me to my spot to glaring at any of the girls who came up to us to ask about Slate.

Mandy's stories had me seeing Ace in a different light. And the embarrassing ones were even better. Like the time they'd gone sledding down the slope behind Mandy's family home in Colorado. It had been a steep incline and they'd been warned many times not to go down there, but the fresh snow had been all too tantalizing not to.

Their punishment had been to walk back up the hill to the house, and when they were young, the trek felt like it was a million miles high. *And* they had to tow their sleds behind them. Ace had thrown up halfway and Mandy had gotten sick from the tears of laughter streaming down her face afterwards.

I learned that she's studying up in New York at a prestigious fashion school. Her outfit made much more sense then. She and Ace are close, his parents often so busy with their jobs in the art world that they spent a lot of time growing up together.

My fingers finally connect with my phone and my head throbs at the brightness of my screen, rivaling the sun's rays spearing through the cracks in the blinds.

And then I see the time.

"Shit," I curse, scrambling for the shoes someone kindly taken off for me. They're piled haphazardly by the foot of the bed.

I'm late for class.

Ugh, I can't even remember the last time I drank like this. It must have been sometime last year because even with all of the wine I consumed during Tipsy Canvas, I hadn't felt this bad. This is a next level hangover.

I brace myself when my hand lands on the doorknob. There's a lock and it's flipped shut. I turn it back carefully, pleased when the click is soft.

When I pull the door open, I freeze in my tracks, my breath catching in my throat. Knox is lying on the couch, his body splayed out in a long, hard line. His shirt has risen from where he's lifted his arm, resting it over his eyes to block out the sun coming in through the windows, and the tugged-up fabric reveals the cut of his hips and the dusting of dark hair from his navel to the waistband of his jeans. Two tattoos are inked into his skin there that I hadn't noticed the night of the rainstorm. Intricate, feathered wings, lining the defining muscle of his hips.

I lick my lips before realizing that in the quiet of the apartment, Knox is fast asleep. The steady rise and fall of his chest gives him away. That, and the fact that he's not snarking at me or shooting daggers in my direction.

It's my one saving grace.

The coffee table shoved in front of the couch is littered with cups and rolling papers, alcohol a puddle across its surface. I have no idea how the glass tabletop has survived the rowdy party unscathed, because I'm pretty sure there was one point in the night where I saw a girl standing on top of it, readying herself to fall into the crowd of people congregated in the living room.

The floor is much the same and I feel like I'm walking through a minefield as I tiptoe around the questionable puddles and garbage. The stench of alcohol in the air makes my head spin and my stomach protests strongly. I press the back of my hand to my nose, trying to block out the smells.

Luckily, I escape the apartment without waking Knox. Unluckily, when I release a sigh of relief, the remainders of my final drink creep up my throat.

I make a dash for my apartment, and thankfully, Rory answers my desperate knocking.

I don't like that knowing look that she's wearing, but she doesn't pester me as I race my way to the bathroom.

Surprisingly, it doesn't take me long to get ready for class.

I told Rory to go on without me when she knocked softly on the door while I had my face in the toilet, but the sound still rang in my head like a gong. She told me she was going to get coffee with Ace before class and asked if I wanted anything, to which I gratefully accepted.

Even though I have plans to meet Reid at the coffeehouse

later, I need something now or I'm afraid I won't make it through the day.

As badly as I want to stay in bed and be a hermit today, I don't want to miss class. Beatrice is bringing in another model and grading our in-class work and I don't want to be docked points for missing out.

And Art History is Art History. There's no escaping the clutches of a near-failing grade.

I doubt Odie will take it easy on me when I show up in my oversized sweatshirt and baseball cap, but maybe if I bring him a coffee, he'll be too preoccupied to tease.

Slinging my backpack over my shoulder, I snag my sketchbook from my desk, shoving all of the loose papers hanging out of the edges back inside. It's a haphazard job at best, but I'm already running too late for my liking, and I can organize them later.

Like while I wait for this stupid fucking elevator the apartment building has.

The queasiness in my stomach has gone down but the piece of toast I forced myself to eat threatens to come right back up when I spot Knox with his own backpack propped over his shoulder, waiting for the elevator.

I can still go back inside and hide, there's definitely still time to—*oh fuck, he's turning around.*

His jade eyes glitter with amusement and I can't shove away the shiver that slides down my spine when he looks at me like that. It feels like a brush dipped in paint dragging across my skin when he trails me from head to toe.

I'm embarrassed, to say the least; more so when he asks, "Sleep well?"

The sound of his voice makes my knees weak. I trip through my next step and my sketchbook goes flying from my hands as I try to catch myself, the papers I just stuffed inside spilling everywhere.

Somewhere in the back of my mind I hear Knox curse in surprise, but all I can feel is the boiling mortification slicing through my body. There are sketches of him in there, fluttering to the ground. One I had drawn while I was supposed to be working on my next assignment for drawing class. He'd been a source of inspiration for me, and there are sketches of him in all sorts of poses, some more precarious than others, and I'm completely and utterly fucked if he sees them.

I drop to my knees, face burning as I scoop the papers closer to me, praying that he doesn't see what's on them. Knox is already crouching low, helping gather some of the drawings, and the fact that this is going to be the first time he's seeing any of my work is overshadowed by the fact that there's a thick piece of drawing paper right next to his boot. It's creased from the fall, half of it turned up at an angle. I can see the lines of his scars I tried so hard to recreate from memory. If he picks that one up, I'll have to transfer schools.

"Don't touch that!" I screech when his fingers close around the edge of the paper. I watch it in slow motion, the clench of his jaw, the way that his eyes flick down to his hands, roughened and scarred flesh on full display. *Oh no.* I think I might throw up all over again when I realize the connection he's making.

He thinks that I mean I don't want him touching my things because of his *hands.*

My throat tightens, heart beating so fast in my chest that I'm sure it's going to burst through my skin. Quickly, I try to rectify my words, pleading, *"No."* My voice cracks around the lump quickly forming in my throat but I push past it. "Knox, I didn't mean it like that."

His face is tight as he stands. I scramble, collecting my

papers in my arms. He towers over me, even when I rise, and I don't like the flicker of muscle in his jaw because he's clenching his teeth so hard.

I don't like the darkness writhing through those green eyes, molten with anger.

He hands out the papers he's picked up and an apology sits on the tip of my tongue. Reaching out, I'm about the grasp them and croak out a thank you when Knox drops them.

I watch them slip to the ground again. The elevator dings and the doors squeal open, but I can't stop staring at my drawings sitting on the floor. I swallow hard, the humiliation prickling at the back of my eyes.

Knox's boots twist in the corner of my vision and he enters the elevator without a single word.

The breaths I'm releasing through my nose to keep calm are harsh and shaky. In a way, I deserved this. Knox thought I was insulting him and he reacted like the hurt man he is. I can't fault him for that.

Except that I can and I am.

Annoyance bubbles underneath my skin. Dipping down, I snatch the papers from the hall floor, not caring if they get crumpled in my haste. The doors of the elevator are beginning to wheel shut but I slip through them before they can close completely, trapping me inside with Knox.

If he thought he was going to avoid the consequences of what just happened in the hall, he has another thing coming.

The tiny, metal box that's grinding down the elevator shaft is filled to the brim with tension. I can feel the stiffness wafting off of Knox's body, even though he's leaning against the wall like he doesn't have a care in the world, his head buried in his phone.

My anger emits in waves and I feel like I'm drowning in

it. What I said came out the wrong way. I had in no way meant it like I didn't want his hands touching my things, but the way he'd gone preternaturally still—that flash in his eyes makes my stomach clench—haunts me. I want to cry because his hands aren't ugly in the least. If anything, they're the most beautiful pieces of artwork I've ever seen: imperfect, yet so, so perfect.

Of course he retaliated the way that he did. I would've misconstrued the comment as well, but there's an itch in my side that's telling me he didn't have to react like *that,* dropping my work back to the ground. Yet another misunderstanding between the both of us.

When I try to speak, there's a screeching that sounds more horrible than usual. The elevator jerks to a sudden stop.

I stumble with the motion and Knox steadies me before removing his hands just as quickly. His touch is searing, and his brows are pinched as the lights in the tiny space flicker before giving out entirely.

"What the fuck?" I question, voice pitched higher because of the nerves that overtake me. We're stuck. The elevator has stopped working and I'm stuck in it with *Knox.* "Oh, my God! We're trapped!"

Knox grunts, punching the buttons on the door. An emergency light flickers on, casting the metal box in a dim, fluorescent glow. Nothing Knox is trying works and I'm officially beginning to freak out.

I watch as he tries to pry the doors open by sheer force, but even with the bulging of his impressive, tattooed biceps, he's no match for the metal jaws of death.

Tossing a look over his shoulder to me, he says, "What are you standing around for, Princess? Call the fire department, or something."

"Right," I respond weakly, scrambling for my phone.

Drawing my gaze away from Knox's muscular form, I dial emergency services. The operator is nice about it, sending someone our way while telling us to remain calm and wait for assistance. Obviously, she doesn't know Knox and I well enough to know that "calm" isn't in either of our vocabularies.

When I tell Knox that all we can do is wait, his eyes narrow suspiciously like I've planned this all along. He looks like he wants to ask more, but he nods instead, sinking down and making himself comfortable against the wall. He looks up at me expectantly, so I sigh, dropping my bag from my shoulder and collapsing to the floor across from him.

His legs are so long that they nearly stretch across the entire length of the elevator, and I can't help but follow the path back up to his eyes, bright in the dimly lit space. I avert my gaze as quickly as possible.

I don't know how long it will take for the fire department to arrive, so I shoot off a quick text to Rory about the predicament I'm in, letting her know that I won't be able to make it to class and to give my coffee to Reid instead. I add a sad emoji because I really, *really* needed that caffeine.

Across from me, Knox's phone buzzes. He reads it and his eyes flicker up to me in a sharp glare.

"Slate seems to think that this is hilarious," he says, and I don't know why the deep timber of his voice feels like fingers brushing across my skin. "Why did you tell him?"

"I texted Rory," I huff, defensively. Crossing my arms over my chest, I level him with a glare of my own. "I don't control who she tells."

Knox rolls his eyes, shutting off his screen.

It's silent for a long time. There are no sounds coming from the outside of the elevator and I wonder if anyone has even noticed that it's stuck. The stupid thing takes so long to arrive at any floor that I think most patrons choose to take the stairs by now, or give up when the elevator never reaches their floor.

"I'm sorry," I blurt when I can't take the quiet any longer. Knox raises a straight, dark eyebrow and I flush. Sheepishly, I continue, "I didn't mean what I said in the hall like that. I just —I didn't want you seeing my sketches."

It's the most I can give him without spilling the truth of exactly what the subject of my drawings are.

Knox's jaw works and it looks like he's contemplating something important with the way that he's assessing me. Maybe he's trying to read me to see if I'm telling the truth, if my apology is sincere or not. The intensity of his eyes makes me want to pull my hat down over my head and hide from his sight.

"It's okay," he says finally, and then quieter, "I'm sorry for the day we met."

Surely my eyes are bugging out of my head with how wide I'm staring at him in shock. I'm pretty sure my jaw has fallen through the floor and is waiting for me in the lobby. I never *ever* thought I'd see the day where Knox apologized for that, and right here, trapped in this elevator, I'm completely bamboozled.

"Don't look so surprised." He rolls his eyes at the way my mouth is gaping dramatically. "It's a long overdue apology."

Damn fucking right it is.

"Are you going to forgive me or not, Princess?" Knox asks when I'm still at a loss for words.

The nickname he uses constantly startles me back into reality and my immediate response is to scowl. "I'll forgive you if you stop calling me that."

"Unlikely," he smirks. "Take the apology or leave it."

I sigh. "Fine, I'll take it."

Knox seems surprised at how easily I accept his apology, but this is all I've wanted all along, a simple acknowledgement of the thing he did wrong. I've been tired of this hanging over our heads for so long, and I feel like a weight is lifted off of my shoulders now that this conversation is happening.

We sit in silence for a bit longer but it's not as charged now. Instead, it's quite nice.

"What are you doing tomorrow night?" Knox stuns me by asking.

"What?"

"What are you doing tomorrow night?" He asks again, as if he doesn't understand how I'm astonished by his question. He's only just apologized for fuck's sake.

Has the elevator getting stuck somehow transported us into the *Twilight Zone?* Is this even really Knox sitting here with me or some sort of changeling?

"Um…nothing?" I respond and he quirks a brow at me.

"Is that a question or an answer, Princess?"

"An answer," I glare. "I have no plans, yet. Why?"

He shrugs nonchalantly, tipping his head back to rest against the wall, as if he's contemplating even finishing his question. He looks like the perfect picture of casual with his hands folded in his lap.

Finally, he says, "I'm having an exhibition tomorrow night. Would you like to come?"

I blink, because this is *definitely* not the neighbor I know. An exhibition tomorrow night? And he's asking *me* of all people?

"Who are you and what have you done with my douchebag neighbor?" I ask incredulously, shifting in my spot.

A wry smile cracks his lips and my heart stutters in my chest. "Still here, Princess."

My mouth twists sourly and I narrow my eyes at him. "Let me get this straight. You want me to go to an exhibition with you—tomorrow night?"

He's staring at me like he doesn't know why I'm shocked at the suddenness of this question, cocking his head when he agrees to the echo of words I've just relayed back to him. "Yes."

"Why don't you ask your roommates to go with you?"

"They don't know about it."

Huh. I wasn't expecting that. I don't know why he wouldn't invite Slate or Ace to an exhibition that he's probably known about for months. Although, I could see Slate wreaking havoc and drinking too much champagne, but Ace? It seems like the perfect spot for someone like him, especially with his parent's connections.

Or rather, why isn't he asking the girl he was on a date with last night?

I don't like the way my body reacts to that line of thinking, my stomach tightening and my fingers clenching into fists as jealously floods my system. I shouldn't be feeling like this over *him* of all people, but I just can't seem to help myself. My mind has always been drawn to thinking about Knox like he's mine.

Maybe the date didn't go well, if he's asking me instead of her.

I mull it over, analyzing him while I decide. Knox allows me the moment, waiting patiently for my response like we have all the time in the world.

Right now, while we're stuck in this awful elevator, I suppose we do.

The green of his eyes is bright. He's never been easy to

read, and even as I search them now, I can't find a flicker of anything telling me that this might be some sort of joke.

I tut, crossing my arms over my chest to stop myself from wringing my fingers in my lap. He makes me nervous. Always has. "Why me?"

"No one better to go with than someone I'm not trying to impress," he answers and I have to ignore the bite of hurt I feel from his words. He has a point though, we've been skirting around each other as much as possible up until this point, and I've just made it known that I'm unwilling to share my artwork with him.

Maybe this is his way of getting me to trust him a little more.

"That doesn't give me a lot of time to find something to wear," I determine.

His eyes flash and I wish I could read that look.

"Is that a yes?"

"It's not a no."

Knox nods and that's that. "I'll pick you up tomorrow at seven, then."

CHAPTER 20
QUINN

When the scent of coffee hits my nose, I'm instantly invigorated.

I thought about canceling on Reid this afternoon after my morning from hell. It had taken the fire department half an hour to arrive at the building and another ten minutes to pry the doors of the elevator open.

By then, Knox and I were no longer speaking. After agreeing to go to his exhibition with him, we chatted shortly about mundane things like the weather and how we think Slate would've reacted if he were in our position. That brought some laughs that I drank in greedily, my heart fluttering at the sound. Eventually, we fell into a comfortable silence, after which I spent the rest of the time reorganizing my pile of crumpled papers. I'd propped my sketchbook on my knees and made sure I was careful enough not to flash Knox any of the drawings.

When the doors screeched open, three firefighters stood staring up at us with consoling grins. Turns out, the elevator had stopped halfway between two floors and I had to nervously slide my body from the surface of the elevator to the landing below.

Even Knox looked less than pleased with that, crouching close as if he was going to jump forward and snatch me up should I slip. The firefighters helped me gain my footing before assisting Knox, questioning us and asking if we needed to be looked at by an EMT.

The man who asked me was handsome. Actually, they all were, but there was something about his deep, smooth skin, the dark braids pulled back from his face. His white teeth gleamed with the grin he gave me when he offered his help. I couldn't help the blush that crawled up my neck. It was once the firemen had made sure that the area was safe and we parted with cheerful goodbyes, that I realized Knox had disappeared.

I should've gone back upstairs to my apartment, but the incident left me wired. Instead, I took a few steadying breaths, shot a cursed look at the devil elevator, and took the stairs the last two flights down to the lobby.

I already missed Drawing, but of course I was making perfect time to arrive at Art History, slipping into my seat with one minute to spare before class started. Odie's shoulders shook as he laughed at my expense, but he quickly zoned fully into the practice test Professor Doff was walking us through.

I've never paid such close attention to class in my life.

"Hey," Reid greets, his colorful eyes roving over the packed coffee house before settling on me. He's dressed in a pair of loose, gray trousers, and instead of his usual sweater vest that makes him look like the most handsome Teaching Assistant around, he's wearing a tight black t-shirt, his sweater hooked over his elbow. The weather is in that in-between stage of chilly mornings and warm afternoons. It's different, seeing him in a color darker than the neutrals that makes his hair appear a ruddy, deep chestnut. The dark shirt looks painted on his skin and I've never noticed his musculature before, but I sure am now.

I have to work to move my gaze back up to his.

Reid's hair is combed back from his face today with a single, unruly wave curling in front of his forehead. His freckles stand out more than usual, the afternoon light drifting in through the window accentuates the speckles.

"Hey." I stumble over the greeting while distracted by his new wardrobe.

"Missed you this morning," Reid says, ushering me into the line. It's longer than I expected it to be, but with all of the pre-weekend partying that seems to go on around the university, I suppose all of the hungover students like me need their pick-me-ups to make it through the rest of the day, so they're once again ready to drink themselves stupid tonight.

"You probably won't believe me, but I got stuck in the elevator this morning," I huff, shuddering at the thought of being trapped in that tiny metal container.

Reid's jaw drops in shock and I nod, grimacing at the memory.

"Rory mentioned something about it in class. Are you okay?" He laughs and the smile I'm trying to keep tucked inside breaks free. "You made it out, obviously, but holy shit, Quinn, how are you even here right now? I would've gone right back to bed!"

Knox's uncommon niceties and disappearing act had kept me from doing just that.

Crossing my arms over my chest, I tut playfully. "I couldn't miss Art History. I have no idea what's going on in the class and Doff sucks ass! I couldn't tell you the difference between a

Romanesque and Gothic cathedral if I'd built them myself," I grumble, thinking about the answers I got wrong on the last test. Odie's tutoring hadn't gone so well, but he promised he'd help me between his own classes and demanding hockey schedule.

Reid snickers. "I'm so glad I don't have to take that. Instead, I get to enjoy History of Architecture and Urban Design. So, if you think about it, it's pretty much the same thing."

"Sounds easier," I mutter, glaring at the backpack of the person in front of me. "Plus, you're naturally good at this stuff, Reid. I'm sure you're killing it."

The freckles on Reid's face glow as his cheeks pinken with a blush. It's cute. "I wouldn't say all that," he trails off bashfully, and it's obvious that he's being modest.

I step forward with the line, counting the number of customers that still have to order before it's our turn. Behind the register is a guy who looks like he would rather be anywhere else, and when I catch sight of the letters stitched into his shirt across the breast pocket, marking him as a frat member, I understand why it's taking so long.

Behind him are two girls scrambling to keep up with the numerous orders coming their way. Unlike the boy at the register, they seem to be a well-oiled machine back there, dancing around each other as if making cappuccinos and lattes is a graceful waltz. I feel a twang of empathy for them even though they seem like they're thriving back there. I have no idea how they can memorize the different drink orders, making them as efficiently as they can and giving them to the customers within minutes.

This is the kind of pressure I would crack under.

I turn back to Reid with a playful glare. "Oh, *come on.* You're one of the smartest people I know!" I don't miss the

way the tips of his ears turn red with my slew of compliments. "It's one of your better traits."

This gets his attention, and he blinks down at me, those
opposite-colored eyes unimpressed. "I have bad traits?"

"While your intelligence is admirable, your sketching
could use some work." I poke fun at him, referring to the last
time we hung out at my place to work on our projects.
Instead, we had spent the night watching a terrible reality
show with the bottle of wine he'd brought. Reid had followed
me into my room where we were supposed to gather my
drawing supplies. He had made a joke that had me laughing
so hard I nearly cried.

My stomach ached too much to get up after that, the wine
making me boneless in my comfortable bed, so the both of us
spent the rest of the night there, joking around and *not*
working on our projects.

Reid quirks a brow. "Is that so? Are you offering to be my
model so I can practice?"

It's my turn to blush now, cheeks hotter than the steaming
milk screaming behind the counter. My mouth parts though
my tongue is a twisted mess from his flirtatious comment,
knotted and thick. I'm not sure how to respond, and I'm
saved by a very punctual throat clearing that comes from the
frat boy behind the register.

"Are either of you planning on ordering?" He asks lazily,
tapping a blunt nail against the register. He's wearing a backwards cap, copper hair poking out from the sides. His brown
eyes drag up and down my body, ignoring Reid's presence
completely and I cringe in response.

I snap my mouth shut, teeth clacking together. So kindly
said for a boy who probably has pre-workout and porn
coursing through his veins.

Reid ushers me to the counter, apologizing for the both of us. "Sorry about that, man."

The boy behind the register looks bored, Reid's apology meaning nothing to him. Frat douche leans forward, flashing his teeth at me in what I assume is supposed to be a charming grin.

It's anything but.

One of the baristas spins on her heel, gauging the way this asshole is looking at me. Her gaze flicks up to Reid and her eyes widen before her lids lower and she glares daggers, ping-ponging between both boys. They're dark, hair even darker. Her skin is the color of espresso, and I wonder how she puts up with this guy all day.

A crash draws my attention away from boy's gross gaze. The second barista is frowning, staring down at the shaker she's dropped to the floor with a clang. The entirety of the coffee house goes silent for a fleeting moment, everyone stopping to see what's going on, but within seconds, murmurs wind throughout the space as she swoops down to scoop the shaker from the floor, dumping it into the sink.

The brunette turns back to the boy at the register. "Quit it, Mike," she barks, a can of whipped cream still poised and ready to add to the Frappuccino in her hand. Those dark eyes flit across mine and her mouth tightens. "Please, excuse him."

Reid glances at her and seems to calm a little, rolling his shoulders. "Quinn, what would you like to drink?"

"I'll have a mocha with an extra shot and extra whip," I nearly spit at the frat boy. "Iced."

With a soft but firm nudge at my lower back, Reid guides me away from the frat rat at the register. I slide down the counter to the pick-up area while Reid pays for our drinks. He joins me a moment later when I've managed to take a few breaths. I won't let that asshole ruin my mood.

"I'm sorry—"

"Don't," I shake my head, cutting Reid off. "Don't apologize for him. *Thank you,* for the coffee."

"It was the least I could do," my friend replies easily, smiling at me.

While we wait, I scour the shop for somewhere to sit. Booths are packed full with studying students, miss-matched chairs and tables stacked with people and their friends. It's a frenzy if I've ever seen one, but the coffee house is a sanctuary for university students, especially during the afternoon hours.

By tonight, the shop will be barren, with all of the patrons getting their caffeine fixes through vodka Red Bulls instead.

"You're taller," I comment. "Do you see any open spots that I can't?" I ask, because there should be more seating behind the loitering line I can barely see over.

Reid scans the coffee house as one of the baristas brings our drinks over to the counter. It's the one with the hazelnut eyes again. She's staring me down, a harsh look on her face that I can't decipher if it's concentration or annoyance. I can't blame her if it's either, focused on the tasks at hand, slinging coffees left and right.

She has every right to be annoyed with the customers who ask for thirteen extra shots of syrup or her coworker who apparently doesn't know how to speak to women. I wouldn't be surprised if he's made comments to the girls he's working alongside, but I'm pretty sure that the one who slams our cups onto the counter with a little too much force can hold her own.

I frown, but she's already turning away, starting the next order.

"There's a table by the window," Reid points to the corner

of the room. I lead the way, a bounce in my step as I move quickly so no one snatches it.

"What a day," I sigh, finally relaxing into the cushy seat. I place my drink on the low table between us, and while it's not the best seat to get work done in, I'm happy to be unwinding before the weekend, chatting with my friend.

Reid snorts at me, taking a sip of his drink. I watch his throat bob around the swallow and I promptly avert my gaze, looking outside the window instead.

There are students walking by in a flurry, a third of them trying to stuff themselves through the coffee shop doors. A woman with a stroller and a dog that's almost as small as my drink. A few girls all staring down at a single phone with beaming smiles on their faces.

"So, what are your plans this weekend?" I ask, playing with the straw in my drink, swirling the ice around and watching the milk incorporate with the tawny coffee.

Reid releases out a long-suffering sigh that has me peeking over at him.

"I'm supposed to be having another family dinner this weekend, but I'm dreading the ride back with my father and brother."

"I'm sorry," I offer sympathetically. Reid shrugs my condolences off. It's not a topic he favors talking about, but I'm still curious about his family. "Does your brother go here?"

He sets his cup down, wiping his palms down his trousers as he clears his throat. He looks like he's preparing himself for war, with the way that he's bracing himself, and I almost feel worse for asking.

"I have three older brothers, actually," Reid says and I nearly spit out my drink. *Three brothers?* I had no idea. "And two of them have gone here, too."

"Wow, your family really likes this place," I mutter.

"Yeah, well, my father is the head of the engineering college here."

"Oh, so you're like Vulcan University royalty," I tease and he rolls his eyes, shooting me a playful glare.

"If I was studying engineering, I would be," he says, moving that glare down to his coffee. His shoulders are tight and I'm sensing that he doesn't want to talk about it, but he continues nonetheless. "Colt, my eldest brother, is getting his Masters in Nuclear engineering, and I'm going into architecture, which, and I quote, *'is for people who can't solve a differential equation.'"*

I refrain from mentioning that I have no idea what the fuck a differential equation is, but Reid must read it clear on my face because he cracks a smile.

"Yeah, tell me about it."

"So, you're telling me that all of your brothers are engineers?" I ask, because the odds of that happening must be some crazy statistic. Almost as crazy as having four sons and zero daughters or knowing how to solve a differential equation.

Across the shop, the bell above the door chimes again, signaling the arrival of more patrons. It's as if I can feel the air shifting with the new presence, coming alive. The feeling draws my attention to the door, where Knox and Mandy have just walked in.

Like a magnet, Knox's gaze finds mine, bright and lush.

It makes me want to shrink back in my seat with the way that they flick beside me to see who I'm with.

The green of his eyes splinters and I can see the way his shoulders tighten from across the room. Mandy must sense the shift in Knox's mood because she's looking around, chocolate eyes pinched together in a threatening way, as if she'll verbally spar with anyone who makes Knox even a bit uncomfortable.

When her eyes snag on mine, her red-painted lips part in a genuine smile.

All I can muster is a soft grin and a lame wave in response, stomach knotting like I've been caught having public sex with Reid under Knox's cold glare.

I pull my focus back to my friend with all my might, but I can still feel him watching me like a hawk.

"Not entirely," Reid shrugs, scooting his chair closer to mine now that the coffee shop noise has gone up with the post-lunch time rush. "Colt is studying for his masters; Foxe is on scholarship at St. Gerald's for wrestling, but on paper he's a communications major, which is funny because every time he talks to someone in the family there's always some type of arguing." He rolls his eyes but the smile that accompanies it tells me that he favors Foxe. "He's never cared about what anyone thinks about him anyway, which is a trait I wish I had."

"Me too," I sigh, placing a hand on his knee empathetically. "Are you close to him?"

"Used to be," Reid shrugs a little. "Oakland is in the Netherlands, taking the semester to study bridge structure. Boring, I know." He laughs at the face I make. "And I'm in architecture."

"Damn," I curse, impressed. "I'm not sure if I'm more shocked by the fact that your entire family are a bunch of geniuses or that two of your brothers are named after animals."

My joke seems to crack the heaviness of the conversation. It's clear that whatever kind of relationships he shares with his father and brothers is a bit strained, but Reid laughs comfortably as we burst into giggles.

"See, this is why I like you, Quinn. You're very easy to talk to."

"Don't forget funny," I chuckle, pairing it with a cheesy grin.

"Right, how could I forget. Funniest person I've ever met," he jokes, nudging me with his shoulder.

"Hey," I whine, shoving him right back. "It's true! I would never lie about something like that!"

Reid smiles broadly, taking another sip of his drink. "You're right, I'll give you that one. But what about you? Any plans this weekend?"

My stomach bottoms out at the thought of my plans. I'm going to Knox's exhibition tomorrow, someone who I've been beefing with since the start of the year. We've only just squashed our issues this morning, so why on Earth did I say yes? Do I really want to spend my Saturday evening with someone who I'm not even sure I can make it through the night without arguing with?

Parting my lips to answer, I'm cut off by a looming figure. Peering upwards, I already know what I'm going to find. Maybe I jumped at the opportunity to spend the one-on-one time with Knox because I want to figure my handsome neighbor out. Knox stands before us, his sharp jaw set in a firm line, eyes blazing like a thousand fires. There's a steaming hot coffee in his hand and I find myself wondering what his order is. I can only assume it's plain black coffee like the attire he's dressed in. Mandy stands a step behind, a sly smirk on her lips that she's not trying very hard to hide.

"I'll pick you up at six thirty tomorrow night." His voice is cold and I frown in response. Reid looks confused, staring up at my neighbor as if he recognizes him from somewhere but can't quite pinpoint it.

I nod shallowly, cheeks hot at the look on Knox's face. I

don't know why I feel like I've been caught in the act of doing something I shouldn't, but him interrupting Reid and I like this is none of his business. He has my number; he could have texted me instead. "Okay."

Knox stares at me a moment longer, then twists on his heel and stalks away, completely ignoring the glare Reid's shooting him and abandoning Mandy.

I follow his form, watching the way he moves with such grace. The crowd parts for him, more sets of hungry eyes trailing after him just like mine. All of the attention on him sends a hot stab of jealousy to my gut. I tear my gaze away, shifting to Mandy, who beams brightly.

"So nice to meet you last night, Quinn." She winks, looking like she knows something that I don't. "I hope to see you again soon." With a flourish of her blonde hair over her shoulder, she trails Knox out of the coffee shop, just as many eyes following her as there were following him.

"Was that your neighbor?" Reid asks, slumping back in his chair. "I thought you didn't like the guy."

I might have complained about him when Reid come over to my apartment the night he told me he ran into Slate and Knox in the hall.

"Yeah," I answer weakly, reaching for my cup again. The words taste funny in my mouth as they come out. "We're working on it."

CHAPTER 21
QUINN

There's a knock on my door at promptly 6:30 the following night and it's the one time I'm thankful that Ace has taken Rory out on a date.

My heart stutters uncomfortably fast in my chest and my hands shake with nerves as I smooth them across the skirt of my dress one last time.

Yesterday afternoon, after I parted ways with Reid, I'd taken a solo trip to the mall in search of something to wear to the opening of Knox's exhibition tonight.

After trying on too many dresses to count, I settled on this one: simple, black, and elegant. The fabric clings to my curves in all of the right places and a rush of confidence has me straightening my shoulders. I look good. Even the store employee had halted in her tracks on her way through, while I was staring at myself in the full-length mirror contemplating on whether it was too much for the event.

The woman complimented me so many times that I wasn't even sure how to acknowledge her gushing after the plethora of nervous "thank you's" I'd offered in response.

I don't know why I'm so anxious. Knox had made it

perfectly clear that he's not trying to impress me tonight, and I shouldn't be trying this hard anyway, but I want to look nice for the occasion. I've straightened my hair and am letting it lie long down my back where my dress is cut low, revealing the length of my spine. I've even put more effort into my makeup than I normally do, going with a shadowy look that makes my hazel eyes pop.

I quickly slip into my kitten heels, flattening my hair and dress one last time. They're short enough to be considered appropriate for the occasion and tall enough to give me a boost of self-assurance.

Eating up some of the height between Knox and I wouldn't be so bad, either.

Another knock comes from the door. It's gentle, not impatient like I'd expect Knox to be. I made sure I was ready on time so we wouldn't start the night off on the wrong foot.

With one last breath, I open the door.

It's Knox, of course, and the sigh I was in the middle of releasing *whooshes* out of me with force as I drink him in.

He's handsome, shockingly so, but tonight he looks like a model. He's wearing a simple pair of black trousers with a matching black button-up. The top three buttons are undone, showing off the beginnings of the tattoos that span across his collarbones.

His hair is clean and brushed, and it looks like he's taken a pass at it with a bit of gel because it's perfectly set in a naturally tousled look.

Knox looks incredible.

Good enough to eat.

Heat floods his eyes and my core goes molten as his hot gaze traces me up and down, drinking me in. I shift in my spot, trying to dispel the need to clench my thighs together as my girlhood whines at me to say hello.

I clear my throat at the tightness lingering there.

Knox blinks once, twice, and his eyes meet mine again.

"You look…" He trails off as if he's at a loss for words. His eyes dip down again and my grip around the strap of my purse tightens so that I don't reach out and tug him to me by the collar of his shirt. "Beautiful," he finishes, and the word settles in my chest like a brick, my cheeks going red.

"Thank you, Knox," I respond softly. I don't invite him in because I'm still too stunned to say anything else. "You look very handsome."

He nods, offering me a soft smile that makes my knees wobble. "Are you ready to go?"

"Yeah," I answer, stepping out into the hall.

I lock my door and follow him to the elevator. The muscles of his shoulders strain against the fabric of his shirt and I wonder if that's why he hadn't fastened any of the top buttons, because they'd surely burst if he had. He pushes the button to go down, the elevator finally back to its normal—and scary—working conditions. I let my gaze travel lower while he's distracted, into betrayal territory, and bite my painted lip at the sight of his taut waist and tight ass.

Good enough to eat, indeed.

"Are we taking your bike?" I ask when we reach the lobby. My dress is snug around my ankles, so I'm careful with my steps, but trying to maneuver my way onto his motorcycle is going to be a problem. "I don't think I'll be able to get on it in this."

"We're taking Slate's car," he tells me, pulling the keys from his pocket and twirling them around one long finger. There are a few keys attached to the ring, along with a fluorescent keychain with the words *'getaway car'* scrawled in white ink. "I hope that's all right."

"More than," I exhale thankfully, taking the hand that Knox offers to help me into the car.

He directs me to mind the rust and the hole in the floor-boards where I'm pretty sure I can see the road. He makes sure I'm all the way in and that my limbs aren't going to get hit by the door when he closes it. He seems so unlike the Knox that I know that I almost ask if the real him has been abducted.

Knox slides into the driver's seat, tucking the key into the ignition. The vehicle starts with a rough cough and Knox waits until it settles before pulling out into the street.

The ride is bumpier than I remember it being the first time I was in this car, but I'm pretty sure I'm being hyperaware of everything happening right now because I'm so nervous.

"Is Slate staying home tonight?" I ask, breaking the silence.

Knox shrugs. He's tapping his fingers impatiently against the steering wheel and I can't help but stare, noticing each groove and scar of his marred skin. The beauty of something so hurtful. I don't know what caused the scarring, but for it to not stop him from creating his art and following his passion, I'm in awe.

"He lets me use his car sometimes, if I let him use my bike."

I raise a brow in shock. "You really trust him on that thing?"

Knox huffs a laugh and my heart stutters. When he glances over at me, it completely stills at the gleam of amusement in those beautiful green eyes. "I trust Slate with my life."

The rest of the short ride is silent except for the sounds of the hardly running Bronco and the tires against the road seeping in through the hole in the floorboards between my feet. If Knox doesn't speak because he's nervous, I don't know. I don't know him well enough to know his tells, but he's still tapping along the steering wheel. Otherwise, he seems as cool as a cucumber.

I, on the other hand, am stewing in my own unease. I feel jittery, on edge the closer we get to the building Knox's exhibition is being held in. It's not far from our apartments, but with each rotation of the tires, I'm becoming just as high strung as Knox.

I shouldn't be reading into this the way I am. Joining Knox tonight isn't anything more than someone not wanting to be alone. I know that he doesn't care much for my opinion, he's made that more than clear, but with the attention on him all night tonight, there's bound to be a little on me, as well.

On the other hand, this feels like more than just an event he needs someone to attend with. The mere twitching of his fingers gives away how important this is to him. I can't help but to wonder again why he hasn't invited his roommates, if he trusts them with his life.

Knox rolls the car to a stop between a packed, well-known restaurant and a jewelry shop. Flanked by each store is an elegant, sleek looking gallery. The outside is covered in black marble and the lighting looks expensive and bright. The sign above the door reads the name of the gallery in large black letters.

OPULENT.

The font matches the name.

There are black curtains pulled down across the large windows beside the door. They must be opening them later in the night or even later in the week when the exhibition is open to the public.

I turn to look at Knox who is staring out the windshield, hands twisted tightly together in his lap.

With a sudden burst of confidence, I gently place a hand on his shoulder. Knox flinches and I rip my hand away, mortified. He looks over at me, eyes wide, and for the first time since I've met Knox, he looks nervous as fuck.

"You ready?" I ask, softly.

Knox nods once, then again, firmly. "Yeah."

He opens the car door for me again and helps me find my footing before he's locking the vehicle behind me. There's a bit of a breeze now that the sun has dipped down behind the large buildings and I shiver a little, more so when Knox places a warm hand at my lower back to usher me inside.

His skin doesn't breach mine, touching only the sliver of silken fabric just above my ass. Knox's palm is a heavy weight against me and the mindless motion he's circling his thumb in has my knees unsteady as I walk, warmth stirring to life between my legs.

My breath catches in my throat so harshly I almost choke, stepping inside of the well-lit gallery. It's empty of patrons, and will remain so until the exhibition begins. Some of the most beautiful charcoal drawings I've ever seen line the walls. Most of them are drawn on large canvases, bigger than my torso, and I can instantly tell how much work and passion has gone into the creation of them because they're simply breathtaking.

"There he is," a man greets us with a broad smile. I tear my gaze from the artwork on the walls as Knox gently nudges me forward. I blush, not realizing that I'd stopped in my tracks in the middle of the doorway. I don't know where to look because it's all so beautiful, but I politely drag my stare to the man headed our way despite wanting to stare at all of the artwork. "The man of the night! And who is this lovely lady?"

His voice is rich and deep, much like the color of his

upswept eyes, glowing bright with excitement. He approaches Knox and I, patting him on the arm as if he knows that he doesn't favor shaking hands or hugging. I watch, waiting to see if Knox flinches like he had in the car when I placed my hand on his shoulder, but he doesn't. There is a tightness to his body and an edge to his jaw that tells me that he might have been anticipating the move.

Knox eases slightly when the man finally removes his hand.

"Silvio, this is Quinn. Quinn, this is Silvio. He owns Opulent."

"Quinn," Silvio greets me with a firm handshake and a knowing look in Knox's direction. He rolls his eyes in response as Silvio turns back to me. "So nice to meet you."

"You as well," I answer politely. I don't know why Silvio had given Knox that look, and I'm not sure I'm going to find out because he's quickly whisking Knox away, talking of some loose ends that need finishing up before the doors open to the show in a half hour.

Knox quickly untangles himself from the silver haired man, making his way back to me.

"Are you going to be okay out here while I go with Silvio?" He asks me and it's almost jarring, how polite he's being tonight. When I wave him off with a nod, he continues, dark brows furrowed like the thought of leaving me alone with his art bothers him. It's blasphemous, I wouldn't dare do anything to ruin this for him. "I'll only be gone for a few minutes. Feel free to look around if you like. I'll bring you a drink on my way back."

"Thank you, Knox," I answer. His gaze lingers before he turns away, leaving me and his exhibition alone.

Assessing the gallery, I'm unsure of where to begin. The only sound throughout the space is the clacking of my heels on the floor. I refrain from pulling out my phone and texting Rory and spilling the entirety of what I'm up to tonight. I'm so nervous I hardly even know what to do with myself. I feel awkward, like an imposter as I decide to view the one nearest to the entrance, keeping a few paces away from the large drawing lit brightly on the wall.

The artwork before me is so dark I can barely make out the forms. The entire canvas is black with deep sweeps of heavy charcoal. The lighter areas of the work have been reigned in with an eraser. I stare at it for a minute, two, allowing the picture to speak to me.

It feels lonely, despairing, almost. The one next to it is an angry stroke of work, lines thick where Knox had clearly pressed harder into the rough canvas as he drew. A puddle of something spilling across a floor in waves. Two eyes ripple in the reflection of the liquid, their pupils malignant and cruel.

It sends shivers crawling up my spine.

Each piece is more beautiful than the last. I find myself both enthralled and rushed, wanting to spend as long as I can in front of each picture while I have the space to myself, rushed because I want to see the entirety of the work before everyone arrives.

The charcoals become lighter, happier, as I follow the path that I'm walking around the room. In the middle of the gallery, well-lit and clearly the centerpiece of the collection, is a canvas so large I'm not entirely sure it could fit through the front door of the building.

It's titled *'Not an Accident'* as the plaque to the side of the canvas reads. It towers over me on the wall and I feel so small, glued to my spot, my throat thick and eyes prickling with tears as I admire the piece, absorbing it's utter, raw beauty.

It's of a pair of hands, fingers intertwined, pressing into

each other in a desperate way, as if seconds from clawing through the skin. One is perfect, smooth, clean skin, while the other is marred, so familiar that it makes my chest ache.

It's is puckered and patterned, tortured by something great, something that is carried by both memory and sight. They're Knox's hands. I would be able to recognize them anywhere, and the unmarked skin of the other must have been what they looked like before the accident changed them forever.

A tear escapes the corner of my eye, but I don't move to wipe it away.

His artwork is a harrowingly beautiful sight.

Footsteps nearly silent against the freshly washed floors capture my attention, but I'm unable to tear my gaze away from the masterpiece before me.

Knox strides up to my side, staring at the artwork with me.

It is a long time before either of us dare speak, but when we do, it's Knox that breaks the silence first.

"Are you ready for the event to start?"

I nod, wiping the lone tear I've allowed to escape. I don't think Knox notices.

"Yes, are you?"

"Yeah," he breathes, finally looking at me, his jade eyes shining with pride. "I think I am."

CHAPTER 22
KNOX

The exhibition is in full swing.

Silvio started the night with a speech, gushing over how long he's been wanting to showcase my art. I've been working endlessly on these images, since I figured I should hone in my drawing skills as the dream of becoming a tattoo apprentice stretches further from me.

I wanted to duck my head at all of the attention when I took the floor, but when I met Quinn's soft hazel eyes through the crowd, the rest of the room seemed to disappear. The overhead lighting shining down on my work was also shining down on her, her blonde hair a golden glow and her encouraging gaze giving me the confidence I needed to continue. The words rolled easily off of my tongue, even if I don't remember exactly what I said because I was distracted by her beauty.

The conversation is loud and the guests seem to be enjoying themselves, a couple admiring the strokes of charcoal streaked across canvas, the harrowing drawings I've made come to life. I can see the way it resonates with people; they may not know my story personally, but each of us carry hurt in our hearts, and they're witnessing mine, something I would have never thought I'd be able to share.

A few times I've found myself looking for Quinn and caught her staring at the centerpiece of my exhibition, her intense gaze watching it with a predatory glint as if she's protective over it. I can tell it's her favorite and I find myself wanting to ask her why she seems so drawn to it.

Instead, I watch her monitor the patrons ogling and commenting, the beauty of her sharp gaze.

It isn't lost on me how she hasn't left my side all night, as if she somehow knows that I need her near me. Her familiarity makes me less nervous around this many strangers who I've allowed to come and judge not only my art, but my life, my *hands*.

I don't have to ask her. The brush of the skirt of her dress against the leg of my pant or the whisper of her bare arm against mine is more than enough. My fingers itch to reach out and cling tightly to hers. I keep a firm hold on the stem of my champagne glass, not a single drop of its contents gone.

It's the same one I hand Quinn when she downs hers during her glaring contest with the guest currently standing a little too close to one of my pieces.

I hate feeling so exposed like this, their eyes on me as they flicker from the drawings to where I walk, slowly winding my own way through the exhibition. I've seen it so many times, lived it, but trying to allow the uncomfortable to become comfortable makes me uneasy.

But I'm trying.

The night is slowly winding down, which is perfect because I'm exhausted from playing host. Tired of fake-smiling and laughing at shitty jokes, tired of people staring at my hands, staring at Quinn, all pretty in her dress. I want to kick everyone out and then kick myself for missing her reaction to every picture hung in this gallery. I should've been there to see if her responses to my other work was as exquisite as the one she gave when she was admiring the centerpiece.

I feel like a circus animal here, so vulnerable with the spotlight on me. People see me as a strong, confident, brooding man most of the time, not to be fucked with. But it's not who I used to be, not before the accident. There was a time where I smiled more, was extroverted, even, when Slate, Ace, and I would wreak havoc across the university grounds. We'd stay out until the sun came up and party until we couldn't see straight.

Ever since that fucking night when my entire world changed, I haven't been the same.

I haven't been that naïve, carefree boy in a long time.

The man before me is talking numbers for one of my pieces. It doesn't sound remotely close to what I want for it, so I peek over at Quinn again to distract myself while he rambles on and my heart stutters in my chest. She's peering down into her champagne glass with a soft smile on her face. Her cheeks are a perfect rose color from the alcohol and a strand of her long, blonde hair hangs down, calling to me.

I want to reach out and brush it behind her ear, to feel the warmth of her cheeks against my skin, to have her prefect eyes on me again.

I can't look away from her. We've come a long way since the night we met, and just like my exhibition, we've managed to find a way to let go of the old and accept this new start. Yes, most of our interactions since have felt forced, but somewhere along the lines I think I found myself trying to annoy her so that her attention would be on me.

I always want it on me.

What Rory said when I freaked out about finding Quinn in my bed rings in my head. *You like Quinn, don't you?*

I do. I really fucking do.

The longer she's looking away from me, the more nervous I become. I *want* to talk to her. I *want* to figure out the unknown draw to her I feel when she's around. I *want* to be able to see the world through her eyes, hear her thoughts about each piece even if it takes all fucking night. I won't be able to sleep, anyway.

"Sure," I respond lamely to the man who is still babbling, complimenting my work as if that will get me to agree to his offer. Some sort of art connoisseur, he claimed. He told me that he could see the next big thing before it happened and that I'm going to shoot up the ladder fast, that he *has* to have one of my pieces. "Let Silvio know that I accept. He will draw up the paperwork for you."

I don't shake the man's hand. I don't shake anyone's hand, but I do place it gently on Quinn's lower back to gain her attention. There are those stunning eyes, finding mine so fast that I feel it in my bones, the electricity that comes with it. Those eyes make me weak. They can tear me down with a single glance—and have before. They break through my walls too easily, so quickly that my only defense against it is to pretend I don't want anything to do with her at all. To piss her off and annoy her so that she can't see what I truly desire.

I answer her questioning look with a nod of my head. I need to offer my thanks to those attending, even more so for the ones that have purchased my artwork, and after that, the gallery will close and the night will come to an end.

I don't want it to.

I want to spend more time with Quinn, but I won't act on that thought.

"I'm sorry, again," I say after the gallery empties out and it's just Quinn and I.

I feel the sudden urge to ask for forgiveness for my dick-ishness again. Although I meant what I said in the elevator, I'm a better man than that, and Quinn deserves a genuine apology.

She deserves a lot more than me.

Even Silvio is gone now, allowing me to lock up after I requested a few final hours with my artwork before it's all packaged and shipped out after the exhibition ends in twelve weeks.

We're sitting against the wall opposite the centerpiece, staring at it, a half a bottle of champagne in. Well, Quinn's a half a bottle of champagne in. I'm driving, so I haven't had a sip, even if I do need the liquid courage because my heart is threatening to beat out of my chest now that we're alone.

My gaze falls on Quinn's shoes at our feet. She'd kicked them off as soon as the last person left the building, before I even had a chance to lock the door behind them, complaining about her aching feet screaming from her dreaded heels.

I can feel her looking at me, watching me. I let her get her fill, find her words before turning my head to meet her gaze. Her hazel eyes are the perfect mix of green and brown, a thick forest of color, honest and raw.

"You're sorry?" She questions in disbelief.

I nod. "Yes."

Quinn huffs, nearly knocking over her glass when she throws her hands out, gesturing to the room. "I'm finally getting a real apology out of you and there's no one here to witness it?"

A smile cracks my lips and her breath catches. I didn't realize how close we were sitting until now, our shoulders brushing with each inhale. Her cheeks burn and she ducks away, turning back to the drawing in front of us.

"I was an asshole that night," I sigh, tipping my head back against the wall. I drain the water in my glass that Quinn had filled, not wanting to feel like she was drinking alone.

"Yeah," she giggles, and something takes flight in my stomach. I fight the urge to lean in and taste the laughter on her tongue. She looks smug, like she might scream that I've apologized from the rooftops. "You were."

I don't know why I offer, but something inside of me forces me to blurt, "Would you care to know why I was such a dick that night?" It's said softly and I immediately want to take my words back when her smile disappears.

She swallows hard and I wipe my suddenly shaky hands down my trousers.

"If you want to," she says, just as quiet. Like it's some secret that will be shattered if either of us dare to speak up.

I don't need to do this. I don't need to explain anything to her, but after how tonight has gone, I want to. I want to tell her everything, be honest about the parking, my failed apprenticeships, the strained relationship with my father, what happened to my hands. *Everything*.

Fuck it, I tell myself. I so desperately want to reach over and snag the bottle of champagne, down it all in one go because my confidence has withered into a fucking puddle. My tongue darts out to wet my lips and Quinn tracks the movement, her pupils wide and fixated.

Taking a deep breath, I try to explain, but the words stick in my throat as the memories are drudged up.

Slowly, gently, but with intention, Quinn takes my hand and intertwines her fingers with mine.

I don't flinch at the contact. The only reason that I had in the car is because I wasn't expecting it, and my mind flashed back to my father's hand when he grabbed my shoulder to haul me around into his fist.

My breath is officially caught in my chest as I stare down at how perfectly her hand fits in mine. She's as warm as I thought she would be, dainty but strong as she squeezes, encouraging me to speak and accepting me if I've changed my mind.

"Sometimes," I start, and have to clear my throat of the thickness lodged there. I can't look at her, but I stare at our hands, my fucked-up fingers twisted with her unblemished ones. "Sometimes, when I drink, it feels like my hands aren't even connected to my fucking brain. Which is kind of why I was such an ass the way we met." I can sense her confusion and continue. "Not because I was drinking, but because of my hands. I was at an interview for an apprenticeship at a tattoo parlor. They told me that my lines were too shaky and turned me down. It had been the third opportunity I didn't get because of this fucking mess." I gesture to the scars on my wrists, the skin grafts creeping up my forearms. My skin is still pink, some of the worse spots a faint purple from where they had to cut back into my skin for a second surgery.

My chest heaves with the deep breath that I take. Anger burns in my chest. I shouldn't be touching her, not with my fucked-up hands, skin stretched too tightly over my muscle and bone.

In a sudden panic, I try to pry my fingers from Quinn's, but she holds firm, consoling me. "Hey. Knox, stop it."

With the way she says my name, I go still.

I don't think I'll ever get tired of it.

"You don't get it, Quinn," I croak. "All I've wanted to do with my life is become a tattoo artist and now my dream is completely fucked because of my step-brother and father." I can't help but spit the words, disgust and hatred lacing my tone. "My step-brother ratted me out to my father about me being an art major instead of the business major he wanted me to be." My voice is thick, wet, and a tightness forms behind my eyes. "I tried to leave before things could get out of hand, but it happened anyway. My father pummeled me into the floor in his foyer, and when I could stand up long enough to flee, I took my bike. It was late and I was terrified, unsure of where to go. Blood was falling into my eyes from a cut in my eyebrow and I lost control. The bike slid out from underneath me before I could right it."

Quinn looks devastated. Tears fill her eyes and I hate myself all over again for doing this to her. But now that I've started, I can't seem to stop.

"I had my helmet on, and that's what saved me, but my hands we're fucked. They had to take skin from here—" I take our intertwined hands and pull up my sleeve, showing off the scars of skin grafts creeping up my wrists, then gesture to my legs. "To fix where the road shredded my hands." I stare for a moment before chuckling wetly because I have to give up my dream of tattooing. Sitting in a room of drawings of the reasons why I have to let it go, it really sets in. "Now, I can hardly hold a tattoo gun for a long period of time, let alone draw a goddamn *straight line.*"

Tears spill down Quinn's cheeks and my chest aches. I hate that I've made her cry, that my words are the cause of this.

I'm shaking like a leaf, my grip tight around her fingers. My breathing is harsh, loud in the otherwise silent gallery, as I muster up the courage to reach out to her like I want.

With a curled knuckle, I gently catch a tear as it rolls down her cheek. She doesn't blink, doesn't break my gaze.

She allows me to do this for her. If this is the only touch I get, I'm thankful.

My voice is tight, a low grind when I try to speak again. "Those drawings," I gesture vaguely around the room. "I drew the ones nearest the door as soon as I could pick up a piece of charcoal after the incident. Hurt like fucking hell." My laugh is wet and fake. "And even more so to clean the powder from my hands." It helped to wear gloves, but when they were still healing the tightness felt like my hands were on fire, melting in the claustrophobic latex.

I don't have as much trouble with them now, other than the trembling.

"Knox," she croaks, but I shake my head softly. Unfortunately, I'm not finished yet.

"This exhibition is about new beginnings," I explain, dragging my gaze across every single piece of work I've created. The despair, the agony, fear, anger, slowly turning into something steadier, stronger, and *happier.* I'm not completely there yet, but I'm hoping that someday I can look down at my hands and be proud of what I've accomplished despite what they've—*I've*—been through.

I untangle my fingers from Quinn's and push to my feet, reaching down to help her up. She stands and I re-twine our fingers, not quite ready to let her go. Instead of looking at the art, she's staring at *me.*

And I can't read the look in her eyes.

It's fitting, how my exhibition is about new beginnings and this feels so much like one. There isn't any more animosity between us; instead, a fresh, clean slate.

Quinn breathes out a hasty, "I'm sorry, too," before her free hand wraps around my neck and she hauls me down for a kiss.

CHAPTER 23
QUINN

The kiss is searing.

It's a desperate attempt to taste each other, devour each other as Knox's lips part beneath mine. Our teeth clack and the sound is loud in the silent gallery, almost startlingly so, but his tongue brushes across mine in an apologetic swipe before dipping in for more, easily taking control of the kiss.

It's urgent, and the taste of him explodes on my tongue, fresh and spicy. I can taste the champagne I've drank and I want to cringe, but when his hands caress my face, keeping me close, the feeling bubbles throughout my body.

I inch closer, pressing myself fully into him. He's a solid wall of warmth that coils deliciously down my body and settles between my thighs.

My heart pounds in my chest as I lose myself in him entirely.

A new beginning indeed.

"Wait," Knox pants between kisses. His words tell me that he wants to pause the kiss that is more dizzying than any of the champagne I've had tonight, but the way his hands keep pulling me closer, the way he continues to press his mouth against mine again and again, tells me that he doesn't want this to end either. "Princess, wait."

I freeze when the totality of his words catches up to me, rocking back from him. *Is he already regretting this?* I mean, I did just throw myself at him like some simpering girl.

Knox's reassuring grip slides down my arms, keeping me in my spot. Tingles skitter in the wake of his touch, and I can't help the part of me that's suddenly terrified of what he's about to say.

He must read it on my face, my worry, because his dark brows furrow like he doesn't understand why my initial reaction would be to pull away. He's stepping into me, plastering himself against my front. I can feel the hard lines of his body, the stiffness of his cock against my stomach.

Warmth collects between the apex of my thighs at the feeling of *that.* I want it pressed a few inches lower and a few inches deeper.

"You've been drinking," Knox breathes, and the pinch to his face becomes more tortured when I slide my hands up his chest, wrapping them around his neck. His eyes search mine with a frantic kind of energy; I don't show him anything but the ache, the need for him that I've been locking deeply inside of myself. "I need you to be sober when I fuck you for the first time, Princess."

"I'm fine," I whine, because holy fuck does that sound good right now. I'm clinging to him just as tightly as he's holding me. I roll my hips to emphasize how great of an idea fucking is and Knox makes a choked noise in response. "I'm not drunk enough to where I'd forget or regret any of this, Knox."

He shakes his head as if trying to rid his mind of whatever

he's thinking. Hopefully, he was imagining fucking me because his pupils grow with hunger.

"Fuck." He squeezes his eyes shut and I grin in triumph. Knox leans forward, pressing his forehead against mine as he confesses, his breath brushing across my lips. "I want to fuck you in a bed, not on some hard floor."

It's a poor excuse and we both know it. I'm more than willing to have a sore back from getting fucked into the marble beneath our feet. It's been far too long since I've last had sex. Knox could fuck me out in the back alley and I'd enjoy it. I'd probably even thank him.

Maybe we should *fuck in the back alley,* I think, as desire rolls through me at the thought of him pressing me into the brick, taking what he wants.

"Just put a canvas down," I suggest, voice hoarse with need. "Let's make some art."

Knox grunts like I've shot him, bucking his hips against me. I can feel how big he is and all I want to do is unleash his confined cock from his pants, run my fingers across the hardness of it, taste him on my tongue—

"Easy," he warns me playfully, but his eyes are dark. There's a strain to his voice that tells me I should keep going. When I do, Knox gently removes my hands form where they've strayed to his belt. I hadn't even noticed that my fingers had moved to his waist all on their own.

"Fuck," I wince. "Sorry."

"Say fuck again," he asks, distracted. The hue of his eyes drip with lust, pupils blown wide as he stares me down. It fills me with a raw heat that has my confidence sparking and I bat my eyelashes up at him like I'm going to make him beg for it. His thumb brushes across my bottom lip, watching me intently as I repeat the word. "Filthy, Princess," he breathes against my mouth. "Every time you called me a prick or asshole or whatever creative curses you came up with, I wanted to taste them off your lips and fuck those words right out of your mouth."

I can't help but rub against him like a horny teenager.

My pussy is throbbing with need. I moan again as Knox gives in, dipping his head and sucking harshly on my neck. The burn of the suction feels so good.

I need to feel it on my clit.

"Shit," I whine. His hands are everywhere now, winding down the length of my back, grabbing a handful of my ass to keep me glued to his front. "Need your cock, Knox," I pant, and he's moving back to my mouth, kissing me so forcefully that the both of us stumble backwards.

"You'll get it, Princess," he promises, hands dragging hot lines across my body. I've waited too long for this, for us to finally be on the same page. I'm about to beg him again, because my failed attempts at convincing him to fuck me right here on the floor are not working, but suddenly, the lights to the gallery cut out, sending the entire room into a pit of darkness.

It's like we're in the elevator all over again.

Knox groans and I can't help the nervous laugh that bubbles up from the back of my throat.

This better not be some horror movie shit.

"What the hell?" I question, turning to look over my shoulder to see if in fact the entire room has succumbed to the same darkness. I don't miss the way that Knox's grip tightens on me as I move like I might disappear entirely if he lets go. My heart stutters in my chest because of it.

"Silvio told me this would happen at midnight," Knox supplies, and I relax a little, knowing that the hooded murder from *Red Grave* isn't about to pop out and slaughter us in the goriest way possible.

Small victories, and all that.

I fake an excited gasp. "My very own Cinderella moment! I've always wanted one!"

The smirk in Knox's tone is clear as day when he answers, amusement echoing in the darkness. "Except, unlike Cinderella, you'll be getting dick tonight."

I swat at him, but hardly connect. Knox chuckles, deep and throaty and the sound buzzes warm between my thighs. Being on his good side is already proving to be spectacular, but he can't keep torturing me like this.

"I think the dark really sets the mood, don't you agree?" I ask as I move back into him, my fingers fumbling to find the top button of his shirt.

"Oh, no you don't," he grouses, catching my hands and guiding me through the dark gallery instead. The flashlight of his phone flickers on and I squint as Knox leads the way, my hand tucked tightly in his as I find my heels and hobble back into them with a soft hiss. They're already aching and protesting the action. "When I fuck you, I'm going to need to see all of those pretty faces you're going to make for me."

I stumble and blame it on my shoes.

Knox swipes our abandoned champagne glasses from the floor and with my free hand, I grab the almost empty bottle. He leads me through the gallery into a back room, which must be the way to the exit at the rear of the building.

Inside is a kitchenette. Knox dumps the glasses in the sink with a loud *clang*.

When I scold him for not washing them, he arches a brow, illuminated by the glaring light coming from his phone. "Oh, now you want to stay longer and clean up?" He questions and I roll my eyes in response. "Is this my punishment for wanting to take you home and fuck you in a nice, comfy bed? C'mon, Princess, you know just how soft it is, don't you?"

I shiver at his words. I do know exactly how comfortable it is. I haven't stopped thinking about his fluffy pillows or the way the mattress conformed perfectly to my body, how the thick blankets and lush smell of him surrounded me.

He's right, I don't give a fuck about the damn glasses.

The ride back the apartment is both the longest ride I've ever endured and also the most tension-filled.

It's difficult to focus on anything other than Knox's hand in mine, the soft and rigid texture of his skin; the way that his thumb soothes gentle circles across my hand where they're intertwined in my lap. He's warm, and it's settling something in me while simultaneously forming a rock in my stomach when I think about what he's endured to gain these scars.

How could anyone, let alone his *family,* do something like that? It's utterly fucking evil and vile and…and…I can't even think of another word to describe what Knox has gone through.

I try to swallow past the lump in my throat, breathing shallowly so I don't make myself sick with the thoughts racing through my mind.

As if he's already so attuned to my body language, Knox squeezes my hand, offering me a gentle smile. It's crooked, where one corner of his mouth tilts higher than the other, but it's easily the most handsome smile I've ever seen. It makes him look years younger, like he's carrying less of weight of the world on his shoulders. It has me wishing I brought my sketchpad with me. When he looks at me like this, it feels like there's a garden of anticipation sprouting in my stomach, a field of colorful flowers.

I frown when Knox untangles his fingers from mine but then he's sliding that large palm slowly up my thigh. My gaze turns sharp but he looks like the perfect picture of innocence, smirk gone as he focuses intently on the road.

The car jumps when we hit a pothole and it causes Knox's hand to slip even higher up my thigh. I wonder if he can feel the heat radiating off of my—

"How are you doing over there, Princess?" Knox asks me, but I can hear the mirth in his voice, see the arousal in his eyes, flashing in the streetlights.

"Peachy," I offer, using both hands to clamp down on his wrist to keep him from coming any closer to my already weeping pussy. The thin fabric of my dress does little to separate Knox's searing touch. "Just peachy."

I skip going back to my apartment, trailing after Knox with my hand still tucked in his.

My heart beats wildly in my chest. The closer we move towards his door, the more confident in my decision I am. I want him. I want his hands all over my body, his eyes and tongue on my skin, his cock plunged deeply into me.

The elevator had been the only option to get upstairs because of my tired feet, but Knox had thoroughly distracted me by pinning me up against the wall and slotting his lips against mine.

We stumbled out onto our floor in a fit of laughter. Now, I'm mostly just drunk off of Knox, his hands, the strain in his pants that's calling to me like a beacon, and that sexy gleam in his eye.

"I'm going to get you some water," he whispers, pressing

a soft kiss to my mouth. We both creeped quietly into the dark apartment, holding our breath and listening for movement. For college students, the weekend night is still young and his roommates must be out because I don't hear any grunts or moans behind closed doors or through thin walls.

His hands settle on my hips, eyes shining with amusement. "And after you drink it, if you still want to—"

"*Yes,* Knox," I cut him off, tone earnest. "My answer isn't going to change."

He studies me, eyes hungry with desire, before he nods, slipping from the room.

I bite back the smile threatening to tear my face in two at the sight of his ass in those black trousers. I can't wait to rip them off of him and find out what's underneath.

Exhaling, I spin on my heel, kicking off my shoes. My feet sigh in relief as they fall flat against the hardwood floors and I wiggle my toes, admiring his room. It feels different this time, from when I'd woken up here hungover as fuck.

The light from the lamp beside the bed is soft, the pile of books stacked in pristine order as opposed to the ready-to-tip-over pile I remember. It's clean, no clothes on the floor like in Slate's room, no pair of panties thrown over the back of the desk chair.

Knox's desk is the only thing I could consider messy, but even then, it's cleaner than what some of my art stations look like when I'm elbows deep in a project. There's a jar filled with chunks of charcoal sticks, a cloth drenched black hanging over its side. There are loose sheets of paper and thick graphite pencils for sketching and a cluster of sketchbooks stacked in a neat order, the one on top open.

Leaning closer, I squint against the dimness of the room to get a better look, and my breath hitches in my throat at what I see.

Sketch upon sketch litter the spread, each one of me. He's made me look so beautiful that I'm not even sure I look like this. Even the ones that have clearly been drawn in a rush are impeccable.

It's me in the elevator, head buried in my sketchbook, hat pulled low over my eyes. It's me when Rory and Ace forced us all to have lunch together, tossing the grape at Slate. I flip the page and it's me, scowling up at him the first night we met. Me sitting on the back of his motorcycle, rain plastered to my head, me—

I all but collapse into the desk chair as I continue to pry. I know I shouldn't, but it's as if I'm in a trance. Some of the pages are filled with larger scale drawings, spanning across the spine of the book. When I'd eaten dinner with Knox, the shock on my face while finding out he could cook.

A hysterical laugh bubbles in my throat. I didn't realize that Knox has been paying as much attention to me as I was with him. The drawings of his hands that I dropped all over the floor are a tribute to that.

"What are you doing?" Knox's voice startles me. I whirl around, jumping from the chair to face him, but I don't move any farther than that. I can't because my knees are locked and my feet are glued to the floor.

He's standing in the doorway, a glass of water in his hand. He doesn't move, either. When his eyes flicker from me to the sketchbook, my chest hurts at the guarded look he wears.

"That sketchbook is filled with drawings of me," I blurt stupidly, still in shock.

I watch Knox's throat work as he swallows. Like he's considering not answering at all.

After a few, long seconds in silence, he breaths out a quiet, "Yes."

"Why?" I ask, trying to resist the urge to wring my fingers together.

"Because I really like you," he answers, and my heart explodes in a flurry of want. My pussy flutters in a flurry of *need.*

All of this time we've spent fighting, when we've secretly liked each other. Every time Rory tried to ask me about Knox had been *deny, deny, deny,* because of this very moment right now. I hadn't wanted to think of him like that, even when I subconsciously was desperate to. I didn't actually want to like Knox, not after what he'd done, but I find myself admitting that I like him a hell of a lot more than I ever thought I could.

Bunching up the bottom of my dress into my hands, I take a step closer to Knox. He's frozen in the doorway, watching me slowly drag the fabric up my body and over my head in a burst of confidence. I'd forgone a bra, and my nipples tighten as the chill of the room washes over me, underneath that piercing gaze.

In the few steps it takes me to cross the room to him, my dress is on the floor and Knox can't stop looking at my body, drinking me in desperately like an artist does their inspiration.

"I really like you too, Knox," I respond softly. This is the most intimate thing I've ever done, bare myself to a man while he's still fully clothed. The ball is in his court and the bulge in his pants has me more than hopeful.

Knox curses. *"Fuck,* Princess. You're making my hands shake."

My solution is a simple one. I take the glass from him and reach over to set it on the dresser. I can feel his eyes rove my body as I move, gaze hot like a knife.

Turning back to him, I slowly, gently take his hands. They're trembling, and it makes me ache for him.

He watches me closely as I lift one of his palms to my

lips, kissing it sweetly. It's followed by the other, and then I'm dragging his hands down my skin and over my breasts, squeezing his hands around them.

Knox's breath hitches and my head nearly rolls back on my shoulders when his fingers twitch as he fights the urge to squeeze harder. I peer up at him. He's so warm, eyes bright and drinking me in like a delight. I want to feel his hands *everywhere*. Right this second.

"They're not shaking right now, Knox."

As quick as lightning, Knox strikes, lunging forward and scooping me off my feet, kicking the door shut behind him.

I arch into his touch, the tightness of my sensitive nipples grazing across the soft fabric of his shirt. I moan into his mouth at the feeling and he swallows the noise desperately.

His room is small, and in two great strides he's placing me on his bed and crawling up after me like a wolf stalking his prey.

I scoot backwards as he ascends over me, until I can't anymore.

Knox follows me like a worshipper to his God.

His hands trail my claves to my thighs where they all but fall open for him. The fabric of my panties is wet and I shiver as the air of his room seeps into the fabric, shivering harder when Knox's hot gaze drags down my body like a brush dipped in paint.

Like this, kneeling between my legs, he's the one that looks like the perfect picture. Soon, I'll have my own sketchbook filled with drawings of him just like this, strands of his black hair falling across his glowing eyes, his tongue poking out to wet his lips.

"My *God,* Princess. Where do I even start with you?" He asks, voice filled with disbelief.

I know his question is rhetorical, but I can't help the whine that accompanies the answer slipping past my lips. "Any-where you want."

As if Knox can't stand the distance any longer, his hips find mine. I can feel the length of his cock through his pants and I keen when he grinds into me, rubbing against my aching core.

His fingers find the buttons of his shirt. They're not trembling now, not as he pins me with those hungry eyes, as if I might slip away if he takes them off of me for a single moment.

As if.

He's torturing me with his slow pace, and it's not fair that I'm the only one undressed here. I lean forward, taking over for him, my fingers frantic to touch the sliver of his chest that he's too leisurely exposing.

Knox's body is smooth, warm, and the ridges of muscle beneath my fingertips feel like puzzle pieces. I know exactly where he's going to fit, pressed tightly against my body.

His shirt slides down his arms, showing me those impressive biceps. Tattoos of all kinds litter his skin and I'm interested in seeing the artwork he's curated for his body for only a moment before he's leaning over me and caging me between his elbows. I can't help but stare as we hover in this limbo, like he's suddenly realizing the same thing as me: that we've spent too much time arguing when all along we could have been doing *this*.

Knox dips down to capture my lips against his in a sweet kiss. "I'm sorry," he murmurs against my mouth, following the words with his tongue.

"I've already forgiven you," I whisper, delirious from the feeling of his mouth on my neck. Knox sucks lightly and my breath catches, my thighs quivering to wrap around his taut waist, but there are still too many clothes separating us. "But if you get inside me right now, I'll forgive you again."

Knox lifts his head and my heart flutters at the grin on his face. I hope I won't always be so surprised to see his happiness, but I can count the number of times I've seen him genuinely smile on one hand, and he's so handsome when he does.

Something blooms in my chest with it; the things I've learned about him, from him, this man who hasn't let his hardships keep him from doing what he loves.

"Don't think you're getting off that easy, Princess," Knox says, and I almost whine when he pulls away from me, but he's kissing his way down my body. I lift my head, watching as he brushes his lips over the tops of my breasts, taking his sweet fucking time. It's frustrating in the best way, and when he looks up at me from below, with his jade eyes all wide like that, I almost shatter right there. But then he's saying, "I have to taste this sweet little pussy first," and my eyes roll back into my head as my body tries to arch into his.

Knox's tongue circles my pert nipple in a tease before he's sucking it into his mouth, grazing his teeth across it. His free hand takes my other breast, and the roughness of his palm combined with the flick of his tongue has me melting even further into his mattress.

My fingers find his bare shoulders and I dig my nails in, hissing when he rolls my nipple between his teeth. *Fuck,* I need his cock right the fuck now, my pussy is throbbing.

"Please!" Apparently, I'm not above begging, but I'm dying up here. My poor pussy has been neglected for so long but I will never admit it out loud. She's well acquainted with my hand, but with all of this foreplay, she's a weeping mess.

Finally, Knox's fingers slip lower. Full body goosebumps

break out across my flesh as his touch dances gently down my sides.

I almost come when he slides them into the waistband of my panties, but he's teasing me again, snapping the elastic against my hips.

"Might have to keep you here all night, Princess, so I can study you with my tongue," he says, leaning down to lick a stripe up the sensitive inside of my thigh. "My hands," Knox continues, and his words are accentuated with a brush of his knuckles down the center of my core. The thin fabric of my panties does nothing to ease the feeling of his touch. I keen deeply, and somewhere in the haze of the storm that accompanies his touch, I don't realize that he's slipping from his pants and boxers, his thick, full length on display. "And my cock," he finishes, rubbing himself against my completely soaked panties.

"Knox," I mewl desperately, but I don't have to wait any longer because he's already prying my underwear down my legs and settling himself between them, admiring the glistening view.

I'm already fisting the sheets in my fingers and it's an effort to lift my head and peer down at him, watching in anticipation as he finally, *finally,* lowers his head to my dripping pussy.

Fucking *fuck,* is Knox wicked with his tongue, sweeping a deep stroke up my slit. He groans and the sound reverberates against my clit and it's all too much already. I figured he was going to be good with his hands, being an artist, but this...the gentle to harsh touches of his tongue against my pussy is otherworldly.

I gasp when he fucks his tongue into me, grinding my hips as I desperately chase the feeling. His hands are planted on my hips to prevent me from scooting up the bed, keeping me held tightly to his face for him to ravage.

It's like he's been starving for years and my pussy is the only thing that can satiate his hunger. He works his tongue, fucking me with vigor. He sucks greedily at my clit and I arch for him. One of his hands is warm across my abdomen, pushing me back into the mattress.

I'm delirious off of the feeling of him. My thighs clench tightly around his head as heat builds in my core, but it doesn't seem to be slowing Knox down, not when he's flicking his tongue so greedily. He must enjoy the desperate noises I'm releasing and the way I'm pulling his hair because his chest rumbles with pleasure when I come all over his face without warning.

Before I can even catch my breath, before I can blink the euphoric spots from my vision, one of his fingers plunges inside of me.

His knuckle brushes the bundle of nerves that light me up like a fucking Christmas tree and I can't control the pleas of encouragement falling from my lips. He takes my praise with pride, working a second finger into me, curling and twisting them, thumb still teasing my clit.

As he works me right to the edge again, tipping me over into oblivion, I thank him. Knox is a giver, that's for sure.

When I'm whimpering from overstimulation, Knox pulls away. He doesn't go far, looking longingly at my pussy as if he's already missing it. My orgasm coats his mouth when he looks up at me, glittering in the light. His thumb strokes a soothing pattern against my hip and I know that I wanted a reprieve from his devilish tongue, but when he's looking up at me like this, my pussy flutters again with need.

"You all right up there, Princess?" Knox teases, crawling his way back up my body. He's following the guidance of my fingers still twisted in his hair, slanting his mouth over mine, sharing the taste of me in a lazy kiss.

I hum into his mouth, blissed out from my orgasms. I peek my eyes open to peer up at him and I find him already watching me, admiring me with a soft curve to his mouth. It makes me preen a little. I'm excited to finally see this side of him, happy and calm. Wrapping my legs around his hips, we share a groan when his cock bumps into my soaking pussy, teasing us both.

"Condom," I gasp, because I've been reduced to one-word sentences with the feeling of his cock against my core. He's so big, and I would be going down on him if it weren't for the way that I desperately need to feel him inside of me, right this fucking moment.

Knox reaches over me, pulling open the drawer of the small table next to the bed. He roots around for a moment and then he's pushing back on his haunches and tearing open the condom wrapper, pulling it out.

"Let me," I offer, and I didn't think it was possible for his eyes to turn any darker, but they do when he passes it over.

My mouth waters at the sight, all perfectly pink and beading at the tip. He's hot and heavy, silky like heaven. I can feel my wetness clinging to it from when I writhed against him.

With a wicked tease of my own, I give his cock a tug, reveling in the low groan that emits from the back of Knox's throat.

"Princess," he warns, and my thighs clench at the deepness of his tone.

I don't wait for Knox to take charge. As soon as I finish rolling the condom over his dick, I guide him closer, ushering him through my slick folds as I stare up at him with big, inno-cent eyes.

"Fuck me, Knox," I breathe. "I can't wait another second."

His lips meet mine in a bruising kiss and he slowly presses into me.

"Fucking fuck, Princess. You're so tight for me." Knox's words are shaky against my mouth like he's struggling to hold himself back from pressing into me all the way.

My only response is his name, a mewl on the breath that's forced from my lungs with each inch he plunges into me.

I'm not all that sure he's going to fit, but the words of encouragement he's whispering in my ear have me relaxing, melting at the praise. The finger he slides between our bodies to play with my clit helps distract me from the way he's stretching me out on his cock.

And then he hits that spot, nestling up against it when I make a noise he likes. I cry out, "Right there, Knox. You feel so good." My fingers dig into the long lines of muscle down his back, trying to hold him closer, as if we're not touching in every way possible already.

Our hips finally meet and I cry out in joy.

"Do you know how many times I've thought about this?" He asks me, accentuating his words with a slow roll of his hips that makes us both groan and my nails grate against his skin. "When you were touching yourself on that side of the wall," he pants, pulling out and fucking back into me slowly, watching my face for any signs of discomfort. "It's all I could think about."

My eyes fly open, gasping when he bottoms out again. "You could hear me?"

His hum is strained. "I hear everything you do over there," he whispers against my mouth, and I shouldn't be excited by that, but when I imagine the way that his cock stood at attention for me even then, a thrill runs through me.

"You'll have to show me how you touched yourself someday, Princess."

I moan loudly at the thought, gripping him tighter. I like the idea of Knox sitting in his chair, charcoal poised above his sketchpad as he watches me with those piercing eyes while I touch myself to the sight of him—like how he's touching me right now, with tight, little circles against my clit.

"I heard you with that guy," he continues, voice darkening with jealousy. His thrusts become harsher, deeper, and I cling to him for dear life as he fucks into me with fervor. "With that fucker from the coffee house. I bet you faked it with him, all that laughing and sighing. I'm going to find out if those noises were real or not."

I shiver at his words, but Knox couldn't be further from the truth.

"We didn't fuck," I pant, bucking my hips up to meet his. Knox makes a choked sound, canting his hips and I scream at the sudden change of angle. And then, because I know it will make him come undone, I say, "All of this is just for you, Knox."

He's fucking me into the bed with abandon. There's a coiling deep in my bones that's so hot I cry out with pleasure. His cock is filling me completely, hitting spots I could never wish to find with my own fingers or toys.

"I'm going to memorize everything about this perfect body of yours, Princess," Knox groans, thrusting deeply. I can tell that he's on the verge of his own orgasm with the way he's picking up his pace, the way he's sliding his hand between us again. He groans like a dying man when his fingers find my clit and I clench around him. "We've got all night. Let me see you come again, Princess. Come all over my cock. Oh, *fuck,* Princess. That's it, Quinn, just like that."

My orgasm rocks through me like a tidal wave, stealing my breath away. I hold onto Knox like he's my lifeline, trembling in the aftershocks. The white-hot pleasure coursing through my veins is incredible, and I wrench my eyes open at the sound of his shaky warning.

Knox follows me into serendipity. His mouth parts, harsh pants slipping past his lips as he comes. He kisses me and it's messy, sharing breaths because we're both so caught up in each other's bliss. I hold onto him tightly, not wanting this night to end.

For the first time, I don't care that it's loud on this side of the wall.

Because I'm on it.

CHAPTER 24
KNOX

Quinn looks beautiful lying in my bed like that, with nothing but her bare body on display.

The evidence of last night is still marked on her skin: bruises littering her form, from her neck to her breasts, from her hip bones to the creamy inside of her thighs. I hadn't left one inch untouched, more than eager to hear all of the different sounds she'd make for me while I traced her skin into the early hours of the morning, and after another around of raucous sex, she'd fallen asleep in the warmth of my arms.

Even with her comforting presence beside me, sleep evaded me.

I don't want her to leave. Thanksgiving break begins later this week and now that I finally have Quinn, touched her, tasted her, fucked her, I don't want to part from her. I can still taste her on my tongue, sweet and fresh, see the faces she made for me and hear the pretty noises that escaped her lips.

Last night must have been some sort of dream because it doesn't seem real. How could I have taken out the girl that has been on my nerves all semester and found something that I actually liked? She showed me a side of her I haven't seen before; the tenderness she displayed, the understanding, her acceptance of my apology I didn't know I truly needed until I felt her tongue on mine.

She broke me down without even trying. I admitted things to Quinn that I don't offer easily to others. Hell, Ace and Slate don't even know the entire story of my accident, and somehow, I found myself admitting every fucking ounce of pain and frustration it brought me.

I still flinch when my friends come up to me and clap me on the shoulder in greeting. It was that exact motion my step-brother had given me right before he told my father the secret I'd been keeping. To this day, I still don't know how Dick found out.

Quinn is a whirlwind of fresh air. She seems infatuated by the scars lining my body instead of disgusted, if the time she spent last night tracing every one of them with her tongue proved anything. She didn't shy away. No, she had kissed them and caressed them, and until then I hadn't realized just how much I missed the touch of someone else. Someone confident and tender like Quinn.

She means more to me than I thought she would.

I held her, long after my fingers began itching for the familiar feel of my charcoals. Wide awake, I snuck out of my bed and over to my desk, flipping through the sketchbook filled with drawings of her—the very same one that had her tearing up—to a fresh page.

I'd gotten lucky that she didn't react poorly to what is essentially my shrine to her. Pages upon pages of drawings of her, in this single sketchbook that I normally keep hidden away on my shelf. How had I been so stupid as to leave it out? *Right,* because I was so fucking nervous about the exhibition that drawing was the only thing that could ease my racing mind and shaking hands.

The apartment is silent, has been all night from what I can remember. I don't care if my roommates had heard us anyway. The amount of times I've overheard Slate taking a girl to "pound town" as he so aptly calls it, is astronomical with these thin walls. He's not shy about it, either, sometimes not even making it to his room before the apartment becomes a symphony of sex drenched sounds and creaking furniture.

Sleep wears on my body, trying to drag me down, but my mind is wide awake. Creative, is what I call it; insomniac, others might say. I won't dare sleep a wink when Quinn is here to draw my attention. She sleeps so prettily with the morning sun cascading over her body as it rises, casting shadows across her skin in the most interesting way, highlighting those marks I left on her body...

For now, the marks are hickeys, but my mind is already flooded with ideas for tattoos to give her.

I take my pencil to the paper. I only have minutes to get this down in my book, if that. I don't know when she'll shift, if the sun will wake her or if everything that happened last night will come flooding in like a nightmare. I wonder how Quinn is going to react when she wakes up, if it will be a poor one where she pouts, or if she'll frown and demand me back into the warm cocoon of blankets she's surrounded herself with.

I just hope that she doesn't regret it.

I shove the thoughts from my mind and focus back on the sketchpad.

I snag a kneaded eraser, blackened with use. There are shards of charcoal strewn about my desk, brushed to the sides for a clean workspace. The chalk clings to my skin and I breathe a sigh of contentment at its familiar texture. Rolling the stick between my fingers, I peer back over to her, the sudden urge to press my sooty fingertips against her perfect skin barreling through my thoughts.

My heart skips a beat at that, the idea of Quinn covered in the essence of my art, of *me.*

The drawings in my sketchpad are both rushed and not. Lazy, languid strokes when I have all of the time in the world to recount how she glared up at me. Quick, harsh lines of a fleeting smile, her gaze brushing mine.

The smooth, cream paper is fresh on both sides, a blank canvas inviting me to soil it with my charcoal. The blackness, like the voice of night I often find myself awake in, instead of letting it calm me to sleep. My eyes ache to fall shut but my mind won't allow it, a thousand different images of Quinn from the night I have yet to add to the rapidly filling book propped over my knee.

I breathe in deeply, letting myself bask in the picture of her again, the sheet twisted around her body, barely covering her sex. I haven't been so fortunate that she kicked it off in her sleep.

Maybe next time.

I'm quick to get Quinn's form down. Her face, a circle for her skull, a smaller one following for her cheek where it's pressed into the pillow. A line that marks the mattress. A box for the window so I can draw the rays of sun washing in over her. Maybe I'll even add a halo to her disheveled blonde hair.

The curve of her body is drawn in such a fluid motion that it surprises me for a moment, but after last night, I feel like I know the dips of her silhouette better than I know my beloved motorcycle. The drawing of Quinn spans across both pages. One wouldn't be enough to capture the raw beauty of her this morning, though I might already have five other sketches of her sleeping from when I found her in my bed a week ago.

I draw the swell of her breasts, her hand, relaxed at her hip, sketching the general shapes of her body before she shifts. Before she realizes that I'm missing from her side.

And not once do my hands shake.

With two quick drags of my chalk, there are her eyelids. My hand moves on its own and I do nothing to stop it. I almost don't draw the fabric of the sheet. Instead, there's a fleeting moment in my exhausted mind where I think about drawing that sweet little pussy of hers but it's gone as fast as it comes, even if my dick does twitch in response. I drape the bending lines across her hips before filling it in with the flat of the stick, using the eraser to mark the highlights and my fingers to smudge the lines until they're buttery smooth.

I love the way that the chalk sticks to me. The onyx dust coats my hands and covers the blemishes adorning my fingertips. It feels like a second skin, a plate of armor against unwanted stares—except for Quinn's of course.

My mind always tends to wander to the self-hatred shadowing its corners when I'm tired. The loud music only helps on some nights, but in Quinn's presence, it seems as if she's scared them away like a beacon of light I've been missing for so long.

Tracing the lines of her fingers, I begin to add the finer details now that I have my base. I study the way the light spans certain areas of her body and hides others, filling in the paper with the thick stick of charcoal. The eraser waits in my other hand, ready to pull out the chalk from the chunk of black I've just colored in.

Occasionally, I blow the soot off of the page. It lifts, swirling around in the rays of the morning sun and I'm distracted by how pleasing it looks. Reminds me of the whorls of ink scattered around my body.

I scrub the powder into the grains of the paper. My hands are a mess and the medium sticks to the eraser I'm kneading into a point so I can carve out the shape of her nipples, tight from the brisk morning air. My gaze flickers to Quinn and back down to the paper again, tongue poking from between my lips as I focus on the important task at hand.

It's a shame that she hasn't woken up yet. I've finished my picture and I don't know what to do now, what to draw because she hasn't yet shifted in her sleep. I think about climbing back into bed with her because every blink feels like there's sand in my eyes.

I know that I need to sleep. I know there are dark circles around my eyes and my skin is getting that sickly look my mother used to scold me about when I was young and stayed up all night studying anatomy on the internet.

Instead, I pull the chair closer to the bed. I can move behind Quinn and draw her backside, but I think better of it, wanting to sketch the more intimate parts of her like her face or where the crook of her arm barely covers the curve of her chest.

I focus on one thing at a time. Her hand. I draw her breasts and the hickeys I left surrounding them last night. Chalk up that tiny scar on her shoulder I have yet to ask about. So many things I don't know about her, but her body is not one of them. I draw the shape of her ear and the piercings punched into them. Sketch the column of her throat, also mottled with marks from my lips.

I wonder if she'll be upset with me when she notices them, knowing that she has class tomorrow.

I smirk at the thought of Reid getting an eyeful of those; of the guy I saw her with at the library seeing the bruises on her skin. I want them to know that she's mine, that she's off limits. It hadn't been my intention when I was kissing them into her skin, but the thought makes my chest puff with protectiveness.

She hadn't had sex with Reid, she told me. That sweet pussy is all for me. *Only me.*

I look at Quinn again, watch her even longer, hand frozen over the page. I'm staring again but she's not awake to catch me.

From somewhere behind me, the buzz of my phone goes off. I place my sketchbook back on the desk and rub my filthy hands on a tissue I pull from the box on the shelf. Black streaks the thin material and it's not enough to clean my skin, but I don't care. I crumple the tissue and toss it into the trash can.

I find my pants discarded haphazardly on the floor. It's too early for Slate or Ace to be texting me, and all of my notifications for social media are set to Do Not Disturb. It's a Sunday, so I'm not particularly sure who it could be.

The screen of my phone lights up with the text and the floor falls from beneath my feet as I read who it's from.

It's my father, and the message accompanying the photo he's sent me makes my blood boil. A letter from the landlord of Third Street Apartments.

I'm not sure how long I stare at the message. All I know is that I snap out of it when Quinn calls my name. Her voice is soft and groggy, confused until she catches sight of me.

When she smiles, my worries seem to melt away.

Everything else can wait when she curls a finger at me, beckoning me back to bed.

"Here you are boys," Rhonda says with a kind smile a handful of days later. She sets a large stack of pancakes with extra butter in front of Slate and a breakfast special before Ace. My hands haven't stopped shaking enough for me to be able to pick up a fork yet, nor the hot mug of black coffee I'm clutching for dear life. Rhonda offers me a consoling glance —she's always reminded me of my mother in a way, with how caring she is, and it makes something pinch in my chest —a feeling I duck away from. "Nice to see you around here again."

I'm thankful that she refrains from asking any questions. I haven't shown up to her diner with Slate and Ace since after freshman year when Slate figured out that he could pull almost any girl he wanted and Ace found other places to frequent, places more sophisticated to the trust fund he's going to inherit next year for his high grades.

It feels like I haven't seen them in ages even though we live together. Ace has been busy with Rory and Slate's been chasing tail as usual, and I've been keeping a lot more to myself than I normally do since we've formed a friendship with our neighbors.

I've missed them.

I texted our special code this morning after seeing Quinn off, the one that would ensure both Ace and Slate would drop everything and meet me here. Quinn flew out with Rory and her older sister, Peep, back to Seattle for the short holiday break. I know I'll see her on Monday, but everything feels too fresh to be apart already. This past week has been bliss, meeting up on campus after classes for coffees and a dinner I cooked her. We even all hung out as a group last night, sharing a bottle of wine and watching movies well into the morning hours. We even found a few more times to fit in some quickies, when Quinn sank to her knees after I told her I sold most of the pieces from my exhibition, and when I gave her three wall-shaking orgasms in reward for when she modeled for me.

Even if she did leave me with a stellar blowjob, I miss her already.

The diner hasn't changed in the two years we've been going, or the fifty years before then. There's a funky neon boomerang pattern adorning the tables, straight from the 80's. The bright blue booths and barstools have been replaced since then, but most of them are still worn with time, their pleather ripped open and showing off a yellow foam inside.

The food is just as good as it's always been, and I don't understand why we stopped coming here, but I always did find solace in the quiet diner and the company of the owner. It became a safe haven for me when I had a bad day and needed a milkshake to make me feel better and was unable to ride my motorcycle. I could barely grip the straw in the cup after the accident and my hands were so weak that I was almost too embarrassed to leave the apartment at all.

A jukebox sits on the far side of the restaurant and I remember shoving loads of quarters into it and setting a queue so long that it had the other patrons moaning and groaning on Friday nights while Slate, Ace, and I sat in this very booth and had the time of our lives.

These days, I feel like I don't know a thing about what's going on in their free time. I don't know how they're doing in their classes; I don't know what grade Slate got on his sculpting project. I don't even know if Ace still works at the art supply store. He doesn't have to anyway, but it was nice to get some free erasers once in a while.

Slate doesn't seem to notice the tension keeping my shoulders rigid, glancing behind him at one of the waitresses ducking into the kitchen with a furrow to his brows. Ace's blue eyes are tinged with only the worry my emergency message could cause, and he hasn't touched his meal.

"What's going on, Knox?" Ace asks me.

"Is it about those noises we heard last night?" Slate tacks on, stuffing a bite of pancakes into his mouth.

I cough. Choke, really. I finally manage a sip of the hot coffee, but it only adds to the blush I can feel fighting its way onto my cheeks. Quinn hadn't been quiet last night, and I hadn't made her, partially because I enjoy the way she was screaming my name, and partially because I didn't realize that anyone was home.

"Slate," Ace scolds, elbowing him in the side. "I told you not to bring that up."

"Two whole fucking years since Knox has gotten laid and you want me *not* to bring it up?" Slate shoots back, glaring. "That's impossible. I'm only a man, Ace. I need details."

Ace rolls his eyes, shooting me an apologetic look. I shrug in response, biting back the smile threatening to appear at the thought of Quinn beneath me again, her nails scratching down my back as she begged me for more.

I shake that thought from my head before my cock wakes from its nap. I watch Ace too closely as he spears his fork into the fluffy eggs on his plate, looking expectantly at me for an answer as to why we're all here.

"I can, uh, go into detail later." I scratch my head awkwardly. *Not.* As much as I'd love to brag about finally getting a taste of Quinn, there's nothing official about us yet. We've slept together a few times, but we haven't talked much about it, too eager to please each other before we had to break apart for the few days off of class that we have. "But that's not why I asked you here."

Slate sighs dramatically and I'm confused for about all of

three seconds until he pulls out his wallet and slides a crisp twenty over to Ace.

At the look on my face, he says, "I thought this would be girl related."

"Sorry to disappoint," I answer, tracing the pattern on the table. My news is much worse than that. "My father came to visit me a few weeks ago and—"

"A few weeks ago?" Ace asks, and he looks hurt, like I've betrayed him. Slate's eyebrows knit, his chocolate eyes brewing with fury at the mention of Travis Foster. "And you didn't tell us?"

"It's not that big of a deal, Ace—" *Except that it is.*

"It *is* that big of a deal! What did he say?"

He almost explodes, and I feel bad about keeping this from them. I hadn't meant to, but nothing is confirmed and I thought he'd leave me alone after I refused to scope out the town for him. After that text a few days ago...well, we've all been so caught up with our own lives that I haven't worked up the nerve to tell them. I haven't even told Quinn yet, and my stomach clenches at the thought of that alone. I've had so many chances to talk to her about it since I received the text on Sunday morning and although my father's purchase of the building is not yet confirmed, it's only a matter of time before the deal is sealed. I can't make her upset with me so soon after I just got her to like me. I'm a selfish prick, and I know it.

Rhonda swings around to check in on the three of us and senses the tension immediately. I can see it in the way her eyes narrow and the wrinkles around her mouth deepen. I offer an apologetic look for all of the commotion.

"Are you boys doing all right over here?" She asks, brushing a strand of graying chestnut hair behind her ear. She stands closer to my side of the booth, a protective wall should I need her.

My chest warms at the sentiment.

Ace's heavy gaze hasn't left mine and Slate is occupied with something behind the counter, craning his neck around Rhonda to see.

"I need to put in an order for blueberry waffles," Ace says, "To go, please."

I deflate in my seat when Rhonda nods, walking away.

"What did he say?" Ace asks, voice low. "Why didn't you tell us?"

My chest twists at the way that he says it. I don't know how to tell them this. They're my best friends for fuck's sake and here I am, sitting in the booth across from them, twiddling my fucking thumbs because I'm too much of a coward to tell them that the rest of our college experience is going to be fucked because of my fucking father.

I decide that ripping the Band-Aid right off of might be my best move. "He's thinking about buying our apartment building."

At their utter silence, I'm starting to think that maybe that wasn't the right way to do this.

Surprisingly, it's Slate who takes hold of the conversation. "When those waffles come out, we're going to the store and getting ice cream, and then we're going home to talk about everything we've missed," he says, and I finally look up. They ordered waffles for *me?* Ace remembered? When I told him that my ultimate comfort food was blueberry waffles and ice cream when we'd gotten that misdemeanor for spray painting one of the buildings on the outskirts of town. We'd only gotten a fine and an escort back into the city, but it had spooked all three of us enough that our reign of spray painting started and ended all in one night. I thought my father would kill me when he was informed, and we found ourselves right in this very booth with enough waffles and ice cream to feed a small army. It turns out that Ace had called his father and pulled some strings so that mine never had to find out, and the incident was scrubbed from our records. "We're sorry you had to deal with that, Knox."

"I'm sorry, too," I admit. "For not telling you."

CHAPTER 25
QUINN

"Hey, dork," Sam huffs, and a second later there's a tiny basketball bouncing off of my head. I whip my chin up, glaring at my older brother who has already turned away, pretending like he didn't just throw something at me as he dramatically makes a shot from the line in the carpet we deemed three points when we were younger. The bright orange ball hits the rim of the mini basketball net hung above the basement closet door and he frowns as it bounces off and rolls away. "Why are you grinning at your phone like that?"

My cheeks burn and I duck my head again. Knox and I have been texting almost non-stop since Thanksgiving break started, and the conversation has somehow moved onto what I have his name saved as before we started sleeping together.

As if I've changed it at all yet. I quite like the contact name *douchewaffle* for him. It suits him well.

DOUCHEWAFFLE:

C'mon, Princess. Tell me.

> I don't think you want to know.

DOUCHEWAFFLE:

Is it really that bad?

> I'll be honest, it's not nice.

DOUCHEWAFFLE:

Is it something you need to be punished over?

I clench my thighs together where I sit on the couch, thankful that Sam's currently distracted by chasing the ball down so he doesn't see how red my cheeks are. I didn't know that Knox had this kind of mouth on him, but I am *very* much enjoying it.

"Oh, just something Rory said," I bluff. Sam sees right through it, narrowing his eyes at me. He looks like he's about to toss the ball at me again but if he does, I won't be so nice about it this time around, so he better watch it. I'm not above kicking his ass at Basement Basketball.

He hums in response, "I'm sure. And do her texts always make you look like a tomato?"

"No," I bite. "But she did say something about Peep being upset with you because you won't text her back."

Just as I suspected, Sam's eyes go wide, fumbling with the basketball as he rips his phone from his pocket. "What? No way, she can't be—*you little—*"

"*Mom,*" I call, grinning at the utter terror that fills my brother's eyes. "Sam's being a dickhead to me!"

"*Quinn,*" she snaps back, shouting down the stairs. I wince, and Sam sticks his tongue out at me. I've made one grave mistake while shouting for Katie Conroy to save the day: I called my brother a mean name. *"Do not* call your brother that!"

I groan, letting my head fall back against the couch. Sam snickers, bouncing the ball between his legs like he's some sort of professional. To me, he just looks like an idiot. I guess it doesn't matter how old you get or what you study, Basement Basketball is for life.

"He was about to call me something worse," I try to defend, swatting away the orange ball when it soars my way. It slaps off of my palm with a loud noise that makes both of us flinch. You do *not* want to be warned by Katie Conroy twice. I'd rather be hit in the head with the basketball again than face my mother's Thanksgiving wrath.

Luckily, the sound of the back door opening and closing signals my father's arrival home, and that should be enough to distract her from our misbehaving. My phone buzzes in my hand and I'm very careful about keeping my smile to myself this time around.

DOUCHEWAFFLE:

Because I'm not above that. I can be very creative, you know.

Stoppppp. You're going to get me in trouble!

DOUCHEWAFFLE:

How is that possible? I'm not even there.

I roll my eyes, furiously typing back.

Sam's wondering why I'm making faces at my phone. He threw a mini basketball at my head, so thanks a lot. I think I might be concussed.

I bite my lip to keep myself from grinning again as I

picture Knox's perfect jade green eyes rolling at my dramatics.

"Quinnie," Sam whines, dribbling the ball across the carpet. "Play one game with me before mom calls us up to help. If you win, I won't bring up whoever you're texting at Thanksgiving dinner. I'm sure grandma would *love* to know what's going on in your life."

I scrunch my nose at him, checking my phone one last time before I give in to his silly demands. I only have a few days left to spend with my family before I'm back on the plane to California, and I'm going to make the most of it, even if my brother can be annoying as hell sometimes.

> DOUCHEWAFFLE:
>
> How about I kiss it better when we get back, Princess?

> I'd rather you kiss a little something further south, but I'll take what I can get.

> DOUCHEWAFFLE:
>
> You can take whatever you want from me and I'll gladly let you have it, Quinn.

> Is that a promise?

> DOUCHEWAFFLE:
>
> Absolutely.

I shove my phone back into my pocket, cheeks and heart warm from Knox's texts. It's only been two days since I've seen him, but I'm already missing those gorgeous eyes, his rough hands hot against my skin. The apex of my thighs ache at the thought of taking exactly what I want from Knox when I get back, but I shake it from my mind, batting at Sam when he pretends to throw the ball at me again.

"And when I win, I'm going to tell everyone at Thanks-giving about you and Peep."

Sam's hazel eyes narrow, and he checks me the ball. "You wouldn't."

I grin, and it's not a nice one. I toss the ball back, a little harder than necessary as my competitive side flares to life. "Try me."

"So, Quinn, I hear your classes are going well," grandma Mavis says from her spot next to me, spreading butter on her roll. I wait for her to finish before politely asking for the knife and promptly chopping the head off of the butter-shaped turkey mom always gets for Thanksgiving. I ignore the disap-proving noise grandma makes because that was way too satis-fying. "What are you taking this year?"

I tuck that sucker's head right down the deep cut in my roll, warm in my hands. Sandwiching it back together, I stuff a bite into my mouth, almost moaning obnoxiously when I chew on the chunk of butter and the flavor explodes on my tongue.

I'm a butter fiend. It is the elite condiment.

Swallowing, I answer, "I'm taking Life Drawing, Art History, Creative Writing, and Critical Thinking."

"That's nice, dear," she compliments, and I heave a sigh of relief when she turns to talk to my grandfather, who doesn't care about what anyone is doing in their personal lives, just about how much turkey he can consume before grandma cuts him off.

"Your mother told me that you're the best in your drawing class," Aunt Gemma beams, and I want to roll my eyes.

Of course mom would say something like that. She only knows what I tell her, and while I am excelling in Drawing 201, I'm not the best in class. They don't know how I second guess every project before I turn it in, how I can't seem to stop obsessively nitpicking my work when I'm supposed to be critiquing my classmates. They don't know that I have the hardest time figuring out what to draw, that nothing gives me the drive to create what I want anymore, because I don't even know what it is that I want.

"It's hard to compare when everyone's style is so different," is what I go with, forcing a smile. "I have this friend, Reid, who's in my class and he's an architecture major. His drawings are so fun to look at because he adds little elements of things he's learned in his own classes. And Rory is quite excellent at drawing as well."

"Right, well, no one is as good as our little Quinnie," she grins, pinching my cheek. It hurts just as much as it did when I was a child. I laugh nervously, eyes flitting around the table, trying to find something to distract her with. I don't want to talk about my classes at all.

My gaze meets my brother's, who's laughing at something grandpa said. In a split decision, I decide that I'll have to turn the tables on him if I want to keep the attention away from school.

"Sam, anything to add?" I ask, sending my brother a pleading look. He appears smug from his spot next to dad, and I don't think he's going to be jumping in and volunteering for the hot seat right now. *Damn.*

Thankfully—and unknowingly—mom comes to my rescue. "Yes, Sammy, why don't you tell us about your time visiting Quinn at school?" She asks, and Sam glares at me. *Sorry,* I mouth, but I'm not at all. At least I didn't have to bring it up to distract them from my failures this semester. "Or should I say when you were visiting Pipa?"

He chokes on his drink, spluttering and pounding on his chest as he looks up at mom with a look of betrayal; dad stuffs a piece of turkey into his mouth, leaning over and slamming Sam on the back to help dislodge the liquid. I don't think that it's his water that's choking him, it's that now the entire family is chatting excitedly, shooting off questions at him like some sort of game show.

"Pipa? As in Pipa Wilson?" My aunt chirps, suddenly interested. "What's going on with you and her, Sammy? Are the two of you dating?"

"No," he gasps, like a fish out of water. I tuck into the mashed potatoes on my plate, hiding my grin behind a large mouthful of the creamy goodness. "Not officially, anyway," he grumbles, stabbing at his green beans.

The conversation throughout the room pitches higher with everyone asking for more details. Sam's face is redder than the cherry pie I helped mom make for dessert, trying to dip and dodge the questions as best he can.

I would totally help him out by admitting my almost failing Art History grade or the fact that I haven't felt any inspiration for drawing since I was a teenager, or how the neighbor I've been complaining about all semester is now something more, but Sam looks like he's doing a pretty good job at deflecting the questioning all on his own.

While everyone is distracted, I slip my phone from my pocket, peering down at it in my lap as I type two quick messages.

> I might've just outed Sam and Peep to the fam. They're still a thing, right?

> Quick. What's the best way to deflect
> attention?

The answers come in just as quickly as I send them.

> RO:
>
> I think so…Peep hasn't wanted to talk about
> it but I'm about to sick Aisling on her. Then,
> she'll really crack.

Aisling is Rory's oldest sister. She and Peep have always been closer, and I remember the amount of times Rory and I snuck around to hear them gossiping about high school things like boys and cars when we were still in middle school. She's hard-headed and confrontational, so if anyone can get information out of Peep, it's Aisling.

The other text follows promptly.

> DOUCHEWAFFLE:
>
> I don't know, I'm sitting at the kid's table.

Knox's response makes me grin. I can picture him, knees up to his shoulders as he squats at a children's table at Ace's home in Colorado, his plate of food much more colorful than all of the kids he's surrounded by. I wonder if Ace has also been ordered to the children's table or if they got themselves banished there.

I'm sure it's nothing like I'm picturing, but it's fun to imagine. I wonder if Mandy is there as well or if she stayed in New York for break.

As I'm about to answer the messages, I'm cut off by mom, scolding me.

"Quinn, no phones at the table. Put that away."

"Yes, ma'am," I salute, offering her an apologetic grin as I tuck it away. "I was just asking Rory what Peep had to say about all of this," I offer, innocently, and Sam looks like he just shit the bed.

Sucks to lose at Basement Basketball.

CHAPTER 26
QUINN

For the third time tonight, I catch myself bobbing my head and mouthing along to the lyrics of the song blaring through the walls instead of reading the words in the Art History textbook that I'm staring at.

Cursing, I toss my pencil into the crease of the book and lay my head in my hands. I've read the same page three times over but I haven't absorbed one ounce of information. It's something about art in ancient Rome and the different ways God figures are portrayed, I guess.

My phone buzzes from the spot next to me and I can't help the smile that grows at the sound. I declined an invite to another one of Slate's infamous parties because I have a test on Monday and I can't afford to fail. I barely passed the last one by the skin of my teeth, even with Odie's help. We haven't had a chance to meet up recently because of his hectic hockey schedule, so I'm on my own for this one. I'll be damned if I don't pass this class with anything less than a B.

Knox pestered me about my lack of presence at said party after Slate beat his own record for longest keg stand, but ultimately left me to focus on my schoolwork, or, as much as the half of my attention on the page can manage.

DOUCHEWAFFLE:

I can't believe you're studying right now. I can't even focus on my drawing. How are you doing it?

You've trained me well in the art of studying with loud backgrounds, don't you remember?

I quickly follow that message with a second.

I should've joined in on the fun instead. I'm going to fail Art History anyway. I could really use a shot right now.

His response pings my phone faster than Slate can turn anything sexual.

DOUCHEWAFFLE:

How about something else that might cheer you up? ;)

A puff of laughter chokes out. Checking the time in the corner of my screen, my smile falls and I want to groan. I've only been attempting to study for a little over an hour.

As mood improving as that might be, I really need to study. This sucks.

To garner some extra sympathy, I tack on a frowning emoji at the end.

DOUCHEWAFFLE:

It's not that hard, Princess.

It's a bold move to reply:

> Your dick? Or Art History?

But I hit send anyway.

DOUCHEWAFFLE:
> Both, but the pair can be remedied.

> Come over.

There's a sudden slamming of a bedroom door through the wall that startles me for a moment, before a grin overtakes my face. I'm in a fit of giggles, realizing how eager Knox is to escape his apartment and see me.

It kicks up an excited feeling in my stomach, butterflies taking flight in a swarm of giddiness. I'm just as excited as he is, shoving my chair back from my desk and bounding from my room to meet him at the door.

Soft light from the lamp in the corner of the living room washes the apartment in a warmth that feels like I'm cuddled up in the comfiest blanket. The rest of my home is dark and empty. Rory had popped her head into my room earlier, asking if I wanted to go to the party next door with her, but at that point in the night I was still determined to study, waving her on without me.

When I tug the door open, Knox barges inside, all but tackling me on the way. His hands find my hips like a magnet and I'm swept up in the heat of his body as it collides with mine. He walks me further into the apartment, kicking the door shut behind him.

"Hurry," he whispers, and his long strides are no match for my shorter legs. I feel like I'm tripping backwards, tangled up in him, but Knox holds me steady and firm, like a rock I've been missing from my life.

It's quite nice.

Knox reaches behind himself to lock the door before he's turning back to me and planting a teasing kiss to my forehead. I pout, wanting his lips on mine instead, and his eyes flicker with mischief. "Before Tye sees me."

I laugh, wrapping my arms around him. He's snug in his usual garb, a black t-shirt that clings to his body like a second skin, showing off the impressive tattoos on his arms. His jeans sit low on his hips, the waistband of his briefs calling my name. The fact that I know exactly what's beneath these clothes is as intoxicating as his blissful scent: nighttime and pine.

"Who's Tye?"

"Old friend," Knox huffs. "He was just arriving at the party. If he saw me, he would've wanted me to tap the keg with him and I'd much rather be here, tapping you, Princess."

I shove playfully at his chest but Knox catches my wrists and pulls me back into him for a proper kiss. I fall into it, relaxing against him and even pressing myself further into his body. His hands slide around my waist and over the curve of my ass where he grabs a handful, sighing in content against my lips.

Knox has been the perfect gentleman since the exhibition, and has even offered to walk me to my classes, though I suspect that has more to do with Reid than not wanting me to walk alone, even though I share most of my classes with Rory.

"Hi," I whisper bashfully when he pulls away. Seeing Knox these days never fails to make my heart race, especially when he rests his forehead against mine, like he doesn't want to be more than a few inches apart. Knox's jade eyes swim with happiness as his heated gaze bores into mine.

I can also feel just how happy he is against my stomach.

"Hey," he answers just as softly. "I missed you."

"It's only been a few hours, Knox," I remind him, but my chest flutters again because I missed him too. I allowed him to walk me home after my last class of the day but had drawn the line at the door that he pressed me up against, using that wicked mouth of his to try and convince me to let him inside. After a *thorough* minute of persuasion, he backed off, leaving me with a cheeky wink and my pussy screaming at me to call him back to finish what he started.

"Yeah, but dealing with Slate feels like a lifetime has gone by sometimes," he jokes, following me eagerly as I lead him through the apartment towards my room. It hits me that he hasn't properly been inside of the apartment before, only having seen it when he walked in on me on accident, because we're usually locked away in his bedroom, with that cloud-like mattress and all.

There will be time to give him a tour later. Right now, I want him in my room. Preferably, in my bed.

"What was he doing this time?" I ask, squealing when Knox pinches my ass, grinning dopily at me when I whirl around to glare at him.

"Sorry, Princess. I couldn't resist," Knox says innocently and I can't help but grin along with him. When the corners of his mouth pull up high, there's a crinkle around his glowing eyes that makes my heart skip a beat. He looks younger, sweeter with that look on his face. Knox is a very handsome man. "He was trying to get me to join in on the party. Think he was trying to rally some girls to play flip cup or something."

Knox frowns when he steps into my room, hearing just how loud the music is. I give him a knowing look and melt at the color that stains his cheeks as he ducks his head, trying to hide his smile from me.

Like I said, Douchewaffle.

309

"Sounds a lot more entertaining than Art History," I grumble, slumping back into the chair at my desk. My body warms as Knox comes to stand behind me, planting a hand beside my notes and resting his chin on top of my head so he can lean over to read my textbook.

"Catacombs," he comments, and I can feel the delicious rumble of his full-toned voice. It makes me shiver in my seat and I wonder if he notices my reaction, how I'm trying to stifle my body's desperate attempts to claw at him as his words wash over me, warmth settling between my thighs. "I remember this. Passed it with flying colors."

"Of course you would be good at it," I groan. Knox slips to my side, planting himself firmly on the edge of my desk. "You're good at everything." When his eyes gleam as he preens, I narrow my own. "Oh, shut up."

"Didn't even say anything, Princess," he muses. "If I help you out with Art History, will you be good for me too?"

I can't help the rush of arousal spilling into my veins like a shot of adrenaline. The way he's staring down at me through lowered lids, smirk turned into a face more serious, it's a taunt as much as it is an offer.

"You wish," I murmur back, because I don't trust my voice to be any louder. There's no heat behind my response because it's all trapped between my thighs that I'm clenching together as tight as a snare.

"I do," Knox responds, gaze fiery.

And, well, those catacombs will still be there tomorrow.

I allow Knox to pull me up from my chair into his chest. His hands find my hips while I wrap mine around his neck, admiring him. It's a soft moment backed by the buzzing bass of Slate's party but I couldn't be any happier right now, with Knox holding me like this in his arms.

Trailing my fingers down his chest, he watches me,

bright eyes never leaving mine as I swiftly slide my hands under the hem of his shirt. I can feel his dick hardening in his pants as I glide my fingers across his abdomen, reveling in the smooth skin of his stomach, dancing over the ridges of muscle.

His grip tightens on my hips but I urge him with a soft tug to take the shirt off. Reluctantly, he pries his hands away from me only long enough to rip the fabric over his shoulders and then they're back, pulling me closer than before.

I trace the line of his jaw and Knox allows me to drink my fill of him. My heart is beating just as fast as his, and with the way that he's looking down at me, all hot desire and burning need, I think I've found my inspiration for my next drawing.

Moving downwards, I follow the planes of his collarbones, fingering the whirling ink there, dark swirls like shadows. They expand up across his broad shoulders and Knox shivers when I lean in and flick my tongue against them.

His breath hitches as I take my time inspecting each and every single one of his tattoos like I haven't done this almost every time we've had sex. They're beautiful, intricate masterpieces, all of them. His dick strains against his pants, but I know he won't move until I'm done with this, allowing me to take my time with him.

Marked beneath the curling swirls are two cupids, bows fully loaded and ready to launch their arrows. On his arm, the tattoo of the female warrior I noticed at dinner, and her counterpart on his other bicep, stare at me.

"Who are they?" I ask softly, and his answer is just as quiet, not wanting to shatter the trance we both seem to find ourselves in.

"Nemesis. The Goddess of vengeance," Knox explains, and my chest stings with grief. He's smiling softly at me though, and tenderly tucking a piece of hair behind my ear.

He nods his head towards his other arm, the other warrior inked there. "That's Eleos, Goddess of forgiveness."

I can't help the urge to surge forward and kiss him. His tattoos serve as reminders of a life he once lived, one filled with rage and hurt, the actions his father and step-brother took against him. The vengeance he must have wanted and the forgiveness he sought after his accident.

Knox lifts me into his arms and my legs wind around his waist without having to think about it. He's kissing me just as passionately as I'm kissing him as he walks us towards my bed.

He places me down and follows me up onto it but I'm not done with my exploration yet. With a little coaxing, I find myself straddling him, pulling away from a dizzying kiss that leaves my mouth a mess of tingles and tasting like him.

There's an image of a winged man falling from the sky on the side of his ribcage. Each and every tattoo is more captivating than the last, and as I hover around the waistband of his pants, I take the moment to lean forward and lick a long stripe over the muscle lining his hips.

"Fuck," Knox curses, hips jolting at the movement. His hands smooth my hair from my face where it's falling with the angle I'm at. He wraps it around his fist and I almost whimper at the thought of him guiding my head while my mouth is full of his cock. "Princess," Knox warns, but the sound is choked. "I thought you were studying."

"I am," I answer breathlessly, unbuttoning his pants. Knox isn't doing a lot to help me focus on that work, and I won't be able to pay it any attention until I've tasted him, felt him like the piece of artwork he is. "I'm cashing in on my reward early."

He hums, helping me rid him of his pants and boxers. His

cock sticks out, thick and heavy. It's pink and leaking at the tip, ready for me to wrap my lips around.

I caress the inside of his thighs, right over where his scars are. Narrow patches of his skin have been grafted to reconstruct his hands after his accident. They're another beautiful addition to his skin, and I kiss over those too.

"You don't have to—" Knox's words dispel into a rough bark when I take him into my hand and lick his slit. The taste of him explodes on my tongue, just as heady and delightful as the rest of him. I know that I don't have to, but with a tug of my hand up his shaft while I suck the head of his cock into my mouth, his fingers tighten in my hair. I want this. I really *really* want this.

I swirl my tongue teasingly around his cock, jerking and twisting my hand down the length of him. On reflex, he tries to shove me further and I allow it, moaning lewdly around him when he hits the back of my throat.

I take him as far as I can, reveling in the noises he makes in response to my movements. When I suction my cheeks, I lave my tongue wet and wildly across his silky length, using my grip on his base to stroke him when I need to pull back for air.

I keep the crown of his cock in my mouth, panting around his girth as I stare up at Knox with wide eyes.

"Princess," he hisses when I twist my hand again. *"Fuck, baby,* need you to stop or I'm going to come."

God, do I want that. Before I can eagerly continue my ministrations, Knox is easing me away from his cock, tearing at my clothing. I'm distracted by the way that his hands desperately slide under the fabric of my shirt, and I'm trying to relieve myself of my clothing so that I can feel more of his touch across my skin.

"Come here, gorgeous," Knox pants, pressing my naked

body flush against his. I slant my mouth over his as I grind against him, my clit aching with need.

"Condom," I breathe between kisses. His hands smooth from my ass up my back and down again, guiding my hips to drag my weeping pussy against him.

"Pocket," he answers against my lips. I strain to reach over the side of the bed and am able to retrieve the condom with ease. I don't even take the time to scoff at him for stuffing three in there before coming over, clearly knowing exactly how this night was going to end.

I tear the corner of the foil off and pull the condom out, rolling it down his cock. Knox's green eyes are hot on my body as he pulls me in for another kiss, his hands caressing my jaw to keep me in place. I'm addicted to his lips, to the feeling of his body pressed up against mine.

His fingers trace me like I'm the finest, most expensive piece of art he's ever had the pleasure of touching. Like I'm going to crumble under the pressure of his hands.

Maybe when my orgasm hits me, I'll crumble, but for all of the right reasons.

The words roll effortlessly off of that devilish tongue of his, good for more than just taunting. "Sit on my cock, Quinn," Knox says, keeping me steady when I swing my leg over his hips, positioning myself right over him. I can feel the heat from where I'm hovering and my pussy drips in anticipation. "Come get your reward."

He doesn't have to tell me twice. Guiding the head of his cock against my center, I tease, brushing him through my wetness. The slick sound it makes has the both of us groaning, Knox's fingers tightening on my hips.

"No time to tease, Princess. You still have to get back to studying."

"You didn't seem all that concerned about my studying

when you were texting me all night," I counter, and before Knox can come back with a witty retort, I sink down on his cock.

Fuck. He fills me so perfectly, all the way to the brim. His cock is nestled so deeply into me that the breath is forced from my lungs. My fingers dig into his broad shoulders as I take the time to adjust to his size before giving a soft rock. Knox makes a choked noise at the motion.

When I'm able to pry my eyes back open and look down at him, he's already staring. His jade gaze is heavy and hot on my own and all of my unspoken questions are answered there, right at the surface.

I'm greedy with it, rolling my hips, grinding my clit against his pubic bone. Knox's words only encourage me further, and soon enough I'm emitting the filthiest noises as I ride him like I've never ridden anything in my life.

"That's it, Princess. Take it," Knox says, his hands sliding up my body to play with my breasts. He squeezes one, rolling my pebbled nipple between his thumb and forefinger, and surges forward to suck it into his mouth. He teethes over it and my head rolls back on my shoulders, fingers finding his hair and burying themselves into its silky softness.

I'm clinging to him like an animal, desperate and needy for an orgasm. I want his come, want him fucking it into me so hard that it leaks out around his girth because there's not enough room.

But the condom will prevent that.

Knox's large hands wrap around my waist, his palms dragging deliciously against my skin. He grips me hard, pulling me down onto his cock with more force and a moan bursts from my mouth when he shifts his hips, hitting an entirely new spot.

I arch into his chest, begging for more.

"Again!"

Knox listens, fucking right into the same spot that has me crying out like a banshee.

I writhe on top of him as much as I can with his iron grip around me, chasing the burning feeling that's quickly heightening.

The room is filled with noise: music from next door, my screaming, Knox's soft grunts as he plants his feet into the mattress and pistons his hips into mine, the hard slapping of our bodies clashing. My bed creaks at how hard we're going at it, but neither of us care about that or the fact that anyone can probably hear us if they listened hard enough.

It's a symphony of euphoria, and I'm loving every second of it.

I come with a cry that Knox desperately tries to swallow, forcing my chin down and pressing his lips against mine. It's dirty and hot, a clacking of teeth that would normally make me laugh but I'm too blissed out to care right now, gripping him tighter with both my hands and my pussy, urging him to come.

"Your body was made for me, Princess," Knox moans, hips stuttering as he releases. He follows that feeling with a few more sharp thrusts, before he's tugging me down to the bed.

I go slack against him, utterly blissed out from the amazing orgasm we shared. Our chests heave against one another and I revel in the feeling of Knox's hands stroking long lines down my sides and back up again, following the motion until either of us are able to string together coherent words again.

Slowly, Knox's body begins to relax under mine. He hasn't pulled out yet and there's this primal part of me that doesn't want him to. I'm enjoying the feeling of his cock inside of me, resting there all warm and perfect. If he weren't wearing a condom, he'd be trapping his come in me and I shiver at the thought alone.

Knox's grip around me tightens even though we're already body to body. His lips find mine, rewarding me with a sensual kiss.

"So good for me," he whispers. He shifts, his cock grazing my insides, and I whimper because I'm not all too sure I can go for another round so quickly, no matter how badly I might want to.

Knox shushes me softly, brushing the hair from my face so he can stroke soothing patterns against my cheek.

"That was incredible. A-plus," I sigh, shutting my eyes, more than content to lie here like this for the rest of the night.

But it seems like Knox hasn't forgotten what I'd been forcing myself to do before he arrived, because he says, "It was. Now, let's clean up and get you that A-plus for real."

CHAPTER 27
QUINN

"**S**o…" Rory trails off and my gaze finds hers in the mirror where I'm brushing on blush. My first date with Knox is tonight and I haven't been able to focus on anything all day. My stomach is a bundle of nerves. "You and Knox?"

"Yeah," I respond softly, trying to fight the smile that's tugging on my lips at the mere mention of his name, but I fail. Rory has known about Knox and I since a few days after Thanksgiving break when she came back to the apartment with Ace in tow, trying to get me to join them for breakfast. When Knox strolled out of my room shirtless, her jaw almost hit the floor in surprise. Rory was sputtering like a child while Ace helped her get her bearings, oceanic eyes glittering as he grinned at his roommate. "Knox and I."

Her eyebrows are furrowed, and I don't like that look. Swiveling in my chair to face her, I question: "Is that such a crazy concept? I feel like this sort of thing happens all the time."

"In movies," Slate pipes up, dreamily. He's sitting on my

bed next to Rory, having invited himself over an hour ago to hang out while I got ready for my date.

I eye him. "What are you doing here again, Slate? Shouldn't you be hyping Knox up or something?"

"Nah, he has Ace for that." He winks at Rory, who only raises her eyebrows in response. "I'm here because I'm seeing you off tonight."

"You're not my dad," I scoff, fishing around in my makeup bag for my mascara.

"But I'd let you call me daddy anytime, Quinnie," he jokes and I shake my head fondly at the brand of humor I've come to expect from Slate.

"I'm sure Knox is going to love to hear that you've been flirting with me again."

Slate hugs one of my pillows to his chest, flipping through a book that I left on the table beside my bed. I wonder if he'll find the page Knox bookmarked for me when he'd been flitting through it, telling me he slipped in a cheeky note for me to find along with the naughty passage.

"He knows what I'm about. If he feels threatened, that's on him. I can just remind him of all the times we used to—" The ringing of his phone thankfully cuts off his sentence and he slides it from his pocket, checking the caller before accepting, his entire demeanor changing as he answers with a quiet hello down the line.

Slate frowns at whatever is being said and I cock my head, watching intently. I share a look with Rory, who is as equally confused and concerned for our friend. I don't think I've ever seen Slate so serious, and with the way his body tenses, I wonder who it is.

"Yeah, I'm on my way," he says finally, hanging up and springing from my bed. He tosses the pillow at the head-board, striding towards the door with a concerning pull to his eyebrows that has Rory calling his name while he makes his way out.

"Everything okay, Slate?"

He startles, like he's completely forgotten that the both of us are here with him. Slate turns, scratching his nape. "I, uh— yeah, everything's fine. I have to go. I'll see you both later."

"So much for seeing me off," I comment when the door slams behind him.

Rory grins, sliding off my bed to join me at the mirror. "Don't worry, I'll be here to do that."

"Thanks," I laugh, capping the mascara and putting it away. Leaning back, I admire my makeup in the mirror. My heart picks up pace the longer I think about my upcoming date, so I try my best to distract myself by asking Rory about her love life. "How are things with Ace going?"

Rory sighs happily. "He's so great. I'm really glad we decided to move here this year, Quinn."

"Me too," I admit, grinning stupidly as we both break out in giggles. If someone would've asked me if I'd be going on a date with the neighbor I swore I'd never even be friends with, I would've laughed for ages. "Ro, will you help me pick out some jewelry?"

Knox told me to dress casually, something with jeans because he somehow convinced me to get back on his motor- cycle with him. Okay, so he didn't have to do much convincing when he was eating me out like a starving man, but I digress.

It's a sunny afternoon, no clouds in sight, and it eases me slightly that I won't have to ride it in the rain again, no matter how much I enjoyed being pressed up against him that night.

Now that we're somewhat of a thing, I'm free to press up against him whenever I want.

Naked, too.

"Here," she says, hooking a pendent around my neck. She clasps it for me and I can't help but stare at the green gem that sits at the base of my throat, glittering in the light. It looks good, like Knox's eyes captured in the stone.

"Is it weird to be nervous?" I ask her, fiddling with the pendant. "We've already had sex but I still feel all jittery."

"Being nervous is completely normal," Rory answers, squeezing my shoulders. They ease slightly under her comfort, pulling away from my ears as I take a deep breath. "You have to promise to tell me all about it when you get home."

"I will," I shoo her, playfully. "I promise."

Rory and I chat about light topics to keep my mind off of my nerves. She tells me about how excited she is for winter break and asks me my plans, as if we don't live four blocks away from each other back in Seattle. In return, I ask her if she knows any other information about Peep and Sam, but apparently, our older siblings are much sneakier than we thought, and we decide to do some major digging over the holidays.

A knock at the door sounds and my nerves skyrocket again. I smooth down my shirt as Rory rounds the corner to open the door, crossing her arms over her chest like a stern mother meeting her daughter's boyfriend for the first time.

I'm thankful that it's Rory and not actually my mom here right now.

I am *so* not ready for that interrogation yet.

Rory squeals when the door swings open to reveal Ace on the other side. I can't help but to deflate a little, hoping it was Knox. Ace is all smiles, sweeping Rory into his arms and guiding her back into the apartment with his hug.

My breath leaves my body at the sight of Knox standing behind him. I swear, he looks better and better every time I see him. He's effortlessly handsome, his black hair fingered through with gel even though he must know it's going to get mussed from his motorcycle helmet. His jade eyes gleam, crinkling at the corners with his smile when he catches my gaze.

He's dressed in a simple black t-shirt, his leather jacket tight over his broad shoulders. It's the same one he wrapped me up in that night we spent in the rain.

Of course, he also has black jeans on, because Knox doesn't know the definition of the word color.

I move to him like a moth to a flame, eagerly accepting the kiss he bends down to give me.

"You look amazing," he breathes against my lips before kissing me again. It's easy to lose myself in him, the warmth of his body and the taste of him on my tongue. His scent fills my nostrils and I love it, the perfect mixture of rain and pine. My heart drops between my thighs as I fist my fingers in his shirt and I'm certain where we're going to end up tonight.

"Thank you," I say when we're finally able to pull away from each other. Rory clearing her throat helped speed that along. "You look very handsome," I compliment, flattening his shirt just as an excuse to feel his chest.

"Are you ready to go?" He asks and I nod eagerly, turning to say goodbye to Ace and Rory. Ace's arms are wrapped around Rory's shoulders, and they're both grinning at us like fools.

"Where's Slate?" Ace asks, finally taking notice of their missing roommate. "I figured he'd be all up in Knox's business right now, playing the part."

Rory shrugs, answering. "We don't know. He got a phone call and left right after." Knox and Ace share a look that I can't read before Rory's continuing, slipping into Slate's role of overprotective friend. "Don't keep her out too late." She points a finger at Knox. He looks like he's trying his best to stop himself from rolling his eyes and I stifle my laugh in the crook of my arm.

"Yes, ma'am," he salutes. "See ya, Ace. Don't have sex too loud tonight. Or on the couch."

Ace is quick to respond, a witty retort rolling off the tip of his tongue. "Why? Is it your turn?"

Rory smacks his chest and I guide Knox from the apartment before she can have a go at Ace for the joke. I've heard worse from Slate, so the quip rolls off of my shoulders easily…but now all I can think about is fucking Knox on the couch.

"If we fuck on any couch, it's going to be yours," I comment as I step onto the elevator with him. Their couch is both bigger and comfier. I wouldn't let Knox suffer on our cheap navy futon that Rory and I got for a bargain.

"Fantasizing about fucking me on my couch, Princess?" Knox hums, his breath hot against the shell of my ear. The elevator feels almost stifling with the heat that simmers between us, his eyes glittering with interest. His hand is searing where he strokes my hip. "We can definitely make that fantasy come true. Do you have any others I should know about?"

"No," I answer all too quickly, and try not to think too hard about the intrigue that flares in his eyes. "How about you?" I counter as the elevator comes to a stop on the first floor, doors creaking open slowly.

I can feel his gaze on my face as he studies me, and he doesn't answer until we've left the building, Knox holding the door for me. "No," he answers, but I can tell he's lying.

It sparks my interest, and when I cut him a glance from the corner of my eye, he's smirking.

Two can play at this game, apparently.

Knox shrugs out of his jacket and I'm taken back to the night when he'd given me a ride home in the storm as he helps me into it, admiring me in the loved leather before he tugs me closer. The smell of him fills my senses, heady and strong and *mine*.

Well, not officially, but hopefully soon.

I'm plastered to his front and I've never felt this carefree, this happy before, especially when he dips his head down for one more kiss. My stomach flutters, and I'm about to drag him right back up those stairs when he pulls away, chuckling when I chase his lips.

Knox plucks one of the helmets strapped to the back of his motorcycle and helps me into it with soft promises of more kisses to follow.

I have to squeeze my thighs together when he shoves his own helmet over that dark hair of his. He looks hot as fuck standing there with his tattoos on display, peeking out from under the sleeves of his shirt. Said t-shirt clings tightly to his chest as if he's worn it only because he knows what it does to me, my ogle trailing appreciatively down the lines of his body to his tight waist.

"Earth to Princess," Knox calls, rapping his knuckles on the visor of my helmet. I startle from my daze, glaring up at him as my cheeks flush with the embarrassment of being caught. My only saving grace is that he can't see how red my face is because of the visor, but it also means that he can't see my scowl. The crinkles around his eyes and the shaking of his shoulders confirm that he knows exactly what face I'm making and is amused. "Are you ready to go?"

"Yes," I answer, but it's muffled slightly by the helmet. Knox swings onto his bike, holding out an arm for me to grab onto. Once I'm settled behind him, he takes my hands and pulls them firmly around his waist.

"Hold on tight," he reminds me, and my heart picks up pace at both the proximity of him and the fact that I've somehow allowed him to talk me back onto this thing. I clench my thighs around him, wiggling closer to make sure I've got a firm grip and he groans like a man shot. "You keep grinding up against me like that, Princess, and we're going to go right back upstairs to that couch."

That doesn't sound so bad, I think. I wouldn't have to endure a nerve-wracking ride on the motorcycle where all I'll be able to think about is how far my body might slide if I fall, and I would get to see Knox's dick.

As if sensing the direction of my thoughts, Knox takes off after a gentle tap to the back of my hand to alert me. I squeak softly despite the warning, squeezing my eyes shut as he pulls away from the building.

I'm pretty sure that Knox can feel the pounding of my heart against his back because at the first stop sign his hands come down to trace the length of my thighs, reassuring me with his touch. It helps me settle enough to crack my eyes open and distract myself by watching the houses pass us by.

At some point during the ride, I actually find myself enjoying it, muscles relaxing, yet my body stays pressed flush against Knox's. I enjoy the feeling of his warmth seeping through my front. I can understand how he feels so at ease like this, like a bat swooping through the night sky.

When we arrive a few towns over, Knox parks against a curb. It's an artsy looking place with murals covering the sides of brick buildings, colorful storefronts calling to me left and right. The road is bright from the streetlights and filled with laughter and a positive aura that stirs excitement in me, even more so when Knox takes my hand, intertwining our fingers.

"Are you okay?" He asks, a touch of concern laced in those eyes. "The ride wasn't too rough, was it?"

I shake my head, winking up at him. "I've had rougher."

Knox snorts, tugging me toward him for a hug that I easily fall into. My heart soars. I never expected someone as closed off as Knox to be so touchy once he's finally opened up, but it makes me feel special. I'm the only one that gets to see this side of him, because even on campus his scowls are his comfort zone with almost everyone except for me.

He guides me down the block with a hand on the base of my spine, ushering me down a set of stairs. The walls are filled with graffiti and I look around in wonder at the small lobby we're in, while Knox checks in with the young-looking boy behind the counter.

I'm squinting at the wall when he rejoins me, trying to discern the oddly shaped letters that are painted onto it. I have no idea what they're supposed to spell out, it's bright red coloring stark against the deep teal wall it's painted on.

"Here you go." Knox hands me a pair of coveralls and I scrunch my face in confusion. He has his own pair, dark gray, and in his free hand he holds two respirators.

"What's all this for?" I ask, examining the beige jumpsuit he's offered me. It's clean and fresh, so I won't complain.

"We're spray painting," Knox answers almost sheepishly. At his tentative tone, I peer up, nearly grinning at the look on his face. His cheeks are filled with warmth and I think this is the closest I've seen him to being bashful.

"We are?" I ask, an eagerness filling my bones. I know spray painting is something that Knox said he, Slate, and Ace have dabbled with, and I've always appreciated the creativity that goes into tagging buildings and trains. I even researched Banksy for one of my high school papers, finding the reasoning behind his works intriguing, but I've never tried the medium myself. "This is going to be so much fun!"

Knox's shoulders fall in relief. Smiling softly, he answers, "I think so, too."

"Where do you get your inspiration from?" I ask Knox, voice muffled through the mask as I watch him paint a long, black line down the wall. The fans in the room are loud, so I have to shout. I was nervous when we stepped inside our assigned studio, cans of spray paint already littering the floor. The walls were filled with intimidating artwork that I hardly had the heart to paint over, but now I'm most definitely enjoying myself.

Knox has been a reassurance from the get-go, explaining that everyone who books time here comes in knowing that whatever they paint is going to be gone when the next guest arrives, so there's no pressure, the only expectation is to have fun.

And it is fun, getting a feeling for the can in my hand, figuring out how hard to press, how far to hold it from the wall. Knox showed me a few techniques, guiding my hands in different motions to create perfect circles, to get the paint drips I was eyeing from someone else's work. The only complaint I have about this date is that the masks make it difficult to kiss Knox, who I've wanted to jump since he pressed his body up against mine when he showed me how to paint the funky letters, his free hand a solid weight on my hip.

I've been in awe of him all night, sneaking looks over my shoulder at what he's painting: a skeleton stallion with a skeleton warrior riding it, sword raised as if leading an army of the dead into war. He's skilled with many mediums and my heart aches as I wonder how it's possible that he hasn't been able to receive an apprenticeship yet.

Something tightens in my chest. The way that Knox draws, paints, tattoos…there's a confidence there that I'm envious of. Every line he makes seems so sure, so well laid like he can see the end result as he's working.

I yearn to feel like that.

"What do you mean?" He asks, beckoning me over to help him with his piece. I begin painting the skeleton horse's eyes a bright neon green, adding whispers of black shadows swimming from its nostrils.

I sigh, abandoning my can of paint and wiping the remnants of the pigment on my coveralls before taking my respirator off. "All this time I've known that I want to be in art, that I want to do something with it, but every time I make something, it never feels good enough. Like I'm not as proud of it as I should be. I don't have a style like you or Rory do, and if I do, I haven't figured it out yet."

Knox fully stops what he's doing to turn to me and I blush at the attention. He takes his own mask off before his hand comes to caress my jaw, tilting my chin to look at him. His eyes are soft with concern and there's a wrinkle between his brow that makes me want to reach up and smooth it out, suddenly embarrassed that I've brought this up during our perfectly good date.

"Is that how you feel?" He asks, and I shrug shyly. Maybe I shouldn't have said anything at all, but it's been something that eats at me day by day. "It sounds like you're missing a muse, Quinn."

I frown because of his words and the lack of his nickname for me that I've come to adore. "A what?"

"A muse," Knox repeats simply. "Something that inspires you."

Something that inspires you. I toss the words around in my head, thinking on it. Surely, I find things inspiring. I wrack my brain trying to come up with something, something that keeps me captivated, gives me the urge to put my pencils to my paper and create something beautiful, but there's nothing.

Well, nothing besides Knox, that is.

"I think that I used to have one," I admit, remembering my early days as an artist. "I loved drawing, always used to have my sketchpad and a pack of markers with me," I chuckle softly, sadly. "My parents used to encourage me a lot, enter me in competitions, and the more I won, the more pressure I felt to be perfect, like I couldn't make any mistakes. Eventually, drawing just felt like work, tedious and something that I had to force myself to do to impress others."

I don't know why I'm admitting all of this right now, in the middle of our date, but the words keep flowing and Knox doesn't stop me, taking my hand as he listens intently.

"I couldn't wait to go to college. I could finally escape from all that pressure and live my life, try and figure out what the hell I'm going to do. I thought that I'd find my love for drawing again once I had a break, but I haven't yet, and I'm scared, Knox, I'm so scared of losing the only part of me I know."

My eyes sting with unshed tears, and I refuse to let them fall because I've already soured the mood enough.

"Quinn," Knox says so softly I'm afraid that those tears might spill over anyway. "Princess, I had no idea you felt this way."

"Because I didn't tell anyone," I answer. "Not even Rory knows how I feel. I'm very stubborn."

His smile eases some of the tightness in my throat. "Don't I know it, baby."

Oh, that's new.

I like that.

"A muse, huh?" I ask, putting my mask back on as I attempt to lighten the sullen mood. Knox looks like he doesn't want to deter this conversation, but I want us to have a good rest of our night, and I think he realizes that because he follows with his own mask, then pats my ass. I can tell that he's smiling by the crinkles by his nose, but the sternness in his eyes tells me that this conversation is far from over. "So, you're telling me that you inspire yourself?" I tease, thinking back to his exhibition. "How very narcissistic of you, Knox."

He rolls his eyes and before I can continue my joking, he's lifting his can of spray paint and marking me with a big heart across the entire front of my coveralls. My mouth drops open in shock but his satisfied smirk makes my heart swell.

"I believe that muses have the ability to change," he answers around the mask, practically yelling. He's staring down at me so intently that it's making me a little nervous. Maybe he's waiting for me to pick up a can of paint and retaliate. Or maybe he's thinking exactly what I'm thinking: trying to find someplace nearby and private to tear each other's clothes off.

"Oh, yeah?" I ask defiantly. I want to cross my arms over my chest but I don't want to ruin his work. In a way, it feels like I've been branded by him, claimed by his artistic talent, and something hot flares within me at the very idea. "What's your muse now?"

Knox doesn't answer but he doesn't need to. The way he seems to be devouring me with his eyes tells me all I need to know about just what his current muse is.

CHAPTER 28
QUINN

"When are you going to ask me?" I ask Knox later, when we're back at my apartment and I'm climbing into his lap after tearing the clothes from his body.

He's distracted with the way I'm pressing open mouthed kisses to his bare chest and sliding my soaking pussy across his hard cock with a swirl of my hips, so it takes a minute for my words to settle. Those jade eyes flick away from where he's watching me grind down on him, his lids fluttering as he tries to focus on me. "What?"

I huff a laugh and his fingers tighten on my hips in warning. Again, I rock against him, our moans mixing together as I melt into his chest.

"When are you going to ask me to be your girlfriend?" I ask, cheeks burning with the question. Back at the spray painting place he had made it seem like I'm his muse, and if that's true, then that means I'm the one who gives him inspiration and drive to create art. I'll be damned if I'm doing all this work to inspire him and I don't even get the title of girlfriend.

His smirk only makes my cheeks flare hotter. Knox leans up, capturing my lips against his in a kiss that almost makes me forget the question I just blurted.

Almost.

"Impatient little thing," he says against my mouth, like he can't get enough of me. Knox bucks his hips and my breath catches, eyes rolling back at the feeling of his crown against my clit. His eyes are hot on me and it makes me want to shrink away, embarrassed about my outburst. "That what you want, Princess?"

I shrug, feeling shy all of a sudden. What if this isn't something he wants? What if it's just casual fun for him? My heart clenches at the thought, but before I can draw back, he's twisting his fingers into my hair and directing my gaze back to his. "If you want."

"Is this answer imperative to how the rest of the night goes?" He asks, reaching between us to rub his cock in a long stroke across my wet pussy. When I arch into him and try to throw my head back on my shoulders, his firm grip keeps me from doing so. Little does Knox know, I'm enjoying the slight burn I feel when my hair tugs with the movement.

There's a light in his eyes, and the way that he's unable to hide that smile, the one that has the corner of his mouth tugging up, has my shoulders relaxing, brings some of my fight back.

"I mean, I can go next door and—"

"Don't you fucking dare finish that sentence, Princess," Knox growls, grabbing my hips to roll us over. I squeal at the swift movement and suddenly I'm pressed into the mattress with Knox's looming form towering over me. His eyes are sharp with a possessiveness that makes my heart skip and my breath catch in my chest. My body tingles with electricity at his following words. "You're all fucking *mine.*"

It's my turn to grin wickedly, to tease him, because if there's anything about our relationship that's guaranteed, it's the teasing. It's always been us, and always *will* be us, the only difference now, is that I think I might be in love—

"If I'll have you, you mean," I nip at Knox's lips, distracting myself to avoid finishing that thought. I stretch, biting the smooth skin between his pectorals as I settle further into him, his warmth and the way that his hands haven't stopped moving along my skin since I pushed him into bed is intoxicating. "Which means that you'd have to ask me, first. See if I even want you back."

"Oh, but I know you do, Princess," Knox's voice takes on a low edge that makes me want to scream. I can feel it vibrating from his chest, pressed tightly against mine. His weight is comforting in the best way, and I'm reveling in it. "I know you want all of this to yourself."

He follows his words by nestling the head of his cock between my folds. I squirm, trying to get him to press further into me, but Knox holds strong, stilling my hips with his hands. My chest heaves with anticipation. I want him inside of me right fucking now, and I'm regretting taunting him already.

The keen that escapes when his mouth moves to my neck betrays my words. "S'not that special," I slur blissfully, craning my neck to give him more room. I can feel his laughter puffing against my skin and I rake my fingers down his arms when he finds that spot that makes me weak.

He hums like he believes me and the vibrations travel all the way down to my toes. Knox's fingers take a torturous path, brushing down the center of my body, slipping between us to tease my throbbing clit. The head of his condom covered cock breaches my entrance and I cling to him like he's the only thing keeping me connected to reality.

"How about I show you how special my cock is, and then I ask you to be my girlfriend?" Knox proposes, fingers scooping up some of my slick, using it to circle his motions faster.

"How about you ask me to be your girlfriend and then you show me how *not* special your cock is?" I counter, but I'll do just about anything to have him pressing all the way in.

"Fine," he relents. "But if I make you orgasm more than twice, you can't call my cock 'not special' ever again. You have to refer to it as 'the most special cock you've ever had the pleasure of coming on,' Princess. Oh, and that it's pretty, too."

Fuck, it really is pretty.

Before I can come up with a witty retort, Knox is pushing in, and the words are ripped from my throat as he works himself all the way into the hilt in one swift thrust. Immediately, my legs wind around his hips, holding him to me as we share a groan of pleasure.

We've been torturing each other.

"Kind of a mouthful, don't you think?" I pant when he begins moving. My fingers are buried deeply in his hair, and I use my leverage to pull his face down to mine, pressing my mouth against his in my own way of trying to distract him.

"More than a mouthful, Princess, as you well know." Knox smirks when we part, and I pinch his side. It's hard because he's all muscle but I manage, not that it affects him in the slightest. *Asshole.* "You want it? You're going to have to agree to my terms."

"Did you want a blood oath, or…" Knox pulls back and I whimper, my pussy clenching around him when his cock is just about to slip all of the way out of me. I scramble, heart pounding in my chest and my eyes flying wide, and I'm clawing down his back, begging to keep his cock stuffed inside of me. "Fine! *Fine.*"

Knox leans down, and the way that his cock plunges a centimeter further into my aching pussy has me gasping, moaning against his mouth when he rewards me with a kiss. I want to bite the smirk right off his lips but he tastes too good, and his tongue is swirling against mine, making me forget. "Was going to ask you to be my girlfriend anyway, Princess, even if you hadn't agreed."

Shifting my hips helps guide him deeper inside me, but it's not enough. I need him moving *now.* I need to feel his cock pistoning into me, stretching me out, shoving the air from my lungs and taking me like he's losing control of his body.

"Well, good for you, Knox," I whine, but he's still not moving. Dammit, has he always been so strong-willed? Quickly sifting through ideas, I realize all too fast that my only option really is giving him what he wants. Sighing, I peer up at him, glaring when I see his lip tucked between his teeth, his face all too amused at my desperation. "I'll take some of the most special cock I've ever had the pleasure of coming on," I grit. "Though that is yet to be determined."

My taunt does nothing to irk him into moving. Instead, Knox releases that lip, letting that wicked yet breath-taking smirk shine. His jade eyes are glittering. "You forgot pretty, Princess. It's pretty, too, isn't it?"

"Come on then, pretty," I whine, on the verge of screaming.

"I don't think so, I haven't held up my part of the bargain yet." His words are followed by him pressing himself the rest of the way inside of me, and I'm sure he's enjoying the way that the tension leaves my body when he's nestled to the hilt again. It's better, so much better being full of him like this, but Knox is still refusing to continue and my poor clit is about three seconds from shriveling up and falling off if she isn't granted the attention she's owed.

I want him to start moving, *need* him to start moving, but Knox has gone all serious suddenly, capturing my hands in his own and pinning them to the bed when I try to snake a hand between us to relieve myself.

"Will you be my girlfriend, Quinn?"

"Yes," I cry out, feeling so full that my heart could burst. He releases my hands as soon as I'm moving, dragging him down to me for a kiss that's hot and desperate and a little sloppy. "Yes, I'll be your girlfriend, Knox. Now, please move, baby, I need your cock."

Knox's gaze goes molten at my acceptance. He pulls his hips back and presses them forward again, finally giving me the friction we've both been desperately craving.

"Of course, Princess. Let's give you what you need."

Things slowly begin to enter a new normal.

I go to class, see my friends, and spend most nights with my boyfriend, licking, teasing, tasting each other on every available inch of skin we can find. The five of us hang out as a group and I've never been happier.

I'm even passing Art History, thanks to Knox's fool-proof system of studying: a sexual favor in exchange for every correct answer I give him when he quizzes me.

For the most part, everything seems like a dream. Compared to the beginning of the year, it is. There's still that nagging feeling of imposter syndrome inside of me that I just can't seem to get over, though.

As I sit in the art building working on my latest project for Beatrice's drawing class, I'm not entirely sure what to do. It's the last project of the semester, and I've started and restarted the drawing three times already, all of my attempted creativity fizzling out as quickly as it comes.

Currently, I'm on the cusp of tears. It's late and I'm frustrated. I don't like anything I'm putting down, and there is only a week until the semester ends. Even if I didn't turn this project in, I'd still pass the class, but that's not the point. It's not so much about the grade—which my parents and GPA might disagree with—but about the art, about the passion that I'm still trying to find for drawing.

It's not from lack of trying. I've been struggling to force myself to tap into my inner creative and find my muse, just like Knox said. I want to create something that I'm proud of, but there's nothing for my heart to grasp onto, no genius ideas that make me want to pour my soul onto the paper.

I'm starting to think I might have to give up art altogether.

Rory offered to tag along, but she finished her project fairly quickly after it was assigned, and things have been a little awkward with Reid since I told him about Knox and I.

Well, he found out, more like.

Naturally, the event occurred after one of our drawing classes. Knox had picked me up, looking glorious in the sun where he stood all leaned up against his parked motorcycle like a badass, sexy as hell in his leather jacket with his helmet hooked under his arm and a second one perched on the seat of his bike, waiting for me.

I can admit that I'm starting to enjoy riding his motor-cycle with him. He's even taken me to his favorite spot where he often goes to draw or think, escaping the stressors of life back on campus like his father pestering him and the apprenticeships he keeps interviewing for.

"Quinn, hold on a second," Reid said, stopping me with a hand from descending the stairs of the building to meet Knox. Rory continued downward after I gently waved her on, but I didn't miss the way that Knox's eyes narrowed.

"What's up, Reid?" I asked, although I already knew what he was wondering. It didn't take a genius to figure out whatever Knox and I started out as is now the complete opposite. He's no longer my infuriating neighbor, but something so much more than that.

"What's going on with him?" He asked, jerking his head to where Rory and Knox were talking quietly. The latter watched Reid and my interaction with intense eyes. "I thought you two didn't like each other, but now you're hanging out with him all of the time? Did I miss something?"

A pang of guilt gnawed at my stomach. I felt bad for not telling Reid about my new relationship with Knox, but I'd been wanting to tell him over coffee or lunch, and with the end of the semester projects and tests coming up, the both of us had been too busy to properly hang out.

My cheeks blazed and it was hard to look him in his eyes when he seemed so confused, so hurt. "Yeah, um, Knox and I are sort of dating now."

He frowned at me, and for the first time in our friendship, I felt like a terrible friend.

Reid frowned. "Sort of?"

"We are." I shook my head, answering him more solidly that time. "We're dating."

I didn't miss the betrayal that flashed through his eyes. "Why didn't you say anything?"

I sighed, kicking and digging the tip of my shoe into the concrete for something else to focus on. I didn't like the way that Reid was looking at me, like I was no longer his friend, which wasn't the case at all. If there was something more to our friendship, he hadn't made it known.

It seemed like Knox had enough, pushing up from his motorcycle to ascend the stairs. His strides were long, sure, and his spine lengthened with each step closer, his chest puffing bigger, his shoulders widening.

"Hey, Princess."

"Knox," I greeted with a nervous smile, accepting the way he tucked me into his side and pressed a kiss to my cheek. I felt them burn quickly with the blatant display of our relationship in front of Reid. "This is Reid," I spoke nervously. "Reid, this is Knox."

The two of them stared, sizing each other up. It made me shift on my feet and Knox's arm around my waist only tightened, showing me off, staking his claim.

It was awkward beyond belief, to say the least. Neither of them greeted each other and it was as if they had both been waiting for the other to break eye contact first so that the other could snap at their neck like a rabid dog. I shot a look towards Rory, but her head was buried in her phone, an enormous smile on her face, completely oblivious to the pissing contest that was happening right up the stairs.

A muscle ticked in Reid's jaw before he ripped his gaze away from Knox to settle back on mine. The caramel eye sharp and confused, the blue sad and untrusting. It made my chest ache, and my words twisted on my tongue. I wasn't able to get anything out before Reid abruptly said, "I have to go, actually, before I'm late. I'll see you around, Quinn."

"Reid," I called, but he'd already turned down the stairs and was brushing past Rory, whose eyebrows furrowed with concern at the sight of him. She tried to speak to him as well, but he brushed her off gently. When she shifted her bright azure eyes on me, confusion swimming in them like pools, I deflated into Knox's side.

I feel similar now to how I did then, defeated and glum. The piece of drawing paper before me is filled with the darkness from my charcoal, my fingers coated in the chalky substance, and the shapes I've been sketching stare back at me, taunting me, because no one is going to be able to finish this except for me.

It's a fairly simple task, to draw yourself as some sort of hybrid animal that represents our inner selves, but as I look in the mirror hanging to my left, I can't seem to figure out what kind of creature resonates with me.

Rory has drawn herself mixed with a dove, for peace and hope. Hope that she'd get over the heartbreak that Max left her with at the end of freshman year. Hope to find someone that would treat her better.

When I asked Ace, Slate, and Knox what they had done when they took this class last year, Ace had said that he drew himself with dragon features, Slate morphed himself with a grizzly bear, and Knox had drawn himself as a bat.

The last time I spoke to Reid before our friendship became strained, he'd been drawing half of his face as a fox, and I'd seen one of the other girls in our class, Wynter, I think her name is, drawing herself as a phoenix. Everyone seemed to light up with their ideas immediately when Beatrice had announced the final project, and I think I was the only one who ducked their head, unsure of what to do.

Voices down the hall startle me from my thoughts. I set my chalk down when I recognize the tenor, the laughter echoing around the silent building. Knox and Slate appear in the doorway to the classroom. Slate is splattered with clay from working on his own final sculpture of the year, something that he's been boasting about but refuses to tell any of us what it is, and the smile that lights Knox's face when our eyes connect is just perfect.

I didn't realize how tense my shoulders were, but the way that they fall at the sight of him makes me realize how exhausted I actually am. There isn't much time left until this project is due, and I'm sure to remind myself that once again: I need to focus.

But the way Knox's gaze drags down to where my hands are settled in my lap, coated in soot from the charcoal, flaring with an impossible heat that makes my stomach flip-flop and my thighs try to shut around the drawing horse I'm strad-dling, I'm forgetting the deadline and the project I've barely started.

I'd like to straddle him instead.

"Hey, Princess," Knox greets, leaning down to press a firm kiss to my mouth. My stomach explodes with butterflies and I can't help but to slant against him, my energy from my long night sapped with his softness.

His hand caresses my cheek and he frowns, concerned as he examines my exhausted and frustrated state.

My heart flutters at the warmth, at the care he shows me. How he isn't afraid to hide his hands from me because I've spent night after night showing him just how beautiful they are.

"Hi," I reply with a soft yet strained smile, turning to Slate next. "Hey, Slate."

"Hey, Quinnie. How's the art project coming along?"

I crumple, leaning further into Knox's warmth. "Not amazing, if I'm being honest."

Knox squeezes my shoulders gently and I'm reminded of the conversation that we never finished, of the one I don't want to finish, the one that I *can't* finish. I shouldn't have brought up my insecurities at all, but he'd been so brave in telling me his, and at the time it seemed like a good idea, until I chickened out.

I think I just accidentally reminded him of it, too.

He doesn't bring it up right now, which I'm thankful for. "What's wrong?" Knox asks, rubbing a soothing hand up and down my back. It feels good, like I could just melt right into his side and hide away for a while. "It looks like you have a solid start."

I crinkle my nose, examining the paper. It looks more abstract than anything, and I wonder for a moment if Knox is just being nice about it. I know him better than that, though, and he would never tease me about the craft so dear to both of our hearts.

"I don't know what I'm doing," I groan. "I've started over three times." All I want to do is throw my head in my hands but I don't want to get charcoal all over my face unless Knox is the one putting it there.

Maybe having sex will help get my creativity flowing?

Knox is silent for a moment, examining my work. I can see the cogs turning in his mind, how he might help me figure out what to draw for my project. Of course, I could easily draw any animal mixed with myself, but I really want this one to have meaning behind it.

"Why don't you take a breather and we can all grab something to eat?" Knox suggests. "A break might do you some good, and Slate and I were going to head over to Rhonda's."

A hot waffle and a large milkshake sounds absolutely superb right now.

I stare at the paper in front of me. I really should stay and put in a few more hours of work, but at the same time I can't stand to stare at it any longer.

A week. I still have a week.

"Yeah, I could use a snack," I agree, picking up my pencil

case from the floor and tossing my sticks into it. "Give me a few minutes to pack up." Standing from my drawing horse, I eye the mess of black on my hands and the clay flecked across Slate's exposed arms. "You should too, Slate. You're covered in clay."

He only grins and I—once again—regret saying anything to him. "The ladies like it dirty, Quinnie. But you already know a little something about that, don't you?"

I try to force the warmth from my cheeks when I think of just how thorough Knox had been the last time I modeled for him. How up close and personal he'd gotten with that stick of charcoal, how up close and personal he let me get with some edible paints I found online.

Sometimes, I love being an artist.

"Fuck off, Slate," Knox gripes, flipping my large sketchpad shut. He helps me pack my things while Slate snickers, and his eyes are hot when I rub my hands together, trying to dispel some of the dust from them. He slings my backpack over his shoulder and my sketchpad under his arm while I dart off to wash my hands at the mop sink before Knox can get any more ideas.

CHAPTER 29
QUINN

Rhonda's is...*bustling* for a Friday night.

Okay, so I've never had the pleasure of actually dropping into the restaurant before, but from the looks of the outside, neon lights busted or dead, a parking lot that is in desperate need of new asphalt, chipping graffiti tags on the side of the building, it's not one that I've ever really considered stopping at.

But, according to Knox and Slate, they have the best breakfast in town.

There are four other tables filled with rowdy college students just like ourselves, except we're not *that* loud.

They must be grabbing dinner before darting off to the row of clubs lining the next block over because it's still early enough that Rhonda's kitchen is open, and no one wants to be the first ones at the bars—that just screams lame.

I slide into the booth, my jeans gliding over the pleather seat as Knox follows me in. He presses our thighs together once he settles, handing me one of the menus stacked in the middle of the table.

I'm not sure I'll ever get used to this nice, *touchy* Knox, but I love it.

Slate takes up the other side of the booth, peering around the diner. I can hear the group of jocks in the corner as they joke about some of their classes that they have no intention of trying in. They seem to think that they'll be able to pass just by the graces of their athleticism, and I pray that they're wrong.

Two older men sit at the bar, chatting quietly. They're drinking milkshakes and sharing an order of fries and it makes my heart melt when their heads tip back laughing when the song on the jukebox switches from something the jocks must have put on to a classic.

The soothing melody along with the feeling of Knox's thigh against mine is settling, driving away some of the frustration I'd felt back at school where I'd been working on my drawing project. There's still that anxious feeling in the pit of my stomach, and I'm not sure how much food I'll be able to get down with the boulder of nerves taking up the space, but I'm willing to try.

The lights in the diner are low and I have to squint to see the menu. Rhonda's reminds me of the kind of place the locals love, and I suppose that everyone who walks in these doors already knows what they want anyway, so they don't need to be able to read the small print on the overstuffed pamphlet.

A disco ball spins in the center of the ceiling, casting colorful blocks of light across the words. I try to use it to my advantage, tilting the menu into the streaks for a better view.

It doesn't help.

"What are you getting?" I ask, leaning into Knox and peering down at his menu. It's the exact same as mine, but I have a feeling he's only pretending to look at it for my sake.

I'm sure that he and Slate have already known what they wanted since they found me in the drawing room.

"Blueberry waffles and a vanilla shake," he answers, and I carefully fold my lips between my teeth as I'm reminded of his contact name in my phone.

I should really change that one of these days.

Knox's green eyes firm with a knowing look. "What are you trying not to grin about, Princess?"

I shrug nonchalantly, straightening myself and hiding my smug smile behind my menu. "Nothing."

Knox hums like he doesn't believe me, nudging me with his shoulder. "Tell me."

"No," I almost squeal. I can't contain my grin now, shoving him back. "It's too embarrassing."

"More embarrassing than the way Slate is going to be panting over the waitress when she comes over here?" Knox asks, and I immediately turn my attention towards the counter, scouring the restaurant for whoever he's talking about. I've never known Slate to pant after any woman. They usually fall into his lap without complaint.

"Shut up, dick," Slate bites, eyes widening in warning. His body goes rigid, and he transforms from sitting tall, shoulders straight and broad, to shrinking in on himself, ducking his head and slouching in tight.

There's a waitress behind the bar, but she's looks older. Much older than us. She's chatting with the two men at the bar and it looks as if the three of them have been friends for ages. It's a little too dark to make out her features, but her dark hair is pinned at the back of her head, pencil jammed in the twist to keep it from falling.

"That one?" I question, nodding my head to show the direction of the woman I'm talking about. After all of these months of enduring Slate's teasing, it's finally time to take my shot. "I didn't know you liked them older, Slate."

He rolls his eyes, but Slate's always been better at dishing out jabs. The tension eases from his shoulders as he jibes, "I *love* them older, Quinnie." He winks and I wrinkle my nose in distaste.

I'm about to retort with some lame comment, but Ace and Rory are greeting us and I'm being guided further into the circular booth by Knox's hand at the small of my back to make room for the two of them.

When everyone's settled, I smile. It's a snug fit for the five of us, but the proximity to my friends helps draw me completely away from the feelings of undeniable imposter syndrome I was experiencing earlier. Looking around the table at each one of them, I feel warm, I feel whole.

Ace and Slate easily pick up conversation while Rory looks over her menu. Knox leans back into me, his voice gravelly and low. "Why were you laughing at my waffles?"

I huff a chuckle at him that chokes off into something more like a hum of pleasure when his large hand settles on my thigh, squeezing gently. His hand isn't just anywhere on my thigh, though, the tips of his fingers are curling into the soft skin between them, his pinky brushing the seam where the fabric of my pants is cinched over my crotch.

Warmth pools between my legs as if he's Pavloved my pussy into thinking that the simplest touch from him means an orgasm. I swallow hard, shooting him a look that he chooses to ignore in favor of tapping he menu on the table like he's deciding between two items. We're trapped in the middle of the bench seat, our friends flanking our sides. If Knox takes this too far, there's nowhere for me to go. I'll have to endure his torturous touches until someone lets me up.

Clamping my hand over his doesn't stop Knox from brushing his fingers across my leg. I press them tightly together, but all it does is trap Knox's hand there. I don't even have to look at him to know that my boyfriend is smirking.

Douchewaffle.

"Your name in my phone might have something to do with waffles," I say, and my voice sounds breathy. Luckily, Ace and Slate are fully engrossed in explaining all of the best items on the menu to Rory. "I thought it was funny."

Knox's brows furrow. "What's my name in your phone?"

I shake my head, refusing to answer when he squeezes the meat of my thigh.

I almost melt into him right there.

Heat creeps into my cheeks, and I'm thankful that the lighting is low because I know they're painted bright red. "Douchewaffle. Your name in my phone is Douchewaffle."

"Douchewaffle? Really?" Knox asks, quirking an unimpressed brow.

I can't help but to giggle in response, which it only earns me another teasing pinch that has my nipples perking up beneath my shirt and my breath hitching in my chest.

With the way that Knox is looking down at me, eyes sparkling with a devilish delight, he knows exactly what he's doing to me.

"What?" I ask, as innocently as I can muster when he's making me feel so scandalous. "Do you think I should add a heart or something?"

He doesn't take the bait, instead, leaning even closer to me. His breath caresses my ear, every stroke of his hand driving me closer and closer to swinging my leg over his lap and straddling him right here in the booth with all of our friends.

"I think you should change it to 'the most special cock you've ever had the pleasure of coming on.'"

"I think there's a character limit," I exhale harshly, and for some reason, I can't stop looking at his lips.

His tongue darts out to wet them. To tease me.

"Oh, Quinn," he whispers, and when he says my name like that, it makes me shudder with pleasure. My eyelashes flutter with the sensation that zips down my back. "You've never been one to complain about length."

I bark out a sharp laugh that has the other three looking our way. I'm sure it wasn't Knox's intended reaction, but he smiles easily, drawing away only slightly so our friends don't figure out what's going on behind our menus. His eyes are still hot on mine, and I know that I'm going to be in for it later tonight.

"Hi there," a cheerful voice greets, the waitress interrupts us before Knox can continue his incessant teasing.

She's pretty, young and youthful, full of happiness. Her bright orange hair is in unruly circlets, barely tamed by the claw clip it's slowly falling out of. It works for her, though, and stands out starkly against her dark uniform and bright eyes.

"I'm Isla, and I'll be your waitress tonight. What can I get you all started to—" Her light tone drops and her smile falls when her eyes meet Slates. She's quick to recover, I'll give her that, clearing her throat and looking pointedly down at the notepad in her hands. "Do you know what you want to order or do we still need some time here?"

I almost rear back in my seat from the sudden change in her tone. It seems forced, and she's chewing on her lip nervously, like it's taking all of her self-control to not sprint out of here.

It only takes one glance at Slate to understand what I'm

seeing, because he's slipped down in his seat and is hanging his head like a scolded child.

"A few more minutes would be great," Knox pipes up, trying to ease her discomfort with a soft smile. "Thanks, Isla."

She nods and skitters away. I hope that she can't feel all of our gazes on her back and she descends into the kitchen like a dog is nipping at her heels, but none of us can seem to pry our gazes away until the door swings shut behind her, then we're all whipping our heads around to stare at Slate.

"What was that all about?" Rory asks, breaking the uncomfortable silence first.

"Nothing," Slate answers all too quickly, and the rest of us share glances.

It's obvious that something has happened between Slate and the waitress, but he's never acted like this in the presence of one of his flings before. Perhaps she was a failed conquest, one that saw through his playboy act. He's fucked so many girls that I didn't even know it was capable for him to feel bad about any of them, unless something really went wrong in the bedroom that time.

"What? You forget her name or something?" Ace jokes. Rory scolds him but Slate ignores them, turning one of the harshest glares—one of the *only* glares—I've ever seen him make on Knox.

Knox's hand on my thigh tenses and even I flinch a little under that look Slate's throwing his way. "I thought you said she wasn't working tonight," Slate grumbles, sinking even lower in his seat. He resembles a kicked puppy, and it's so unlike him that I'm feeling concerned on his behalf.

Knox only shrugs, wrapping his arm around my shoulder and drawing me against his side. "I didn't think that she was."

"Fucking douchewaffle," Slate mutters, and I hide my grin in Knox's shoulder.

After Slate has eaten his bodyweight in pancakes, we head over to one of the bars only a block away. It's packed with people, which Slate preferred when we offered to go to a less popular bar or even when we offered to all go back to the apartments and drink the rest of the night away.

It seems like he's more than ready to forget about whatever the fuck happened back at Rhonda's.

The air is hot with bodies and laughter. As we make our way through the throng of people, I'm glad that Knox talked me into a pit stop at the apartment so that I could put my things away before we went for our late dinner.

My hand is tucked tightly into his as we shove through the crowd to the dance floor. Rory is leading the charge, tugging on my other hand while Ace had gone off after Slate to apologize and make sure he's getting everyone drinks and not just himself.

Knox isn't usually one for parties, and I'm worried that he'll be uncomfortable here, especially as Rory draws us into the center of the crowd. Peering over my shoulder, I'm pleasantly surprised to find Knox easing his way through the dance-floor, shoulders lax as the clubby music washes over us. It's bass heavy, which isn't unlike the music I've heard him listen to through the wall, but I know that he prefers hard riffs and lyrics that are screamed so loud it makes my eardrums rattle.

He tosses me a smile that he only reserves for me.

I can feel his gaze on me while I dance with Rory, letting

the beat of the music wash over me, drawing the rest of my unease away. I know I'll have to face my project again tomorrow, but for now, I revel in the feeling of being free, being with all of my friends.

Ace hands Knox and I drinks when he returns. I take a sip of mine and hum in approval. It's something fruity and I can barely taste the alcohol, which means it's dangerous. Delicious. There is no Slate in sight and Ace shrugs, pulling Rory into his side when he shouts that he's still by the bar, taking shots with a group of girls that stopped him.

I roll my eyes because that is very much like Slate. Knox pulls me into his front, plastering his broad body up against mine. His free hand slides around my waist, pinning me to him in a possessive way, and when I peek up over my shoulder, I catch him glaring at a guy a few feet away, whose face drops when they flicker down to the way that Knox is holding me and then back up again.

I can't help the giddy feeling that erupts in my stomach and I use the brim of my cup to hide my grin when the boy turns away and slithers back through the crowd with his tail tucked between his legs.

I roll my hips with the rhythm, my ass brushing up against Knox's front where I can feel the beginnings of his interest against my hind. His grip on me tightens, tugging me even closer and steadying me against his chest when I stumble.

"Falling for me hard there, Princess?" Knox teases, his thumb slipping underneath the hem of my shirt to trace my skin. A shiver zips up my spine despite the heat of the bar and I lean into him, relaxing against his strong body.

I ignore his jibe but can't ignore the way his cock is jabbing my backside. I roll my lip between my teeth, biting back the moan that threatens to slip from them. We only just arrived and Knox is acting like he's ready to drag me right the hell out of here and all I've done is wiggled my hips a little.

Sometimes, he's too easy.

"Think Slate is coming back?" I ask over my shoulder, trying to distract myself from the wetness gathering between my legs when Knox subtlety rubs against me again. His hand at my waist has gone from a soft swipe of his thumb to his palm flat against my stomach, the tips of his fingers trying to wedge themselves into the waistband of my panties.

I squeal at the sudden abruptness of Knox spinning me around. My drink sloshes over the brim of my cup and down my arm as I stare up at him wide eyed and confused.

The song changes, melting effortlessly into the next one. It's quicker, sexier, or maybe I'm just thinking that because Knox is gluing our bodies back together, his hips circling, his large hand guiding mine in a slow grind.

His eyes are all pupil and he uses the curve of his knuckle to close my dropped jaw, the other wrapped firmly around me again, keeping my hips pinned to his as we dance to the music.

Knox's breath is hot as he nips my earlobe before whispering, "I don't want to hear another man's name come out of your mouth right now." He rubs his cock against me with intention; I gasp and he smirks. "Now, close that pretty mouth of yours before I shove my cock in it."

My head falls back on my shoulders at the thought of that perfect cock of his pressing into my throat, pushing the air from my lungs, praising me as I take him all the way to the hilt.

It's all I can do to keep the moan from creeping up my throat, but the music helps drown it out.

"Knox." I mean to scold, but it comes out like a whimper.

Fuck, I've only had two sips of this drink and I know it's not already going to my head. It's Knox. He's my undoing, what I thought I'd never find. I've had boyfriends before, and hopes to find one that treats me like he does, that supports me and learns with me and adores me like he does.

He doesn't even have to touch me. He could just look at me with those big green eyes and I'd melt for him. I wrap my arms around his neck as we lose the night in each other, his forehead pressed against mine, his breath a soft pant against my lips.

My nipples tighten beneath the fabric of my shirt and I know he feels them pressing against his chest from the way that his eyes gleam, the way that his tongue darts out to wet his lips. He looks like he's still hungry, and I'm his next meal.

I fucking love it.

I lose all sense of our surroundings as we grind against each other in the middle of this dance-floor with the lights beating down on us and the music drowning out the noises he keeps drawing from my lips. As far as I'm concerned, we're alone, his body pressed up against mine in the midnight hours, like we're meant to be.

"What do you want, Princess?" Knox asks me, staring down at me intently. He towers over me, and I love the way he's holding me so tightly, like I might just slip away at the stroke of midnight.

"You," I answer immediately, because there's no need to think about it. There's no other answer. I want him at all hours of the day, throughout the night. When neither of us can sleep and we're curled around each other, whispering into the dark like it's our safe haven. I want him and his shaky hands, the ones that make *me* tremble. I want his dark hair and broody nature, the way he only opens up for those closest to him.

"Do you know what I want?" He asks, voice throaty and

low. I wouldn't be able to pick it up over the music if he weren't right in my ear.

"Me?" I guess, and his laugh makes my heart soar.

"Yes," Knox chuckles, nipping the shell of my ear playfully. "But do you know what I want to do to you?"

Fuck, I might just come right here in the middle of this dance-floor like some whore. The way we're grinding up against each other like a couple of horny college students, which we are. Like our friends aren't in the same bar as us, like there aren't other people watching us.

Someone bumps into us and my drink sloshes over the rim of my glass again. Knox straightens to glower at whoever it was, but the iciness of my drink sobers me a little. Enough to have a witty reply on the tip of my tongue when he steps back into our bubble.

"Draw me like one of your French girls?" I ask, fluttering my lashes up at him.

Knox smirks and my knees go weak. The threat in his eyes makes me vibrate with pleasure.

"First, I want to take you home," he says, and his hand strokes a long line from the base of my back up my spine, his fingers fisting my hair at my nape. My fingers scrabble against his shirt, almost tearing into the fabric as he directs my head the way that he wants, his lips trailing a teasing line up the column of my throat.

I'm fucking *dripping.*

"Then—" Knox's breath is so hot against my skin that I can barely even focus on the words that are coming out of his mouth. All I can feel are his fingers tangled in my hair, his lips on my skin, and his cock grinding into my stomach. "I'm going to strip you of all of these clothes—" His other hand grabs a handful of my ass and I didn't even realize that his drink has disappeared from his grip until now.

The thought doesn't last long, because Knox is still talking, still trying to ruin me with words alone.

And I think he might just be able to.

"And I'm going to ask you to ride me, Princess. I want that tight, drenched pussy on my cock as you take what you want, everything that you want, because you're my needy girl, Quinn, aren't you?"

The sound of my name on his lips has me rolling my hips faster, grinding on him harder.

"Yes!" My nails rake down the back of his shirt.

"And when you're coming on my cock, squeezing me tight, I want you to—"

"Your drinks," Slate says gruffly, interrupting *everything*. I've never been so frustrated, so horny as I am when he shoves an arm between us, effectively breaking us apart.

I don't think my glare has anything on Knox's, but Slate doesn't seem to care at all, shoving a drink into my empty hand before doing the same to Knox. Now I have two, but my first one is almost empty, having spilled more of it than I actually drank.

I can't miss the way Knox is adjusting himself, shooting me an apologetic look before turning those daggers back on his best friend. I gulp down as much air as I can but it's humid and gets stuck in my throat.

"Thanks," I answer, dazed. Slate doesn't look any less calm from the shot—or *shots?*—he'd taken at the bar. His brows are pulled tightly together and there's a scowl on his lips that doesn't go away when he takes a swig from his own drink.

Knox seems to realize the mood his roommate is in, and although he gently maneuvers his way back to me, pressing a reassuring hand at the base of my back, his confused attention stays on Slate.

"You okay, man?" He asks, cautiously. I don't think he's ever seen Slate like this either.

"Fucking dandy," Slate grunts in response, eyes grazing down to where Knox's hand is, to how he's standing slightly in front of me. I think I see Slate's lip curl in response but he's quickly bringing his drink to his mouth, glaring at us all the way, while he empties the contents of it in a few large gulps.

Knox stiffens beside me.

What the hell is going on with him?

Before either of us has a chance to ask, Rory's pushing through the crowd, towing Ace behind her. A girl makes a face as she passes by but Rory doesn't seem to notice, eyes red-rimmed in a way that makes me start surging toward her and abandoning the boys behind me.

What the fuck did I miss while I was completely consumed by Knox?

"Ro, what happened? Are you okay?"

She shakes her head, giving me a sad smile. She's clutching onto Ace like he's a lifeline, wrapping one arm around me when I hug the daylights—nightlights?—out of her. "I'm okay, just ran into a little trouble."

My heart sinks. She doesn't need to elaborate for me to know she's talking about her douche of an ex, Max.

"Where is he?" I ask frantically, rolling onto my tiptoes to peer around the bar. It doesn't help much, and I can't see through the mass of bodies surrounding us, but when I find him, I'll—

"Already taken care of, Quinnie," Ace answers a little too smugly for Rory's liking, if the gentle elbow she hits him in the side with is any clue. I can't help but grin along with him, thankful that he was able to help her out while I was lost in the feeling of Knox's body pressed up against mine.

357

Glancing over my shoulder to check in with him, I find him avoiding my gaze, but not on purpose. He's staring at Slate still, who refuses to meet any of our eyes, glaring around the room like all of these people are his own personal enemies.

"We're going home," Rory tells me, shifting wearily on her feet when she picks up the tension swirling around our group. She looks just as worried about Slate as I feel, but he refuses to acknowledge any of us. When she shoots me a questioning glance, her ocean eyes still glossy, I shake my head.

I have no idea, either.

"We'll join you," I answer, reaching my hand back for Knox's. He immediately attaches and twines our fingers together. I gently thumb over one of the ridges of his scars and he squeezes back. The moment we had only a few minutes ago was ruined, but I think we might still be able to make up for it, as long as nothing else goes wrong tonight.

"You coming, man?" Ace asks, clapping Slate on the shoulder.

All Slate does is hunch further, shrugging Ace's hand off.

Something has grabbed his attention, and he doesn't look happy about it, tossing over his shoulder, "No, I don't think I will."

We stare after him, shocked. He's already disappeared into the crowd. Well, as much as any six-foot-five man can disappear. But the boys can see better than me so I'm sure they're catching where he's off to.

"What's his problem?" Rory asks, rubbing at her red eyes. It makes me ache for my best friend.

I hate Max.

Knox shakes his head, tugging me in the opposite direction, towards the door. "Not a fucking clue."

CHAPTER 30
KNOX

Quinn falls into my bed with a breathy gasp that I eat up as I follow, prowling towards her.

She's scrambling to the headboard but reaches forward, not letting our lips part from the searing kiss we share. Like she can't get enough of me. Like we didn't annoy the fuck out of each other months ago.

And *fuck,* the way my name rolls off her tongue, all needy and hot—it's not filled with hatred anymore. Now, it's a heady whine that makes my cock harder than stone. I might just crumble under her touch like a delicate piece of charcoal, and I'd let it happen, too, all to hear those pretty moans, taste those pretty lips, touch that pretty skin, soft as silk.

I want to be wrapped all around her, embedded in her skin like the chalky substance I hold so dearly. I want to ink her skin with my touch, with my come—

Quinn's nails graze down the length of my back when I settle my weight against her. A shiver drags down my spine as a fleeting thought flashes through my mind: one of her, naked and sitting on my cock, her fingers wrapped around my tattoo gun as she presses it against my skin, marking me as hers.

I'll teach her how to hold it, and let her have free reign with it, because anything that she gives me, I want. I want her glares and her harrumphs, her curses and her arms crossed over her chest, her quips and her quivers.

I squeeze my eyes shut, trying not to burst from that visual alone. If anything, I can't wait to coat her virgin skin in my ink. There is so much canvas for me to work with, all smooth and perfect, practically begging for a tattoo or two.

But more than that, I want Quinn's smiles, the laughter that sounds better than any song or sound I've ever heard. I want those lavish hazel eyes on me at all times, her hands on my skin, gently tracing my scars as if they will tear open at the seams. I want those drawings of me she's been hiding, and I want to model for her. I want to be her muse. The very thing that she's obsessed with and can never get enough of.

She's already that for me.

I want to take away her fear, the anxious look she gets when she's drawing. I can tell that she loves it with all of her heart and that she's struggling. It's something that I've been meaning to bring up, but haven't found the time. The semester is almost over, and in a few weeks, the both of us will be in different states for the holidays. She deserves to know that she's not alone, that I feel similarly with the apprenticeships that have gone nowhere.

I need to tell Quinn that I don't think my dream of becoming a tattoo artist is feasible anymore. How I've stayed up many late nights, thinking over it all. Every interview. Every piece I've given since the accident. My hands shake too goddamn much to tattoo, but not to draw, something I've always loved doing, and still do. I can make a living off of it,

I know this because of the exhibition. People enjoy my art. *Quinn* enjoys my art.

And I don't think anything other than that matters to me anymore.

Quinn grinds her hips up into mine and I revel in the way that she takes what she wants, tells me what she needs without words, how her body rolls up into mine, demanding my attention.

I've been a fucking fool all this time. A goddamn fucking fool. I could've had her like this, milking my cock dry, making these sounds that threaten to tear down the walls. I could've had my hands all over her, because she seems to like the way that I'm touching her, even with how shaky and scarred they are.

Quinn makes me feel like they're not. Like there's not a single thing wrong with me. Like my hands aren't a fucking mess most of the time. Like I'm not still riddled with nightmares of my accident. Like my father isn't prowling around campus like a fucking bloodhound, trying to buy this building, reminding me that I'll never be able to get away from him, no matter where I go or what I do.

I touch her everywhere I can, slipping beneath her t-shirt because the need to feel her is a fervent one that I can't contain. I hum into Quinn's mouth, her warm skin against mine. It burns across my scars but she feels too good to stop.

Slipping my fingers around her back, I unclasp her bra, parting my mouth from hers with a harsh breath. Quinn's quick to turn her head away from me when I graze my teeth across her jaw, offering me more room to work. The ease in which she opens up for me makes my cock twitch and I groan as I rut against her.

I shove up the hem of her shirt and her bra under her chin.

I could let her sit up and slip the garments away, but I'm too focused of the taste of her skin on my tongue, the sweet scent of her filling my lungs with each pull of air I take. She smells like summer, fresh linen swinging with the easy breeze. There's a hint of fruit, like pineapples or kiwis.

She's the perfect taste.

Reaching my intended destination, I mouth across her breasts, avoiding her pert nipples, just to tease her a little more. As much as I want to rush through this, I also want to draw it out, to make it last, because I've never been as happy as I've been with Quinn in my arms.

The way her fingers scrape against my scalp in frustration is amusing. I hide my smirk against her skin, enjoying the impatient whimper she releases when she tries to grind against me and I pull away completely.

"Knox." She's breathless, just like she'd be if my cock were in her mouth right now.

I pick a spot close enough to the rosy peak of her breast but far enough to torture her a few moments longer, sucking harshly to leave a mark. I hum and she squirms.

"Yes, Princess?" I ask, plastering on my most innocent face. My Quinnie sees right through it because she's glaring at me, eyes narrowed, pupils wide.

Her chest heaves as she tries her best to catch her breath. I bet I'm making that difficult by the way each of my exhales breeze over the wet mark I just licked into her skin.

"Please," she swallows harshly, begging. "Touch me."

Something inside of me roars to accept her soft-spoken request, but I resist.

I have plans for my girl.

Instead, I lave my tongue over her pebbled nipple, reveling in the keen she releases as her head falls back onto the pillows.

My free hand works around the other, tweaking, pinching, twisting it in time with what I'm doing with my mouth, licking, nipping, sucking.

Quinn seems to be enjoying it, by the noises she makes, and I'm enjoying her enjoyment.

She's fucking amazing.

I've not nearly had enough of my fill when Quinn begins getting restless again, hands planted on my shoulders as she tries to push me down her body.

Greedy little thing.

I *suppose* I can grant her this one demand.

"No," she whines when I pull back, lifting myself back onto my knees so I can stare down at her like the beautiful piece of artwork that she is.

All mine.

"Take your shirt off, Princess."

"Only if you do too," she barters, and I nod, following her lead.

Those deep eyes, my new favorite color, drink in every inch of my body. She looks like a huntress, locked on her prey, pupils dilated, her tongue darting out to dampen those sweet, swollen lips. The intense look sends electricity zipping down my spine, right to my core.

I'm honored to be her next meal.

And I analyze her in too, all curves, all woman. Every time she's laid bare before me, the need to study her grows tenfold. I want to trace her skin, first with my eyes, then with my hands, and again with my mouth.

"Perfect," I breathe, because I can't help myself. I can't stop it, these feelings rushing through my body, nor do I want to.

I swear I can feel the heat of her blush from all the way up here. There's no need for her to be bashful about what I've just admitted, she's beautiful and she needs to see that, or I'll just have to make her.

Quinn takes my hand, tenderly drawing it up to her lips and placing a soft kiss against one of my scars. Goosebumps break out across my flesh.

"You're the one that's perfect, Knox." Her eyes sparkle when she grins, and now it's my turn to blush, heat racing up my neck to fill my cheeks. *"My masterpiece."*

Fuck. I didn't know that I could come from words alone, but if she keeps speaking like this, keeps kissing down the length of my scars, I might just come in my pants, and that would ruin our fun.

For only about twenty minutes, but still.

"Show me how you touched yourself that night I heard you through the wall," I say, voice coming out rougher than I intend.

Quinn moans at my words and I think I might just come after all.

While I'm distracted by her parted lips and trying to keep my cock from exploding in my pants, Quinn surges up, hands latching around my neck as she pulls me into her. My hands fall to the bed to brace us, but she doesn't seem bothered by the weight of my body on top of hers, especially when she hooks a leg around my waist and tries to flip us over.

My girl wants to be on top.

I can give her that.

My hands find her hips and I twist, maneuvering us so that Quinn's sitting pretty on my cock. Unfortunately, it's still trapped in my pants, and she has hers on as well, and the two layers of clothing between us are two too many.

Maybe I didn't quite think this one through.

"I don't think so," Quinn teases, dragging her hands from

my shoulders to the waistline of my jeans. My muscles coil beneath her touch, and I love the way she greedily drinks in the way I react to her. Her voice is low, a sultry tease. "I want what you promised me at the bar, Knox."

My head falls into the softness of the pillows beneath me at her brazen demand. The tips of her nails dance across the skin above the waistline of my briefs and I squeeze the meat of her ass with a grunt of approval. "Fuck, Princess, you're perfect."

She's stolen my signature smirk, the corner of her mouth quirking upwards and damn, does she look pretty like that.

Quinn doesn't hesitate, deft fingers undoing the buttons of my jeans like she was made for it. She drags the zipper down next, paired with a light scrape of her nails brushing over my heavy cock through the fabric of my briefs.

The noise that comes out of me is guttural. But not embarrassing, because if there's going to be anyone to hear these noises from me, *make* these noises spill from my mouth, I'm glad it's Quinn.

She snaps the waistband of my briefs against my hips and it's sharp. I startle, eyes narrowing as she stares down at me with those wide, faux innocent eyes.

That debauched smile gives her away, though.

I decide to forego teasing her back in case she decides to change her mind about riding me, and help her with her own buttons instead. I make much quicker work of it, helping her slide off of me so we can rid ourselves of the fabric barriers.

My cock bobs, springing from its confines, and Quinn's gaze is laser focused on it, finally bare herself.

She's watching me with an intensity that I feel all the way to my very core. I wonder if Quinn can feel it too, with the way she's taking my cock in that soft hand of hers and leaning over to lap up the pearl of precum that's glistening at my tip.

I bite back the hiss that threatens to slip as she works, licking and sucking my cock. I nearly bite through my lip at her wicked tongue. My fingers twitch to wrap her long, blonde hair around my fist and hold her steady, fuck my cock into her obedient little mouth like I so desperately want.

My fingers also itch for my charcoals. I want to remember this moment forever.

"So, so prefect," I compliment, caressing her cheek when she pulls away, automatically moving into me like the six inches of space between us is too much. I feel it too, the consuming need to always have her near, to always be touching her in some way or another.

I draw her in, claiming her mouth with my own. It's a slower kiss, and I pour all of the feelings bubbling up in my chest into her, willing her to understand what I'm feeling without having to outright say it. How much she means to me, how she's already changed my life for the better.

Quinn waits patiently as I rifle around for a condom. She takes it before gently poking at my chest, signaling for me to lie down. I follow obediently, because watching her rip open the packet while she eye-fucks my cock has me on edge.

Rolling the rubber onto my length, she slowly climbs back on top of me. I guide her, hands on her hips, but let her grind herself down against me, the both of us sharing a plea-sured moan as she plants her palms against my chest, prop-ping herself up, hovering over my cock.

I'd prefer if we were chest to chest so I could wrap my arms around her, plant my feet into the bed, and fuck up into her with abandon, but I let Quinn carry on for now.

I'm unable to remove my hands from her waist as she

gives me a rough tug before guiding my cock through her slit. She's warm, wet, and all mine; I grunt at the feeling.

As she lines the head of my cock with her pussy, notching me into place, I hold my breath to try and calm my racing heart. Quinn's presence makes it beat like a drum, all wild and brash. The gasp she sucks in as she begins gingerly lowering herself onto my throbbing cock is one I want to replay over and over forever.

Fuck, she's tight as she descends onto my dick. I feel the way her walls hug me, squeezing with pleasure. My fingers dig harsher because it's the only way to keep myself from bucking up into her.

"Oh my God, Knox," she whines when she's fully speared on my cock. Heat courses through my body like a lance and I force it away, letting Quinn take her time to adjust. I grit my teeth when she gives a swirl of her hips, her head falling back on her shoulders as she bobs softly.

She all but collapses against my chest, reaching forward to kiss me again. We can't keep away from each other, drawn to the other like magnets.

I slide my hands up the expanse of her back, trailing across the dips and valleys of her body as I hold her closer to me, careful not to move my hips. Over the round of her ass, the curve of her spine, across her breasts, all the way up until I'm caressing her cheek, keeping her still as I slowly dip my tongue into her mouth, kissing her deeply.

Kissing Quinn ignites a fire in my soul. It's passionate, fervent, and full of all of the feelings I haven't had the gall to admit to yet. The ones that cross the line into something I'm terrified of giving away, something that I haven't experienced in a long time.

Love.

With my mouth against hers, I pour all of those emotions

into her, hoping that the way her fingers curl into fists against my chest means that she understands exactly what I'm trying to convey.

Bucking my hips causes Quinn to make a noise that I greedily swallow. She lifts up, dragging herself off my cock and I can't help but shudder at how slow she's going with her exploratory little bounces.

One would think I've never fucked her before.

She arches fully into my body as she sinks down again and with a cry of pleasure, our lips finally part. Quinn trails kisses down my throat and across my collarbones as she makes her way to sit up again, trying a different angle that makes her breath hitch. The rush of cool she leaves against my skin makes my chest heave, hands trailing back to her hips like I'm the belt keeping her from falling off this ride.

She's absolutely stunning in the soft light emitting from the lamp. Her golden hair is disheveled, hanging across her shoulders. Her hazel eyes don't leave mine as she rises and falls again, but her lashes flutter with the movement. All of her creamy, soft skin is on display, dusty nipples, rosy lips, the apples of her cheeks filled with a healthy glow.

I brush a lazy circle against her clit with my knuckle and it really spurs my girl into action, kicking up into a pace that makes my balls tighten.

Her full breasts bounce with her movements and I reach out, getting a handful of one, dragging my thumb across her tightened nipple. She emits a keen, her hand coming up to cover mine, to knead against mine, showing me how she wants me to touch her.

I have no problem doing that.

Focusing my attention on her breasts, I pinch, twist, and tease her with my touch. It makes Quinn moan, makes her hips grind harder, her bounces becoming fast and messy instead of controlled and calculated. Always overthinking, my girl. I'm glad that I can fuck it out of her, have her complete putty beneath the hands I've spent so much of my life hating.

I find her hips again, not only to slow her down before I prematurely orgasm, but to help guide her. Quinn plants her hands on my forearms to steady herself, and I love the feeling of her nails digging into my skin.

Her head rolls back as she releases a pleasured mewl, shifting her hips as she searches for new angles. She's moving more frantically now, a slight furrow to her brows as she tries to chase that feeling.

"That's it, Princess. Take what you need," I encourage, unable to look away. I'm desperate for her, for everything that she gives me. I cherish it. *Her.* "Take everything that you need."

"I need *you,*" she breathes, just as delirious with arousal as I am. I can feel the warmth in my gut, the way that her tight pussy grips my cock, fucking down onto me as she chases her high.

Her nails drag down my chest, leaving long lines of red in their wake, puckered and raised. As I peer down at them, licking my lips, I wonder for the first time if I should get a tattoo with color, because these marks look pretty damn good.

Quinn's request is all I need to hear for me to take over, holding her closer, tighter, and I plant my feet into the mattress and begin fucking up into her, faster and harsher, as deeply as I can go.

She feels too good, better than anything I've ever experienced. And the way that she clings to me, just as tightly as I am to her makes me proud, like she might love me just as much as I do her.

The cry she releases when I hit that spot inside of her is

loud, drawn out as I plunge myself deeper, focusing my movements on that exact site. Her hands against my skin turn desperate, a scramble of pleasure that she's nearing. Her eyes are squeezed shut just as tightly as her pussy is clamped around my cock, and I can feel myself hurtling towards my own orgasm.

"Mark me," Quinn begs. And I do.

Rolling the both of us, she cries out but I'm already bending forward, marking her with my mouth, sucking bruises into her skin. I bite into the meat of her shoulder, not hard enough to break skin, but enough to leave an imprint of my teeth. Her fingers pull harshly at my hair as she moans, long and hard, but I don't care. I'm on a mission and I will not be deterred.

I hook a hand under Quinn's knee, pressing it higher to give myself a better angle. Her eyes are rolling into the back of her head and her hips are moving to meet my strokes thrust for thrust, only heightening our shared pleasure.

Quinn marks me back, her nails against my arms, my sides, my spine, adding to my quickly growing collection. Every time I press into her, I gain another pretty piece of artwork from a quickly crumbling Quinn, who I know is on the verge of orgasming because of the way she screams "Right there!" when my fingers find her clit, begging for my attention.

I circle the nub, darting down to kiss her roughly before she shuts those pretty eyes while she comes. I press my forehead against hers, sharing a breath, watching Quinn intently as my hips piston into her and my thumb strokes her over the edge of oblivion.

My arms tremble with my own impeding pleasure, holding myself above her, caging her in while I work her to the brink.

"Mark me," she says again, desperately.

"What?" I pant back.

The words roll off of her tongue in an urgent cry. "A tattoo that reminds me of this," she whimpers, and I almost buckle. "Of you. I—" Quinn's words are silenced with the moan that drowns out the rest of her pleas. Her pussy tightens around mine, body shaking with her orgasm.

It hits me like a wave, her words, rattling in my head. She wants me to give her her first tattoo? Even with my fucked-beyond-belief hands, even though she knows how much they shake, how many times I've been rejected apprenticeships, she still wants me to be the one to ink her skin...

Fuck, if that doesn't make me want to come with her.

Pulling out with a groan, I rip off the condom, fisting myself down my length as I come with a throaty groan, painting Quinn's body in white streaks, dotting her perfect skin.

It has always been far from my favorite color, but I think it could become my most treasured if I get to keep seeing my come splattered across her body like this.

Collapsing next to her, I wrap an arm around her waist and drag her into me. I'll get up and clean her off in a bit, but right now I just want to lie here and admire her, revel in the words spoken with the remnants of my ebbing euphoria.

Quinn's touch is soft, nails scratching lightly up and down the arm I have draped across her body. Her eyes are closed and she has a soft smile on her face, a content one, one that I wouldn't mind seeing every night for the rest of my life.

The noises we shared are ones that would have definitely had Quinn pounding on the plaster separating us at the beginning of the semester. Now, we're on the same side of the wall, cuddled up tightly, sharing more than just words. I think about how moments ago she was a writhing heap under me, begging for my touch, my tattoos, and it all hits me so full on that the only thing I know how to do in this moment is to kiss her again, giving her all of me as the realization rears its head.

I love her.

I really fucking love her.

CHAPTER 31
QUINN

"Quinn?" Knox asks when we're both cleaned up and back in his bed.

My head rests on his chest, the steady beat of his heart lulling me towards sleep. The moonlight streams in through the blinds we have forgotten to close, painting Knox's face with stripes of soft light. I admire the straight bridge of his nose, his lips, his dark eyes when I shift to look at him only to find him already staring at me.

His fingers dance across my forearm where it's resting between his biceps, a gentle pattern that makes me feel safe and loved.

"Yes?"

"Did you mean it?" He asks, and the softness of his voice in the dark feels like a secret, and the fact that he used my name instead of the endearing 'Princess' he so often calls me has my body tensing before I can stop it.

Knox feels it anyway.

I wrack my brain, trying to figure out what he's talking about. I shift through the haze of tonight, the things he said, the things *I've* said. Through the all of the touches and kisses and promises pressed into skin.

And then it hits me.

"About wanting you to give me a tattoo?"

Knox's eyes shutter as if he's thinking about it. I don't fail to notice the twitching of his cock beneath the sheet, pressed against the leg I have slung over his thigh.

My pussy clenches in response. I bite back a smile, enjoying the way that he reacts to my words.

"Yes," he answers, almost nervously.

I brush a few strands of damp hair from his forehead. When we went to shower, Knox showed me a thing or two, sinking to his knees between my legs until I could barely hold myself up. Then, he proceeded to lather my body in soap, massaging it into my aching muscles.

Knox catches my hand, intertwining our fingers and presses a chaste kiss to my palm. I never thought that he'd turn out to be so tender and kind beneath that harsh exterior he normally wears.

My stomach flutters at the thought of him so soft and compassionate only with me.

"Yes, Knox," I answer and he smiles. My heart soars at the sight of him so bright-eyed. "I meant it."

I squeal as he rolls us, caging me between his forearms. His cock is thickening against my leg, but I don't have time to really appreciate it because he's slanting his mouth over mine, thoroughly distracting me.

A quick sweep of his tongue parts my lips and my fingers find their way to his hair, digging in deeply. I keep him close with an encouraging noise, wrapping my legs around his waist as Knox rolls his hips.

"I'll give you something good, Princess," he says against my mouth, rubbing his cock through my slit, easily finding my arousal waiting for him. I melt into the pillows, the soft mattress in bliss. I'm just as ready for another round as he is, and at this rate, we won't be sleeping at all tonight.

As long as I'm with Knox, though, I don't care.

I snort at his words, shaking with laughter. "Yeah, right. You'd be more likely to tattoo a dick somewhere on me."

"How about somewhere *in* you?" He asks, teasing my entrance with his tip. My fit of giggles dissolves into a moan, the feeling of his cock, bare against my wet pussy is immaculate.

I pull him down for another desperate kiss.

"Yes, please," I say, somewhere between breathing and kissing. Knox removes himself from me and I whine, but he's shushing me softly as he reaches into his bedside table for another condom. Sitting back, he rolls it on his thick length with ease while I take an appreciative glance down his body.

Knox is back on top of me within seconds, stealing a peck against my mouth before pulling away, eyes serious. I don't know how he can take anything seriously right now, but I give him my attention anyway.

"I'll give you whatever you want, Princess."

If he wasn't talking about tattoos, I'd swoon.

"Even if I want something silly?" I ponder, moaning loudly when Knox doesn't hesitate to align his hips with mine and shove forward. My legs wind around his waist, pulling him even closer to me, tracing his smooth skin, the rippling muscles of his back as he begins moving.

Knox's hum against my throat sends shivers skittering up my spine. "Even if you want something silly," he promises, speaking through the kisses he's peppering across my body. "I can see you with something more meaningful, too, if you want. Something that represents you as you are." His mouth finds mine and our hips slap together in a rough thrust. His eyes are soft, determined, and proud. "Something that shows your grace, your beauty, your *innocence,*" he jokes, climbing back up to nip at the tip of my nose. I laugh, but there's something about his words settles a piece of my heart.

It's something that I thought I've lost. Something that's been tamped down since I turned thirteen and won first place in the art fair for my drawing of two swans with their beaks pressed together, forming a heart. One of them was dark, and the other was a pristine white, opposites, just like Knox and I.

"Knox," I gasp as it hits me like a wave. His compliments, how he's described me like I'm his dream.

He makes a noise of agreement, unaware of the sudden burst of creativity he's given me.

"That's it, Princess. Say my name just like that."

"Knox," I whine a little this time. "Baby, baby, wait a second," I pant, shoving at his shoulders. I want him, and I'm absolutely planning on finishing this with my boyfriend, but I need to tell him what's come over me.

He pauses, pulling away.

His dark brows are furrowed with worry and I'm quick to soothe him. "Did I hurt you?"

"No." I shake my head firmly, offering him a consoling smile. "You've given me the best idea. I know what I'm going to draw for my project."

Knox grins, kissing me excitedly. I can't stop beaming, finally feeling the exhilaration I've been yearning for all these years. I'm jittery and nervous, but it's thrilling, my heart beating heavily in my chest.

I feel full.

It makes me want to laugh when Knox looks down between our bodies where we're connected. His eyes flick back up to mine and I grimace a little. Parting from him sounds less than appealing.

"Do you need to go right now?"

This time, I can't help myself, laughing, full and happy. Knox groans at the fluttering of my pussy clenching around his cock. He buries his face into my neck and I thread my fingers through his hair, enjoying the solid weight of his body on mine. "Oh no, Knox, I'm not leaving you until you've fucked me so thoroughly, I can only see stars."

I can feel his lips curling into a grin against my skin. I can't help but to smile along with him.

"That," Knox says, pulling away with a wicked smirk, his eyes gleaming beautifully. "I can do."

"Quinn?" Knox asks me sometime later when we've managed to clean ourselves up again and actually try to sleep.

It's not coming easily.

That jittery excitement still buzzes beneath my skin. For the first time in years, I'm feeling creative, like whatever I make next is going to be groundbreaking, and once I put my pencil to the paper, I'm going to be unstoppable.

To say that I don't know where this is coming from would be a lie. Knox's whispered words have embedded themselves in my brain, in my heart, and every time I close my eyes to attempt to fall into the sleep trying to drag my eyelids down, they ring in my head over and over until I'm biting back an eager smile.

"Yes?" I answer, not moving from where I'm resting my head on his chest. Apparently, sleep isn't coming very easily to Knox, either, but I'm unsure why.

His fingers stroke my hair again, a soothing motion he's been doing since we settled in this position. I enjoy the occasional brush of his blunt nails against my scalp, scratching my head.

"Are you still awake?"

I want to snort so badly at his question. "Wow, nothing gets by you. Did the fact that I answered you when you called my name make you think I was asleep?"

I squeak at the teasing pinch to my cheek he gives me, swatting at his chest that's shaking with laughter. I can't help but join him. I enjoy this side of Knox, the happier, freer side that he doesn't show anyone outside of his trusted circle.

"You could've been saying yes to anything." His tone takes on that familiar teasing one that makes my aching thighs clench. We might have gone too many rounds tonight, is what my tender pussy is telling me. "Could've been having the best dream about me stuffing my cock into your drenched pussy, Princess, begging me for more."

"Stop," I beg, even though my body is going hot with his words. Knox buries his fingers in my hair with a deep chuckle, holding me close. "I can't go another round tonight. You've ruined me."

I ignore the way his chest puffs with pride.

"Back when we had our date," he starts, and I know where this is heading. The night of our first date when we went spray painting a few towns over, I'd blurted out about the imposter syndrome that had taken root so deeply I wasn't sure I would ever know what life would feel like without it again. I'd clammed up, cutting the conversation short, but it's been looming between us ever since. "We haven't had a chance to talk more about it. I want to know how you've been feeling since then?"

My heart soars in my chest. This man is incredible. He hasn't forgotten our conversation, and even though I may have wanted him to because I was embarrassed about it at the time, he's been thinking about it. Thinking about me.

I'm overcome with emotion.

"Good," I answer, smiling softly. "I think I've finally found my muse."

"Oh yeah?" He questions, peering down at me curiously. "What is it?"

"I think you mean to ask *who* is it?"

He takes the bait. "Okay, *who* is it?"

"Guess."

"Quinn," Knox grumbles warningly. He's not one for dragging out teasing unless he's the one keeping me on the edge of orgasm until I'm crying and begging like a harlot to come. This is nothing like that, so he doesn't need to be so moody.

His thumbs brush across the sensitive skin around my nipples, drawing them into tight circles that make me hiss. I want him to touch them, to pinch them and kiss them and bite them.

Knox gives me a knowing smirk in return for the glare I shoot him.

Apparently, two can play at this game.

"It's you," I breathe out, more than interested in the way his fingers roam my body sensually. They're rough against my skin, dragging in the most delicious of ways. I love everything that he does to me, and that thought awakens all of my nerve endings.

"Me?" He teases lightly, but his touch is a taunt. It's moving lower, a hand slipping through our legs, the tips of his fingers brushing the insides of my thighs that his hips are pinning open for him. My pussy is a weeping, aching traitor. "What made you decide that?"

"What you said earlier changed my way of thinking. It

reminded me of exactly why I loved drawing in the first place." I think back on my first drawing competition where I took home the first-place ribbon for my piece of the two swans. What I felt at the time was a pride so intense that I carried that ribbon around all weekend, showing it to anyone who would give me attention. My parents and brother were happy because I was happy. I drew that swan because I wanted to, and I drew it for me.

I won that competition because I loved my work because of *me.* I spent those hours putting in the effort and it didn't matter if I won or lost because I was proud of the finished product.

"Somewhere along the way," I continue, playing with his hair. "I stopped drawing for myself and started doing it for others. I started drawing what they wanted to see, what they suggested. I stopped drawing what I really wanted and started pleasing those around me, and sometimes it wasn't even people who knew anything about art at all." I want to snort, because the thought of letting someone who doesn't know a fucking thing about drawing critique my work is totally ridiculous. "Your love for your own art is inspiring. You don't let anything get in your way or keep you from trying to achieve your goals, not even your past. You don't care about what other people think, you are completely and unabashedly yourself, Knox. And I love you so much, for that and so many other reasons," I rant, blurting out the thing that has been on my mind for a while but didn't think would come out during a conversation like this.

It feels good, finally admitting it to him, but when Knox's body goes tight against mine, my heart drops into my stomach.

I sit up quickly, my mind racing. I hadn't meant to blurt

them out like that, but it doesn't make them any less true. I thought he felt the same way. I thought—

"I'm sorry, I—"

"Quinn," Knox calls, and I haven't managed to untangle myself from the sheets before he's following me, locking his arms around my waist to pull me back into him. My chest is heaving, blinking away the stinging in my eyes. Knox's breath is hot in my ear. "You're not going to admit that and think I'm letting you leave, right Princess?"

"I didn't mean to say it," I answer quickly, my anxiety rising again. The fact that he'd only stiffened against me and still hasn't said it back has a sick feeling crawling up my throat. I can't be here if he doesn't feel the same. "It just slipped out," I manage weakly, slumping against him when it's clear he isn't going to let me go.

Maybe it's a good sign.

Knox maneuvers me easily and I hate the way that my pussy clenches at his bulging muscles. He pins me to the mattress, draping himself over me so there's really no chance for escape.

The room is dark but through the soft light coming from the street lamps outside, I can make out his serious face, the straight of his jaw and lips, his intense eyes focused on me.

"But you meant it. Right?" It's not a soft question, but a stern one, like I should choose my answer very carefully.

I swallow harshly. I want to reach out, to brush back the onyx hair falling across his forehead, fix it on the top where it's been mussed from our earlier endeavors. I want to rub that crease between his brows because now that I've had a little taste of loving Knox, it hurts to see him so stoic again.

My voice is loud in the quiet of the night even though it's barely a whisper. I swear my heart is beating louder than the admission that passes my lips.

"Yes."

It takes all of a millisecond before Knox is shoving himself forward, connecting his lips with mine. A zip of electricity passes through us and my limbs wind around his of their own will, pulling him even closer.

The kiss is hot and heated, a battle as our tongues slide over each other.

"Say it again," he begs me, and I do.

"I love you," I repeat, and this time he's tasting it directly from my lips. Knox's hands are tight where they're holding me, like I'm still trying to run away. His cock is hot and hard against my thigh, and I might be working up to another round after all.

When Knox finally pulls away from me, his eyes are sparkling and he's sporting the biggest smile I've ever seen. He's utterly breath-taking when he's happy.

"I love you too, Quinn."

My jaw falls slack but I don't stew in my surprise for long because his mouth slants back over mine and we're rolling, touching everywhere, the both of us losing ourselves in each other.

"You love me?" I question, breathing heavily when we finally manage to pull apart.

I feel so full, so excited and love-drunk and dizzy. I kiss Knox again because I can't help myself. *He loves me.*

"I love you so fucking much, Princess. More than I've ever loved anything."

"Even more than your motorcycle?" I tease, and he rolls his eyes at me, tickling my sides.

I squeal, writhing underneath him. The movement makes his cock brush my entrance and we're both dissolving into moans, the amusement melting into a heavy arousal that screams loudly in the dark.

"Even more than my motorcycle," Knox answers, his eyes heated with desire. He kisses my cheek. "Even more than tattooing." He works his way across my collar bones to the other side of my face and I arch up into him to reach his soft lips. Knox shifts so our mouths are millimeters apart, so I can taste his next words as he says them. "Even more than drawing."

CHAPTER 32
QUINN

I've forgotten how good this feels. How freeing it is to draw and not care about anything except putting down what I want, dirtying the crisp, white paper with thick, heavy lines, experimenting with smudging the chalk however I feel like smudging it.

I feel like I'm young again, with not a care in the world. The music from my headphones blasts in my ears and I'm singing loudly, uncaring that my boyfriend is probably sitting on the other side of the wall wondering how crazy I am.

Whatever. He's stuck with me now.

After another round of slow, sensual fucking, Knox and I reveling in our love for one another, I decided to spend the day embracing this newfound creativity, and have been working on my final project for drawing class all day.

It's been going incredibly well. I've never been so focused, so excited for the final result. Not even the looming deadline can shake me from this feeling.

Sitting back with a happy sigh, I admire what I have so far. Only a few more finishing touches until I'm done, and I can't wait. I'm thrilled with how it's been going, letting my hands do the work while keeping my mind from straying.

For my final Drawing 201 project, I chose to morph myself with a swan. Not only for the fact that it had been an ode to my younger self, but also because of their representation of the awakening of power and self-esteem. I've learned so much this semester about myself, and in the beginning, I was unsure of where I fit in in the creative world, but after learning the stories of so many around me, Knox's included, it has made me realize that I need to create art that *I* love and that *I'm* proud of, and not let others dictate my decisions.

I also chose to morph myself into the swan because of their grace. Grace in dealing with others—Knox's gnarly attitude, Slate's cheekiness, Ace's cockiness, Reid's snark, and Rory's hidden relationship. I've learned a lot of patience and made some amazing friends this semester.

I've come such a long way since then, especially now that I'm deeply in love with the neighbor that had been a thorn in my side for all these months. Knox is as sweet as ever, though he still distracts me from my work these days, it's no longer with rowdy music.

Speaking of, the song cuts out as my phone rings and I decide that now is as good as any time for a break. My mom's contact picture flashes and I smile. It's been a week since I've last talked to her. I've been so busy with studying for finals and projects that I haven't had a chance to call.

Dusting my charcoal laden hands on my pants, I can't help but think of how Knox had done the same thing when I climbed into his lap one night while he was working on his own drawings.

I shiver as I remember the hungry look in his eyes at the charcoal fingerprints he scattered around my body.

"Hey, mom," I answer, shoving that thought far, far away from my mind.

"Hi, Quinnie," she greets cheerily, and the sound of her voice makes me ache.

Only one more week until I'm home for winter break and I couldn't be more excited. Rory and I booked our flights long ago, and as sad as I am to be apart from Knox, I'm excited to see Sam and my parents and the rest of our family for the holidays.

Knox isn't going home. Instead, he's going to Colorado with Ace to spend the holidays with him and his family. It's something they've done the past few years, even before Knox's father found out about his secret art school status. He and his father haven't seen eye-to-eye in a long time, and when I offered my sympathy, he only brushed it off, saying that I shouldn't feel sorry for him because he's more than happy with the decisions he's made.

"How are you doing? How are your classes?" Mom asks, always straight to the point, always wondering about my future in art.

It's something that I know I have to talk to her about, these feelings that I've been harboring inside of me since I gave up drawing for myself. It might be a hard conversation, but it's one that I know will have me feeling lighter in the end.

"They're good," I answer, trying to appease her. I wince, already falling back into old habits. "Actually, I'm glad you called, because I wanted to talk about that."

"Oh no," she gasps, already thinking the worst. "You're passing all of your classes, right Sweetie?"

"Yes, mom," I sigh, rubbing my hands down my jeans again in a nervous motion. I stare at the streaks of charcoal embedded into the denim and smile. "I, um, don't really know how to have this conversation," I admit, and she must hear the slight quiver in my voice because she sounds alarmed when she responds.

"Quinn, are you alright? What's going on?"

"I'm fine, mom. I just—" I sigh, moving over to my bed and falling onto it. The ceiling is drenched with afternoon sun and I count the stripes where my blinds are casting shadows between them. "For a long time now, I haven't been feeling like I could be the artist everyone wants me to be."

There's a pause on the other end of the line and I chew my lip, worrying about how she's going to respond.

"Sweetie, what do you mean?"

I take a deep breath and admit everything to her. I admit that I've lost my way in the art world, lost my spark, and that I've been struggling to find it again for as long as I can remember.

"Quinn, I had no idea that you've been feeling this way," she says, and I hear the concern thick in her tone. It makes my heart twinge with guilt.

"That's the thing mom, you wouldn't have known because I hid it for so long. I was afraid to disappoint everyone, especially you and dad, when you've both done so much for me and my art career."

She makes a choked sound that I think is her trying to smother a sob. It makes my own tears spill and I wipe them from my cheeks, uncaring that the charcoal left on my hands is going to mix with them and leave me with dark streaks down my face.

"I wish you would've told us sooner," she murmurs, and I hear her shuffling throughout the house, the opening of a door. Her voice echoes and I know she's entered her bathroom, probably searching for a box of tissues. "We will support you however you need, Quinn. Even if it means following a different passion of yours."

Those words hit me harder than I thought they would. Of course, I know that my parents would support my decision to give up art if I wanted to, but I also know that I'd always feel that dread-like cloud hanging over me like I've disappointed them when they've poured so much into helping with my art career.

I swallow thickly. "I know that," I say because it's the only thing I can.

"So," mom says, clearing her throat. When she continues, she sounds stronger, more than ready to listen. "Is this the end for artist Quinn?"

The thought is like a twist of a hot knife to my gut. I love being an artist and have since I was a child and the thought of giving it up isn't something I've ever actually considered. I always had hopes that my creativity would come back, that my love for art would always be here. It has, finally rearing its head again, and while it may not be the exact same feelings I remember from when I was younger, I'm more than ready to accept the newness of the creativity sparking in my veins and rolling with it.

"Not a chance," I answer her, unable to keep my grin tucked between my teeth. But there's something else tugging at my mind; something else I want to share with her.

"Your head was always stuck in that drawing pad of yours," mom chuckles wetly and my nostrils prickle with emotion. It's never easy hearing her upset. "You hardly ever wanted to play with your brother. Sam had to drag you away from your drawings to get your attention, and it only worked when he offered you a different craft or a bowl of ice cream."

She's right. When I was younger, I didn't care about anything besides art. Drawing, coloring, painting, I loved all of it. I remember always begging my mom to buy me something from the craft aisle, even though most of the things I picked out screamed that a mess was to be made while playing with them, she always encouraged and supported my desire to explore the arts.

We laugh together as we reminisce and my shoulders ease. "I remember that. Actually, I think he still owes me a bowl or two."

"I'll be sure to remind him the next time I talk to him," mom says. "Maybe over winter break the four of us can go get some together."

"I'd like that," I answer softly, wiping a tear from my cheek. My phone buzzes in my hand and I pull it away from my ear to check the screen. A text notification from Knox is sliding away, the name *Douchewaffle* making me smile. "Hey mom?"

"Yes?"

"You know that neighbor I've been complaining about this semester? The one who stayed up really late and was always playing loud music?" I chew on my lip, unsure of why I'm suddenly nervous to tell my mom that I'm dating the man I swore to hate for the next two years of my time at Vulcan University.

"Yes…" She answers, somewhat uneasily. "What about him?"

"Well, his name is Knox, and he's my boyfriend now," I breathe, squeezing my eyes shut tight as I await her response.

It's silent on the other end of the line for so long that I pull my phone away to make sure our call hasn't disconnected.

And then my mom bursts into laughter.

"Oh, of course he is, Quinnie."

"Hey," I grouse, "What's that supposed to mean?"

"Quinn." Mom's voice takes on a scolding note that makes me feel like I'm ten again and arguing with her about bringing my markers to the grocery store. "I've never seen you move so fast as to when you were shoving your father into your apartment after they showed up on your floor. You were blushing bright red after you slammed that door in their faces. I'm pretty sure you're the only one in the room who didn't know you were head over heels for that boy back then. Leah and I talked about it almost the entire way home."

"Oh my God," I slap a palm to my forehead, utterly mortified.

"What?" She answers my groan, "It's perfectly normal, Quinn. He's cute and I can't wait to formally meet him. Maybe he and Rory's boyfriend can come up for New Year's."

"Really?" I ask, surprised. My family always spends the night celebrating the new year with the Wilsons. It's an extravaganza with a lot of food and even more drinking and it's always the best time. Mom's suggestion of inviting Knox and Ace makes my heart kick happily in my chest.

"Of course, Quinn. You deserve to be happy. I love you, Sweetie."

"Thanks, mom. I love you too. See you soon."

"Thank you for meeting me," is the first thing I say to Reid when he sits down in the seat across from me.

He looks good. He always does, and I don't know why I'm acting like it's been an eternity since I've seen him when we share the same class two times a week. His hair is a little longer, fluffier today, and his eyes are just as vibrant as they always are, even though they're filled with a hint of sorrow.

Things have been tense between us since he found out about Knox and I. We still sit together in class, but he always chooses Rory to be the buffer, sitting on her other side as we work through our class periods.

I'd be lying if I said it didn't hurt. I've missed the easy banter between us, teasing each other about our majors and our lives over coffee.

I slide a cup of his usual over to him and he thanks me with a tight smile.

"Reid," I sigh, unsure of what route to take with this. We're friends, and if there's some hidden feelings, I haven't been made aware of them. I know that he's hurt because all I've done all semester is complain about Knox, but I wasn't expecting to fall so hard for him either. "I'm sorry."

His brows furrow as he looks out the window. The sun streaming inside makes the freckles dotting the bridge of his nose more noticeable. "You have nothing to be sorry for, Quinn."

"What?" I almost splutter my drink, pounding on my chest to dislodge the drops from my esophagus. "Explain, because you've been acting weird around me since you found out about Knox and I."

Reid winces and I immediately regret phrasing it like that. He did seem like he was upset about the entire encounter. He even walked away from me after Knox showed up outside of class to pick me up that one afternoon

"I'm sorry that it came off that way," he starts, fingering at the cardboard sleeve wrapped around the hot cup. "I've been going through my own shit, and finding out that you're dating Knox felt like maybe we weren't as close of friends as I thought," he sighs, settling back into his seat and I feel like a total piece of shit for being so caught up in myself that I didn't even notice Reid was acting out of character because of his own problems in life.

"I'm sorry, Reid. I should've told you but it was still shocking and new to me at the time. I didn't know how to tell you. Is it your family giving you trouble again?" I ask, reaching out and placing a consoling hand on his arm.

"Amongst other things." He shrugs, and I don't miss the way his gaze flits over to the counter where the same barista from the day that frat bro had made a fool of himself is making drinks. Her piercing eyes are already on us, lashes narrowed. She startles when I catch her, ducking her chin back into her work.

"*Oh,*" I tease, crossing my arms over my chest, unable to hide my shit-eating grin. Reid stares at me like he's begging me not to bring it up, but I can't help myself. I think he understands this, too, because he rolls his eyes at me before I can get a word out. "Does the 'other shit' involve a certain pretty barista? You should ask her out."

"*Yeah,*" he scoffs. "Someday, maybe." Reid checks his watch before shoving his chair back and offering me a hand. "C'mon, time for review. Are you ready?"

"Yep," I answer, and he seems surprised at my cheer. I haven't been excited for a drawing critique this entire semester.

"I can't tell if you're happy because it's the last critique of class or because you're actually excited about your project," Reid says, leading me towards the door with a hand against my lower back.

I peer up at him over my shoulder, "Definitely the latter, Reid." Then softly, to myself, I echo, "Finally, the latter."

CHAPTER 33
KNOX

"Knox!" Quinn calls in surprise, and the smile on my girl's face when she sees me makes me perk right the hell up.

"Hey, Princess," I greet, bending down to kiss her when she's close enough. Her hands wrap around my neck while mine frame her face, demanding a longer kiss than I should in public, right outside of the art building.

"What are you doing here?" She asks, breathless when we part. I don't let her go far, wrapping my arm around her shoulder as Rory and Reid trail behind. Quinn's cheeks are a pretty shade of pink and I can tell that she's flustered over our display of affection but the truth is, I can't keep my hands off her. She loves me, and I her, and I'm going to let everyone know.

I smile at Rory and regard Reid with a polite nod. Quinn told me that she was going to talk to him at the coffee house the other day and afterwards mentioned something about him having a possible crush on the barista there and that I needed to stop "pulling my cock out" every time Reid came around.

So, a nod he gets.

Reid tries to smile at me but it looks more like a grimace. I guess we're both on the same page of trying to accept each other's presence for the sake of Quinn. I can see Rory and her rolling their eyes from the corner of my vision but I ignore it, letting my shaky hand trail down her back to give her ass a playful pinch. She doesn't notice the slight tremor because my palm is pressed flat to her jeans. The motion gets me an elbow to the stomach, but it's well worth it.

"Came to meet you to hear all about how your Art History final and critique went," I tell her, leading her towards the pathway to our apartments.

To be honest, my head's been a mess all day and I'm more than thankful that I've finished my finals already because I can't stop thinking about the message I received from my father days ago, rubbing it in my face that the deal has gone through and that Third Street Apartments is going to be getting a facelift over the summer by the person I consider to be the Devil in disguise.

I thought that the walk to campus was going to help me clear my head of the dreaded news I have to break to my roommates and Rory tonight, but the trek didn't help in the slightest.

Quinn beams but her hazel eyes are knowing. We talked about it last night when we were cuddled up in her room and were taking a break from me quizzing her on her Art History cards. She's improved tremendously since we started studying together, but I know she was still a bit nervous going into the final exam this morning.

I brush a soothing circle against the small of her back with my thumb, craning my neck down to murmur, "I don't know how to tell everyone."

Her eyes soften and she pulls my hand from her back, intertwining our fingers instead. When she notes the minute tremble, her brows furrow and she squeezes in sympathy, letting me know that she's here if I need her.

Fuck, I love her so much.

"I think the best way to do it is going to be coming right out and saying it." She offers this solution gently so the others don't hear, and I nod, biting the inside of my cheek.

I've never had trouble telling Ace and Slate the things that I've needed to, but this somehow feels worse than recounting the night of my accident and my asshole of a father to them. The fact that he's still haunting me after I've all but told him to fuck off from my life is more than frustrating.

No wait, I'm pretty sure I've actually told him to fuck off before.

Why is he so obsessed with me?

I nod at Quinn. She's right. We've planned a dinner for the five of us and decided to tell everyone then. I don't want to be the source of this bad news, the fact that we're all going to be scrambling to find somewhere new to live during the spring semester makes my stomach twist. I don't want to add to anyone's stress, but I know that I can't handle it all on my own.

Quinn told me that all of them would rather share this burden than let me go through it alone, letting it eat at me. The guys will notice something is up with me eventually, and I know I'll feel even worse if I keep it from them longer than I should.

"You're right." I want to sigh. I really, really hate this.

My girlfriend winks up at me, bumping me with her hip. "Always am."

The answering scoff I make gets me a pinch to my own ass.

We come to a fork in the sidewalk. To get to Third Street

Apartments we need to head left, but Reid says his goodbyes to the girls and begins heading to the right.

Ugh. I really hate what I'm about to do.

"Hey, Reid," I call after him. Rory and Quinn both look at me surprised. I'm sure they didn't even know I knew his name.

Reid turns, his brows furrowed and wearing a frown. I should probably be thanking him for being a good friend to Quinn during the semester, especially when I was trying my best to do everything in my power to annoy the fuck out of her, but extending this olive branch is going to have to do.

"We're throwing a party Saturday night to celebrate the end of the semester; you should stop by."

My words hang heavy in the air between us. Quinn pinches her arm, probably to see if this is a dream, and I bite the inside of my cheek to keep from chuckling. Rory's eyes are nearly bugging out of her head, and I wish I had my phone out to snap a picture and send to the group chat.

Reid stands and stares, dumbfounded. He looks like he's one second from looking around and trying to figure out if it was actually me or not, even though he just watched the words come out of my mouth. I know he wasn't expecting me to offer something like this, but hey, I'm trying, even if it is for Quinn and not because I actually want to form a relationship with the guy.

See? I can be nice.

"Yeah," he answers, but it doesn't really sound like he means it. Maybe he thinks that this is some sort of joke or something. Either way, no skin off my back if he doesn't show. At least I can say I was nice about it. "That'd be cool."

"Cool," I echo. "You probably know where I live." Okay, so maybe I'm still a little bit of an asshole.

"Yeah," he winces, trying to smother it by scratching his head. "Thanks. I'll see you there."

I nod, guiding Rory and Quinn down the other sidewalk as Reid returns to his own path.

The girls are still gaping like some sort of alien has taken over my body and is pretending to be me, and it kind of makes me want to laugh.

"What?" I sigh, wanting to get this over with.

"You seriously just invited Reid to one of your parties after you've been beefing with him all semester?" Rory explodes, and maybe I should take offense at how shocked they are about this.

"Yeah? You're both friends with him, so I thought I would be nice and invite him along," I explain, and they almost swoon.

Woah. These quickly changing moods are throwing me through a loop.

"That is *so* sweet," Rory coos and Quinn laughs. "I'm going to text Ace right now and tell him how sweet you're turning out to be under all of those black clothes."

I frown, glancing at Quinn, who hasn't said anything yet. To be honest, her silence is making me a little nervous, so I lean down to ask her, "Is that okay?"

"Yes, of course," she answers quickly, "I just wasn't expecting you to do that."

I look both ways before crossing the road, swinging my hand in hers, trailing Rory as we go.

"I know that there's no man on campus you love more than me, so I'm pretty confident that we can have Reid around without it being an issue," I muse, and she shakes her head, laughing along.

This is what I needed after being left alone with my worries all day. My girl and a little laughter.

"I do love you, Knox."

"I love you too, Princess."

"Awe, you two are so freaking *cute!*" Rory exclaims. I hadn't realized that she turned around and is now walking backwards, her phone propped up in her hands to take pictures of Quinn and I. "Say cheese!"

"So, what's this all about?" Slate asks, loading another slice of pizza onto his plate.

Okay, when I said dinner, I didn't mean that I was going to make something. No, that's saved for Quinnie and the occasional guy's night when we feel like something more than wings or 'za.

Tonight, I'm too nervy to cook, but I did pay for the pizza, so same thing.

"What do you mean? Why does me buying pizza for everyone mean that somethings up?" I question, ignoring the look Quinn shoots me. Fuck, I'm too nervous. I've barely even eaten a slice, and at this rate, Slate's going to demolish the rest of them before I can even manage one.

I'm not even sure I'd be able to pick up my slice anyway with how badly my hands are shaking. I've stuffed them under my legs for now, and Quinn's not the only one who's noticed.

"Because you were adamant about all of us showing up," Ace adds, talking around his own food-filled mouth. Rory scolds him and it normally would make me laugh but tonight I'm too on edge. "Some of us had plans tonight."

Slate scoffs. "Yeah, a fuck-fest on the girls' couch doesn't count as plans, Acey boy."

He's still been acting strange lately, but in better spirits since the night we all spent at the bar. I'm not sure what's up with him and I haven't gotten the chance to catch him alone to ask. When I try, it's like he's avoiding me, taking phone calls or telling me he's on his way out to meet someone.

It's more than frustrating at this point, and it wounds me. And now I know what it's like when my roommates have to put up with me.

Looks like I might have some more apologizing to do in the near future.

Quinn sets her hand on my leg where I haven't stopped bouncing it beneath the table, trying—and failing—to dispel my nerves. I look over at her and my worries seem to fade with the soft smile she's giving me, her wide hazel eyes encouraging me to say my piece.

I take a deep breath, opening my mouth to speak, when Ace cuts me off, firing a glare at Slate. Rory's head is in her hands but I can feel the heat of her embarrassment all the way across the table. No one is ever going to let them live the couch-fucking incident down, even if Quinn and I also spent some naked one-on-one time on my couch, without all of the hubbub of someone walking in on us.

We're sneakier, and I prefer to keep it that way.

"At least I have a girl to fuck on the couch."

Slate goes still in his chair for a split second that only I catch because my attention is on him. Before I can delve into his reaction, he's stuffing his face with more pizza and shooting back. "I could have three girls here in ten minutes for a fuck-fest on the couch if I wanted."

"Please," Quinn interrupts, silencing the table with her stern voice. It makes my spine tighten and my cock twitch at the authoritative tone. I kind of want her to use that in the bedroom sometime. I can imagine her telling me how to

move my tongue while she's sitting on my face. "I think Knox was trying to tell us all something, and I'm trying to eat, Slate."

"Ace started it," Slate mumbles, which is certainly not true.

"Anyway," Quinn says, making stern eye contact with both of my roommates so that they know she means business. I don't know why this is turning me on so much, watching her come into herself since rediscovering her passion for drawing again, but goddamn it's so fucking hot. "Knox, if you'll please."

"Thanks, Princess," I say, smiling at her softly. She squeezes my leg and that's all it takes for me to untuck mine from beneath my thigh and clasp my fingers with hers. I'm definitely feeling like I need her support right now, especially with the way that everyone else is staring at me.

"You're very welcome," she replies, pleased. She's having no trouble at all tonight, picking her slice back up with her free hand and taking a bite. I watch her swallow, wishing she was doing that around my cock instead.

Head, meet gutter. Now get the fuck out of it.

I clear my throat, fighting the heat that threatens to climb from my throat to my cheeks when I catch Slate, Ace, *and* Rory all looking at me, their eyes sparkling with amusement.

I suppose I better speak up before any of them dares to say anything about the way I was staring at Quinn.

I decide that ripping the Band-Aid off is the best way to go. It's not so much as a planned sentence as it is me nervously blurting out what my father has done, but it gets the point across just the same.

"My father's bought the building and is evicting all of us at the start of summer."

I wait for the cries of outrage, the pizza slamming back into plates, the groans and glares, but nothing comes.

No one seems all that surprised by my news.

"Isn't anyone going to say anything?" I ask, more confused than ever.

The last time I talked to the guys about this, my father was only looking into the building. It hadn't been a confirmed notion, but maybe they've used all this time to wrap their heads around the idea that this might become a possibility.

I look between Ace and Slate.

Ace shrugs. "We kind of figured this was going to happen."

"Yeah, man," Slate chimes in. "Your dad is a total prick."

Stupefied, I look at Rory, who ducks in her seat, squeaking. "Quinn kind of filled me in about it already."

I look at Quinn, eyebrow raised.

She shrugs innocently. "Sorry!"

I'm pretty sure no one is expecting me to burst out laughing, which is why they all startle in their seats when I do.

"Sorry," I gasp through my laughter. My stomach hurts and my trembling has calmed down. "I've been a nervous wreck all day and you all knew? This is great."

Ace shifts in his seat like I'm scaring him. Maybe I am. Maybe I don't know what else to do besides laugh at this utterly fucking shitty situation that's happening all because of me.

"Knox," Quinn starts, trying to pull her hand from mine, but I won't let go. "It's okay. We're all going to be fine."

"Nothing's going to change except that we won't be living next door to each other anymore," Rory promises.

"And we have no plans of letting you go, man," Slate says, finally having dropped his pizza to his plate. His full attention is on me, and his chocolate eyes are serious, something I haven't seen often in one of my best friends. It's almost as jarring as I thought my admission would be. "You're stuck with us."

"Stuck with you?" I ask, and I don't like how insecure it comes out.

The sounds of my friends' acceptance ring around the table. Each one is an assurance that has my shoulders dropping their defenses and my heart surging with happiness.

"Yeah."

"Yup."

"Of course!"

The only person who doesn't answer is Quinn, and my heart races double as I turn toward her.

She's looking up at me with so much love in her eyes it makes it hard to breathe. She's perfect, everything about her from her annoying questions when we first met to the bottoms of her toes. I've spent too much time with my head up my ass when it came to her, and I'm never going to let that happen again now that I have her. I'm never going to let her go.

"Yes," she says softly, lovingly. It's apparent she feels the same about me. "There's no getting rid of us because we love you, Knox. And we'll choose you over some silly apartment building with a sketchy elevator any day."

Dammit. I hate showing emotions in front of so many people. It makes me feel too vulnerable, but these are my friends, my family.

Which is why I don't hesitate to lean over and sweep Quinn into a passionate kiss in front of said family, who only cheer obnoxiously.

They're stuck with me too, and I wouldn't change it for the world.

EPILOGUE

QUINN

Seven Months Later

"Knox," I sing-song, bursting in through the open front door of his new home.

After Travis Foster bought out our apartment building to renovate over the summer, the five of us—along with the other residents living in Third Street Apartments—were granted the rest of the spring semester to stay. One week after classes end, we need to have all of our belongings removed from the building for the new construction to start.

None of us renewed our leases for next year when the building is set for a grand reopening.

Knox's father hadn't even tried to convince his son to stay, but that didn't matter at all to Knox. The only thing that he or any of us cared about was that we'd no longer be living next to each other come summer.

The three of them—Knox, Ace, and Slate—found a house to rent on the outskirts of campus. It's gorgeous: a modern number that looks like it costs more than an arm and a leg and has more bedrooms than they need.

Ace's parents are well-known in the art community. So well-known that he doesn't even need his job at the art supply store in town. I'm sort of proud of him for wanting to have his own income, even if all he spends it on is booze and Rory. The latter I definitely accept; she's been needing someone in her life like Ace.

Ace had been adamant about Knox and Slate moving in with him, even though they were wary about how expensive the home was. Knox was the hardest to convince, but in the end, Ace won out, telling them that his parents wanted to do this for them, that it's only one year, and that they're like his brothers.

He even tried to convince Rory and I to move into an apartment building nearby, but it wasn't the right fit for either of us. We wanted something homier than the new high-rise with perfectly straight lines and cookie-cutter to every other apartment in the building.

We wanted something close to campus, something walk-able because neither of us have cars. We like the lived-in feel, having the memories of others' stories shared in the chips in the floor or the dents in the walls.

I miss our old apartment dearly, saddened by what Mr. Foster is going to make it into. Sure, the elevator was a death trap in itself, and sure, the walls were thinner than paper, but it was home, where I found love with my grumpy next-door neighbor, though I'm sure that in Knox's version of the story, *I* was the grumpy one.

The five of us had spent our last night at the building together, drinking and eating until our hearts were content, stomachs filled with waffles and ice cream from Rhonda's. It was the perfect night to end our time in the building, but also to end the semester.

I passed Drawing 201 with flying colors, and I've been beaming since that night I spent with Knox when my inspiration finally struck again. The swan portrait that I merged with myself was a project I never thought I'd be able to finish, let alone be so proud of. It's been a long few years since I've felt this good, this light, and I can only hope that it's not a fleeting feeling. I want this one to stick around for as long as possible.

I even passed Art History, and I don't know who was more excited, Odie or myself when I texted him about it after receiving my grade. I still owe him my coffee order and probably a six-pack or so, maybe even a trip to one of his games, but I definitely couldn't have done it without his or Knox's help.

In a few days, Rory and I head back up to Seattle for the summer, although I see a few flights back to California in our future. Maybe even the boys can come and visit us. I know Knox is staying around Vulcan U for the summer and Slate is going back to Hawaii to spend time with his younger sister and parents he hasn't been able to see since Christmas. Ace is traveling with his parents for a spell and even invited Knox along, but he declined, graciously thanking Ace's parents for the offer but that he's diving deep into his next set of drawings for an exhibition he wants to put on sometime next year.

Since he's had to put his dream of becoming a tattoo artist on hold because of the lingering effects of his motorcycle accident, he's decided that his next showcase is going to be drawings of all of the tattoos he wishes he could give some day.

Knox has also decided to restart physical therapy to work on the shakiness of his hands in hopes of one day making those dreams come true.

Rory is taking a four-week painting class at the Royal Academy of Arts in London and I'm sad to see her go for so long, but I'm so incredibly excited that she's gotten this opportunity because her portraits are simply breath-taking. I know she's going to kick some major ass out there, and when she returns, I'll be waiting with open arms and a case of Seattle's best tasting vodka, which is basically just vodka we can get from any liquor store in any state, but it's the thought that counts, really.

And as for me, I'm not sure what I'm going to be getting up to this summer, but I expect to find myself with my head in my sketchbook now that the ideas are flowing so freely. I'm excited to spend time with my parents and see Sam again, and I know that Rory and I will always find something to get up to in our neighborhood.

I turn towards the living room where I hear Knox calling my name, heading deeper into the house. I've already been given the grand tour, already helped christen Knox's room a few days ago when they hadn't even moved in one piece of furniture yet.

That had been a lot of fun, and my legs are still sore from our endeavors.

I come to a screeching halt at the sight of Knox and Slate bare-chested as they carry a couch between them, moving further into the living room.

My gaze zeroes in on Knox, his chest glistening with effort. His tattoos look absolutely delicious right now, as do the muscles flexing underneath them. I suck in a sharp breath and lock my legs together, trying to ward off the heat of arousal washing over me.

It's move in day for the boys and they've been lugging boxes and furniture from Third Street Apartments all morning.

Knox looks godly in the light spilling in through the large glass windows overlooking the yard. The parties at this house are going to be next level coming the fall semester. It's all that Slate has talked about since they signed the lease, commenting on how their housewarming party is going to rival that of *Project X.*

"Hey, Princess," Knox winks, catching my wandering eyes with his own. I can only beam, not bashful at all about checking my boyfriend out. This stroke of inspiration has really helped me come out of my shell a little more, feeling more settled in my own body than I have in years.

So what if he's caught me admiring his chiseled torso? He's all mine and I can stare if I want to. Although, the sudden dampness between my legs that has me shifting on my feet does make Knox's smirk widen, those jade eyes going molten.

"Can you two stop eye-fucking for one minute?" Slate groans dramatically, acting like he's struggling under the weight of the couch. He could probably easily carry it by himself, actually, with how ginormous he is. "This thing is fucking heavy."

"All right, let's put it over here," Knox directs with a sigh, guiding them a few more feet into the room. They place the couch in front of the giant television Ace splurged on, and I know movie nights are going to be insane in here. Two words: surround sound. It will be just like we're at a movie theater, without all of the extra bodies, and with twice as much popcorn.

A thump sounds from upstairs and the sound of Rory's laughter drifts down the staircase.

So, maybe this new house isn't that much more private than our old apartments.

As soon as Knox lowers his end of the couch, I'm

flinging myself into his arms, wrapping mine around his neck tightly. Knox laughs and swings me around before planting me back on the ground and leaning over to kiss me silly.

The flooding warmth that spreads throughout my body only intensifies as he steps closer, pressing into me and grinding my hips against his with a firm grip around my waist. It allows me to feel how happy he is to see me, and damn, I don't think I'll ever tire of this.

"Hi," I grin when we part.

Knox's eyes glitter with amusement. "Hi, Princess. How was your morning?"

My hands snake down his chest, brushing over his nipples as I go. I don't miss his reaction to my touch and it makes me giddy all over again. I hook my fingers into the waistband of his pants, turning my smile sultry, enjoying the way his eyes darken with need. "Much better now."

"Is that so?" Knox quirks an eyebrow. He looks like he's two seconds away from dragging me upstairs to his new room and breaking his bed in. He hasn't gotten a new one but a new room calls for a new fuck, and I love that soft as fuck mattress he has. I wouldn't mind it one bit at all if we abandoned this moving stuff and found our way up there. "Do I want to know why you're so cheery this morning?"

"You already know," I grin, rolling onto the tips of my toes to kiss him on the nose.

When I try to pull away, Knox growls, tightening his hold on me to keep me close.

I almost purr.

"You can't say that and not want me to fuck you, Princess," he replies roughly, dipping down to whisper in my ear. His breath is hot across the shell and I shiver in his arms, eyelashes fluttering at his whispers. I have to swallow back the moan crawling its way up my throat.

We startle apart at the sound of a loud crash, turning to find Slate all but glaring at the both of us, having just dropped a box of books to the ground purposefully.

"I thought we were supposed to be moving," Slate tosses over his shoulder before yelling up the stairs. "I can't have *both* roommates fucking already. There's still so much shit to move!"

"I'm *coming,*" Ace shouts back and I crinkle my nose.

"Ew." My joking reaction makes Slate crack, a smile twitching at his lips. He's still been acting weird but won't tell anyone why, insisting that he's completely fine even though all four of us can see through his lie easily.

Slate props his hands on his hips, still staring down at Knox and I like he's scolding us. "I knew I made a good decision in befriending you, Quinnie."

"More like forced yourself into my life," I grumble playfully, following him out to his rusty Bronco, stuffed full with boxes.

"Just for that, I'm giving you a heavy box," he teases right back, but he isn't kidding because my breath is nearly knocked out of my chest when he hands me the next one. It's falsely labeled *'Knox's room'* because I'm pretty sure it's actually filled with bricks.

Knox glares at his roommate as he rids me of the heavy box. I give him heart eyes and try to convey that I'm totally going to go down on him later for carrying the weight of the world—that box—for me.

His answering grin shows me that he understands *exactly* what I'm trying to tell him.

While Knox carries that inside, I sneakily slide out a box that says *'couch pillows'* on it instead. It takes me back to the day Rory and I moved in to our last apartment, how the living room box had been the last one I brought inside before my very first—and very terrible—run in with Knox.

The smile I wander inside with is a nostalgic one.

"Are you ready?"

"Yes!"

"Then why are you acting like I've already put the needle to your skin?" Knox argues, sitting back in his chair.

I'm lying on the dining room table, shirt pulled up to my neck, waiting for Knox to put the tattoo gun to my skin. I keep squirming, not quite comfortable on the cold table top, but it's the best we've got. Lying on the couch or Knox's bed would probably make me feel less uneasy, but I wanted him to have the flattest surface to work with because I know he's nervous about fucking this up with his shaky hands.

It's not his hands that I'm worried about. I don't care what the lines look like and I know he'll make them perfect. I'm worried about the sudden indecision creeping along my spine.

It's my first tattoo ever, and I'm hella nervous.

It's taken me months to decide on what I want it to be of, and Knox has been nothing but patient, not pushing or pestering me once about it, no matter how badly I know he wants to be the one to put my first ink on my skin.

The sound of the gun is intimidating as fuck.

I sigh loudly and Knox shuts the tattoo gun off, placing it on the table. He rips the gloves from his hands and helps me sit up, guiding my shirt back into place.

"Maybe we should wait," he suggests softly, soothing the skin of my hands with his thumbs.

"I want one," I huff, sadly. "But I don't think this is the one anymore."

Knox's hand falls from mine only so that he can grip my chin and turn my face towards his. He's looking down at me sternly and presses a firm kiss to my lips before answering.

"That's okay, Princess. There's no rush. You don't even have to get one, if you don't want to."

"I do," I whine in frustration. I've had it planned for weeks and now...I just can't go through with it. It doesn't feel right anymore.

I slide off of the table into Knox's lap, resting my head against his chest while he holds me tight. I let the soothing beat of his heart calm my racing thoughts, the rubbing of his hands up and down my back a relaxing gesture. It makes my heart swell with the amount of love that I have for him, and I'm really going to miss him this summer.

Knox brushes a strand of hair from my face when I finally lean back. He's studying me with those intense jade eyes that I've come to love. I can always tell what he's thinking these days: his annoyance, his happiness, his anger, his lust. But right now, I'm not all that confident in what he's pondering.

"I want to show you something," he murmurs softly and I frown.

"Okay," I answer tentatively, but his hand is sure in mine as he laces our fingers together after helping me from his lap.

Knox guides me up the stairs and into his room.

"Knox," I can't help but tease, because the lingering traces of my nervousness are still making me feel jittery and unsure. His hand in mine helps. "I already know this room too well," I continue, alluding to when we'd gotten every-thing moved in and Knox fucked me over every surface in here. It was pure bliss, one of the best nights we've shared together.

A good fucking might help my nerves right now, come to think of it.

He puffs a breathy laugh and guides me to sit on the edge of his bed. I follow his instructions with obedience, covering my eyes when he tells me to.

"How many fingers am I holding up?" Knox asks, and I roll my eyes behind my lids.

"Um, two?"

His grumbling sounds like it's coming from the other side of the room when he answers. "I was thinking two."

I bounce giddily on the edge of his bed, grinning in his general direction. When I hear his scoff, my smile only widens.

"Easy, Princess."

I stop my bouncing but not my grinning.

"What is it?" I ask, thrilled now rather than nervous.

Knox's laughter still sends butterflies shooting off in my stomach to this day, and I don't ever want that feeling to go away.

"If I told you, that would defeat the purpose of me asking you to close your eyes, Quinn," he tuts and I swear I can hear him rolling his eyes at me. "But you can open them now, Miss Impatient."

"Hey, that's my middle name—" My words stick in my throat as I stare at the canvas he's holding.

I'm in utter awe at the artwork he's showing off, the lines he's so confidently drawn. I'm transported back to the night of his exhibition, when he'd shared the deepest parts of his soul with me in both pictures and words.

Similarly to the centerpiece of his exhibition, the charcoal drawing in his hold is of two hands intertwined. His, with his rough scars and grafts, clutching tightly to a flawless hand, a more feminine hand.

My hand.

Knox shifts nervously on his feet. I can feel his eyes on me and all I'm doing is staring at the artwork, open-mouthed and awe-struck.

"I wanted to give it to you before you left for Seattle," he explains, looking from me to the picture, more nervous that I've ever seen him. "So you can take it with you and have something that reminds you of us while we're apart."

Tears well in my eyes as my heart constricts in my chest. "It's—" I choke, pressing a hand to my aching chest as if that's going to be the thing that will make it stop feeling like it's going to explode. "It is so beautiful, Knox."

He breathes out a soft sigh of relief, just managing to move the canvas out of the way when I spring up and collapse in his arms, sobbing into his chest. It's not even pretty crying, either. It's full-blown ugly crying that's fucking up my makeup, but neither of us really care.

Knox cradles me tightly against his chest, his lips peppering soft kisses to my hairline. "Shh, Princess. I'm sorry, I didn't mean to make you cry."

"I'm crying because it's perfect," I say, pulling away. My fingers stay locked in tight fists, the fabric of his shirt balled between them.

Knox brushes my tears tenderly, wiping softly at my wet cheeks. He studies me, eyes glinting with concern as he drinks me in, calming me down. *"You're* perfect. And I love you."

"I love you too, Quinn," he answers, his voice a rasp that makes me lean in closer.

And even though I'm too chicken to get a tattoo today, Knox is there, tattooed on my soul. He's inked in the love that I hadn't known I was missing until we met. Through all of the arguing, the late nights spent at each other's throats and in each other's arms, we found love.

And I fucking love Knox. So, *so* much.

"Yeah?" I ask, cheeks pinkening at his words. It still feels surreal, how we went from hating each other to loving each other so fiercely. I'm thankful for him every single day. "You love me?"

"I love you, Quinn Conroy," he repeats. "I think maybe I always have."

"That's *so* not true," I laugh wetly, trying to swat at his chest. Knox catches my hand in his and kisses my palm, eyes shining with adoration.

"Okay," he concedes with a grin that makes my heart skip. "Maybe not *always,* but for a long time now. It's us, Quinn." We both turn to admire his drawing again before looking down at where our own hands are clasped tightly between our chests. His scarred one, my smooth one. Opposites, yet somehow perfect together. "I want us. For as long as you'll have me."

"Forever then?" I ask, because I don't even need to think about it. I'm not letting this man go.

Knox nods, leaning down to kiss me. It's an unspoken promise, one that settles in my heart like a tattoo when he agrees.

"Forever, then."

ACKNOWLEDGMENTS

There were many instances I had of my own imposter syndrome during the process of writing this book. I won't bother writing all of the thoughts that were running through my head while working on this story, but just know that if you're a creative and struggling with your work, I feel you, and this one is for you.

To Paigey, the best sister anyone could ever ask for. Thank you for lighting a fire under my ass to work on this novel (and keeping me on track when my mind wandered to the mass number of other ones I dream of writing some day). You are both my biggest support and my second harshest critic, and I thank you for it. I love you so much.

To my mom, who supports me through all of my creative endeavors (and just life in general), even if they don't always work out. Thank you for giving me the space to learn and work through things on my own and always being there for me when things go amazingly well or horribly wrong. You've always been my biggest cheerleader and I love you dearly.

To my dad and brothers, I love you all. Thank you for the support throughout anything and everything I do. You don't need to know every gritty detail of this book to have supported me, and I don't think I want you to know every gritty detail of it either, so if you've made it this far maybe we shouldn't talk about what happened in chapters twenty-three, twenty-six, and thirty. Ever.

To Chlo, who, without Tumblr, I never would've met. Our

love for writing fanfic about a certain series really kicked off our friendship and it's felt like I've known you my entire life. Thank you for letting me shoot ideas, ask questions, bitch, and complain. Thank you for always hyping me up when I'm feeling down, beta reading, and so much more. I miss you dearly and I promise I'm coming to visit you soon.

To Hannah and Abe, thank you for being my best friends and sticking by my side through all of my creative chaos. I miss you both so much and I hope you enjoy this book as much as I enjoyed writing it!

To Pam and Alyx, my work best friends, who are always checking in on me and where I am in the writing process that week. The both of you bring me so much joy and I'm thankful to even know you, let alone get to call you my friends. The anticipation is over, it's finally here!

To you, the readers. If you've somehow found me from the internet, congratulations! If you don't know me from my *many* years as a fanfic writer, it might be best not to go down that path because there is *a lot* out there...I'm only a delusional girl who loves self-inserts, after all.

To Jeanie and the Ripped Bodice. Jeanie, your classes have been a huge part of my journey, and thank you to the Ripped Bodice for hosting those classes. They've helped me through my own sense of imposter syndrome, when I was just starting out and nervous beyond belief, when I had so many questions, I didn't even know what to do with myself. Thank you for meeting with me and guiding me through the process of getting my first book out into the world. I did it!

To Books and Moods for the incredible cover! I'm obsessed and can't wait to work more with you in the future.

And to the next novel...I'll see you soon.

ABOUT THE AUTHOR

Lanie Tech is a graphic designer by day and author by night. Her writing stems from many years spent as a fanfiction author and she's sorry if it shows. She is currently in her contemporary romance era but hopes someday to dip into the romantasy world with her novels. *Midnight Muse* is her first novel.

She currently lives in SoCal with her younger sister and enjoys strawberries, traveling, creating delusions during walks or work, and loves anything and everything creative.

Connect with her at lanietechauthor.com

Instagram: @lanietech
TikTok: @lanietechauthor

CONTINUE READING FOR AN EXCLUSIVE SNEAK PEEK AT BOOK 2 IN THE VULCAN UNIVERSITY SERIES, COMING SOON!

RORY

Cabo's warm sun beating down on my bare shoulders does nothing to brighten the sour mood I've been in for the past two weeks.

My body is a mess of self-induced nerves, jittery and sick at the mere thought of the boy who broke my heart at the last party of freshman year at Vulcan University. I haven't been eating well, each bite settles in my anxious stomach like a block of concrete. I can't sleep either, haunted by the images of Max, the argument we had that led up to our breakup after seven months of bliss.

I haven't been hiding it well, either. My older sisters pester me with questions whenever they can and my mom tries to use her maternal sway to influence me into speaking about it, but I refuse. Dad's the only one who refrains from saying anything, but I suspect it's because he never really liked Max anyway. He's been a solid wall of comfort when I need to be around someone who isn't going to speak about my current state of mess, and I'd like to stew in it a bit longer, overthink some more, maybe try one more time to fix it before finally telling the rest of the Wilson clan the whole story. If I break the news to them now, there will be no world in which I could bring Max home again and have my family welcome him.

Despite the lack of sleep, I still haven't fully processed the entirety of the situation. How we had gone from seeing each other most nights, laughing and kissing and more, to the shell-shocking We're Over™ speech in Max's upstairs bedroom the night before I left back to Seattle for the summer.

My phone buzzes and I check it all too eagerly, deflating when my best friend's name appears: Quinn. Her contact picture is a candid that I took of her mid-bite of what I consider is the epitome of burgers. The thick patties leak juices down her forearms and the bun is overflowing with outrageous toppings that seemed blasphemous to be included on a burger. She didn't care though, and was a trooper at the hodgepodge taste that twisted her face into a grimace, making me laugh so hard I nearly peed my pants.

In return, Quinn had her own good laugh at the sight of my bangs when I cut them after that dinner. Well, it was much later in the night, after she helped me pack for my family vacation and fell asleep to reruns of our favorite match-making drama. I swear, I want to sign Quinn up for it one of these days. She'd be perfect: all hard-headed and gorgeous. I know that my best friend would give the men a run for their money and the viewers an entertaining season.

She really should've threatened to tell my parents on me when she was attempting to stop me from ruining my hair.

Bangs fucking suck.

"Get that pretty head out of your phone, Rory Wilson," dad commands, rapping his knuckles across the brim of my baseball cap as he leads the way away from the check-in counter towards the elevators. There's no way I'm going to be caught dead without a hat this summer until my hair grows back in. "Quinn can wait until later. C'mon kiddo, you're in Cabo! Time to soak up some sun!"

The resort is nice: the lobby vast and open, letting the fresh air filter through the entrance. The view of the ocean is incredible from this floor alone and I bet it'll look even more striking from our hotel room. The sands are clean and white, and if I didn't know any better, I'd say that they have someone on staff who combs through the beach after every patron so much as leaves a footprint on it.

But I don't care about the sand and the perfect weather or the sun tan that I'm going to get that will hide some of the freckles dusting the bridge of my nose. I don't care about family dinners at sunset or the bonfires on the beach Peep hasn't stopped talking about. I don't even care about the tropical drinks.

Okay, that's a lie. I care *a lot* about the tropical drinks.

"Aren't you and mom going to the spa and leaving us to fend for ourselves?" I ask, sourly. I don't know why I'm feeling abandoned by my parents within the first hour of arriving to this luxurious all-inclusive. I should be happy to have a few hours to myself before they start pestering me about Max again.

I swallow thickly at the thought of him, wondering what he's doing right now. If he's missing me.

He's not going to text you, so get your head out of your ass and enjoy the sun.

"Fend for yourselves?" Dad scoffs, rolling his whiskey-colored eyes. "As if I didn't raise *three* incredibly strong-willed women who know exactly what they want. I figured you didn't want to hang out with your lame old parents, but if you'd like to join your mother and I at the spa, I—"

"Honey," mom cuts in before I can answer, shooting dad

a stern look. Her bright blue eyes that I've inherited are piercing, and I bite my lip at the wave of amusement that surfaces. She turns her attention to me, face softening as she loops her arm through mine. "You're almost twenty years old, Rory. I think you can find something to do with your sisters for a while, right? Plus, I think I saw some cute boys over by the pool." She wiggles her eyebrows.

"Yes, mom," I answer, trying to keep the annoyance from leaking into my voice. Now that she's brought up boys again, I feel like jumping right into the enormous pool shaped like a horseshoe and drown in it. Maybe I should jump into the ocean instead. Nope, *sharks*.

I slide out from her grip, following behind my family as I give myself a mental pep talk. The air is warm with summer and sunshine as I take a deep breath, releasing all of the negative emotions that I can with my exhale. Now isn't the time to be sulking about the boy I envisioned a future with. It's about spending time with family and making the most of my summer vacation.

Come on Rory, you can do this.

Making the most of my time doesn't last nearly as long as it should.

Trailing my sisters into our hotel room, I abandon my luggage by the door and drag my feet all the way to the queen bed closest to the window that Pipa's already claimed. I face plant onto the mattress, reeling over the story Max just posted to his Instagram that I'd so stupidly checked in the elevator. It took all of my effort to keep from bursting into a pool of hot tears at the sight of him and his friends with a group of perky looking girls. According to the location tagged, he's down in Panama City Beach for the time being.

I didn't get too good of a look at the story, immediately swiping away as soon as I noticed the girls hanging all over my ex and his friends, but from what I did see, I noticed how they all somehow managed to buy their bikinis two sizes too small. *Lovely.*

The worst part is, Max didn't look heartbroken at all, like the last seven months we spent together meant nothing to him.

"I can feel your brooding from all the way over here," Peep huffs from her side of the bed. It's an unspoken rule that she and I share, not because Aisling is the oldest, but because she has a mean jimmy leg and whoever winds up with her won't make it through the night without one or two new bruises.

I feel bad for whoever she ends up marrying someday.

My response is dry, muffled by the fluffy pillows. "It's not that big of a bed."

"Come *on,* Ro," Aisling sighs. She's using her *'mom's not here so I'm in charge'* voice, except that it sounds nothing like mom and more like a motivational speaker. "You can't spend all summer sulking."

I don't see why I can't, but I indulge my sister anyway. "Why not?"

I know she's glaring at me. I can feel it prickling the side of my head. Aisling Wilson is not a woman to be messed with. She's a defense attorney for fuck's sake.

Before Aisling can read me my rights, Peep pipes up. "Let's go down to the pool," she suggests, ever the peace-maker. I can hear her emphasizing her words at Aisling, which means her chestnut eyes are comically wide as she tries to get her point across. I have no doubt that if she gets me alone, she'll put that psych degree to good use. "Have a few Piña Coladas."

"Can't," I sigh, even though drinking my thoughts away does sound pretty fucking nice right now. Maybe I can find a hot man of my own and post a picture of him on my story. *Yeah,* that will show Max. "Not old enough."

"Ro, it's Mexico. You're legal here."

I lift my head from the cloud beneath me, taking in my sisters' matching grins. Mom and dad might care, but they're not here right now. I have hours to get properly drunk before we meet up with them for dinner. "Fuck it, let's go."

With three matching squeals, we race for our bags. I haul my suitcase over to the far corner of the room, staking claim before either of my sisters can. By the end of this trip, it's going to look like a tornado crashed through this place: clothes strewn about, shoes kicked off in every direction, and don't even get me started on the bathroom. Three daughters, and none of us use any of the same products.

It's going to be a hellscape.

Plucking one of the bikini's out, I hold it up with a frown. It looks nowhere near as skimpy as the ones that the girls in Max's pictures wore, and suddenly I feel self-conscious. While I don't look anything like those girls, I do have an appreciation for my own body, but I can't help but to compare. They looked like Miami supermodels, with their bleach-blonde hair, pouty, plump lips, and perfect tans. And well, I'm just Rory Wilson from Seattle, where it rains more than shines.

With a sigh, I toss it back into my bag, rummaging around the case I packed my swimsuits in. There's a new one-piece that I bought specifically for this trip that I consider stuffing into the bottom of my bag completely. If I'm going to make

Max jealous, taking thirst-traps in a one-piece is not the way to go.

Next.

"Ro, hurry up," Aisling exclaims from somewhere behind me. *What? How the hell is she dressed already?*

I voice that thought. "You changed already?" I ask, whipping my head around to stare at my sister. She's looking at herself in the mirror, rubbing in the last of her sunscreen to her cheeks.

She shoots me a smug grin. "Wore my suit on the plane."

"Ew." I wrinkle my nose. That sounds uncomfortable as shit.

Aisling scoffs. "It's not that long of a flight. I came prepared."

If that's what you want to call it, I think, turning back to sort through the rest of my bathing suits. The fact that she isn't calling Peep out for lollygagging is bullshit, but expected. They've always been closer to each other, and I didn't make it any easier when I expressed more interest in painting than playing princesses with my sisters. Unless the princesses got to have their make-up done or sit for a still-life; those were my favorite scenarios when we played.

Aisling didn't appreciate sitting still for long and Peep always rushed out of the room after about ten minutes, claiming that she had to use the chamber pot.

Who said I was the only creative one in the family?

I contemplate the bright orange bikini, not because I'm thinking about wearing it, but because I'm contemplating who let me purchase this monstrosity in the first place. It's God-awful. *Next.* There's a blush pink one with cute flowers adorning the fabric but that's all it is. *Cute.* Not sexy like I'm needing it to be while I'm on my mission to be the pettiest person at the resort.

Tucking that suit aside, my breath catches in my throat and my cheeks burn as I hold up the final bathing suit.

Quinn fucking Conroy, I love you so much.

She must have slipped it into my bag when I wasn't looking, that sneaky bitch. I'm forever grateful right now because it's the skimpiest, sexiest thing I've ever seen. It's like the swimsuit equivalent of the little black dress: the little black bikini. *Perfect.*

I change quickly, applying my sunscreen and readjusting my bangs under my hat. With the suit, I look the perfect amount of casual and sexy. I grab the book I swore I would read this vacation, my sunglasses, and a towel, and then my sisters and I are off to the pool. I'll have one of them take a few pictures of me with a book in one hand and a colorful drink in the other, looking just as unbothered by the breakup as Max is.

Yes, it sounds pathetic. I should be enjoying my vacation with my family instead of trying to get back at my ex, but I can't help myself. I want to make him feel the way that I feel. I want to show off what he's missing out on, which is a really sexy Rory who *hasn't* cut her hair into bangs.

Aisling and Peep are quick to drop their towels off on the first empty loungers they see, taking the few steps into the lavish pool and wading over to the submerged bar with a call over their shoulders that they'll bring one back for me. It's perfect, honestly, because I have no idea what kind of drink I should be ordering. My go-to at school is a basic vodka tonic, and I'd prefer not to taste the harsh cut of alcohol right now. I want it masked by sugar and fruits. I want my tongue blue or green or purple.

Settling onto the expensive-looking lounger, I peer over the top of my sunglasses, keeping myself ducked below the brim of my hat as I assess the rest of the vacationers, mindlessly running my fingers over the pages in my book.

There's a family splashing loudly at the other end of the pool where it's shallower. Two young sons and their father are laughing and chasing each other around while the mother watches fondly from her own chair. It's an endearing sight.

Swinging my gaze towards my sisters, I notice the plethora of young men and women lounging around a few of the tables built into the pool. Music plays, something that's bass heavy and keeps the vibes riding high. The drinks are clearly flowing because one of the men stands on a stool and backflips into the water. Everyone cheers, but it wasn't that impressive. He mostly back-flopped.

With a heavy sigh, I turn my attention to my book. I don't really know what's happening but I'm still in the early chapters, where the main character finds herself in a pickle that only the man of her dreams can help her out of.

When I looked up at him, the breath from my lungs ceased. He had the most luxurious blond hair, and the urge to run my fingers through his perfectly tousled locks was almost overpowering. It must have been some sort of magic holding them in circlets like that. And his eyes—his eyes were like the merging of two oceans, deep, blue waves warring with each other. His lips, plush like a rose, and if I only rolled up to the tips of my toes, I might have been able to catch a taste—

Something across the pool snatches my attention from the words on the page. No, it's some*one*. My mouth runs dry at the sight of him, looking all too much like the love interest I just read about. He's tall, I can tell even from where I'm sitting on the other side of the branch of the horseshoe-shaped pool. He looks like he embodies the word *'summer'* with his perfect golden glow and salt-kissed blonde hair that puts the waves of the ocean to shame. His eyes are hidden behind dark sunglasses, and I take the chance—as I hide behind my own —to drag my gaze across his sharp jawline and down his body.

The man is toned. He's not as broad as Max, but still has a good amount of muscle packed onto those arms and chest. I can even see a bit of his thigh, creeping up his shorter swim trunks and I'm *incredibly* happy with that trend for men's fashion right now. I'd love nothing more than to wrap my legs around that very waist, see if I fit as perfectly between those cutting hips as I bet I would.

As if he couldn't be any dreamier; he has tattoos. *Drool.* I'm unable to make them out from my vantage point, but the blots of ink scattered across his skin make him even sexier.

If I were a man, I'd whistle.

Of course, Beach Babe takes this exact moment to look up. *Directly at me.*

Or, at least, I think he's looking directly at me.

I watch the smile curving his lips and I *definitely* know that he's looking at me.

Squeaking, I quickly fumble to lift my book in front of my face, ignoring the sudden rush of heat that flares in my cheeks from getting caught ogling him all the way on the other side of the resort. I clamp my legs shut tight, ignoring the preening between them from his smile alone.

I'm no longer able to focus on the words on the pages, forcing myself to reread the last paragraph three times before I peek back up over the bridge of my book—only for my gaze to collide with Beach Babe's, who stands directly in front of me.

I'm pretty sure that my mouth is agape. I hadn't heard him splash into the pool over the sound of my thundering heart, but it's clear that he swam over here by the way his hair is plastered to his head and the droplets of water streaming down that smooth, glowing skin. I trail one of the droplets over his pectoral and I want to lean forward and lap it up, use it to wet my throat. From this close, I can tell that he must be around the same age as me.

"Like what you see?" He asks in a teasing manner, but his deep voice settles right between my legs. He pushes the sunglasses up to rest atop his head and I'm stunned by the gorgeous blue of his eyes. The look exactly as my book described, the warring of two oceans, a clashing of blue hues.

I take a swim of my own, forgetting that he's asked me a question. I blink when that dashing grin returns to his lips, and then again when there's a loud splash of water behind him. *That's* what draws me back to reality.

"Oh, um, hi," I say, because apparently, I've forgotten how to speak.

Quickly, I look around for my sisters that have been gone *way* too long. I don't see them by the bar or anywhere within the general vicinity. *Great,* so now they've abandoned me too. *Am I destined to spend my entire summer alone?*

"Hi," the man answers and damn, is his smile dazzling. Each of his teeth are straight and white, like perfect pearls. "What's your book about?" He asks, taking a seat on the recliner next to me. He props his feet up and leans back like I've invited him to join me. It's a smidge off-putting, how he's acting like we've known each other for more than a few minutes, but I don't own the resort and my sisters' towels claim the two chairs on my other side, so there's not much that I can say. He looks like every woman's wet dream laid out like this, all long and hard…and there I go again.

"I don't…I don't know," I admit, when I should probably lie. "I haven't really been paying much attention to it." *Because you keep thinking about a certain boy that's in no way thinking about you,* my mind supplies, unhelpfully.

He offers me a sympathetic smile that I don't want, nor need from strangers. "Lot on your mind?"

"Like you wouldn't believe," I answer drily.

"I hear Piña Coladas are the best for mending heart-breaks," he says easily, sliding his sunglasses back over his eyes. *Is he really going to sit here with me?*

I start, because how the hell did he guess? Am I really *that* transparent? I haven't even cried since I got off the plane, no matter how badly I wanted to when I saw that picture of Max and his new best friends.

"You don't look like the kind of guy who's ever had his heart broken," I comment, because this man is unquestionably the one doing the heartbreaking.

His head rolls my way and I know that he's winking at me even though I can't see his eyes through his sunglasses. "That's why I said *heard,* Darling."

My nose scrunches. *Darling? As if.*

Snapping my book shut, I gather my towel and stand. The man doesn't seem fazed by my sudden departure, but he does call out after me, his words stopping me in my tracks. "If you need to de-stress, maybe want to make that ex of yours jealous—" his words make the heat from my core rush to my face. I grit my teeth. "You know where to find me."

I spin slowly on my heel, but he's no longer watching me. Instead, his face is tipped up towards the sun, basking in it like it's his full-time job.

"Are you propositioning me?" I ask tightly, and I'm not so sure I find his smirk endearing anymore. Okay, it's still incredibly fucking hot, but *hey,* who the fuck doesn't introduce themselves before offering such favors? Not that that's *not* what I'm looking for while on my *family* vacation. *Jesus, Ro, maybe you need a nap instead of a drink.*

"Glad you finally caught on. I'm Ace," he says, but I'm

already stalking back towards the hotel, boiling with annoyance to the tip of my ears. *Men.* Ace calls after me when I ignore him. "You're going to want to remember that, and my room number, but I'll give it to you later!"

I flip him off over my shoulder and ignore the kick-start my heart gives at the raucous laughter that follows me all the way to the elevator.